HUNTING AFTER GHOSTS

TALES OF THE ROUGAROU BOOK 4

JULIE MCGALLIARD

Hunting After Ghosts
Goth House Press
Copyright © 2022 Julie McGalliard

Edited by Shannon Page
Cover art and design by Julie McGalliard

Library of Congress Control Number:
ISBN:978-1-951598-06-8

For my Grandparents
Who probably wouldn't have liked this book at all

1

TRAUMA MORPH

"Hyup!" my brother Nicolas barks out a brief warning before tossing me across the field in Bayou Galene where the Varger gather for events. Every full moon day is a party here, but today is special: I'm getting a chance to prove I mastered the trauma morph enough to be allowed unchaperoned into the outside world.

My back connects hard with the metal supports of the viewing platform. Most of my ribs, plus a couple of vertebrae, crack, then heal almost instantly. Gasps from the audience as I fall to the grass, hard and crunchy after a few days of brutally hot and strangely dry weather, then applause as I hop to my feet, curl into a crouch preparing for a new assault. On the opposite side of the field Nic gets into a crouch himself, ready to launch himself after me again.

A female wolf I don't know steps forward from the audience and skewers me through the gut with a thick, rusty spear made from part of a cast iron fence. It makes an absolute hash of my soft internal organs. Inside me, the wolf reacts with shock and fear.

Let me take this threat

No, me

She listens. No trauma-based shapeshifting.

Emboldened by my success resisting her, I rush toward Nic, throw him across the field. I have been told it looks somewhat comical when I do this, since I'm a foot shorter than he is. Most of my half-brothers, sons of my father Leon with a number of different women, are built like Nicolas: tall, broad-shouldered, and athletic. Nicolas had a Black mother, and in spite of his freckles and coppery hair, it sometimes surprises people to find out we're siblings. But if you look in our eyes, you can see the kinship.

Cheers and clapping. Most of the audience doesn't understand what this fight is supposed to accomplish. They're cheering me for holding my own against a larger and stronger opponent, something they respect, not for resisting the trauma morph, something most of them don't know anything about.

I find Steph in the audience, look for a smile of encouragement. But she has her arms folded and her face knitted into a fierce frown.

My gut, barely healed from the skewering, churns in panic. What is it? What's bothering her?

The distraction allows my brother to attack again, more intimate this time as he wrenches my leg out of its socket. I collapse, unable to walk for a moment, until it heals.

With a surge of painful effort, I push myself to my feet and manage a single step.

A white van drives onto the field and its door slides open, releasing my brother Rufus already in wolf form, jaws open wide and headed straight for my throat.

Shit he's going to kill us for real

The wolf and I have the same thought at the same time, and—

A moment, impossibly brief, as I feel the shift take hold, try to pull it back, *nonononono*—

She shakes him off, growls, makes hard eye contact, a

green flash. He concedes immediately, rolls onto his back in a show of submission.

Rufus returns to human form half a second before I do, rises, offers a hand. I stand up, everyone cheering and clapping and whistling, as if I won. Because he conceded, right? If you didn't know what I was actually trying to do, it looked like a win.

Somehow, it's more depressing to fail and get cheered for it.

I slump forward with a sigh, as Nic comes to drape a black silk robe around my shoulders. He's already wearing his own identical robe. The Varger must have gotten these robes cheap at some point, because they seem to have dozens.

"Good fight." Nic hugs me. "You'll get it next time."

"Next time." I groan, sink my head into his chest. "That's a whole month from now." Trauma morph trials are traditionally held on the day of the full moon, when the wolf is strongest.

"Four weeks," Nic says. "I know you can do it."

"Easy for you to say."

He continues hugging me for a while, rubbing my shoulders, which is very welcome. We heal rapidly, but we still get tired. Our bodies prioritize, healing first the parts we need to survive, and after that, the parts we need to hunt. Some things, like feeling really well-rested, get pushed back, waiting for a calm moment when nobody's trying to kill us. I've been doing the trauma morph training for three months now, stressing my healing abilities to their limit, and we never get to the calm moment.

"Abby, I believe in you, you're going to get this," Nicolas says. Then he leaves me alone.

The wolf who stabbed me approaches. She's dressed in hipster black, long dark hair peppered with gray, and even before I hear her thick New York accent, I can tell she wasn't raised here in Bayou Galene.

"Sorry you didn't get it kid, but that was a real good effort." She shakes my hand. "You're gonna get it for sure next time for sure, you bet."

"Thanks. Have we met?"

"Roxanne Peters, usually of Brooklyn. That's why they brought me in for this, they knew we didn't know each other. I'm what they call a dark wolf. No known wolfy ancestors, then, boom, one day I wake up naked in the cemetery next to one of your people from the Brooklyn maison."

"Wow. Amazing."

"Yeah, kid, I know you're not impressed." She laughs and gives me a light punch in the arm. "I hear you woke up in the middle of Seattle, no wolves around anywhere, had to make your own way."

"That's what happened, yeah."

"See, I really respect that. You gotta have guts to make it on your own like that."

"Thanks." Flash of memory: Steph frowning, why was she upset? "You know what, I'm going to go find my loufrer. See you later."

I find Steph with her brother Morgan, pouring himself a cup of aged imperial stout from a keg from the new Bayou Galene microbrewery.

"I just don't want to stay much longer," Steph says, agitated.

"I'll drink it fast. It's really good, though, you should try…" He trails off. Sometimes he forgets that she's an alcoholic who can't try a sip of the imperial stout this one time just because it tastes really good. He notices me, sloshes his drink in a kind of cheers gesture. "Abby! That fight was amazing! Just like in the movies. Is it always like that when your people fight each other?"

"Well, the stabbing is a bit novel, but we do tend to toss each other impressive distances and come back right away from otherwise crippling injuries." I try for a light tone, but Steph shudders.

"It looked pretty brutal to me, kiddo. Are you hurt? Can I hug you?"

"Sure, instant werewolf healing, hug away." We embrace. "It's okay, Steph, it's just play fighting. You know. Like what puppies do."

"Puppies bite ears, they don't bite ears *off.*"

I reach up to my ear, feel the earring stud from when Steph took me to get them pierced. It was January, early in Mardi Gras season. Only a few months ago, but it feels like forever. If you look closely at my wolf form, she is also wearing little earrings. "I'm sorry. I didn't know it would bother you so much."

"I'm fine," she says, not convincingly. "I just wasn't expecting it to be so violent."

Now that I'm at my (probably) full adult height of (almost) five-two, I'm tall enough to rest my head on her shoulder. "I invited you out here because I really thought I had it this time. I thought I'd prove my mastery of the wolf and then we'd all go into town for my birthday."

"Oh, sweetie." She strokes my hair. "We can celebrate your birthday whenever you're ready."

"What about Terry? It's his first birthday. You didn't bring him?"

"No. I didn't know. I thought all the blood and violence might be upsetting to a baby. He wouldn't understand."

"I guess not. It's fine." I inhale, speak without thinking. "Steph, who's that man? Are you dating somebody?"

"What?" She startles, pulls away from me.

"The man I smell in your hair. New boyfriend?"

"Oh, don't you start. Yes. I am seeing someone, his name is Irwin and I've been seeing him for three weeks. My dear brother does not approve. He seems to think every guy I date from now on is going to be the second coming of George. The last thing I need is the two of you ganging up to try to keep me living like a nun."

"I'm not, Steph. I really didn't mean anything by it. I just noticed him is all. Hair, you know, it holds scent really well." I'm babbling. I can't believe what a horrible mess I'm making of everything today. "It doesn't matter, please. I'm sure he's great."

"Look, I know he seems nice," Morgan says, pointing emphatically with his beer hand and splashing dark liquid on his fingers. "But George seemed nice at first. If something like that happens again, we have to be ready."

Steph shakes her head. "See what I mean? I think maybe we should go, brother. Keys?"

"Oh. Yeah. Sure." He hands her the keys to his truck, drains the rest of his drink, gives me a brief hug. "That really was a great fight, Abby. Absolutely fantastic. I had no idea you were so—I mean, I know you're a werewolf and all, but I had no idea you were that strong. Or tough! It's just like in those superhero movies. I had no idea."

He leans in close and I can smell the beer on his breath. He's really pretty drunk. I don't usually see him like this. Maybe the imperial stout threw him off. "Say, Abby. I know there are some differences between born werewolves like you and bitten werewolves like down at the Hammerfit, but how big are the differences? Can the bitten wolves fight like that?"

"Hammerfit? Morgan, when have you been to a Hammerfit?"

"The one on Rampart, it's pretty new. I've talked to a couple of guys there."

"About being bitten wolves? That's something they just talk about?"

Morgan laughs. "Not to just anybody! But these guys, I was watching them and I kind of knew, so I dropped a few hints, then we got talking. Remember I'm looking for new hunting buddies?"

"I do remember that, but I had no idea you were doing it by talking to random bitten wolves in a brand new Hammerfit." It seems disturbing to me in a way I can't fully put my finger on, and I'm still trying to puzzle it out when Pere Claude and Leon approach.

"Miss Steph, Mister Morgan, nice to see you again," Pere Claude says.

"You too, Mr. Verreaux." Steph takes his hand, smiles warmly. She always seems calmer about the whole werewolf thing when my grandfather is around. "Have a nice, um, a nice time tonight?"

"'Good moon' or 'good hunt' would be traditional."

"Well then, have a good moon. All of you." She gives us a vaguely apologetic smile. "See you soon I hope. In town." She hustles Morgan away.

I watch them go with a crushing feeling in my chest. Steph didn't like it. And she's right, isn't she? It's brutal, what we do. Violent. Shocking. Bloody.

"Is something wrong, Abby?" Leon asks.

"I failed the trial. Dad. Obviously something is wrong."

"It was a good effort. You'll get it next time. Have some champagne in anticipation of future victories."

He holds out a bottle, already uncorked. The good stuff, based on the smell, with a vivid yellow-orange label and a French name: Veuve Clicquot.

"Thanks." I take the champagne, drink straight out of the bottle. It is good. Fine, crisp, dry, fruity.

"It took me two full years to master my wolf, I don't think it will take you that long," Pere Claude says, giving me a hug.

"And I never did master mine, so you've got me beat," Leon says.

"Yeah. Thanks. How long has there been a Hammerfit on Rampart?"

Leon answers, "A couple of months. It's a rebranding and expansion of the traditional gym that was already there. I believe you've been to it?" I nod. That gym is where I met Nic for the first time. "We thought it would be helpful, with the current outbreak, to have a place in town where bitten wolves know they can go for support. The Hammerfit chain has started to become known in the, the bitten-wolf world I suppose you'd say, as a resource."

"Is that why Roman and Rufus are here? Because of the Hammerfit?"

Leon turns evasive. "It might be. I'm not sure."

"There are so many bitten wolves now," Pere Claude says, shaking his head. "It's not like when I was young. We usually killed them back then."

"Right, and that was bad," Leon says.

"Of course." Pere Claude stares into the distance. "It was bad."

After an awkward moment of silence, I change the topic. "So, what do you guys do in the trauma morph trial if there isn't a fully mastered wolf like Rufus around?"

"We improvise," Pere Claude says. "You don't know Rufus well, even though he's your brother, so he seemed to be a good choice for the attack."

"He was, in a way. I did think for a second he was going to kill me for real. But it doesn't seem entirely fair, does it? If there was no Rufus, I would have succeeded." Boy I sound whiny. I sip from the bottle again. Roman and Rufus approach, as if talking about them has summoned them. Rufus is wearing a black robe like mine, but on him it's almost indecently small.

Roman pumps my hand in an exaggerated hearty way that seems artificial. "Abby, good show. You very nearly succeeded."

"Thank you."

"That was a solid fight." Rufus seems sincere when he takes my hand. "I think you're almost there."

Roman and Rufus are twins, Leon's oldest children. In

spite of being non-identical they look very similar, taking after their grandfather: tall and strongly built men with golden hair and heavy chests, smooth tans, no freckles. But the twins are fitness-obsessed even for werewolves, so they look like body builders, toned and sculpted as well as massive.

"Thanks. I really wasn't expecting you guys to just show up like that. And driving a car onto the field. That was novel."

Roman laughs. "Abby, you of all people should expect that sort of thing. Aren't you the one who popularized the saying that cars are werewolf kryptonite?"

I grimace. "Did I? Probably I did. Sorry about that."

Roman says, "My son Raymond is around here some- where, I wanted to introduce you. Hey! Raymond!"

I've met Raymond before, briefly, but I don't bother reminding him of that. It wasn't much of a meeting. Raymond was clearly unimpressed with me at the time and we exchanged no words.

A young male wolf—like his father in coloring and features, but slight and not tall, maybe because he's young still —walks up, face in his phone. "Yeah?" he says, still clearly unimpressed.

"Raymond, this is Abby. Your aunt, technically, although I believe you're around the same age."

He gives me a half-hearted wave and a smirk. "'Sup, auntie. Good fight. But they're telling me you failed? I don't get that. Wolf-you totally pwned his mangy ass." He directs this at his uncle Rufus, who scowls briefly, then forces a smile.

"Colorful idiom," he says.

Roman smiles. "It's true, Ray. Your big, powerful uncle was bested by a little girl who looks like a cheerleader. That's the reality of wolf-shifter combat. Once we go to wolf form, all the rules change. That's the power of the trauma morph."

His expression is a fierce glower, causing me to wonder if he resents Rufus for having the trauma morph when he doesn't. What am I thinking? Of course he does. And Rufus resents Roman for having a dominant wolf, when he doesn't. They've probably been sniping at each other since they were fifteen or sixteen, when their wolves first appeared.

I try to lighten the mood. "Cheerleader? You have got to be kidding me. What about me says 'cheery' to you?"

Rufus laughs. "Listen to you. 'Oh, I'm small and perky and gymnastic and I'm dating a star quarterback, but how could you say I'm anything like a cheerleader?'"

"Running back, excuse me. If you mean Edison, he's a running back, not a quarterback."

Everybody snickers at that, as if "running back" is a punchline. I don't know what they think is so funny. It's not like I told them he's a tight end.

I speak up. "Raymond, this was a trauma morph trial, which is supposed to prove that I can resist the urge to go to wolf form when injured. Because if I can't resist it, the theory goes, I might turn into a wolf unexpectedly, in public, at any time, any place. Football half time act, presidential inauguration, Jazzfest headliner, that sort of thing."

Raymond responds to my half-hearted joking with a laugh. "That would be pretty funny all right. And then you'd be naked up there in front of everybody."

"Right. Because of that, unmastered trauma morphs are basically quarantined. Under house arrest. Not allowed to leave town, unless we have a chaperone, meaning, a senior wolf who agrees to stick with us basically every minute, and take a bullet for us, should that be required."

He thinks for a moment, laughs. "Take a bullet for you, huh? Sure, okay, I get it. But how often does that come up?"

Leon and I share a glance and a slight smile. Leon says, "The answer might surprise you."

Roman says, "There's so much you need to learn about the power of your wolf, son."

Raymond shrugs. "I guess." He looks at me. "Dad wants

me to apprentice in the French Quarter for the next few months."

"Well, you should do that. They're great. Etienne knows more about scent tracking than maybe anybody ever. I'd be out there in the French Quarter maison right now if I'd mastered my wolf fully."

As if summoned, key members of the French Quarter maison crew approach: Vivienne, Etienne, Nicolas, Babette, and Barney. Nic is wearing clothes again, which probably means he's going back into town with them.

"Barney!" I haven't seen him in a while and give him a hug. "I thought they sent you back to the Meriwether maison."

"Temporary." He grins. "Just helping the wolves there transition into running their own Snarlaway franchise. Apparently the good people of Meriwether continue to need rats gotten out of their church buildings and black widows out of their garages."

Babette steps forward to hug me. "Migarou. You will succeed next time, I know it." She takes the bottle out of my hand and drinks from it. "Just champagne? You can't get drunk on that with your wolf awakened again, let me get you something stronger."

"It's fine, Babs, I like champagne, I don't need anything stronger." I take the bottle back from her. It's noticeably lighter.

"Oh, before I forget, what does this smell like to you?" She leans in so that she can wave her silk scarf under my nose. The maison recently got some kind of massive perfumery kit from France, to aid in training for scent tracking. Babette has been using it to blend odd and very specific perfumes.

"Um, used bookstore with an espresso machine?"

"And?" She waves it again.

I close my eyes, inhale deeply, get a hint of... ozone? "There's a thunderstorm coming?"

"Perfect! Migarou, you really are the best. I can't wait to be working with you again."

"So, how's it been going, you guys?" I hear the wistfulness creep into my voice. When my wolf was gone for a while, I was training with them as a scent tracker at the French Quarter maison. It was fun and I was good at it. It's nice to have the wolf back, in some ways. But I really miss my time at the maison.

"Busy," Vivienne says. "But less busy than it was. I think the Flint Savage outbreak is finally dying down."

Nic rolls his eyes slightly, sighs. "Maybe. But nothing like this has ever happened before so we're not entirely sure what to expect."

Viv folds her arms and gives Nic stern lawyer-face. "Which is also why we shouldn't assume the worst."

"Not assume, just prepare!" he snaps back. I get the impression this is an argument they've been having a lot. "Vivienne, you're a smart person, but you're not a scientist, and a lot of the things you think you know about bitten wolves are just folklore and you know it!" He turns to me with a slightly apologetic smile. "I'm sorry, Abby. It's just extremely true that nothing like this has ever happened before."

"Please, don't stop arguing on my account."

"Mr. Etienne," Roman says, addressing the director of the maison. "Are you still willing to apprentice my son Raymond as part of your team?" He wraps his arms around Raymond's shoulders. Raymond is visibly annoyed.

"Of course." Etienne smiles at Raymond. "You were raised by your father and uncle in rural areas of the Pacific Northwest, I understand?" Nods. "So, all this must be very different for you?"

Raymond laughs. "Well, no mountains. And the trees are all wrong. But you guys are in central New Orleans, right?"

"In the French Quarter," Vivienne says, "Thickly inhabited historic tourist district. There's nothing quite like it in the Northwest, or, really, anywhere else."

Roman says, "The maisons are part of a larger system they call the track and chase teams, which are intended to prepare and respond to unexpected new wolves on the full moon. They need a mix of wolfless—" he nods at Barney, "wolves who will stay human on the full moon—" he nods at Etienne, who hasn't transformed for five years after getting a head injury, "and wolves who will transform." He nods at Viv, Nic, Babette.

"Sure." Raymond shrugs. "Why not?"

"I want you to experience the traditional Bayou Galene hunt tonight," Roman says. "I'll take you into town tomorrow."

Big group hug from the maison crew, and they all wave and turn to leave.

I feel a sudden gut-churning emptiness, a loneliness that I can't fully explain, like something being pulled out of me. They're only going into New Orleans, less than two hours away by car. And I'll see them again soon. But still I want to cry.

I drink from the champagne bottle, notice how empty it is.

"Babette drank half my champagne, that lush."

"We'll get you another bottle." Leon makes a little follow-me gesture and starts heading back toward town.

"No, it's fine, I'll—wait, yes, let's get me a new bottle of champagne."

Bayou Galene is a very small town, if it even counts as a town, but the Grand Maison is still more than a mile up the Galene Road, at least ten or fifteen minutes of walking. The land here clings to the paths of the rivers, little fingers trailing out into the gulf. On a zoomed-out map, Bayou Galene looks very close to similar towns like Montegut and Chauvin, but unless you're a bird, they're far away from each other. To get to a different one you would have to go up a bayou road for miles, and down another bayou road for miles.

Walking up the unsheltered road, sun beating on my head, it's hot. I flap the edges of the robe, sigh. "I think I got bit by something on the grass, there are red marks on my ankles and they itch."

"It'll heal," he says, after a brief glance.

"Of course it'll heal, I was just complaining."

"You're upset because you failed the trial."

"True, but also my ankles are itchy."

"Abby, I wanted to talk to you about something."

My heart flutters in apprehension. "Well that's never good."

"It's about the trauma morph training. Are you experiencing the permanent black moon?"

"Why do you ask me that? Just because it happened to you?"

He shakes his head. "You seem... different."

"Different from what? We barely know each other. Dad."

"Abby, we spent a lot of time together when you were in Los Angeles recovering from your gunshot wound. Maybe you didn't feel like you got to know me, but I got to know you."

"Yeah? And what do you think you know about me?"

He stops walking for a moment, takes a deep breath. "Please, just listen to me. Assume, for the moment, that I care about you."

I stop walking, drain the champagne bottle, fold my arms. "Fine. You care. And?"

"You're seventeen. You have the black moon, and a powerful wolf. You're working to control the trauma morph and it's making your black moon worse. I've been there, okay? Exactly there. And when I was there, I made some foolish decisions. Things I regret to this day."

"Thanks for the vote of confidence. Dad."

He sighs, shaking his head. "Please, could you—I'm actually trying to be a dad, here, all right? A counselor, not an authority figure. I'm not trying to tell you what to do."

"No? I guess you'd eye-flash me if you were." I stop, think about it. Maybe he's sincere, but I don't want to admit it. It kind of annoys me when Leon tries to "be a dad" as he puts it. Maybe that annoyance is my own problem? Etienne acts like a dad to me sometimes, and it never annoys me when he does it. "Have we ever dominance-flashed each other?"

Slight smile. "No. We haven't."

"Worried about who would win?"

Small chuckle. "Oh, no, I'm not going there with any of my kids."

"Really? None of us? Not even Roman?"

"Not even Roman." We start walking again. He looks thoughtful. "Why did you ask about Roman specifically?"

"I don't know, he's the oldest, he has a dominant wolf, I thought maybe it would've come up sometime."

"Unfortunately, Roman's mother and I were no longer together by the time his wolf arrived. I did try to prepare him and his brother for what was coming, but I wasn't their hunt leader while they were young wolves." He seems a little sad.

"You regret that?"

"I do. It's part of what I mean when I talk about foolish decisions."

"But you weren't seventeen when the twins were born?"

"No, I was twenty."

"Well. There. You see? You never really stopped making foolish decisions, did you? Maybe the foolish decisions are a 'you' problem."

He grimaces. "I suppose I deserved that."

We walk for a while and something strikes me. "You think it was the black moon that caused your foolish decisions, not your red moon? Because I don't even have the red moon."

He laughs. "No? I guess you don't. I made foolish decisions under the red moon, too, but they were different. Less calculating, you might say." He turns a bit red, embarrassed, and I make a guess.

"The red moons were when you slept around?"

He nods. "I did other foolish things too, but that's probably the one with the most serious lasting consequences."

"You mean all your kids? Yeah, as one of those consequences myself, I guess I have mixed feelings about that particular aspect of your werewolf bipolar." I stop. Think about it. "Wait, it's the full moon today, shouldn't you be having a manic episode?"

"No." He shakes his head. "I don't really get the red moons anymore. Not since you restored my wolf."

"Is that good?"

"It's good." He smiles broadly. "It's very good."

We stop again, having arrived at the Grand Maison. Most of the buildings in town aren't particularly old or fancy, but the Grand Maison is impressive, a stately two-story structure of brick and wood painted white, framed by majestic live oaks. Letters carved into the entrance above the lintel announce:

LE GRAND MAISON VERREAUX
1798

The lower level of the house is raised up to to protect against flooding, which puts the wine "cellar" at ground level. The stone walls feel cool and damp when we enter. A single bare bulb dangles from the ceiling and Leon pulls the chain, illuminating the interior with a weak light. He heads straight for where they keep the champagne, hands me another orange-label Veuve Clicquot and takes one for himself. I pop the cork on the new bottle, consider going outside again. But it's cool in here and I like the smell of old wine, so I lean against a bare spot in the chilled stone of the wall, start drinking. Leon does the same.

"You know, I always wondered about those giant bottles of champagne." I point to three prominent bottles, with the Tattinger label. "I've seen them in the wine section of the grocery store and they're always so expensive. And they've got these important-sounding Biblical names. Jeroboam, Rehoboam, Nebuchadnezzar. Why?"

"The larger bottles are for aging. I don't know why they have the Biblical names."

I look around the cellar. "I thought Pere Claude kept all his Scotch in his home office, but there's a bunch in here too."

"He keeps a seasonal selection in his office." Leon takes a sealed bottle of Scotch from the shelf. "So he's still got his honeymoon Scotch."

"Honeymoon Scotch?"

"He and my mother went to the Scottish highlands on their honeymoon. They really liked it there. Particularly a little town called Drochlemore just north of Inverness. They brought home this bottle, intending to open it on their..."

He trials off and I smell the distress in his sweat.

"Some anniversary they never made it to?"

He nods, sadly.

"I'm sorry," I say. "I don't really know what else to say. I'm sorry about what happened to my grandma."

"Thank you." A moment of silence, then he says, "She was an extraordinary woman. I think you would have liked her."

"I was possibly possessed by her, remember?"

"Yes. I remember." He nods. Sips the champagne. I can't quite read his expression. Then he says, "We would use the term 'ridden' in such a situation. You invited her. 'Possession' implies something unwilling, unwelcome."

"I'm sorry, I didn't mean to be offensive."

"You didn't offend me." He smiles, more broadly. "I was worried about you. That your religious background would lead you to contextualize what happened in a negative way."

I shrug. "No problem. Grandma's welcome in my head pretty much any time." I look around. "You know, it seems increasingly ridiculous to keep thousands of dollars' worth of alcohol in a place that's going to get flattened by a hurricane within the next twenty years. Maybe we should open the Jeroboam now."

"This one is a Balthazar. That's four times the size of a Jeroboam." He briefly strokes the bottle with an anticipatory smile. "How about when you master your wolf?"

"Okay. When I master my wolf."

2

LUPUS COR LEONIS

Just before moonrise I head to the bunker, a concrete building on the north edge of town, built in the 1960s to hold the modern communication technology that forms the basis of the track and chase teams. It's got a space age look, like the Science Center in Seattle, and a forest of satellites and antennas sticking out of it.

It's also one of the few buildings in town with modern air conditioning. In just the silk bathrobe I feel chilly, so I head to the wardrobe closet, put on the smallest Snarlaway olive green jumpsuit, roll up the cuffs.

As I leave the wardrobe room, Jason Hebert, one of the bunker directors, almost crashes into me. He stops short, sips the iced coffee that splashed onto his hand. "Abby! What are you doing here, you didn't get shot in the head again did you?"

"No, I just thought I might stay human tonight, help out maybe?"

"Sure, yeah." He runs his free hand through his hair, making it stick straight up. "Is something special happening?"

"Not really." Now I feel stupid. "Never mind. If I'm in the

way here I can just go back to the others and do the regular wolf thing."

"No, no, don't do that!" He holds out both hands as if to physically prevent me from leaving. "You're not in the way. I was just surprised. We can find something for you to do." He sighs, takes a sip of the coffee, runs the other hand through his hair again. "Come on, Mimi and Oscar are working tonight, they'll be glad to see you."

I follow him into the main control room, monitors on every available spot of wall, computers on every flat surface, a dozen people in headphones. The bunker is staffed mostly by the wolfless, Varger who don't change for whatever reason, and it's got a very different energy than the party in the big field. The wolves are giddy and high energy, like people ready to see a big music show. The wolfless in the bunker are tense, sharp and focused, frowning, highly caffeinated.

A few months ago, when I worked here, it was different. Not so many people and the atmosphere was relaxed, laughing and joking, everybody ready to eat pizza and play video games all night unless something happened, with the expectation that nothing would.

Tonight, it feels more like a NASA control room when the mission has already started to go wrong.

Mimi notices me, takes off her headphones and comes over for a hug. "You didn't get shot in the head again did you?"

"No, why does everybody keep asking me that? You know I'm a partially mastered trauma morph, I can stay human on the full moon just because I want to."

"Oh yeah? I forgot you could do that. Well... good for you."

"It seems kind of tense in here, is something wrong?"

"Oh, nothing, just the biggest bitten wolf outbreak in... ever." Mimi fans herself with a sheet of paper and throws herself into a retro-looking olive green office chair, which poofs up a stale smell as it rolls backward.

"London is settled," announces one of the people I don't know, a dark-haired young man with a stubble of beard. He takes off his headset and tosses it onto the desk while the room cheers and claps and he rubs his eyes with the heels of his hands. He looks exhausted, sweaty and gray and hollow-eyed, but otherwise handsome.

"The first person to make *An American Werewolf in London* joke gets pelted with stale donuts," announces someone else, to general laughter.

"That counts as the first joke," another person says, and stale crumbs of donuts all fly toward the speaker, who laughs and ducks. For a minute there's a donut fight, then Jason good-naturedly says, "You'll get crumbs in the keyboards y'all" and the donuts stop flying.

"I'm beat, see you guys in a month." More clapping as the first young man leaves the room.

I stare at his monitor, showing a generic London image of the Big Ben clock tower. "You had an outbreak in London? What time is it there? We don't have a maison anywhere in Europe do we?"

"We don't," Jason says. "But we did have one of our people, wolfless, who just happened to be backpacking through England and was able to get to London before the night was done. Rene talked him through it, but we got there pretty late, I would bet anything there's going to be a secondary."

"Talked him through it? Through what? What was he able to do, without the equipment? He wasn't able to get tranquilizer darts or anything like that?"

"No. But he was able to get a butcher knife and colloidal silver."

My stomach lurches. "A butcher knife?"

"He didn't kill the new wolf, don't worry." Smiles tiredly.

"I saw that look. But, and I know this is going to sound disgusting, we find that doing a lot of damage, especially taking off limbs—arms, legs—then treating the wounds with colloidal, usually gets them exhausted to the point where they calm down enough that we can bind them up and take them elsewhere."

"Arms and legs? And they heal from that?"

"Usually."

"Bon Dieu." We sit with that for a moment. Then I say, "You've, uh. You've had to do this a lot?"

He sighs, shrugs. "That and more. We've had to develop a whole new set of combat techniques on the fly. Every moon it's something new. A month from now we'll have somebody stationed in London, but who knows? By then the outbreak could be in Paris. That's the frustrating thing. We've tried to run algorithms to predict, but we just don't have enough data." He sighs. "Well, it's almost moonrise on the East Coast, let's check in with Brooklyn."

A new face on the monitor, a young man I don't know. "Hey, how ya guys doin?" he says, in an accent I recognize from Roxanne.

"Good, you?"

"We're ready. We got three last time, but I think that was a fluke, two of 'em were tourists." He makes a show of cracking his knuckles.

Jason nods. "Good. Thanks. Miami?"

Another monitor pops up with a new face, a young woman I don't know.

"Miami checking in." She holds up an iced coffee, wipes her forehead with it. "It is hot down here."

"Hotter than Louisiana?"

"Somehow, yes."

"All right, countdown. Everybody?"

Brooklyn leads the countdown, based on their local moonrise time. "10—9—8—7—6—5—4—3—2—1!" And we all pause, listening. For what?

Sirens. In the background. Miami turns to check something, turns back toward us with a sigh. "We're up, there's an incident at a dance club. Could be cocaine or howler or something, but we have to assume the worst. We'll keep you posted. Annalee, you ready?"

A collar feed pops up in the corner. I hear a female voice say "ready" and the video walks out the door.

"Annalee is a mastered wolf like you," Jason says. "Ideally we'd have a couple at every maison, but there are too many maisons now and there just aren't enough of y'all."

"Shit." Brooklyn chimes in. "Showtime, everybody. Incident at a Yankees game." Another collar feed hooks in and heads out.

My gut is fluttering. This seems so different from when I started. So many incidents, everybody so intense. "And this is all still the Flint Savage outbreak?"

"Flint Savage epidemic, more like," Mimi says. She rolls the chair again, spins it around, staring at the ceiling with a weary look.

"I'm sorry." I think back to the moment I brought in my first bitten wolf, Andrew, who turned out to be the first known Flint Savage—victim? That doesn't seem quite right. Andrew is happy as a wolf, or at least, he was the last time I talked to him a few months ago. "We should have stopped Flint Savage sooner."

"I don't know how you could have." Mimi gives me a tired smile. "You were pretty much the only reason we stopped him as soon as we did. Getting the Cachorros and the Lobos to help, doing the parade sweep during Mardi Gras, even backing up Pere Claude, that was all you." She sighs, shakes her head. "*You* are not the reason this is all happening."

"I'm not? But somebody else is?"

They cast furtive glances at each other. "There's no real point in blaming anybody," Oscar says cautiously.

Mimi scoots the chair in my direction. "Oh, stop beating around the bush you guys." She leans in toward me. "Abby, there are rumors. You've been spending all your time doing that trauma morph training, I guess, so you probably haven't noticed. But those of us without wolves, we notice things, hey? The rumor is that Leon came back home to take over as hunt leader from his father."

The bottom drops out of my stomach. "Bon Dieu, of course he did. Shoot. Leon should not be the pere."

She frowns at me. "You think? But some people think he might be a good change. I know you're loyal to Pere Claude, and nothing against him, he's a great man, but he's been hunt leader since the 1960s. That's a long time. We think he's starting to seem a little—you know. Tired."

I take a deep breath, force a smile. Another wolf would know I'm furious by the smell of my sweat, but I don't want to show that to the people on the track and chase teams. They didn't do anything wrong, and I don't want them to not be honest with me because they're afraid I'm going to take their heads off.

I answer carefully. "Maybe. But, Leon as hunt leader isn't the answer."

"Why are you so sure about that?"

I don't know exactly why I'm so sure. But I am sure. I reach for the first thing that comes to mind. "He abandoned his people for forty years. I don't think that speaks well of his leadership."

They all nod thoughtfully. "Good point," Mimi says. "So who do you like as the next pere?"

"I don't know, maybe my brother Nic if he wants it. Or Etienne."

"No, Etienne can't do it, you need an active wolf," someone else says.

"And a dominant wolf," someone else points out.

"A mastered wolf is ideal," Jason says.

A pause, and all faces in the room turn toward me, most of them grinning. Like it's a big joke. They know I fit the bill, or will as soon as my wolf is mastered, but they still think it's ridiculous, the idea of me as hunt leader. And it is ridiculous. I'm seventeen and raised on the outside. But I still feel a little hurt that they all think it's so funny.

"Absolutely not," I say, trying to keep my voice light. "As soon as my wolf is mastered, I'm outta here."

They laugh. My phone buzzes. "Oh, it's my Seattle loufrer. I should take this, do you guys need me for anything right now?"

"Not yet. We know you're available, we'll call you if something comes up."

I head to the employee break room, a grim, windowless space featuring an extremely stained automatic drip coffee maker and the world's oldest microwave. In the winter it's dreary, but in the summer, I enjoy the fact that it's a dank underground tomb.

I answer Deena's video call. "Hello?"

"Hey, Abby!" She's smiling, recently freshened up her hair color to be a bright, full rainbow. "What's up? Are you an official free citizen of the universe yet?"

"No, I failed the trial. Still a prisoner in Bayou Galene."

"Is it pre-moon or post-moon there?"

"Pre moon but just barely. I'm planning to stay human though."

"Why, so you can mope?"

"No, so you can call me on the phone."

"Well if you want to mope at me, go right ahead, I'm very supportive of moping. Oh, Izzy just came in, you want to say high to Izzy?" She turns the phone around to show her girlfriend Isobelle Quemper, who she met when she was in New Orleans visiting me.

Izzy leans in close to wave. "How y'all doing out there? Did you pass that trauma morph thing?"

"Not yet."

"You'll get it next time. What?" She speaks to somebody off camera. "Oh, I thought I fixed that! Sorry, Abby, gotta go deal with the app. We should talk when it's not the full moon!" She waves again and leaves, presumably to work with the rest of the technical crew on one of their many apps. With such an explosion in new bitten wolves, all the track and chase teams have been really stressed, but their technology has also exploded.

Deena turns the phone back around to show her own face. She smiles a little sadly. "That's my girl, the computer genius."

"Is college still in session?" I ask.

"For another couple of weeks. Right now we're at the Georgetown maison, check it out." She spins the phone around to show the repurposed warehouse that houses the Seattle maison, originally intended as temporary to deal with the outbreak I caused by biting Steph's ex husband George. But temporary maisons don't break up until thirteen moons with no new bitten wolves, so the Seattle location is still going strong. Like the bunker, it seems much busier than when I was there last.

"Is Edison around?" I hear a pathetic whine of longing creep into my own voice and hate myself for it. The last time Edison and I were together we were getting really close, going on our first official date, kissing afterward. But the Flint Savage problem got really intense after that and even though we saw each other a few more times, it was always part of a larger group with no opportunity for romance.

"No, he's got a gig with the band and he's out getting ready for that."

"A gig? On the full moon?"

"Yeah, Abby, local music venues don't watch the moon calendar." She snickers. "The maison told him it was okay, since we've got Officer Dan on board. Did you know that? Dan got the trauma morph from you—well, from George—well, from whoever George bit—and didn't even know it until he started comparing notes with all the other wolves and thought to check it out. So now he's doing that whole staying human on the full moon thing. Anyway, I sort of have a job, but since I'm not semi-wolfy like Edison or a computer genius like my girlfriend, my job involves hanging around and staying sober in case somebody needs to get driven in a car somewhere."

"Well, that's important. I mean, if they bring in a wolf who's more than a few blocks from the maison, they need a van to put them into."

"Yeah, except I'm the backup driver, so mostly I end up getting people snacks."

"Snacks are also important. Wait—"

"What is it?"

"Moonrise." I close my eyes for a moment, listen to the silvery howling. I shudder. I want to go with them. When I hear the howling, there's a part of me that always wants to go with them.

But I tell the wolf no.

That's what I've been practicing for months, after all.

Pere Claude once told me, when the wolf was sleeping after my head injury, that I was very good at telling her no, but not so great at telling her yes. Eventually I did tell her yes, when my grandfather and I brought down Flint Savage together. But now we've spent months going back to where I was before, telling her no.

"Do you need to go?" Deena's voice cuts through my thoughts. "We can talk later."

I take the suggestion. "Later. Yeah."

I end the call, drop my head onto my arms. I want to cry for no obvious reason. Then my phone buzzes again. I look down. The control room is calling.

I pick it up. "Hello?"

Jason's voice. "Abby, the cemetery group needs more fuel for the generator, do you know where we keep the propane?"

"Sure. I'll bring some out there."

As I'm heading to the cemetery with the canister, I call Deena again. "Guess what they have me doing?"

"Does it involve snacks?"

"Maybe. Delivering propane to the cemetery."

"Why the cemetery?"

"You'll see." I set the propane down, swing my phone camera around to show the cemetery, built in classic southern Louisiana style, surrounded by a brick wall topped with spiky iron fleur-de-lis, fancy crypts and mausoleums visible above the top of the wall. "Notice anything?"

"The name worked into the front gate says Bayou Galène with an accent, have I been saying it wrong all this time? What does the accent mean?"

"Everybody around here says 'Bayou Gall-een' so you're good. But I was talking about something else. It's big, isn't it? Relative to the size of the town?"

"You're right. How small is the town?"

"I'm not sure exactly. Around a thousand people?"

"Huh. That is small for a town. It's a lot of werewolves, though. Did it used to be bigger?"

"No, smaller."

"Do a lot of people... uh... die... there?"

"Not really. There's a different reason the cemetery is so large, you'll see it soon."

I wedge the propane under my arm to give myself a free hand, tap the code into the door lock on the outer gate, slip inside, make sure it latches firmly behind me. Once inside, I stop at the Verreaux family crypt, swing the phone up to show the statue on top of it: a winged woman in a draped gown, crown of thirteen stars on her head, large wolf seated at her feet. Her hands are clasped at her breast, left hand in a fist around the top of a sword which is pointing downward, right hand closed around the outside of her left fist. The motto beneath her feet says LUPUS COR LEONIS which I have been told is very bad Latin for "the heart of the wolf is a lion."

"Family crypt, check it out."

"Wow. You come from a family with a family crypt, that's so Gothic. I've never seen an angel like that before. She's got a sword!"

"We're not sure what all the symbolism means. Apparently nobody bothered to write stuff like that down back then. They just assumed people two hundred years later would know, I guess. Or that it wouldn't matter. Anyway, see this enormous mausoleum, how it dominates the center of the cemetery?"

"Wow. That is huge."

"There's an interior, let's go." I reach another elaborate wrought-iron door, tap in another digital code, enter the mausoleum.

Just inside the doors an enormous gray wolf, Josie, makes eye contact with me, an amber flash. If we didn't know each other she'd be chasing me out right now.

I blink slowly, lower my gaze, look away. The wolf takes this as a signal that I'm not here to cause harm, and steps aside, lets me approach the final gate. Another coded lock, then we're in a raised courtyard, partly grass, partly brick. Two more wolves, Amelie and Sylvan, greet me at this new location. Once again I lower and avert my gaze. The wolves press their noses into my free hand, then depart.

"Wait, where are we now?" Deena says. "Why are there so many kids, is this a day care center?"

"Moon care center. Remember, we don't start transforming until we're in our teens, so where do the kids go when their parents are on the hunt? They come here."

Colbert, a wolfless man who often stands guard, steps forward. "Abby. Is something going on?"

"No, just delivering propane for the generator."

"Oh, thank you." He takes the propane with a smile. "It wasn't so urgent, they didn't have to send you."

"Well, I'm also showing my Seattle loufrer the cemetery."

He half-laughs, waves into the camera. "Oh, yes? Hello Seattle friend, how do you like our little nursery, hey?"

"It's basically the coolest thing I've ever seen," she says enthusiastically and he smiles in response.

I wander through the courtyard, showing all the details: barbecues and generators and coolers and patio furniture. The older kids tend to be deep into their phones, while the younger kids run around playing, mostly pretending to be wolves themselves.

"Are all the kids out here?" Deena asks.

"Nobody over the age of thirteen comes out here unless they're helping take care of the younger kids. Thirteen is the youngest age when the wolf is thought to appear. So they end up acting like outsider teenagers, really. Just sort of hanging out, not children anymore, but not adults yet. They like to steal their parents' beer and go down to the end of the spit. There's some ruined houses, perfect teenage hangout spot."

"What's going on over there? The wolf lying down on the blankets?"

"This way." I take the phone over to where a nursing mother is sprawled on large wool blankets laid across the bricks of the courtyard. A chubby human infant with curly red hair sucks noisily on the swollen teat of a large gray wolf. "This is Zepherine and her son Alcide."

Zepherine turns toward me at the sound of her name. Alcide giggles, pats his mother's fur, and begins crawling toward me. I sit down and let him crawl into my lap, while his mother watches intently. She knows me. She trusts me. Otherwise she'd have driven me well away. Still she watches me. The intense focused gaze of her golden eyes is a little unnerving, even to another wolf. Because her eyes, her posture, her teeth, her taut body language all tell me: one wrong move and I bite your throat out before you can exhale.

"The Varger are very protective of their children." I tickle Alcide who lets loose with a shrieking, excited giggle.

"I guess they would be, huh?" Deena says. "I mean, your babies aren't any tougher than regular-people babies, are they?"

"Not really. And except for weirdos like my dad, they don't usually have big families. So they treat their children as precious." I hear my voice choke up a little.

Deena says, "That all makes sense. But why guard them in the cemetery?"

I give Alcide a last tickle and return him to his mother, who nuzzles me briefly, an acknowledgment that I behaved correctly with her child and we are not enemies. "That's another thing nobody knows for sure. There's a practical reason—three gates and wolf guards, so no strangers are getting in on foot. But also, look." I swing the phone around to show the top of the mausoleum building, where each corner has a sculpture of a winged wolf, perched and watchful, gaze outward.

"A wolf with raven's wings, is how I've heard them described, and they're oriented toward the compass points. The Varger have this whole mythology regarding ancestral spirits. At one time, I guess, they kind of thought the spirits of the ancestors would watch over the kids. So that's why you'd put the nursery in the middle of the cemetery."

"This is amazing. What?" She says this to somebody off camera, I hear indistinct conversation, then she turns back to me. "Abby, sorry, I guess I need to go pick up a pizza." She rolls her eyes. "My extremely vital role as bringer of pizza. Talk to you later. Thanks for the tour."

"Yeah. Enjoy."

I turn off the phone and sit for a moment, staring at the wolves, the kids. I feel blank, shut off. I had a purpose, to deliver propane and to show Deena our cool cemetery during the full moon, and now... now what do I do?

They don't need me here.

They didn't really need me at the bunker.

Nobody needs me anywhere.

"See you all later, have a good moon." I head back to my room in the Grand Maison. It's not much of a room, really. They call it a "cabinay" which is probably French and spelled "cabinet" but I've never seen it written down. It's a tiny little room more like a hallway between two larger rooms, one used by my grandfather as a private home office, and the other used by Vivienne as a bedroom when she's in town. The bedroom is almost always empty during the day, and the office is empty at night, so it's not too awkward having to go through another room to get here. But, once I'm there in the cabinay (or cabinet), I get sort of—stuck. I can't think of how else to describe it. I stare at the clothes in my makeshift wardrobe, the books on my little bookshelf, the computer on my desk, try to think about what to do next, and it's just too much. Instead I sit on the bed and stare blankly at the wall.

This is a depression symptom you know

It sounds like the voice of a different person talking in my head, another voice: older, sensible, a little snarky. I've heard that voice before. It's the voice that first told me to leave New Harmony.

"Shut up," I tell it, out loud. Going to wolf form and back again took my hair out of its French braids, so I decide to comb it and put it back, which takes a while when it's this long. Nine whole months without anybody shaving it off me. I briefly regret that I don't have a braiding-each-other's hair kind of friendship with anybody here in town. Steph has braided my hair for me. My mother used to do it. Then, after my mother died, my older sister Chastity did it.

I wonder what Chastity is doing right now? My step-mother Meekness and my older brother Justice seem to have stepped right in to the remains of the John Wise evangelical empire, I know this because I've seen them on talk shows a couple of times. But what happened to the rest of my family in the cult? My brother Great Purpose was eighteen when the cult was destroyed, where did he go?

I should ask somebody who's good on the Internet, Izzy or Barney, maybe they can find out what happened to my other siblings. But not tonight, obviously, they're busy. And why am I only thinking of this now? It's been months. I must be a terrible person.

Hair secured, I glance at my phone for the time. It's ten p.m., probably almost the full moon in Seattle, right? Or is it? Seattle is two hours behind New Orleans, but a lot farther north, and the relative times of our sunsets vary a lot depending on time of year.

I feel so low all of a sudden and I really want someone to be holding me, someone who I know loves me, somebody I feel safe with. Three people flip through my mind: Steph, Edison, Pere Claude. Pere Claude is the only one who's physically close enough for that to be practical. I should have gone to wolf form. I should be hunting with the others. I'm useless here.

I consider going back to the bunker. Maybe they don't need me for anything in particular, but maybe they have other little chores, like propane delivery. It's something to do at least.

As if on cue, my phone rings.

"Abby? We do need you, it turns out. We've got strangers in town."

3

BECKFORD MANOR

"We have this camera outside the bunker trained on the main road." Jason points to a screen showing a puddle of light, empty pavement. "It's very narrow right there, no other way in or out, so we see every car. We just had one drive south."

"Oh no." My heart thumps. "What are they doing? They're not heading to the hunting grounds?"

"Probably tourists." He smiles reassuringly. "It was a Honda Civic. If they meant to go onto the hunting grounds they would have brought a truck. They should turn around when they reach the first gate. Make sure they do." He hands me a heavy, elaborate, gold-colored badge that identifies me as a "Federal Wildlife Officer."

I weigh it in my hand. "This looks real."

"It is real. Once you're south of the gate you're part of the Petit Galou Swamp Federally Managed Wildlife Refuge, which we are authorized to enforce. Congratulations, you are now an officially deputized officer of the law. Go get a uniform from the wardrobe. And take the white truck." A pause. "Do you have your license yet?"

"Um, except for the parallel parking. You don't need me to parallel park, do you?"

"So the answer is no?" Slight smile. "We'll send Oscar with you. Oscar, you're up!"

As usual, the smallest uniform is a little too big for me and I have to roll up the cuffs. Oscar, wearing a similar uniform, gives me a quick once-over, then a thumbs up and a smile. We climb into the white truck, drive until we reach the DANGER! ROAD CLOSED BEYOND THIS POINT barrier.

"Look at that." He points to obvious drag marks in the red dirt, where somebody moved the barrier aside and then moved it back.

"Sneaky. Clearly we need a heavier barrier?"

He sighs, shakes his head. "I guess so."

Beyond the barrier ourselves, it isn't long before we spot the strange car down at the spit, parked in front of the largest of the ruined houses, a big white mansion ornamented with pillars and wrought iron, stately in its decay.

"Hang on, I'm going to hit the red button," Oscar says, with a grin. It turns on a flashing red light and a siren. The strange car shakes for a moment and a woman gets out of the driver's side, face panicked, whitewashed by our headlights. Oscar's voice booms out over a loudspeaker. "Remain inside your vehicle."

The woman fumbles her way back into the car, slams the door.

"I've always wanted to do that," Oscar says. "Okay, let's look at her ID, run a quick name check, give a very stern warning, and send her on her way."

Oscar and I approach the car, me on the driver's side and him on the passenger side. I rap on the glass. "Roll down your window."

From inside a muffled voice, "I'm trying! The key isn't— okay, there it goes."

The window crawls down, releases smells of hairspray, clove cigarettes, stale coffee. The driver is young, with long, dyed-blonde hair, gothic-style makeup, pale skin, dark eyes, dark lips. "God, you scared me," she says. "Are you a cop?"

I flash my badge. "Petit Galou Swamp Wildlife Management. Can we see some ID?"

She hands over her license, and a student ID card for good measure. Jennifer Albertson. LSU. "It's okay, I'm just doing a ghost hunting thing for my film class."

Oscar and I exchange glances over the top of the car. Ghost hunters are the last thing we need around here. Looking for proof of the dreadful rougarou, I suppose. I take a picture of both pieces of ID, send them back to the bunker. Oscar shines his flashlight inside the car, illuminating film equipment: lights, microphone, open laptop computer.

"You're trespassing, Miss Albertson?"

"Trespassing? But it's an abandoned house."

"This is a wildlife management area. Access is restricted. The road's unsafe. Didn't you notice the warning sign on the gate?"

She makes a scoffing noise. "They put those up after hurricanes and then just leave them there for months at a time, it doesn't mean anything."

The bunker texts back:

```
Student ID checks out, go ahead and send her
                                         away.
```

"All right, it looks like we can let you go with a warning," I say.

"Let me go? But I was going to be here until midnight."

Oscar and I exchange frowns. He asks, "What happens at midnight?"

"The ghost wolf appears." She laughs a little. "If he's real, anyway."

Oh, absolutely not, the last thing we're going to do is let you stick around and catch footage of the "ghost wolf." I say,

"I'm sorry, Ms. Albertson, I doubt there's a ghost wolf, but if there is, he's protected wildlife and you still have to leave."

She grumbles, but puts the key in the ignition, guns the engine. The wheels spit mud, but the car doesn't go anywhere. After a few repeats of this, she sighs. "Can you guys get me out of this? If you're going to make me leave."

"Sure," I say. "Let's see what we've got in the truck."

Oscar and I go back to the truck and rummage through the equipment in the back, but fail to find anything that looks like you could use it to pull a car out of the mud. "I could have sworn we had a chain or something," he mutters. He glances at me. "Do you think you could use wolf strength to do it? Just, like, push the car?"

"Maybe, but don't you think that would be a bad idea to do right in front of somebody with a camera?"

He laughs. "Right, right, I wasn't thinking. Well, shoot. Looks like we have to call in a tow truck from Houma and keep our ghost hunter busy until it gets here."

"Houma? There isn't a tow truck here in town?"

He shakes his head. "Not really. I'll make the call, I've done it before and I know the guy. You keep our ghost hunter distracted."

"Sure." I go back to the car, slip in on the passenger side.

She yelps. "What are you doing in my car?"

"We have to call in the tow truck from Houma, we might be here a while."

She sighs, then brightens. "Can we at least get out of the car then? Maybe the ghost wolf will come early."

"No, you cannot get out of the car," I say. "What part of protected wildlife area are you still not understanding?"

She makes a disgusted noise. "Come on, what do you think I'm going to do? Step on a protected snake or something?"

"It's for your protection too. You should see the size of the alligators we get around here."

"Alligators?" She seems intrigued. "How big?"

"Big enough to eat you. They're not like the alligators you meet on those swamp tours. The ones who like marshmallows and hotdogs? They're practically tame, and they'd still take an arm off if you're not careful. The wild boars would eat you too, if you let them. And the wild cattle won't eat you, but they will trample you to death if you get in their way."

"Sounds real dangerous," she says, voice sarcastic. "Look out for the cows!"

"If your ghost wolf is real, he'd eat you too." I say.

"Not if he's a ghost," she says.

"Why don't you tell me about the ghost wolf?" I say.

"You want to hear the story of Beckford Manor?" she perks up.

"Sure, why don't you tell me the story of Beckford Manor."

"The current structure was built in the1920s as the Holy Magdalene Catholic Home for Girls." She gestures at the white mansion. "But before that it was the site of a terrible massacre during the Civil War. A group of enslaved people were trying to escape a Thibodaux sugar plantation. They intended to leave the country by boat, and were hiding, waiting for their boatman in what was then an abandoned fishing cabin. But before the boatman arrived, hunters caught up with them.

"Normally, they would have been captured and taken back into slavery, which is bad enough. But instead the hunters slaughtered them all. Beheaded them. Every single man, woman, and child. And do you know why they did that?

"According to one of the hunters, who was just a boy at the time, as he was recalling it decades later, it was because they had already been cursed by the rougarou. Come the next full moon they were going to change, and there would be no controlling them.

"So instead they were murdered. Thirteen people in all.

They separated their heads from their bodies and threw them into Petit Galou swamp for the alligators to eat.

"The cabin where it happened sat empty for a few years, as the war raged on. Without upkeep it crumbled. But it was on high ground, which is at a premium around here, so in the 1920s the home for girls was built on that site.

"And yes, it's exactly what you're thinking. The girls sent here were pregnant or otherwise deemed a trouble to their families. Mary Kelly, one of the girls sent out here, remembered it later. These are her words."

She stops, puts her voice into a vaguely Irish lilt.

"Oh, sure, it was beautiful out there, with the flowers and trees and the ocean just right there. But none of us could rest easy. Some of the girls took to sleepwalking. Me, I had a nagging sense of dread I could never explain. Just a sense all the time that something terrible was going to happen, and no amount of prayer could make it feel better.

"That summer I started to see a little Black girl in a white dress with a red ribbon tied around her neck and her hair in pigtails. She would look at me and laugh and run off, like she was playing hide and seek. She had such a pretty laugh. At first I thought she was a local girl, just swift on her feet. I would see her in the middle of the day, so I thought nothing of it.

"But then, one day, a dreadful hurricane was on its way, everything all battened-down and the skies going dark, and I saw the little girl, and I worried about her, so I followed her, thinking to make sure she made it home safely.

"I watched her run straight through a wall.

"Not two seconds later, the gales drove a great tree branch through the window upstairs, right where my bed was, and it killed the other girl who shared the room with me, that Paula Anderson.

"The little phantom saved my life. After that, I never saw the girl again, but I would hear that pretty laugh sometimes, coming faint and far off. And I started to wonder about that red ribbon she kept tied around her neck, and what might be underneath."

She pauses for a moment. "Where's the tow truck?"

I check my phone. "They're getting one. Go on with the story."

"The home for girls closed during World War II and the property sat empty until the early 1950s when it was taken over by Deacon 'Deek' Boudreaux. Deek had made a lot of money during the war, but doing what? Nobody ever knew for sure. Arms dealer, was the rumor. He wanted to make the property a resort-style hotel, but the project seemed cursed from the beginning. His workers would report hearing strange noises or having the unpleasant feeling they were being watched.

"The resort, when it finally opened, was a failure. Guests didn't want to spend the night there, it turned out, and the rooms were never more than half full, even at the height of the season.

"Deek turned it into a card room. Gambling was illegal in the state at that time, but he figured nobody was going to bother coming all the way out here just to bust him.

"The illicit casino was successful for a while. But gambling often brings out the worst in people, and almost every night somebody was in there trying to knife somebody else. There were murders and attempted murders. And people swore the house wasn't fair. Stacks of cards or stacks of chips would get knocked over for no obvious reason. People would report hearing strange noises. A few people heard the pretty laugh girl. Ghosts, or a rigged house? It's hard to say. But either way it's hard for a gambling spot to live down rumors that they don't play fair. So that closed too.

"The building sat empty for almost twenty years until Argan Beckford came along. He was a Texas oil big shot who got lucky, retired young, came out here to the end of the earth to raise minks.

"Why minks? Good question. Beckford had an advantage when it came to the mink trade: he was born without a sense of smell. And one of the things about a mink farm, it's the worst thing you've ever smelled.

"It was the 1980s by then and nobody believed in ghosts anymore, but Beckford had the same trouble people always had when they tried to have work done on that piece of land. Workers kept quitting on him, saying they didn't feel right working out here, like they were being watched all the time. Sometimes they'd see red eyes glowing in the dark. And they swore, if they were there on the full moon after dark, they heard the rougarou, the werewolves of the swamp, howling for blood in the distance like the wailing of lost souls. Got so they wouldn't work after dark on any night, full moon or no.

"Well, at a certain point, Beckford got tired of waiting for the remodel to be finished, called it good enough, and moved in with his seventeen-year-old daughter Lunora and his twenty-five-year-old second wife Amber Lee.

"Now, Lunora and Amber Lee didn't get along too well. Rumor was, Amber was a bimbo, a gold digger. And Lunora was still in mourning for her mother, who had died of an extremely rare malady, fatal familial insomnia.

"A strange disease. No cure, no treatment. Once symptoms start, you have, at most, three years to live. You sleep less and less, and eventually stop sleeping entirely.

"If you stop sleeping, after just a few days it hits your brain like a bad drug trip. You start to hallucinate. By the time you die of fatal familial insomnia, you've gone entirely mad."

She pauses, gives me an intentionally mad-looking smile. My phone has text from Oscar:

Tow truck on its way.

"We should wrap this up," I say. "Tell me about the ghost wolf before the tow truck gets here."

"Oh, sure, sorry, I was slipping into tour guide mode. All right, Beckford's wife ran off and there were rumors he had money problems. Beckford and Lunora were fighting all the time, according to their housekeeper. Then one day she went in and nobody was there. She found Beckford's body in his study, ripped to pieces by a wild animal of some kind. And while she stared in horror at his body, she heard a girl behind her laughing. Thought it was Lunora. But when she turned around, there was nobody there.

"That was forty years ago now, and nobody has touched the property since. But the local kids say that if you go down on the full moon at midnight, you can see a white wolf pissing on Beckford's grave."

A pause. I check my phone. The tow truck is getting here soon. "That's the ghost wolf?"

She nods. "That's the ghost wolf."

"Is there footage of this wolf?"

"No, I would have been the first." She sighs. "Can't you help me?"

"How many times do I have to say no? Look, the tow truck is here, let's go."

We get the truck hauled back onto paved, solid road, and she verifies it will drive forward. Oscar and I follow in the white truck, just to make sure she doesn't get it into her head to turn around and drive back down the spit.

Then, for good measure we park the white truck sideways across the road, just north of the too-easily-movable gate.

"Well, that's probably our excitement for the evening," Oscar says. "I'm going back to the bunker, what about you?"

"Not yet, I want to go down, check out Beckford Manor."

He smiles. "Looking for more ghost hunters?"

I smile in return. "Looking for ghosts."

Back down to the spit on foot. All the buildings down here,

no matter how fancy they were to start with, are now abandoned and crumbling into the sea. But the white mansion is obviously the most fancy. It squats with an air of self-importance, surrounded by flowering vines, mature live oaks, a stretch of lawn.

Pepper and lightning, a smell distinct and familiar, from behind me. I turn to see Pere Claude as a wolf, enormous and pure white, standing on the bridge over the canal, looking out over the whole spit, commanding, breeze ruffling his fur.

He nods at me, a greeting, but my presence doesn't change his purpose at all. He pads down, heads to the front porch of the ruined mansion, sits there for a moment staring out with a regal look. His eyes flash red. He howls, once, a howl that says, this land is mine. He climbs down the stairs and begins marking his territory in the usual way, urinating at various points around the circumference of the house, almost as if he's performing a containment spell.

He finishes. He makes eye contact with me, pauses briefly to put his nose in my palm, then takes off again to rejoin the rest of the pack.

4

THE VENERAY

After Pere Claude's wolf leaves, I move to investigate the ruins of Beckford Manor myself, taking pictures along the way. Crumbling white facade and broken statuary, covered with layers of spray painted graffiti as well as mildew and a proliferation of trailing vines. The half-finished remodel leaves it awkward, sturdy brick bones showing through a disintegrating and vaguely Roman facade of plaster.

Up the stairs to the grand entrance at the top of a porch, I make note of the columns overrun by a kind of trailing vine, thick and woody like wisteria, flowers with ruffled flutes like datura, white barely tinged with a strange luminous color that seems to be, somehow, both yellow-green and pale lavender. In moonlight they glow. But the most striking thing about them is their smell, a syrupy high-end sweetness like jasmine, troubled underneath by a hint of bitter earthiness, like old blood.

On either side of the front doors, a parade of white marble statues, most of them missing heads and hands, darkened by moss, mildew, trailing vines. One of the partially intact heads seems to be staring at me, hollow eyes spray-painted red with silver dots in the center that throw back the moonlight.

Cautiously, I enter the main house, stepping on a floor that creaks loudly, spongy and warped. I imagine taking a wrong step and a rotted plank giving way, tumbling me to the mud below. But the room, which must have been some kind of sitting or reception room, is curiously intact, still dominated by a white leather sectional couch and an assortment of antiques. The top layer of wallpaper, a peach color, is peeling away to reveal multiple layers of elaborate paper underneath.

Nobody, human or wolf, has been inside recently. Rats, nutria, birds. But I'm starting to pick up on the faint, faraway scents of the family that lived here forty years ago: a man, a woman, and a teenage girl.

The teenage girl was a bitten wolf.

I'm very nearly sure of it.

I close my eyes to focus on scent. It's the full moon so the wolf is right there, ready to take over, as the smells swirl around me. Bright and recent smells tug at my awareness, but I'm looking for the faint, the faded, the background. Etienne has taught me many tricks for this, ways of separating out the different layers of scent information. It feels a bit like trying to look at the paper instead of what's written on the paper. Dusty, dank and faded, like the rot on a forest floor. Then—

A pop of sharp, dark red, a familiar person-smell: my father Leon.

It's faint, and far away, but I'm almost sure of it.

I follow the smell upstairs, test each step before trusting my weight to it, avoid a couple of missing stairs. The wood creaks like a sigh, exhaling a shadowy damp rot, a smell that oozes like mud.

Once I reach the upper floor, instinctively I open my eyes to see where I am. Green-flash, my heart pounds, another wolf, invisible to my nose somehow?

No, the green flash was something else. I approach, eyes adjusting to the point where I can make sense of things again. Luminous mold or mildew, that's it. Flecks of an eerie phantom green speckled here and there on the walls, the clothing and draperies left behind. I'm torn between wanting to take back a sample, look at it under a microscope, and a curious loathing that makes me want to avoid touching it entirely.

Leon's trail leads me to a pile of clothing, smudged and glowing with that foul mildew. I touch it gingerly, moving items aside, until I uncover a T-shirt that poofs up a strong scent of Leon and clove cigarettes. I unfold the T-shirt, from a band called The Cure, touring an album called *Faith*. I'm almost certain that Deena has played this band for me before. As I shake it, something drops out, as if it was folded up inside the cloth.

A photograph. A thick, squarish photograph that still has a chemical odor, one of those instant-developing photos I think. The angle shows it to be a selfie, a boy and a girl, both around my age, some of the boy's pale arm visible in the corner. They are mugging hard for the camera, heads down, glowering upward, gothed up: teased black-dyed hair, heavy black eyeliner, blood-red lipstick and white, white faces, the boy's makeup not entirely concealing thick freckles.

Bon Dieu, this is my father.

I take a picture right away, just in case it crumbles to dust the instant I touch it, and text the picture to Deena:

GUESS WHO THIS IS

The photograph goes into the breast pocket of my uniform.

Exploring the room, this one bears the signs of someone having moved out in a hurry, clothes strewn around, closets and drawers open. The girl's scent is strong, clinging to the clothes and the bedding. She was not a wolf for most of the time she was here. The not-wolf person smells are deeper, baked in, and the wolf smells sit lightly, a sprinkling added at the last minute.

I can guess what happened: Leon made her a wolf, she came back, packed, and left. Well. Came back, maybe killed her father, packed, and left.

Down the hall I find a tremendous bedroom, luxurious still, in spite of the rot and the animals that have nested in here. A peach satin bedspread, discolored, still shiny. Beckford and his young wife slept here, at least for a while.

Continue down the hall to the final room, push open a door that's been shut forty years. Long-sealed smells rush out, overwhelming me: Scotch, cigars, rotting books, old leather, the girl as a bitten wolf, blood, shit, fear-urine, death.

After a moment I recover, start to take in the details. Padded leather armchair, dyed a maroon like old blood, studded with brass, shredded by animal claws, a wolf. She killed him in this chair. His fear soaked into it, along with his blood. She spent time making him feel afraid before she killed him.

My throat tightens. She had a reason, she must have. When she killed him. Did he deserve it? He probably deserved it.

Shying away from the armchair, I head toward his desk, massive but not well made, not solid wood, veneer over particle board, now warped and peeling. I sit down in his chair, nicer than the desk, genuine antique, thick and heavy, solid wood. Rusted from the damp, rollers make a hideous squeaking noise.

Unexpectedly I'm gripped by fear: he's going to come in, he's going to catch me, sitting in *his* chair, *his* desk, I have to leave, to get out—

Father Wisdom. That's who "he" is in my mind. The cult leader who raised me, my stepfather, he had a study like this. No Scotch and cigars, and the fine leather books were mostly Bibles. But it felt like this. A sanctuary for the boss, the patriarch, a room where he and he alone gets to retreat into a carefully ordered world of pleasant things, where it's always quiet and clean and nobody will ever bother him, because they know what will happen to them if they do.

A resentful rage stirs, and I move impulsively to shove everything off the desk onto the floor. Pencil cup, old-fashioned desk phone, paper blotter, sectioned tray of paper clips and push pins, all of it clatters dramatically to the floor. For a moment I feel foolish, wondering why I did that. But the clearing-away has revealed something: a square yellow sticky note still affixed to the surface of the desk, writing on it clear even after forty years. Cryptic, ominous:

> Venuray
> Venaray
> Venerrey
> Veneray
> June 4
> Call the boys

I pull the note up off the desk surface, put it in my pocket next to the photograph, explore the rest of the desk. Drawers locked, but decayed latches give way easily under force. Inside, nothing as intriguing as the "veneray" note: financial records for the mink farm, reference to Thibodaux Taxidermy.

I know that place. I've been there. My grandmother was killed in wolf form by hunters who took her body to Thibodaux Taxidermy, but Leon tracked them down and killed them. Afterward the shop sat empty for forty years, until last summer when my sister Opal, the Frat Boy Killer, tried to use it to engineer another massacre, or at least, to get Leon and Pere Claude to kill each other. She failed in that. The only people who died during the attack were Strigoi, members of the Russian mafia.

Leon told me that "hunters" killed his mother, but was one

of them his girlfriend's father? Because he never mentioned that.

I find myself constantly glancing at the armchair. When I turn my back on it to examine the contents of the shelf, I keep turning around, like it's watching me.

I don't believe in ghosts. Not actual literal ghosts. But the smell. The violence, rage, death, fear. It bothers me, even though I'm pretty sure that Beckford wasn't a good guy and might have deserved to get eaten by his own daughter.

The books on the shelves are mildewed, but otherwise untouched. The gilded edges of the paper must be real gold, impervious to the forces of decay, gleaming in the dark. One of the bottles of Scotch is intact and full of golden liquid. Still good? Maybe. I'll take it for Pere Claude. The cigars are a lost cause, foul-smelling and rotten to the touch.

But that armchair.

It bothers me.

I want to leave the room where it is.

Anyway, I think I've figured out everything I'm going to figure out. Downstairs again, sweep quickly through the other rooms, the palatial kitchen, the epic laundry. Out to the back porch, overlooking a large grassy field surrounded by live oaks.

More of that flowered vine with the odd smell, and another smell, one that's very old and very, very foul. Follow the scent trail, find ruins that could have been a chicken coop, rotten wood and twisted wire. The stench that lingers is unlike anything I've ever encountered: sharp and fecal, lots of ammonia, bitter. When I close my eyes it becomes an intense but ugly yellow, and so prickly, so rough, like a carpet of pins. I can hardly imagine what it was like when new. It must have driven the wolves crazy.

I snap a few pictures, notice my text to Deena hasn't gone through. Morning is getting close and I'm starting to feel drained, tired. Back to my cabinay and right to sleep.

WHEN HE TELLS HER HE'S A WEREWOLF, SHE HASN'T SLEPT IN *three days and she thinks she might have misheard.*

You mean vampire, don't you?

Vampires don't exist. Why would I be a vampire?

It fits. You're pale, nocturnal, kind of scary, I think I've seen you hissing at the sunlight...

He laughs. You do the same thing and you're not a vampire.

Are you sure? I feel like I might be. I'm something anyway. Everything's all...

She trails off, makes a gesture to indicate the world is shaking, unstable. After three days without sleep she's starting to hallucinate, as if she dreams while still awake. She sees movement in the corner of her eyes, maybe just her own hair, but she keeps thinking it's going to resolve into some creature: a spider, an animal, a ghost, a monster. But always when she turns to look at it straight on, there's nothing.

She sucks deeply on the clove cigarette, hot acid taste, smoke tickling her nose. Sometimes she experiences an emptiness where her sense of smell should be, but most of the time she doesn't notice. Right now she notices. He tells her the cloves have a very strong smell, one he likes, but to her it's nothing, a sharpness, maybe, and that's it.

I'm serious about being a werewolf. Do you want to see?

Does it involve you taking off your shirt? Then, yes.

He laughs, rubs the hair at his temples where natural red is starting to push out flat, artificial black. She likes the effect and tells him so.

It's like your head is on fire at the roots and burnt out to charcoal at the ends.

He nods, but seems distracted. Do you want to see?

I told you I did.

All right.

He begins stripping out of his clothes, quickly, as if he's practiced it a lot. The Cure T-shirt, the one from the concert they went to with his mother, that comes off first, moving up over his head, dropping to the floor.

Belt, jeans, underwear, shoes: all move down in a single gesture and he is standing in front of her completely naked.

She feels herself blush, look down, away from his genitals, somehow she wasn't ready. Is this how they're finally going to do it then? Is that what he means when he says he's a werewolf, that he's ready for this? That he's going to throw her to the bed and…

Pay attention. His voice is snarling, irritated. Look at me.

Why do I have to look at you? Now she's annoyed. I know what dicks look like.

But that's not what I'm showing you.

She does look, and yelps when she sees what he's holding: a knife. Gleaming, sharp, but old, tinged with fire. A strange curved dagger, has he shown it to her before? It looks somehow evil, as if it's absorbed a murderous intent from the past.

Are you going to kill me? She tastes the words, sharper than the cigarette. She's fascinated by them. Maybe she likes the taste of them. The disease will kill me anyway, before too long.

That's why I'm doing this. He grits out the words and then plunges the dagger deep into his own gut.

Blood and other fluids spurt out. She stifles a scream of horror and frustration, kill me, I said kill me, why are you killing yourself? He drops to the floor on all fours, panting, and she watches, fascinated and scared. Is this how I'm going to watch someone die for the first time? She pictures her father dying. He's in his favorite chair, brass studs on leather the color of dried blood. She pictures him dying in that chair.

Wait.

Her nose tickles, not that she smells anything, but she feels it, like spider fingers reaching up inside, and she wants to sneeze. The air feels hot and slippery.

Where he was, instead of white human flesh, there is a white wolf. Not so very different from a big dog, but still, she knows. A wolf. It's there in the sharp ears, the focused eyes, the long fierce jaw, the oversized paws. Like a dog in its raw form, a dominant predator, before we bred them into being our friends.

She never really liked dogs, found their slobbering friendliness oppressive. A dog needs you too much.

But a wolf. A wolf stands alone.

She looks deep into his eyes, they flash green and her heart stops.

Then it starts again.

She touches the fur of his neck, finds it warm, coarse, thick, inviting, she wants to run her hands through it. She buries her face in his neck. Her nose tickles sharply again, but still she doesn't smell anything.

Do you understand the words I'm saying? She says.

He tosses his head, briefly opening his mouth to show teeth.

She has never seen teeth like that.

Thick and long and sharp as daggers, they make him look prehistoric, an ancient monster. Briefly he's nothing but teeth. His mouth closes again. Teeth hidden, once more he could be a large dog.

He seems to be waiting for something. She feels like she ought to say something.

Okay, yes.

Was that what he was waiting for? Whatever it was, the wolf bows down, in a classic stretching position, the air goes slippery again, and he becomes a young man. He rises.

Do you understand now?

You're a werewolf. For real.

If I bite you, you might become like me. And if you become like me, it might cure your illness.

I WAKE UP.

The dream fades rapidly, leaving me with a vague sense of displaced emotions. I was her. Lunora. The girl in the house. I felt her terror over the the fatal illness, the strange emptiness where her sense of smell was not. And a nausea.

Wait, that's hunger, I didn't eat before going to bed. When was that? What time is it?

I pick up my phone. It's 1 am, so I must have slept all day. Wow. My steps creak in the old house as I head downstairs and out to the courtyard, then into the public house. It was built around the same time as the bunker and has a similar geometric concrete assertiveness, plus air conditioning. The lower floor is mostly small meeting rooms and offices. The school meets here, and it's where the mayor of Bayou Galene, by tradition the pere, keeps an office that shows up as a mailing address on outsider paperwork. The second floor has the library, plus a big dining hall and a large commercial-style kitchen.

By convention, the kitchen is always open, and if you're hungry, you can forage anything in the smaller of the two refrigerators. I find yogurt, the fancy kind Vivienne likes, mix it with granola, start eating while I climb another set of stairs, to the smaller third floor we call the raven's nest. It's built in a hexagon and during the day large windows provide a spectacular view of the surrounding area. But right now the windows are just black mirrors. Another stairway leads to a deck on the roof, and I was planning to eat outside. But Leon is here in the nest, laptop computer open, collection of pere diaries spread out across the surface of a table, one of his own notebooks open in front of him.

"Abby." He glances at me with a slight half smile, then goes back to frowning at the notebooks, tapping a capped fountain pen against the paper. "Don't spill on the books."

"You're going through the pere diaries? Looking for anything in particular?"

"Anything that might help us with the Flint Savage outbreak," he says, with a sigh. He frowns, shuts the notebook, looks at me. "Did you want to talk?"

"Why did you close the notebook?"

"Abby, please."

"Keeping secrets? Hoping I won't find out about... this?" I take the photograph of gothed up teenage Leon out of my pocket and place it on the cover of the closed notebook. His face turns a gratifying shade of shocked gray before his expression becomes a smile and he gives a subdued chuckle.

"I was going to ask where you got this, but I think I know where. The manor out on the spit. Bon Dieu. I had forgotten…"

"About your unfortunate fashion choices? I bet you have. And don't think you can just quietly make this disappear, I already sent a copy to Deena."

Another smile. "I'm sure she'll put it to good use." A long, heavy sigh. "I suppose you have questions?"

"Yeah. I do. What did you do to get your hair to floof out like that?"

He looks perplexed for a moment, then bursts out laughing. "Back combing and way too much hairspray. Also, the dye damaged it, gave it a bit of a rougher texture."

"I have other questions too."

"Of course." He pushes back in his chair, sets down the pen. "It's been forty years, I have no reason not to answer them now."

"No? Okay. The girl in the picture is Lunora Beckford, right?"

"Right. How do you know the name?"

"Ghost hunter. You heard about last night's ghost hunter, didn't you?"

He nods. "I did."

"Were you dating Lunora behind Pere Claude's back?"

"Yes. Behind her father's back too. My father didn't want me dating a wolfless human. Her father didn't want her dating at all."

"So you made her a bitten wolf?"

"It wasn't so we could date. She thought she was starting to suffer from the fatal familial insomina that killed her mother, and we both hoped becoming a wolf would cure her."

"So you bit her. Is that one of the things you were talking

about when you said you did stupid things when you were my age?"

He grimaces. "Yes. It is."

"Do you regret making Lunora a wolf? She didn't start an outbreak did she?"

"No, no." He shakes his head. "It wasn't that. It was just— the way it all happened. You know."

He's obviously being evasive and I think about pressing him harder, but don't want to forget about the "veneray" note. "I also found something weird in her father's study."

I hand him the small yellow square and his face goes gray again, blank. No chuckle this time.

"You found this in the house?"

"In the study. At his desk, under a bunch of other stuff. Do you know what it's about?"

"The date is the full moon when my mother was killed. 'Call the boys' could be a reference to the hunters who did the dirty work. Beckford was—he and my father had what you might call a feud going. My father objected to the smell of the mink farm. Beckford objected to 'all these dogs' running around free so close to his minks. He lost a few to coyotes, he blamed our people. Our 'dogs.'" He shakes his head. "But the Veneray, that's something different." Deep sigh, and he leans back, stares at the ceiling as if looking for inspiration. "I thought they were fiction. My father used to talk about them. Werewolf hunters."

"Werewolf hunters? What kind of werewolf hunters? How would you hunt werewolves?"

He shrugs. "I don't know. That's part of why I never believed in them. According to my father they were started in the post-Civil-War period and might have ties to the Klan. But he was just telling the story his father told him. A children's tale, I thought. 'Behave or the rougarou will get you' to a Cajun, 'behave or the Veneray will get you' to a Varger."

"But the rougarou legends are based on real werewolves.

What if the Veneray legends are based on a real group of werewolf hunters?"

"You could be right. But if true, it changes… everything." He sighs, starts tapping the pen again. "My father instituted the trauma morph restriction to keep us hidden from people like the Veneray, and I thought he was being ridiculous."

"What? Pere Claude started that? I thought it was traditional."

"No. The methods of training to control the trauma morph are traditional, but the ban on uncontrolled morphs in the outside world without a chaperone, that was his own idea. My father became pere in the mid 1960s, and his thinking was based around the mass media of the time. He very much had a nightmare scenario in mind of something like the 1969 moon landing, all the planet tuned into the same live broadcast at the same time, and a wolf transformation caught on camera."

"Wow, this is blowing my mind. I was picturing everything all wrong. No wonder you hated the restriction so much. It must have felt like your father was picking on you special. Torturing you. Keeping you a prisoner."

Long, slow nod. "That is how it felt. Yes."

"But if the Veneray are real, maybe he was right the whole time. Maybe we do have to stay totally hidden, or this secret group of werewolf hunters will come after us."

"It's not that simple. Because I'm also right. There will come a day, very soon, when things change for us no matter. Somebody will capture a wolf transformation on video, and the wrong people will see it, believe what they're seeing, and take action. Or we'll have to move. One badly placed hurricane could wipe us off the map."

A moment of silence, while I eat my yogurt and he stares at the photo and the note. Then he yawns. "Well, I don't think we're going to solve the Veneray problem tonight." He stashes the photo and the "veneray" note in a pocket in the back,

closes the book, wraps the elastic around it. A gesture of final-
ity. He gathers the notebooks into a stack, lifts up a bright
orange bench to reveal a storage area, puts the books inside,
closes it, locks it, pockets the key. "If you still can't sleep, I
would recommend the pere diaries written by Joseph Baptiste
Verreaux. He was not the most compelling writer, although his
level of detail regarding animal husbandry is fairy
impressive."

He leaves. I stare at the locked storage area. It's probably
nothing important, nothing that would matter to me at all, but
the mere fact that he didn't want me to see the diary he was
working on, makes me want to know what's in it.

5

END OF THE WORLD

She inhales, deep and long, against the fading intense pain of the teeth, a deep, full-body bite, down to the bone, and laughs, giddy, as the world shimmers and he regains his human form. She leans against the wall in a kind of afterglow, spent, not from pleasure but from pure intensity, the pain, but it's gone, the aftermath is… it's a rush. She laughs.

That was it. That was what I always imagined it was like to be bitten by a vampire, she says.

He shakes his head. I told you vampires aren't real. Anyway you won't live forever.

But maybe I'll live to see twenty, she says. Sighs. Inhales, exhales, inhales—her nose tingles with something strange that reverberates through her mind, like a sounding note, a crashing wave, something huge, over-whelming, she feels undermined, clutches at the wall. Is that—is it smell? Already?

What is it? he asks. What's wrong?

She looks down to her arm, where the marks of his teeth are already healing rapidly. What is smell—what is it supposed to—to smell like?

He laughs. I don't know how to explain it. You think your sense of smell is coming back?

Not coming back, I never had one. Remember?

Right, right. But you think you're starting to get one?

Maybe. I don't know. Is smell... is smell bad?

I WAKE UP, TEN MINUTES BEFORE I'M SUPPOSED TO TRAIN WITH Pere Claude. Luckily, trauma morph training is done in the smallest and oldest of the Bayou Galene gyms, which is also the one nearest the big house. These days, trauma morph training is almost all it's used for, and until we started using it a few months ago, it seemed very stale.

It has none of the amenities you expect in a modern gym. No air conditioning, no machines, no TV, weak internet. It doesn't even have a bathroom, just a sink and a water cooler. It reeks of old sweat and werewolf blood. Three of the walls have the traditional leather padding typical of sparring rooms, but no reinforcements in the walls. The fourth wall is paneled in thick wood, aged and stained and dark, weapons hanging in rows: axes, swords, daggers, hooks, spears, flails, chains. Like an exhibit of medieval torture devices, or a serial killer's party wall.

Whenever I enter the old gym, my attention is drawn instantly to the wall of weapons, morbidly fascinated by the smell of blood and pain that radiates from it, like a malicious ghost. Even though the weapons are kept in good working order, sharpened and oiled, in my memory they always become dark, damaged, crusted in blood and rust, like something from a horror movie.

Pere Claude is already sitting on one of the benches near the water cooler, wearing his full moon robe of silver-embroidered white cotton. It came from somewhere far away, maybe Morocco? The first time I saw him in it I joked that it made him look like Gandalf. He looked perplexed for a long time and then said, "Oh, yes, the fantasy movies. Vivienne took me to see them. The mountains were very beautiful."

"Abby, welcome." He stands, holds out his arms and I go

to him for a big, enveloping hug. It's reassuring. Maybe too reassuring. Maybe that's why I failed the trial. When Pere Claude comes at me, even when it's with some bizarre hooked chain from the serial killer wall, there's no part of my brain that wonders whether he's going to kill me for real.

I pull away. "What are we working on today? After my failure?"

"Not failure. Attempt."

"An attempt that failed."

He shakes his head. "Dwelling too much in your failures just invites more of them. Let's start with animals."

"Sure, animals."

Pere Claude says, "The wolf sleeps."

I curl up into a little ball on the floor, imitating the wolf nose-to-tail sleeping position as best I can with my human body.

"The wolf wakes up."

I uncurl and imitate a wolf or dog waking up, with movements similar to the downward dog of yoga, kicking out and stretching first one leg and then the other.

"The wolf sees a crow."

I lift my head up, as if I'm looking at something in the sky above me, and several times rise up onto my legs, then go back down to all fours.

"The crow leads the wolf."

Imitate a crow, arms out and then down to my sides as if flapping, move forward in an exaggerated birdlike way hopping from one leg to the other.

"The wolf meets a bear."

Briefly, I'm the bear, moving on all fours like the wolf but with a different, heavier gait and a more rounded body position.

"The bear chases a rabbit."

I move swiftly for a few moments as the bear, then transition into being the rabbit, move with a hopping gait.

"The rabbit meets a frog."

More hopping, but with my legs splayed out instead of tucked under me.

"The frog leaps to catch a fly."

Huge leap into the air, body splayed out, arms reaching as if to catch something out of the air.

"The fly is caught in a spider's web."

Crouch, fall to the floor with all my momentum, jarring, a little painful.

"The spider repairs her web."

Spider is my favorite animal to do, because I'm really good at it. I can actually crawl up the padded wall, using the irregular spots as shallow hand-holds.

"The egret tries to catch the spider."

Drop to the floor on one leg, lean forward as if trying to catch something in my mouth, hop to the other leg and do the same thing.

"The alligator tries to catch the egret."

Alligator is a challenging position, like a very low plank where I change position moving just my hands and feet.

"The alligator is bitten by a snake."

Snake is fun, where I keep my legs tightly together and my arms against my sides, move by wriggling my whole body.

"The wolf catches the snake."

Back to all fours, imitating the way a wolf runs and pounces to catch a smaller animal. A different hunting move than "wolf catches the buffalo."

By tradition, by the time we're back at "wolf" the animals workout is over.

Pere Claude gives me a big smile. "Very good. Now, we speak to the wolves."

"Wolves? Plural?"

He shakes his head for a moment. "Apologies. The traditional way—we speak to our own wolves and also open ourselves up to listen to the ancestors. In past sessions I have modified it for you, to be speaking only to your own wolf. I thought you might find it too much like the prayers of your childhood, to speak to the ancestors in that way."

Anger coils in my throat, and my voice comes out in a thick growl. "You've been doing that the whole time? Training me wrong? No wonder I failed!"

He shakes his head, holding out his hands in a calm-down gesture. "Abby, please. If you're ready to speak to the ancestors, we can try that."

"Okay. Sure. Thanks." I feel embarrassed now. Why did I get so mad? And at Pere Claude too, one of the least enraging people I know. "How much like a Christian prayer is it really?"

Slight smile. "I'll lead you through one traditional mediation and you can tell me. Join me on the floor." He lowers himself, a little stiffly, to sit cross-legged on the padded floor. I lower myself to sit facing him. "Spine straight, don't slump. Close your eyes. Listen to your heart beating."

I do.

Thump thump

Thump thump

For a moment I imagine: what if my heart stopped beating?

"You're afraid, why?"

"You noticed that? I, um, I don't know, I just wondered for a moment what would happen if my heart stopped beating and it made me panic for no reason."

"Listen to your heart, it's strong. Take my hands."

We reach out, clasp hands. "Eyes closed, repeat after me. We honor the gifts of the wolf, which come to us from the ancestors in their wisdom."

"We honor the gifts of the wolf, which come to us from the ancestors in their wisdom."

"Wolves of ancient days, we honor you and welcome your counsel."

"Wolves of ancient days, we honor you and welcome your counsel."

"In silence we wait to hear your voices."

"In silence we wait to hear your voices."

I wait for another line. Nothing. Oh, right, he just said we wait in silence.

I'm not sure what I'm waiting for. Something to happen? Nothing to happen? He was right, in a way, that it feels more like a prayer than what we usually do, but it doesn't bother me like prayers to Wisdom's Christian God. I feel pretty neutral about it, actually. If there are ancestors out there who have something to say to me, the channel is open.

Grandma, you there?

Nothing. Well, I didn't really expect anything. Did I? Last summer, when I reached out to what might have been my grandmother's spirit, it felt as natural as reaching for my own wolf. I didn't have to do anything special. And now? Now I just don't know.

Faces seem to dance in the darkness before my closed eyes, morphing and changing, human to animal and back again.

Once upon a time all humans could become any kind of animal.

The words echo in my mind like something I heard aloud once. Once upon a time.

But if it was ever true, why did we lose that ability? Everyone but the wolf shifters, it seems.

No, there are others. Other shifters.

Who is that? Grandmother?

I seem to smell something, like exotic spices and dead flowers, a faint ghostly perfume.

Grandmother is that you?

A feeling, comforting and bothersome at the same time, like something stirring in my guts, something tingling at the back of my head, a sense of urgency, a question I need answered, and in my mind I seem to see white men in suits, laughing, drinking, in a fancy room, like a nice bar, and their laughter goes right through my ears like knives.

"The Veneray, tell me about the Veneray."

My voice. My eyes are open. I didn't mean to speak out loud or open my eyes, it just sort of happened. Pere Claude tenses up, sweat giving off a hint of fear. Wolf fear, different from the yellow curry scent of regular-people fear. Wolf fear is red. Dangerous. If we fear something, our instinct is to kill it.

He opens his eyes. "Where did you hear about the Veneray?"

"I found a reference in a note at the ruined mansion on the spit. Beckford Manor. You go there as a wolf, don't you? Every full moon, you claim the territory as your own."

He looks down, seems moderately embarrassed. "I suppose I do. The man who had my Leah killed, he lived there."

"Did you know he was involved with the Veneray?"

"I did not. I thought our feud was entirely over his mink farm. We hated the smell. He thought we were sending 'dogs' after his precious minks." A scowl. "They were killed by coyotes, but he didn't care." He stares into the distance, troubled. "I was never even sure the Veneray were real."

"But you were told about them?"

"I heard the stories from my father, who heard them from his father. When my own father was killed, he was killed by a land mine during the hunt. Were the Veneray responsible? I never knew. But afterward, as the pere, I was determined that we should update our protections for the modern era. We built the bunker and the public house, we formed the track and chase teams, we began to police our own lands more rigorously for strangers and suspicious activity. The world was changing, fast. Communication technology, transportation, if we didn't seek to master these things, I knew they would destroy us."

He closes his eyes. "I've done my best, Leah Evangeline, but you would say it's not enough. It's never enough."

He spends some time weeping, and I put my arms around his shoulders. He cries for a good long while, then falls silent.

"Are you still feeling up to the training?" I ask.

He raises his head, seeming confused. "Training? Right." He looks around, nostrils flaring. "This is the old gym. And you're my youngest granddaughter Abby."

"Right, Grandpa. You're training me to master the trauma morph."

He smiles. "You're doing very well. But do you think we could stop for the day? I'm feeling a bit overwhelmed."

"Of course. Let's go back to the public house, it's super hot in here today."

Arms around each other, we head to the public house, spend the rest of the morning chatting with the people there who come and go. He seems fine. Normal.

But I remember what the people in the bunker said, about him being tired, and I worry. Because he's so strong, so solid, I've never before thought about how old he really is. Eighty years, if I'm doing the math right. And that seems pretty old to me.

AFTER LUNCH I WANDER DOWN TO BECKFORD MANOR AGAIN, find Leon already there.

"Investigating?"

"Yes." He sets down an item that I recognize as a cassette tape. I pick it up, see the label is hand-drawn, an image of an explosion, the words END OF THE WORLD.

"What is this?"

"A mix tape." He smiles slightly. "Think of it as a playlist, only recorded on physical media."

"Right. I've heard about mix tapes. Why the explosion?"

He says, "It's a mushroom cloud." I continue to stare. "You know, like what a nuclear bomb would cause?"

"Oh, right. There was a picture of an explosion like this on the cover of one of the paperback editions of *The Late, Great Planet Earth* we had at the cult."

"During the 1980s we all thought we were going to die in a nuclear war. It shows up in a lot of the music."

"Yeah? Were people worried about global warming?"

"Almost nobody."

"What about deadly global pandemics?"

"Only Stephen King fans." He smiles slightly, holds up a battered paperback copy of *The Stand*. "Are kids your age still reading King? In the early eighties he was a huge phenomenon."

"Well, I don't know about other kids, but I read him. I haven't read that particular book, though." I pick it up, think about reading it, realize it smells too strongly of book rot, set it down again. "Have you read it?"

"Yes." He nods. "I've read most of his work."

"So that's something we have in common."

He nods. "I suppose it is." He holds up the tape, examines it. "I remember the day Lunora and I made this tape together. Her father wasn't home and we got into his Scotch." A slight chuckle. "I wonder if the bunker still has the equipment to play it?"

"The bunker? Sure, they have everything." I take it from him, put it in my own pocket. "I want to hear what music you were listening to back then."

"Well, I hope you enjoy it." He picks up an object, a chipped plate that has a picture of former president Ronald Reagan on it. "I remember this. Her father got it for giving a lot of money to the Reagan campaign."

"How much money?"

"I don't know."

"Did her father spend money stupidly?"

He holds up the plate. "Absolutely, he did."

My eye has been caught by another object, a thick cartridge of some kind, with what looks like album artwork for a band I've never heard of called REO SPEEDWAGON. I hold it up. "This is recorded music of some kind, right? What kind of a thing even is this?"

Leon takes it from my hands. "It's an 8-track tape. I didn't realize people were still making them in the 1980s. They were designed for playing in the car, I think."

"But isn't that what cassette tapes were for? Is this from before cassette tapes were invented?"

"No. But you know how it is with technology. The old things hang around for a while even after the new things are invented. Sometimes the old things even outlast the new things that were supposed to replace them. I hear your generation buys vinyl records again, but not compact discs." He puts the tape down.

"Edison buys vinyl, so I guess you're right. He likes to get weird records you've never heard of from the thrift store." I pick up a flat black plastic square, five inches or so. The printed label says FLEXI-DISKETTE and somebody used a red marking pen to write the word "pong!" on it. "What the heck is this?"

"Computer storage. Pong was a very early computer game. You can probably find a version online somewhere, if you want to see how it was played."

"This was for a computer? You're kidding. How much storage?"

He takes it from me. "Looks like 100 kilobytes."

"How much is that?"

"I don't know, not very much. A couple notes of a song?" He laughs.

I take a picture to send to Izzy and Barney. They might be amused. Then I take a deep breath. I have to ask something that's been on my mind since the full moon. "Leon, did you come back home because you want to be the next pere?"

"No." He answers quickly, firmly, shakes his head. "I know why you might think that, but it's not true."

"Okay. Why did you come back home then?"

"I came back to help my father. It's true, I think he will have to step down as hunt leader within the next few years. But I'm not my own first choice for pere." Slight smile. "That's not false humility."

"Okay." I shrug. "I guess I believe you. How do we get a new pere anyway? When it happens, I want to be prepared."

"The people go out on the hunt on a full moon night, with the old pere leading, and his, or her, seconds right behind. Then, when the time comes to lead everyone home again, it's one of the seconds who leads, and that person becomes the new pere. Return leadership is from behind, so the new pere is the last wolf to return."

"What happens to the old pere?"

"Nobody knows."

"Are they killed?"

"I just said nobody knows."

"Hmm. I'm extremely skeptical about this bit of information, but okay." I pick up a different waterlogged paperback, *Interview With the Vampire* by Anne Rice. "Deena likes this book I think. How did you avoid Pere Claude figuring out you and Lunora were dating? I noticed Steph had a new boyfriend just because I gave her a hug. Apparently that seemed creepy and pissed her off."

"I would go swimming in the bayou after we'd been together. Then I would smell more like the bayou than anything else. A very strong scent tracker like Etienne would probably have known. I think my mother knew. But she never said anything." He picks up a small waterlogged magazine called TV GUIDE, holds it up. "You've probably never seen one of these, have you? A weekly magazine just about what was on television?"

"Nope." I laugh. "I've heard of it though. *Dallas*, that must have been a TV show?"

"It was. There was a trend at the time for something they called the 'nighttime soaps.' I haven't thought of them in years." He frowns at the cover. "Lunora and her father came from Dallas. He used to dress a bit like this. The white cowboy hat and the gray business suit. We made fun of him behind his back." A pause. "Your loufrer Steph was upset with you?"

"She got mad when I asked about her boyfriend. I don't know why." I pick up a squarish black plastic chunk with the faded remnant of a brightly colored sticker on it, start working the sticker off with my fingernail. "Are we creepy? What we do, I mean? Knowing things because we smell them?"

He shrugs. "In popular folklore we are portrayed as monsters."

"Dad. That was not the answer I was looking for. Do you know what this is?" I hold out the black plastic thing. He takes it, examines it closely.

"I think it's part of a dismantled Rubik's Cube. Do you know what that is? Do they still make them?"

"Maybe I've seen it in toy sections?"

"Well, in the early 1980s it wasn't just a toy. It was a phenomenon. Everybody had one. My father had one." He sets it back on the table. "Abby, I'm really not the person to ask about creepy. That photo you find so amusing? Obviously I went out of my way to be seen as creepy, at least at one time."

"Do you still?"

He shakes his head, looks up at the ceiling. "I don't know. It can be useful to make somebody afraid of you in the right way."

"What's the right way?"

"They're scared of you, so they leave you alone."

"What's the wrong way?"

He has to think a while before answering. "They're scared of you, so they try to destroy you."

"How do you know the difference? How do you know you're scaring people the right way instead of the wrong way?"

"I don't know. I used to think I was good at scaring people the right way, but maybe I just got lucky. This whole Veneray thing has got me questioning everything." He picks up a tea tin that shows Princess Diana in a wedding dress. "Do you remember Princess Diana?"

"Remember? No. I remember adults talking about her. She was killed by the Illuminati."

"Killed by the what?"

"The Illuminati. They're some kind of big secret international conspiracy I guess? Apparently they do satanic ritual child abuse and Princess Diana was going to stop them? It's been a while, so I'm not sure of the details. My mother thought Princess Diana was a pure heart. That was the phrase she used. A pure heart. And they killed her because of that."

He frowns, tea tin in hand. "Did you hear a lot of that kind of thing growing up? Conspiracy theories?"

"I did. But it was funny. My father—Father Wisdom obviously—was part of all kinds of societies and organizations dedicated to promoting his type of Christianity in government. Project Blitz and the Congressional Prayer Caucus Foundation and The Fellowship and the Association of Christian Fathers and the Circle of Angels and others I don't even remember. He had prayer circles and power brunches with senators and presidents. They'd, like, eat pancakes and share each other's secret direct line phone numbers and talk about what kinds of laws to pass or not pass. That's a conspiracy, isn't it?"

Leon shrugs. "I suppose you could say that. But those aren't exactly secret, are they?"

"Secret enough. Have you ever been to one of their meetings?"

He shakes his head. "No."

"Did you even know they existed before I mentioned them?"

"Congressional Prayer Caucus maybe? But not the others. The one called Project Blitz sounds particularly, uh, ominous."

"It should, they're a bunch of Christian nationalists who are always working to get their propaganda into schools."

He frowns. "And they just went ahead and called themselves Project Blitz? Seriously?"

"At one time they did. But who knows, maybe too many people have heard about Project Blitz now and they renamed themselves the Super Freedom Patriot Fun Club. It doesn't matter. There are conspiracies and secret societies all over the place. Most of them involve men. That's the pattern I notice. There's only one real conspiracy, and it's men."

He chuckles slightly. "I guess you're right. Why aren't women part of more secret societies?"

"You tell me. You're a white man with money, don't they invite you?"

"Sometimes they do. I turn them down. They all sound very tedious. I have no interest in eating pancakes with men who bore me. But if the Veneray are real, they're different. The Veneray know how to kill us."

Silence for a moment, as both of us think about that. Not perfect silence. A dripping, creaking, sighing silence, the silence of a house decaying around us. I hold my breath for as long as I can, then exhale. "Does Pere Claude know?"

"What? Does he know what?" His sweat turns stressed out and I think I have my answer.

"About you and Lunora. He still doesn't know, does he?"

He chews on his lower lip for a moment, makes a gesture to flick his hair out of his eyes, even though it's too short for that. For just a moment, I see the self-conscious emo teenager who got together with his secret girlfriend and made a mixtape about the end of the world.

"It's not the dating." He sighs. Picks up a fragment of broken glass, sniffs it, frowns, puts it down again. "It's the taboo."

"*The* taboo? There's only one?"

"Might as well be. The taboo is against making bitten wolves. Obviously it happens accidentally sometimes. But you don't do it on purpose."

"Why not?"

"Well. The Flint Savage outbreak should give you a clue."

"But, he was kind of a special case wasn't he?"

"It only takes one." He picks up a brass sculpture of a rearing horse, stares at it for a moment, shakes his head and puts it down again. "Or so the thinking goes. Like a lot of things my elders told me, when I was seventeen, I thought it was ridiculous. But now I just don't know. Maybe my father always did know what he was talking about." He takes a look around the room, as if scanning for anything else of interest. "Etienne and Régnault are coming out from New Orleans later today, to help Viv and me search the manor in a more formal way. Not just scent tracking, but photographs, chemical samples, that sort of thing. We shouldn't disturb too much more before they get here. You want a ride back to the house?"

"Sure."

Once I'm back I collapse onto my little bed, wake a few hours later with the house full of people: Leon, Vivienne, Etienne, and Régnault. I hurry downstairs, find them in the main sitting room drinking iced coffee and chatting, animated.

"Abby," Viv greets me first. "You can join us, we're talking about what we found at Beckford Manor."

"You all went down to Beckford Manor without me?" I glare at Leon. "You didn't tell me you were going without me."

He and Viv exchange looks. Viv sighs. "Little one, have you ever tried to awaken you when you're not ready to get up? It's not a particularly enjoyable or fruitful activity." She pours me some iced coffee from a pitcher, hands it to me, a pacifying gesture. "Anyway, remember, you're still in training. If you can't follow the direction of your senior investigators, you can't be on the team."

"But I'm not in training right now." I flinch in disgust at the whining in my own voice. "I'm stuck out here."

"Trauma morph training," Leon points out. "That is part of your training for the track and chase teams, yes?"

"I guess."

Etienne jumps in. "Of course it is, Abby. With a fully mastered wolf, you will be an enormous asset to our team."

"Fine. What did you guys find out anyway?"

Viv says, "Lunora killed Argan Beckford, and she was a bitten wolf at the time. Also a trauma morph, since it appears that Lunora entered the room as a human, but killed her father as a wolf."

Leon says, "We found his safe. It wasn't in his office, it was in the bedroom. Beckford was deeply in debt, far more than I realized at the time. And apparently he was dealing cocaine."

"Cocaine? Wow. Actual cocaine has just been sitting there for forty years?"

"Trace amounts only."

"Did you find out about the Veneray?"

"Yes and no," Leon says. "We're certain now that Beckford was in contact with them. But who his contact was, and whether he was giving them orders, or they were giving him orders, is still uncertain. We're almost sure now that the Veneray are connected to the death of my mother, but we don't know for sure that she was the intended target, and if so, we don't know why."

Régnault stands up, looks at Vivienne. "I believe, cher, that we are done here?"

"Of course, go back to the city, thank you."

Etienne jumps up. "If it's okay, Mr. Régnault, I'd like to go back into town with you." He glances at Viv, who nods.

"Yes, Etienne, I think you've given us all the help we need, thank you."

They leave, and it's only now that I consciously notice: "Wait, where's Pere Claude? Isn't he part of this?"

Viv and Leon give each other pointed looks. Leon sighs. "We're taking you and Pere Claude along to to the next phase."

"The next phase?"

They glance at each other again, then Leon says, "The storage locker with my mother's things. After forty years, we're finally going to clean it out."

6

LEAH EVANGELINE

Viv and I take her car, heading east in roughly the direction of New Orleans, bundle of unfolded cardboard boxes in the back seat.

I ask, "Why are Grandma's things in a storage locker?"

"When a loved one dies, things that smell strongly of them create the illusion they're still alive. This can be confusing and painful. Everyone responds to it differently. Some people hang onto everything as long as they can, some give it away, some burn it up in a pyre. We put everything in a storage locker. The idea was to keep it there until the pain wasn't so raw, then sort through it."

"But you kept it there forty years."

She gives me a small, sad, ghost of a smile. "There never came a time when the pain wasn't so raw."

"Okay, I get that. So why are we doing it now?"

"Well, Leon's finally here for one thing. And a few months ago, we got this." She pulls a folded letter out of the inner pocket of her jacket, places it on the seat between us. I scan it quickly.

"They're going to put a bunch of houses there? Really?"

"It's high ground, which I guess is considered increasingly valuable around here. People have started to look at flooding data when they decide where to buy houses. Anyway, they offered to move the contents out to their Kenner location near the airport, but that would be expensive and we didn't really trust them to do it anyway. The project seems more urgent, now that there might be something in her things that sheds light on this Veneray business."

I study the paper. "Is it really so urgent? It seems urgent to me, but I'm stuck out here with nothing to do."

"Nothing to do? Aren't you training to master the trauma morph? And shouldn't you be taking classes? That high school diploma isn't going to earn itself, you know."

"Am I earning a high school diploma? I missed that somehow. Is somebody teaching me algebra and I didn't notice? Because that would be kind of cool, if I could just learn algebra in my sleep or something."

"Hasn't anybody talked to you about this? Bayou Galene operates a highly regarded secondary school. We get outsiders applying all the time and getting turned down, which, I must say, enhances the mystique. You could get your high school diploma, even go to college there, get a respectable Bachelor of Arts without ever leaving town."

"Is that what you did?"

She nods. "Before going to law school. And Nicolas, before getting his epidemiology PhD. You've been in town long enough, I assumed—" she sighs. "Sorry, I think I'm the one who dropped that particular ball. Anyway, it's not too late to start. You can work on getting your GED, then a BA in English literature or history or something like that, whatever seems most interesting to you."

"Hmm."

"You don't sound interested."

"Well… do I have to stay in town? What if I master the wolf before I get my BA?"

She laughs. "You can study in New Orleans, if that's what's bugging you. Or Seattle. Or anywhere."

"Seattle? I could study in Seattle? Are you serious?"

"After your wolf is mastered, you can go anywhere at all. Seattle. Los Angeles. Paris. London. Backpack across Europe for a year. Anything you want."

Overwhelmed and dizzy, I sink down into the seat, folding my arms. "I don't think I can handle that much choice. What if I make the wrong choice?"

"And what if you do? But, come on, you want your freedom more than anything, don't you?"

"I thought I did."

"Well, you'll get it soon. Enjoy it while it lasts."

"While it lasts? Why, what's going to happen to it?"

She shakes her head. "Never mind. Just feeling my age I guess. When you get older, a lot of your freedom starts to... I won't say disappear. It's just, you get hemmed in a little bit. By everything that's already happened, you know?"

"Feeling your age? You don't seem that old."

"That's kind of you, but I know teenagers think of all adults as equally ancient and out of touch."

"That's not true, Viv. I mean, aren't you and Steph around the same age?"

She laughs. "Oh, see, now I know you're trying to flatter me."

"That means you're older than Steph?"

She shakes her head. "Little one, I'm old enough to be her mother. I'm Leon's age. Well, a couple of years younger. Probably."

"Probably? How do you not know how old you are? You weren't born in a cult, were you?"

She laughs. "Close enough. Haven't I told you the story before?"

"Obviously not."

"I was abandoned here by nuns, presumably after being

abandoned to the nuns by my birth mother. Unless my birth mother was a nun herself. I really have no idea."

"Nuns? That is like being born in a cult. Wow. Were they terrible?"

"I don't remember them being terrible. I don't remember them being anything at all, really. My memories from before they took me out here are a little fuzzy. I sort of vaguely remember reading comics in the back room of the gas station/bait shop/convenience store up in Beniet, which is just north of Bayou Galene. The gas station attendant asked me, 'Weren't you with the nuns honey?' And me saying, 'Yes, the nuns brought me out here.' He read this handwritten note that was pinned to my coat, which apparently said, 'For the rougarou.' So he drove me down to the Bayou Galene public house and dropped me off there. The public house was pretty new at that point, this was the early 1970s."

"They just left you there alone? How old were you?"

"Seven. We think."

"Bon Dieu. Jerks."

She laughs. "Jerks? Maybe so. I think they were scared. Anyway, to me, the public house wasn't much different from the Beniet bait shop, I curled up on a couch and kept reading my comic. I fell asleep, then Leon found me there. He was only ten, but you know how old a ten-year-old seems when you're seven? He took charge of the situation. Asked me why I was there and where I came from and things like that. He had been with the group in the cemetery, but he went to the public house because he wanted to watch something on TV. This was the 1970s, you couldn't just watch TV on your phone.

"After we talked for a while he decided that I should be presented to his mother. We walked down the road to the big field. It seemed to take forever. But once we were there, he howled for her and she came. An enormous wolf with the most beautiful red coat."

"Were you scared?"

"I don't remember feeling scared. I was apprehensive. I didn't know what was going to happen. But she didn't act scary."

There are tears in her eyes. "We, uh, we bonded instantly. She curled up around me and I went to sleep nestled in her fur. I didn't wake up again until the other wolves started to come back to the field. She stood up and stared them all down when they came over to investigate the stranger."

"Did she growl at them?"

"She didn't have to. None of them threatened me at all, they just wanted a sniff. But I could tell that if any of them had threatened me, she would have made them back down. The last wolf to come home was Pere Claude. He was so large that I thought he looked like a bear. That was the first moment I was scared. Not because I thought he was going to harm me. I knew she wouldn't allow it, and I knew he didn't want to anyway. I was scared he would make me leave, that he would say I didn't belong there. Somehow I knew he was the big boss.

"But then I looked from him to her, the white wolf and the red wolf, and they were staring each other down. I saw the eye flash, her green and him red. And he dipped his head in this little way, you've seen it, you know what it means. He conceded to her. They nuzzled each other, then came over to nuzzle me together." Her voice breaks. "I knew I'd found my true parents. I chose them. They chose me."

"Did you know they were people?"

"Not really. I was seven, having wolves for parents seemed kinda normal? But they became human again pretty soon after that."

"Did you grow up knowing you were going to be a were-wolf yourself?"

"Yes and no. They used to argue about it. My mother thought the nuns had some reason to think I belonged with the rougarou, maybe because they knew my parents. She

thought my nonchalant reaction to being surrounded by werewolves on the full moon was proof. But my father thought the
nuns simply didn't want to take care of me anymore, hadn't
found me an adoptive home, and invented an elaborate way to
pretend to themselves that they weren't just killing me."

"Huh. They both had good points."

"They did. That's why, when I was nineteen and still no
wolf, I thought my father must be right, and left town for a
while."

"Like Leon."

"Like Leon." She nods, looks thoughtfully out the window.
"Anyway, you already know I spent a while in Los Angeles
acting under the name Roxy Void. Until my wolf came after
all and I went home."

We arrive at the storage place soon after. It's part of a sad-
looking strip mall, mostly shuttered businesses and a big
"Coming soon!" billboard advertising the housing develop-
ment. The only businesses still open are the storage place and
a gun shop.

Leon is standing outside a big, white truck, frowning up at
the brutal sun from under the brim of a black cowboy hat.
Black jeans, black sport coat, plain black T-shirt tucked into
the jeans. He looks like the guy in a gangster movie who shows
up to kill you. I remember what he said about making people
afraid of you in the right way. The sport coat has to be incred-
ibly hot in this weather. But nobody looks like a badass in just
a T-shirt, do they?

Viv and I get out. She carries the cardboard boxes and I
carry a smaller pack of lids. We follow Leon and Pere Claude
to the storage place, which is organized like a motel, most of
the doors opening directly outside, but some opening onto an
indoor hallway.

"The interior doors are for the climate controlled spaces,"
Leon says, in answer to my unasked question. He punches a
code for the outer door, and we enter a dry, air conditioned

hallway, shockingly cold after the heat outside. He punches another code. An orange door slides open to reveal a shrine to my grandmother.

Like a museum exhibit it's lovingly curated, arranged just so, to look like a bedroom a person could return to at any moment. Clothes, books, a little desk with a manual type-writer on it, paper loaded in, half-finished watercolor painting, fountain pen sprawled across an open notebook, ink bottle nearby.

The family did not put my grandmother's things here in order to save themselves the pain of running into them daily. They moved them here to create a sanctuary where they could go to pretend she was still alive.

The person who's spent the most time here is obviously Pere Claude, and he goes, practiced, to sit in the middle of the bed, tears coming into his eyes. He picks up a pillow and cradles it. "She's gone, isn't she son? She's gone."

"She's been gone a long time, Dad."

"A long time."

Leon puts his hand on his father's shoulder, and Viv embraces both of them. I stand a little outside this family group, bow my head for a moment, eyes full of tears that are mostly echoes of their grief. I never met my grandmother, and that makes me very sad. But my grief isn't the same as their grief. Leah Evangeline left a hole in their lives much more like the hole my own mother left in mine.

Viv looks up at me. "Abby, my mother was very close to your size, if you see any clothes you like, try them on. If they fit, please take them. She had some nice things. I used to wear them myself until I got too tall."

I inhale, go straight to a pair of red cowboy-style boots that still smell like Viv, hold them up. "Like these?"

"Oh, God, the boots!" She shakes her head with a little laugh. "They were the last thing to go. I wore them even after they started to pinch my feet. They're really well made, it killed me to have to stop wearing them. You've got to try them on."

Five minutes ago I would have sworn cowboy boots weren't really my style, but this pair is really compelling. The lines and the color are beautiful, the red color deep and vivid, the swirling design stamped into the leather subtly enhanced by an artfully applied darker color.

They fit extremely well. Better than any other shoes I have. I kneel down to take a closer look. "Each one has a zippered pocket on the inside."

"That's right." Viv nods, smiling. "Big enough for a passport, keys, some money." Her expression turns solemn. "She said that her mother's experience fleeing the Nazis made her think, you never know when you're going to have to leave somewhere quickly, with nothing but the clothes on your back.

"Fleeing Nazis? As in actual Nazis? Original Nazis?" I try to do the math. How old was my great-grandmother, that she would have fled the Nazis?

"What other Nazis are there?" Viv frowns.

Leon inhales deeply, nostrils flaring, sweat taking on an angry shade of red. "In Idaho? Neo-Nazis." He glances at me. "But yes, our grandmother Jeanne-Moreau fled the original Nazis. Her mother put her on a train from Paris to stay with relatives in New Orleans. She was only seventeen, I think."

"Nazis," Pere Claude says, with a growl. "Leah hated Nazis."

"I thought everyone hated Nazis," I say. But I glance at Leon's glowering expression and feel foolish, and young. "Until about a minute ago I thought that."

"Can you imagine wanting to kill someone just because they're Jewish?" Pere Claude shakes his head. "It's so horrible."

"It is horrible," Vivienne says, taking his hand. "It's horrible, Dad. Some of the things people do to other people."

I'm struck by something. "Wait. Was Grandma—Great-grandma, I mean—was she Jewish?"

Vivienne nods. "She was. Yes."

"But does that mean you're Jewish? Does that mean I'm Jewish?"

Viv and Leon look at each other, frowning. Leon says, "That depends on what you mean. Vivienne and I were not raised in the Jewish culture and we know very little about it. But we were not raised as Christians either. Would a rabbi consider us Jewish? Probably not. Would a Nazi consider us Jewish? Maybe."

"So, how did the werewolf genes get in there? Are there werewolves in France?" I ask.

Leon says, "Maybe, but our grandmother originally married a Cajun man from around here, so our mother is half Cajun. But the marriage fell apart and when Leah Evangeline was just a child, her mother left her first husband and went to stay with another branch of the family in Brooklyn. She remarried, and her second husband was Jewish, so our mother was raised in the faith. But she was never particularly devout herself. Emphatically not a Christian, though." He gives me a sidelong grin. "You would have liked that about her."

"Leah was from Brooklyn," Pere Claude says. He laughs. "She was so bold! A very dominant wolf, in spite of her size. The folks around here did not always know what to make of her. But she knew how to win them over. She was always so charming." His voice drops to a whisper as his eyes fill with tears. "So charming."

"She was," Vivienne says, squeezing his hand. "She was, Dad."

"I wonder," Leon says. He sits down at the desk, glances at the typewriter. "Oh, this is her Gothic novel." He picks up a half-finished watercolor painting sitting next to the typewriter, holds it up toward me. "Look familiar?"

The painting, mostly in shades of dark green and blue, depicts a young woman who could almost be me: long, white dress and long, red hair flying in a strong wind as she runs down the steps away from Beckford Manor, glancing over her shoulder as if afraid of what might be following.

"Why was she painting Beckford Manor?"

A sad laugh. "There was a Gothic romance boom in the 1970s. Here." He goes to the bookshelf and pulls out a handful of titles like *The Secret of the Dark House* and *The Demon Lover*, which all have cover images similar to the painting: a young woman with abundant hair running away from a fore-boding mansion. The "Demon" book indicates that the publisher is something called "Avon Satanic Gothic" and my jaw drops.

"They actually called it that? Satanic Gothic? Satanic? For real?"

"They did."

"And Grandma was writing one?"

"Well, I don't know how Satanic it was," Leon glances at Viv. "I never read more than a few brief excerpts, did you?"

"It's unfinished," Viv says. "But it does have BDSM themes and explicit sex, that's probably the Satanic part. And before you ask, yes, it is very awkward reading your own mother's half-finished kinky sex novel."

Leon chuckles sadly. "Any good?"

Viv shakes her head. "Not really? But she never got all the way through the first draft, so who knows how good it might have been after some editing."

A moment of sad silence, then Leon says, "I think we can get everything except the furniture into the two cars, let's go. Abby, are you up for helping us pack?"

"Of course."

"Good, just try to keep things together as much as you can when you put them into the boxes. Everything's very well organized right now, and I'd hate to lose that. Except, when you find papers or notebooks, or anything that seems like it might be related to the Veneray, put them over here."

Viv, Leon and I start packing. Pere Claude mostly watches us in silence, possibly too overwhelmed to help or to say much. Every once in a while he points to something we're holding and says, "I remember that," or, "Leah had that."

"We're taking good care of everything, father," Leon says. "We're being very careful."

"Good. That's good."

"Where are we putting this stuff when we get back to Bayou Galene?" I ask. "It should go somewhere climate controlled, right?"

"Right, there's a storage room in the public house that I've mostly cleared out."

I pick up an acoustic guitar. "She played guitar?"

"Not very well," Viv says. "I mean, maybe she would have gotten good, if she had time." She sighs. "Shit, no wonder we've never done this before."

"It's painful," Leon says. "Yeah. Here." He pulls a flask of Scotch from the back pocket of his jeans, hands it to her. She takes a sip. I wonder if it's the wedding Scotch and don't have the courage to ask.

My grandmother, it seems, did a little bit of everything, but wasn't an expert in most of it. Macrame. Calligraphy. Guitar, fiddle, harmonica. Watercolor. Fiction writing. Beading. Country line dancing. Bird watching.

Leon picks up a pile of letters. "She corresponded with people all over," he says. "I wonder if—well, we'll go through them all."

"And all these groups she was part of," Vivienne says, setting down an armful of papers. "She led the only Girl Scout troupe we ever had in Bayou Galene. I think that was for my sake. When I was young, I had a bit of a hard time adjusting. The other kids had been raised in Bayou Galene and I was abandoned at the age of seven by nuns, so we didn't really understand each other."

I locate a scrapbook that seems older than the others,

black, bound in stitches rather than spiral-bound. Intrigued, I open it and gasp in shock at the first picture. Huge, filling the page, in crisp black and white, it appears to show me and Izzy, in 1960s period garb, getting arrested by cops. Then I realize what I'm looking at. This is my grandmother and Izzy's grandmother, getting arrested during a Civil Rights demonstration.

I pull the picture carefully out of the black corners that hold it, see on the back it's signed:

To Leah Evangeline,

Keep fighting the good fight

Love, Espero

"Who was Espero" I hold up the picture and Vivienne gasps.

"A very famous photographer in the 1960s," she says. "He took a lot of pictures of the Civil Rights Movement, captured some very iconic moments." She exhales, takes the photo from me gingerly, in a way that makes me think it must be valuable. "This looks like his own print. It's absolutely gorgeous." She exhales a shuddering breath and carries it over to Pere Claude. "Look, Dad. It's that time Mom and Aunt Charli got arrested, remember? And they ran it in the paper and everything?"

He looks at it and frowns, then suddenly laughs. "Oh, I remember that! I was so upset." He looks sad now. "She, I thought it was dangerous for us to involve ourselves in outsider business like that. But she was right. She was always right." He clutches Viv's arm. "She was right about you. Do you remember that night? The night the nuns left you all alone?"

"I do remember."

Leon takes the photo from her, carefully. "I brought some document sleeves in case we found anything like this, I'll take care of it. Abby?"

He gets me to help him put it in a clear envelope, with a

hard back to keep it from getting bent. He asks, "Do you know the significance of this photo?"

"Well I know a little bit about the Civil Rights Movement." I shake my head. "But a lot of what I think I know was probably lies I was told in the cult, so I'm not going to say anything more. It's a beautiful picture, though. And it captures something. You can tell who the heroes and the villains are just by their body language."

He nods. "You know, we should find out what Charlaine Quemper wants to do with this. Maybe it should go to a museum."

"Right. And I should send a copy to Izzy, lay it flat." I take a picture with my phone, text it Izzy, Deena, and Edison:

> GUESS WHO THIS IS

Izzy texts back almost right away:

> Oh my God, that's our grandmothers, isn't it?
> Are they getting arrested?

> Yep, Civil Rights march. 1960s.

> Wow. Grammy never even told me about that,
> the stinker, she's going to hear it

Deena adds:

> Your grandmas are the best. And the outfits!
> I could die.

Edison says nothing. Is he busy? I tell myself not to worry, go back to packing.

7

SHORTHAND

Packing up everything from my grandmother's storage locker is strangely exhausting, even worse than trying to learn algebra. By the time we've got everything ready to go, my brain hurts. When we return to Bayou Galene it's late enough that I go right to sleep. But just a couple of hours later I wake up, hungry, with the vague sense of having had another nightmare. My sleep schedule has been really strange the last few days. I go to the public house kitchen, grab some more of Viv's yogurt, find her and Leon up in the raven's nest with a bunch of their mother's diaries spread across the table.

"Abby." Leon glances up. He's tapping a capped fountain pen against the paper of the notebook. "If you can't sleep either, maybe you can help us."

"Help you what?"

I sit down next to Viv who glances, sniffs, says, "Is that my yogurt?"

"You put it in the public refrigerator."

"I did? I thought the other one was the public one. Anyway, it doesn't matter. You can eat my yogurt. It's just that I have to go all the way into the city to get the kind I like."

"We're trying to figure these diaries out." Leon holds one

up. "My mother kept formal diaries, similar to the pere diaries, but she also had a series written in some kind of code. Cryptography isn't something either of us knows much about. The dates are written in plain English, though, so we know they seem to start when she went to Bayou Galene for the first time and go all the way to right before she was killed."

"You think I can help you with crypto? You've got to be kidding."

"You might think of something we missed," Viv says. "Here's the first diary."

The intro is written in neatly printed plain English, and I read it out loud. "This is Vol. 1 of the private diary of Leah Evangeline Arendt. I assume you're reading this after my death, because if you're not, and I find out, I will kill you."

Viv and Leon glance at each other, smiling. "That's her sense of humor all right," Viv says.

I turn to the next page. "This isn't code, it's Gregg Shorthand."

"It's what?" Leon stares at me. "Did you say shorthand?"

"Yeah, it's like a—okay, I guess it's kind of a code—if you want to write something out fast. Like if you're taking dictation. If you get good you can write as fast as people talk. I never got quite that fast writing it, but I can read it pretty well."

Viv says, "But how do you know shorthand? You're just a kid!"

"I'm seventeen."

"No, that's not what I mean. I've heard of shorthand, but nobody was learning it anymore when I was your age, how did you come to learn it?"

"They taught me in the cult. To be a good helpmeet, right? To take dictation from my father and eventually my husband?"

"How old was Father Wisdom?" Leon frowns. "I thought he was younger than me."

"I don't know how old he was. But if it's old-fashioned, it's not the only old-fashioned thing we did in the cult, you know? Anyway, even with computers, I use it all the time. Taking notes in class, or when I was answering the phones for Snarl-away. When did people stop using it?"

"In the 1980s I think," Viv says. "By the 1980s if some executive wanted to dictate a letter, he'd do it into a tape recorder and then give the tape recorder to the secretary to type up. Remember those mini tape recorders they used to have? Like Dale Cooper in *Twin Peaks*?"

Leon says, "Abby, does that mean you can read this?"

"Sure." I point. "That says, 'My first day in Bayou Galene' and then—oh." I laugh.

"What, what?"

"It says, 'if you want to know where Bayou Galene is, drive out beyond everything, then drive some more, then drive some more, then keep going until you hit the middle of nowhere. Then keep going until you hit the Gulf of Mexico. That's where you'll find it.'"

Leon shakes his head, a complex look. "She always used to claim she was happy here. That she didn't miss Brooklyn at all."

"Well, look at the date, she hadn't fallen in love with Pere Claude yet." I flip to the next page. "Here. She calls him a 'mountain of a man.' And, get this, says he's not her type. Not her type at all."

I keep flipping, scanning for the thing I know is coming. "Look, here's where he asks her out on a date! And she says yes, but she describes it as being curiosity. Just curiosity. Wait, he's not the pere yet! She describes his father. 'A similar-shaped mountain, but slower moving and more quick to anger.' This is good stuff. But it's very personal. She talks about her period."

"She does?"

"Yeah, she just mentions it in passing. 'It's the 1960s, they never heard of tampons out here?'"

"I can hear that delivered in her voice," Viv says. "Wow."

I pick up diaries with later dates, flip through until I see what I'm looking for. "Here it is! Pere Claude proposes! But not Pere Claude, sorry. Just Claude Verreaux. She writes:

Well, it happened. I could smell it coming. Mr. Claude
Verreaux proposed marriage to me today. I told him
my price. If he wanted to marry me, we were going to
live in Brooklyn. He left, then. I crushed his heart I
guess. He was so sad. I didn't want to make him sad. I
really do like him. But I'm serious about Brooklyn. I
don't care how much I like a man, I am not moving
out to the ass-end of nowhere for him.

Viv snatches the book out of my hands. "She says ass-end of nowhere, really?"

"Yeah, uh, shorthand is phonetic, you leave out most of the vowels, so it's basically just the 'ss' sound, but how would you interpret s-nd f nwhr?"

"Ass-end of nowhere," Viv agrees, wonder on her face, as she stares at the scribbles I know she can't read. "That's so weird. I called it that. When I was twelve and just starting to feel restless. I don't remember her ever saying it out loud, but she must have, I must have gotten it from her. Wow."

I skim through looking for highlights. "Well, later on they go to Brooklyn, and stay there for three months. She can tell he's not comfortable, but she's impressed with his sincere effort to enjoy it. And he does like New York. He's just not at home and she can tell."

I pick up the next diary. "Here it is! They were in Manhattan, it was July, they were walking through Central Park looking at the fireflies, and somebody tries to mug them. Jumps out the bushes all 'give me your money' and they both growl and flash him at the same time. Just instinctively. And he yelps, and runs off. They start laughing and can't stop laughing." I swallow through a rush of tears. "That's when they agree to get married for real. That's when she says, 'For him I'll go to the ass-end of nowhere. Because that stupid little town is his home, deep down in his bones, and we both know it. He's going to be the hunt leader someday. And I love New York, but I think I can love New Orleans almost as much. So that's settled. I'm going to become Leah Evangeline Verreaux and I'm going to spend the rest of my life fighting to make the ass-end of nowhere a better place to live.'"

We all sit with that for a moment, swallowing tears.

Leon asks, "Abby, can you type?"

"Of course. Helpmeeting skills. You want me to transcribe the shorthand diaries?"

He nods. "Do you know how long it will take?"

"I really don't know, sorry. This is a pretty big pile."

"All right. Start with the last diary and work backwards. The last one is most likely to have the information we're looking for."

"Sure thing." I gather them into a pile and head back to the cabinay.

I assume I'm going to do an hour or two of transcription before going to bed, but Grandma's secret diaries are too fascinating. It's just her, her thoughts, uncensored. And they are funny, direct, angry, and without any hint of... propriety, I guess. She talks about crying when Martin Luther King was assassinated, and crying when Ronald Reagan was elected. She talks about sex with my grandfather, which makes me feel a little uncomfortable, since they're my grandparents, but at the same time, it's really sweet to read. She presents herself as having fallen in love with him almost in spite of herself. When she describes her two miscarriages, she sometimes goes into grotesque detail. She also describes pregnancy and childbirth in extremely blunt, informative terms. She and Pere Claude were so happy when Leon was born, it makes me want to cry.

And the things she did! My grandmother not only marched for Civil Rights with Izzy's grandmother, she marched for women's rights, and environmental protection. She went to plays and movies and art museums and baseball games and literary speakers and music concerts. She was there at the first Jazz and Heritage Festival, in spite of having words to say about the sponsor, Shell Oil. She saw David Bowie and Nina Simone perform live (not at the same time).

And she helped people, especially young women. She describes traveling with a couple of younger women from Houma all the way to New York so they could get abortions, and she's really blunt about that too.

My grandmother was pretty much everything I could ever want to be.

But she wasn't like me in some important ways. She seems to have had no trouble striking up conversations with strangers. She often writes these conversations down in her diaries, verbatim, and had a good ear for dialect and accent. One of her favorite things was to sit in a coffee shop or some other public place and listen until something caught her ear, then write down everything people said to each other.

It's all so fascinating that it's work to drag myself away from skimming the other diaries to start typing a full transcript of the final one. But when I do, a narrative starts to emerge right away. Grandma was pissed off about all the oil refineries going up in this area, and talking about the environmental impact, and how it was tied into racism, and she had a particular hatred for a state representative called Edwin A. Duke. She bothers to write out his name in regular English the first time, but calls him "EAD" after that, sometimes "dEAD." She calls him a "real good ole boy Louisiana type. Racist, sexist, infamously corrupt, apparently in office for life even though everybody hates him."

Oh.

Oh shit.

The final entry. Not too long before she was killed. She writes:

> Well, that's it. I'm going to do it. I'm going to take his seat away from Edwin A. Duke. I'm going to run for office!

I run all the way back to the raven's nest and find Leon and Viv still there, although they've opened a bottle of red wine and seem to be chatting more than examining the formal diaries. They startle when I burst in.

"Abby, why aren't you in bed?" Viv asks.

"Transcribing, duh." I wave the diary over my head. "I know what it is! I know why Grandma was killed!"

"What? Why?"

"This." I point to the name EDWIN A. DUKE. "Grandma was running for office. Against this guy. He must have known that, and he must have been afraid she might win."

8

SERIAL KILLER PARTY WALL

Leon takes his mother's diary from me and stares at it, although I know he can't read the shorthand. "You think a politician had her killed?"

"That happens right? In real life, not just in the movies?"

"It does happen. And if it was connected to the oil industry around here, that means money." He glances at Viv, who nods.

"Money, for sure."

"She didn't mention her political ambitions to us at all. I guess she never got the chance."

"Do you guys know anything about Edwin Duke?"

Viv frowns. "I think I remember her mentioning his name in a negative way, but I don't remember any details. I'll start researching, there might be some things to turn up." She shakes her head in despair. "But even if he did do it, ordered a hit on our mom, I don't see how we can ever get justice. That's probably why they killed her the way they did. No human remains means almost no possibility of a murder conviction."

Leon inhales deeply and his expression turns to a pure

glowering hatred, sweat sizzling with murderous fury. "If we can't get justice, we can still get revenge."

"After all this time?" Viv puts a calming hand on his shoulder. "Is it worth it? Trying to get revenge on a well-connected politician just seems like it's asking for trouble."

"It might be," he says, voice rough, growling. "Will you try to stop me?"

"Leon, you know I can't stop you from doing something if you've made up your mind to do it. Nobody ever could stop you, as I recall. But think about this. You're not seventeen anymore. What would you be trying to accomplish? We know the truth now, or at least we think we do, and that's probably all we're ever going to get."

He closes his eyes, makes a tangible effort to calm down. "All right," he says. "I'll be cautious."

After a long, tense moment I yawn hugely.

"Get to bed, little one," Vivienne says. "Thank you."

Over the next few days, I finish transcribing the diaries while Vivienne and Leon look into the history of Edwin A. Duke. They even travel to Baton Rouge once. But, other than the fact that Edwin A. Duke is dead and his son, Edwin A. Duke, Junior now holds the same state representative position, they don't get much.

Grandma's diaries, meanwhile, remain fascinating, but also don't provide anything more that seems relevant to her death. I do find out things about Leon, and about Vivienne, that will probably embarrass them when they get around to reading the entirety of my transcript. Leon was right that she knew about him and Lunora dating, and there are passages where she considers what to do. She talks about taking them to that Cure concert, the one with the T-shirt and the photograph:

> I wore black and stayed a goodly distance away, so
> hopefully they didn't look too much like they had been

driven there by a mom. I know I'm technically Leon's chaperone, but I don't have to humiliate him. The venue was quite charming, an old movie theater in the Carrollton-Riverbend neighborhood that had been converted into a nightclub. I enjoyed the music too, although I'm not sure I should tell Leon that, it might spoil his fun.

She also talks about her ongoing efforts to find out about Viv's parentage:

I tracked down one of the nuns today and we had words. She claimed at first not to have any idea what I was talking about, but then I put the stare on and she spilled it. She called V's mother a "loose woman" and a drug addict, said they did everything they could for the child, but the child was too wild, she wouldn't behave, she wouldn't be quiet in church.
She's just a little girl, why do you expect her to be quiet in church?
She howls like a wolf, like the loup-garou, you never heard such demonic howling
Howling?
When we put her to bed without supper, or when we switched her, or when we put her in isolation, she would howl like she was trying to raise the devil himself.
At that point, I nearly strangled this little old lady with my bare hands.
She cried when she was hungry, when she was in pain, and when she was lonely. And you blamed her? You blamed *HER*?
I must have showed the wolf too much, because the nun started to tremble in fear, crossed herself. Mercy, she said. Saints, mercy. She backed away, crossing

herself and muttering nonsense the whole time. But
eventually I got a name out of her, Ruby-Ann, that's
the name of V's mother. Not that it tells me much.
Damn Christians.

I think my grandmother just might be my favorite person,
ever.

I'M ASLEEP, BUT NOT ASLEEP, PADDING THROUGH THE VAST HALLS
of a mansion too large for the number of people who live here, looking for
something, I can't remember what. I hear a voice, two voices. Leon and
Roman.
   She's dangerous, says Roman.
   We're all dangerous, Leon says.
   I mean dangerous to you, to your plans.
   What do you know of my plans?
   I wake up.
   Through some trick of acoustics, I hear Roman and Leon
talking in another part of the house, but can't hear what
they're saying, just a rumble of deep voices. In my dream they
were talking about me, but it can't have been real. In the
dream I heard their words, but I can't hear their words now.
Their words must have been part of the dream, in spite of the
way they echo in my head.
   She's dangerous.
   We're all dangerous.
   I mean dangerous to you, to your plans.
   There isn't a window in my cabinay, but the overall light
levels tell me it's probably dark outside. My phone tells me it's
12:04 a.m. Late but not too late. Pere Claude is snoring in his
bedroom down the hall, deep and even.
   Now that I've noticed them, the rumble of voices is

distracting, keeps me from falling back to sleep. I keep trying and failing to make out what they're saying.

It's going to keep bugging me until I resolve it. It's hard to sneak up on a werewolf, so I probably can't catch them saying anything too incriminating. But I know this house pretty well. I know how to move lightly through its spaces, where to step so that the floor doesn't creak. And I live here, so my smell is all around, they might not notice me getting closer.

Step, carefully, on the very tips of my toes, hardly breathing. At the base of the stairway I start to be able to make out their words.

Roman says, "Definitely. There's another one"

"Hmm." Leon makes a grumpy noise, and I hear the sound of something squirting. "But you're sure Flint Savage didn't have a Florida partner?"

"As sure as we can be. If he had a different partner, not me, wouldn't he have set that person up to inherit his property?"

"Maybe." Leon makes another thoughtful grumping noise. "Thank you. I'll have to think about our next step. Are you going to stay in town through the next moon?"

"If you want me to."

"Would you be willing to help train Abby to master her wolf? I think I want her in New Orleans as soon as possible for the scent-mapping project." I hear another squirt, hold my breath. If they are talking about me behind my back, here it comes.

"Of course. But I thought she was training with Pere Claude?"

"She has been. And you saw it during the trial, her wolf is very nearly mastered. But she's emotionally close to my father, feels too safe with him, I think. She needs a different trainer to get all the way there."

Damn. I want to be upset, but how can I be? These are just my own thoughts, echoed back at me.

Roman chuckles. "And she doesn't feel safe with me, is that it?"

"Well, no. You two grate against each other. Am I wrong?"

"No, no. You're not wrong at all. I find her annoying and she finds me… I don't know, exactly, but it's obvious that she tenses up whenever I'm around."

"In the cult, her older brothers were often the administrators of physical punishment. It may be that you put her in mind of them."

I lose my balance, take a careless step forward, hit a stair with a creak loud as a gunshot.

"Abby?" Leon calls out. "Is that you?"

"Hey." Yawning, I enter the kitchen. "I heard you guys talking down here and couldn't sleep."

"Sorry. Did you hear we were talking about you?"

"I heard my name." I shrug.

Leon sips from a small glass of dark liquid. From the smell, it's that imperial stout Morgan liked so much. Now I notice that the counter has several growlers arranged in a line, and that he and Roman are drinking out of very little glasses, like they're doing a tasting.

"Right there." Roman points and Leon squirts from a bottle of yellow disinfectant, releasing a sharp chemical smell, leaving a small black ant drowning in a puddle of liquid. The ant stops moving immediately.

"The ants are always worse when it's dry and hot like it has been," Leon says, then turns to me with a smile. "Abby, you want to taste test the beer? We're trying to figure out the best one to enter into a competition."

"Oh. That's what you're doing?"

"That, and killing ants." Roman spritzes another ant. "Does Snarlaway have ant poison?"

"We do, but we don't tend to use it here in Bayou Galene. There might be some in the bunker, I guess I could check."

"Don't bother right now. The sanitizer is working well

enough." Leon spritzes another ant then pours me a two-ounce glass of pale golden liquid. "They're arranged from light to dark. This is a lager."

I accept the taster. "Roman, you're back."

He nods. "I'm back."

"You were in Florida, right?"

"Dealing with Flint Savage's affairs, yes." He smirks. "It seems that even after our falling out, he didn't update his will and other legal papers, so I am now the proud owner of a struggling chain of Florida plastic surgery clinics, as well as his extensive notes about the injection exposure process."

"Wow. He kept the notes in Florida?"

He gives me a disgusted look. "No, he kept the passwords to his online accounts in a master account, and the password to that was kept in his will, which was read to me in Florida."

"His will? But he died in wolf form, how did they know to read a will?"

Leon jumps in. "Transforming wolves, when we make our wills, usually include explicit provisions for what happens if we simply disappear. Because that's what happens when we die as wolves. It looks like the human vanished into thin air."

"I guess it makes sense, I just never thought about it before."

Leon says, "Abby, Roman is interested in training you in trauma morph mastery, what do you think?"

"What do I think? Do I think I'll learn faster if I train with somebody where we get on each other's nerves?"

Roman smirks. "So you heard that."

"You knew I heard it." I pour another beer sample. This one is red, carmely. "Can't sneak up on a werewolf, right?"

"It is difficult," Leon says. "But we drop our guard some-times, just like other people."

"I trained my brother," Roman says, pouring himself some yellow beer, an IPA by the smell. "We had very little to go on, just what Leon had already told us, but it worked beautifully. My brother mastered his wolf in a few months. But that's from start to finish, you've already started, I don't think it would take you even that long." He lifts one of the growlers, and a dozen ants go scurrying. "Ew."

Leon drowns them with his spritz bottle.

I sigh. I don't really want to train with Roman, but maybe it will help my training to do something I don't want to do. "Fine, I'll train with you."

"Great. Meet us in the old gym tomorrow morning at ten a.m. Be prompt. I've heard that's a challenge for you. And don't eat breakfast."

"No breakfast?"

"Breakfast after. My training method involves training hard as soon as you wake up, then eating whatever you want, then a nap."

"A nap? Seriously?"

"Only if you want to, of course, but I'm almost certain you will want to if you train hard enough. After sleeping, rise, and spend the rest of the day however you want."

"Why that particular pattern?"

"My brother and I have experimented with training methods for people with a wolfen nature. We've found the wake, train, eat, sleep pattern works best. But we haven't trained a lot of women and girls, so if it doesn't work for you, I apologize in advance."

"Sure. I'll give it a try." I pour another beer, a dark malty brown. "Are we not looking into Edwin A. Duke anymore?"

"I wouldn't say we've given up entirely, but for the moment we have reached a bit of a dead end," Leon says. "Viv and I both have a few inquiries out there, we'll see if anything pays off."

"Edwin A. Duke?" Roman says. "Is that a name I should know?"

"He probably had your grandmother killed," Leon says. "But otherwise, no."

I set down my empty glass. "Okay, Roman, see you first thing tomorrow morning."

The next morning I dress in my nicer, newer sweats, the ones Vivienne picked out for me. I take the time to French braid my hair close to my head so that it looks neat. At 10 a.m. promptly I walk into the old gym and find Roman, Rufus, and Leon waiting for me there. Rufus and Leon sit in folding chairs drinking coffee, while Roman circles the room, picking up different items, letting his nostrils flare, putting them back.

"The blood on these is old," he says, with what sounds like approval.

Leon nods. "The building was constructed at least a hundred years ago. Abby, good morning."

"Dad." I nod at him. "So are you training with us, or just watching?"

"Watching. Roman suggested that it might be helpful for me to see his techniques and I agreed. My father's techniques are traditional, but traditions can often be improved I think."

"I guess so. Don't the Lobos have their own techniques?"

"No, they don't have any formal tradition for training trauma morphs. But it's a more common gift among their people. The tricks for how to master it are more general knowledge and less a specific training discipline."

"And they don't care about unmastered trauma morphs in the outside world?"

He shakes his head. "They don't. That seems to be specifically a concern of my father's."

"Maybe because of the Veneray?"

"Maybe so."

"So what about full mastery? Calling the wolf at will? Do the Lobos train for that?"

"Again, not in any formal way. But most trauma morphs do fully master the wolf."

While Leon and I were talking, Roman took down an

implement that I think of as the stabby thing, began to roll it around on his hand, very casually, as if he was thinking about buying it from the stabby-things shop.

Now he lunges forward, but I'm ready. His body language signaled his intent, and it's no challenge at all to resist the wolf. She basically yawns and shrugs.

Shoot, I think I made a mistake wearing my nice sweats today. Now they're covered in blood.

Roman withdraws, wipes off the blood, my gut knits up. He gives me a cold look like I'm a specimen he's examining.

"What does it feel like?"

"Getting stabbed in the gut? Here, let me show you."

I reach out for the weapon and he laughs, puts it back on its hook on the Serial Killer's wall. "I know what it feels like to get stabbed in the gut; I meant, when the wolf wants to come. The trauma morph. What does that feel like?"

"It's, uh, it's like—" I sigh. "It's like she doesn't trust me to take care of it. She thinks, 'this looks like a job for me' and just takes over."

"So, your feeling is that it's a power struggle between you and your own wolf." Roman nods thoughtfully. Picks up another weapon, the one I think of as the fancy axe, starts playing with it. "Rufus?"

Rufus shrugs. "That's not how I would describe it. My wolf doesn't think in words."

Roman dives toward me again, going up under the sweatshirt, slices a gouge out of my hip, like he's carving me up for dinner.

HURTS

oh, God, how can something hurt this much...

I gasp and the pure shock very nearly summons the wolf, but instead I take a step backward, stand on my not-injured leg, lean against the wall, panting, until the wound starts to heal with a ferocious tingling sensation.

"Ow. That hurt." I use a deadpan voice, make it sound

like a joke, to show he didn't throw me. Nobody laughs, although Leon smirks a bit.

Roman bends down to pick up the bit of flesh he sliced off. "Interesting." He holds it up. "The flesh doesn't heal when it's taken away from the rest of the body. It's just meat."

"We're not zombies, Roman."

"No. But what are we? What does it mean to be a wolf shifter? Where does our power come from? The healing? The speed? The strength? The shape-shifting itself?"

"Um. Magic?"

Roman sneers at me in obvious distaste. "Magic. Like in your series about the boy wizard?"

"No, that's a totally different kind of magic. The boy wizard kind doesn't exist, as far as I know. I don't see how it could, not in the world we see around us. But our kind obviously exists, because here we are."

"But then why do you call it magic? No. If it's real, it's science. Something we don't understand yet, but something we could understand, if we worked at it."

"Our brother Nicolas is creating a wolf-specific lab in New Orleans." I shrug. "I guess we'll figure out the science of it there."

A moment of a familiar slippery feel in the air, smell of lightning, and Rufus, in wolf form, attacks from behind, sturdy chomp on the back of my leg. I fall forward, gasping in pain. He knows how to bite to make it hurt, worrying the flesh a little, maximizing the amount of damage a single bite can do.

I look up, see Leon watching, with a frown. We make eye contact. He nods. "Abby, you're doing well, it doesn't look like you're struggling to resist the wolf at all."

"Not really, no."

Rufus releases my leg.

"Now call her," Roman says. "The wolf was right there a moment ago. Call her."

I reach. And don't find.

"I can't. I told her no and she went away to sulk."

"She doesn't get to do that. Are you her master or not?"

"Apparently not."

We spar. Roman comes after me with the fancy axe and I pick a different axe, we clash. It's obvious he isn't trained with the axe and I am, which gives me a bit of satisfaction. Sure, he's enormous and in extremely good shape, but I could still maybe take his head off in a pinch.

Then it hits me: the wolf can't use the axe. No hands. If I'm going to learn to call her at will, I can't rely too much on other weapons.

I start to practice dropping the axe and picking it up again, which possibly baffles Roman as a combat technique. But when he says, "Call her," I do. We fall to the ground, shake ourselves out of our clothes, bite him gently on the arm.

Human again, I rise, giddy, laughing. "I did it."

"You did. Now. We fight and you do it again, but not until I say."

We fight, all three of us, Leon watching. But now it seems weird that I'm naked, Rufus is naked, and Roman and Leon are clothed. No wonder traditional Varger combat just has everybody get naked right from the start.

Roman says, "Now."

I call the wolf.

"Good, good. Now, we fight again, and call the wolf when I say."

After the third time, he nods, shakes my hand. "Good job. Get dressed. High protein breakfast and then a nap."

I WAKE UP, HEART POUNDING. I WAS HAVING A NIGHTMARE, something — a giant spiderweb dripping blood. And I was surrounded by it. Trapped inside of it.

At least I wasn't Lunora this time.

I check the time. It's midnight. I slept for almost twelve hours, and I'm starving again.

I head to the public kitchen, grab the last of Viv's fancy yogurt, climb up to the raven's nest, find Leon staring into a laptop computer, making notes on a paper notebook.

"Don't you ever sleep?"

"I'm middle-aged, so not really."

"What does that mean anyway? Middle-aged. How do you know you're middle-aged and not just a regular adult?"

"Because you're older than fifty and never sleep." Small smile. "We do start to lose some of the wolf's gifts with age, if that's what you're asking. Mostly healing speed. That slice Roman took off your hip would have laid me up for a bit longer."

"That was pretty brutal wasn't it? Pere Claude stabs me and all that but he's never cut anything *off* me. It seems different. More psycho."

"It does seem a little extreme, doesn't it? But the sheer fact of our extraordinary abilities seems to demand a kind of brutality. It takes so much to bring one of us down." He gestures toward me. "You have lost a foot during a fight, you healed it, kept on fighting. A great gift. And yet the loss of the foot is still there in your mind. The blood, the pain, the grotesquerie."

"Grotesquerie. You're still such a goth." I snicker. "It's weird about the foot, though. For the longest time, my brain kept trying to tell me that the new foot was different from my other foot. Not in any particular way. Just different. How do our bodies know what shape to go back to?"

"Nobody knows."

"Pere Claude says the wolf knows."

"That's the same as saying nobody knows."

"Roman got mad when I said we were magic."

"Roman is a strict materialist."

"Is that like being an atheist?"

"Yes and no. I'm an atheist in the sense that I don't believe in some all-powerful God in charge of everything who demands worship, but I'm also not completely shut off to the possibility of the uncanny, the supernatural. I believe you might have been ridden by the spirit of my grandmother, for example. Roman would say, it was all in your head, no question. You see the difference?"

"I do. So, that whole ancestor worship thing, do you believe in it?"

He frowns. "Not worship. No. Wolves don't bow down, not even for our own ancestors."

"Oh. Okay. So what is it then?"

"Veneration, maybe. Honor. Respect. Communicate with?" He shakes his head, seems a little frustrated. "I don't know, we don't give it a name. Most of us don't believe in it literally anyway. Have you heard the Varger slang term 'peregard'?"

"I have." I think about it for a moment. "It seems to mean something like 'what you just did or said was very shocking' but it's usually used as a joke, like, when what you did wasn't really all that shocking."

He nods. "It was originally 'les peres regardez' meaning, 'the fathers watch,' as in, 'the ancestors saw you do that.' It might have reflected a sincere belief at one time, but now it's just an idiom. Figure of speech. You know?"

"Sure, like how a lot of atheists still use Christian swearing." I think about it for a moment. "But what about the Lobos? Do they talk about the ancestors?"

He frowns deeply for a moment then says, "You know, they do, I think. But my Spanish isn't very good, so a lot of the nuances are lost on me."

"You don't speak Spanish? Why did you call your pack the Cachorros then?"

He smiles, that proud-dad smile he gets sometimes. It

always makes me a little uncomfortable. "They called themselves that." A pause, then he asks me, "How do you think it went today, training with Roman?"

"Good. I guess. Yeah, it was good." I think about it. "I mean, Roman and I still get on each other's nerves, but that's okay, isn't it?"

"In this context, yes. So you're interested in continuing to train with him?"

"Sure. Yeah." I think about it. Nod more vigorously. "Definitely. He's pretty much the opposite of Pere Claude, and that's probably exactly what I need right now."

He nods, smiles. "All right. I'll let him know. I think it went well too."

9

THE NEW MOON

For a while, we fall into a routine. I train with Roman and Rufus, sleep for twelve hours, get up in the middle of the night and wander around a little before going back to sleep, waking up, and going back into training.

We try things, the more extreme the better. Sometimes it feels like Roman is daring me, asking, "Are you tough enough for this?" and I always answer, "Hell yeah."

Because I can't back down in front of Roman. He brings out my pride, my stubbornness, and I think I bring out the same feeling in him. Not that he consciously sees a tiny teenage girl like me as a real threat. But he knows my wolf. He feels challenged by her.

The experiments get weird. One time Roman and Rufus bind me up in chains, like a mummy, heavy boat chains. It's the weirdest fight, as I have to throw my whole entire body around, using moves that I learned as "snake" while training with Pere Claude. Then Roman says, "Shift, see if it will get you out of those chains."

I do. But it's not a normal shift. It's slower, more like the way the bitten shift. Not more than a few seconds, but long enough for me to be conscious of a sensation of stretching, contracting, twisting, maneuvering, until the wolf stands, shaking herself free and growling a challenge. '

Back in human form, I put on one of the silk robes. Roman nods approval. "Shifting to get out of a trap is really useful if you can do it." He glances at Rufus. "We've never managed to prove it, but I have a theory that it should be possible for a fully mastered wolf to do a partial shift. A hand into claws, or a jaw elongated to hold more teeth, and nothing else."

"Bon Dieu, really? Have you ever seen it happen?"

"I think so, but it was so brief it was hard to be sure."

One morning I go into the fighting room and nobody's there. I check the time, just in case I lost track again. It's a strange day, dark clouds and a heavy silence in the air as if a storm is coming.

In the raven's nest I find Leon drinking coffee and staring at a computer screen.

"Aren't we training today? Where's Roman?"

"Roman went into town. It's the new moon, we don't do trauma morph training on the new moon."

"Oh yeah. Because we don't transform. Do we? Or do we?"

"The general thinking is no."

"General thinking? So nobody is sure?"

"It's hard to be sure of anything one-hundred percent. As Reina and Nicolas are both fond of reminding me, our overall numbers are so low that everything could be an outlier. But either way, there's not much point in training." He pauses, gives me a knowing look. "You didn't realize it was the new moon until I told you."

"I lost track of the days. What? It's not like anything changes out here."

"That's not it. You have the black moon. You should notice when the new moon hits because you're in a bad mood. Worse than the previous day."

"Your point? No wait, I know your point. You think I have that permanent black moon thing. But what if I do? What am I supposed to do about it? Run away from home for forty years? Stay in this one little town for the rest of my life? Because those seem to be my only options. Unless you've got some treatment for the black moon that you've been holding back on?"

Uncomfortable, he looks down, away. "Nothing that I'd recommend. "

"Nothing you'd recommend? But you do have something?"

"I used berserker drugs that way. When I said I misused them? That was how. Treatment for the black moon."

"And they work?"

"I told you I don't recommend them."

"They work but there are side effects?" He nods. "Memory loss, right, you've mentioned that one. Other things?"

"It's hard to explain. Personality shifts, I guess, would be the easiest way to describe it."

"Permanent?"

"The personality shifts? I don't think so."

"Which leaves us right back where we started. It sucks being inside my own brain and there's nothing I can do about it except master my wolf as quickly as possible so I can stop training."

"Right. But I also wanted to remind you that your judgment is compromised right now. You might find yourself feeling paranoid or hostile where it's really not warranted."

"Bitchy, is that what you mean? When I'm depressed I'm a bitch?"

"That's not where I was going with that." He gives me a very small smile. "But it does seem to prove my point, that you're reading the worst possible intent into everything I say."

He closes the computer. "Anyway, today I'm just as depressed and bitchy as you are, we should go for a walk."

"Can't we go into town?"

"You mean New Orleans?" He shakes his head. "No, not today, sorry."

"But if we're not going to transform anyway, why not?"

"Because I have plans with my father later today."

"Fine. Let's walk."

We start heading down the Galene Road, toward the ocean, smell coming strong on a light breeze. I inhale deeply.

"You like the ocean," he says.

"I do. You?"

"I bought a house in Venice Beach, what do you think?"

I give a small laugh. "Good point. And it is a nice house."

We continue walking. Soon, we've left the town behind and find ourselves walking on open road, a dirt road full of potholes and weather damage. The Varger have no motivation to make this road easy to drive on.

"Do you know what used to be there?" I wave toward ragged skeletons of wooden structures.

"Back in the 1970s when I was a kid, there used to be bait shops and fishing concerns along this stretch of road. The butcher shop was down here too. But that's all shifted north."

"Was this a good place to grow up?"

"Good enough, I guess. When I think about my child-hood, describe it to myself, it sounds ideal. Two loving parents, a nice house, plenty of food. And we had fun. My mom's kind of fun, where we'd go into town and go to a museum or a play or something, or my dad's kind of fun where we'd stay in town and just explore. We used to walk around like this. He'd tell me about the animals, the trees, the patterns of weather. Sometimes he'd tell me stories about the old days. Or he'd daydream about traveling. He liked to travel, he said, but as pere he didn't feel right leaving the people for too long. I think that's why the Scottish honeymoon ended up meaning so much to him. It was the last time he got to travel seriously with my mother, before becoming the pere. But we did go camping sometimes, as long as it wasn't far away."

"Did you like that? Camping?"

He grimaces. "Not... really? I tend to think humans invented indoor plumbing and electricity for a reason."

"Hmmph, some werewolf you are." I'm teasing him, but he looks genuinely upset for a moment.

"And you enjoy camping, I suppose?" he says, sarcastically.

"No, of course not." I laugh. "The cult was basically a permanent Bible camp and I hated it there. I guess I always did take after you more than my mom."

"Sorry about that." A small smile. "Nature over nurture, huh?"

"I guess. But it's weird, I cannot picture you and my mother together at all. What did you even have in common?"

"We met in Los Angeles. At a party. And she was, I guess, going through a phase. She was entertainment at the party, part of a burlesque troupe. She called herself Jezebel Ruin."

"Oh Bon Dieu, now you're just making things up."

"Why would I make up something like that?" He seems honestly confused.

"To bug me?"

"Why would I put any effort into bothering you? It's so easy to bother you without trying." He sounds cranky, but then he smiles. "Sorry, I told you I was feeling bitchy today."

"Yeah, okay. So, did you and my mom actually date-date or was it just a fling?"

"I don't know how to answer that."

"Okay, I'll try again. Did you know her real name?"

"No."

"For sure? You never saw a driver's license or anything?"

"I didn't."

"So you just called her Jezebel Ruin the whole time?"

He sighs. He's trying to suppress memories of lust, I can

tell. I appreciate the effort, but it still makes me feel uncomfortable.

"Jessie," he says. "I called her Jessie. I have no idea if that nickname had any relation to her legal name."

"To me she was Mother Blessed. So neither one of us knows her real name. That's kind of weird, isn't it?"

"Our whole relationship was weird. She was—quirky."

"A weirdo, you mean? People tell me I'm a weirdo."

"She claimed to be a witch."

"What? No kidding, she really was a witch?"

He frowns. "I never saw any evidence of magical powers."

"That's not what I mean. As part of her testimony, I mean her how-I-got-saved-by-Jesus story, she claimed to have been a witch, before she met John Wise and found Jesus and repented and all that. 'Dabbled in witchcraft and demonism' was how she put it. 'Abusing the holy gift of prophecy' was another one. She and Father Wisdom wrote a book of prophecy together. I think they wanted another total game changer like *The Late, Great Planet Earth*, but for some reason it never sold like their child-rearing books."

"Prophecy." He shakes his head. "She did claim to be psychic. She would tell me her visions sometimes. They were nightmarish."

We're beyond the bridge now, approaching the ruins of Beckford Manor. Against the heavy dark backdrop of the storm clouds, it squats with a pale living malevolence. The heavy odor of the strange flowers, alternately sweet and rotten, surrounds us.

"Do you know what kind of flowers those are?" I ask.

"I don't. They do smell peculiar, don't they?"

"Peculiar is one way of putting it. But Beckford couldn't smell anything, so that couldn't be why he had them."

"No, I think they're from before his time. Maybe back in the 1920s when the basic structure of the building was built?"

"What about the luminous mold?"

"We called it foxfire. It seemed to appear in places where the wood of the house had been water damaged and was rotting."

"Did you ever see a ghost? Or hear a ghost?"

"No."

"Not even the pretty laugh girl?"

"No, I never heard the laugh. Lunora claimed she did."

"Claimed. You think she was lying?"

"No, but by then she might have been hallucinating."

We stare at the house. Both of us are fascinated by it, not wanting to go inside, but not wanting to leave. It makes a heavy impression in our minds. It has a personality.

"It's not really a beautiful building is it?" I say. "It makes all these gestures toward being beautiful but they're all wrong somehow."

He nods. "Lunora thought so too. She said it was like Hill House. Alive in its own way, malevolent."

"Did she claim to be psychic?"

"Yes." He pauses. Gives me a look. "You're suggesting I have a type?"

"Don't you?"

"Most of the women I dated weren't like that. But the first and the last, Lunora and your mother, you're right, they did have some unusual things in common."

"Wait. My mother was the last woman you dated? Nobody since her?"

"No. You're my youngest child, remember?"

"Huh." I think about it. "I guess it makes sense but it still feels surprising somehow. Like, I've spent all this time thinking you messed her up. That dating you was such a traumatic experience that it broke her and she went running straight into the arms of a cult leader. But maybe it was the opposite. Maybe she broke you."

He frowns, chewing on his lower lip, tosses his head to get

rid of phantom bangs. "I don't know. It didn't seem that way at the time."

"No? Something broke you, though, didn't it? It wasn't too long after that, you tried to kill yourself."

His rage starts to simmer. "I don't want to talk about that."

"No?" I turn toward him, starting to get angry myself. "You've spent all this time warning me about the black moon but you don't want to talk about the worst thing it ever did to you? Hypocrite."

"That's not what hypocrite means." He delivers this exactly like a sullen teenager. But he seems to catch himself, and laughs slightly. "You want to know why I tried to kill myself? The truth is I don't know."

"You don't remember what was going through your mind?"

"I do, but it doesn't make any sense. After your mother left, I tried to find her, but I didn't have much to go on. I knew she was from around here, somewhere in Cajun country. So I got this idea in my head, that I could master the wolf and finally return home. After more than a decade, I resumed trauma morph training, and used the berserker drugs to treat the permanent black moon, as I had before. But they didn't work the way they used to. Instead they made it worse. And that's—well, that's what happened. I wouldn't blame your mother. We both went into that relationship with our own problems."

A long pause while he stares into the distance, once more brushes phantom bangs out of his eyes. I start walking toward the ocean, with a mind to go out as far as I can, until the land literally ends in the waters of the Gulf. Leon follows along. After a while I ask a question that has often been on my mind: "Was my mother crazy?"

"I don't know how to answer that. She managed to act mostly normal most of the time. She saw visions, but she didn't wander down the street shouting about them to nobody in particular."

"Was she religious when you knew her?"

"Yes and no. She presented herself as having come from a strict religious background, and having rejected that to become a diabolist, a libertine. It was a pose, I think now. Or something she was trying to be, that she never truly became."

"Did you love her?"

"Not the way you mean. I'm not sure I ever loved anyone that way."

"Not even Lunora?"

"Not even Lunora."

"Did she love you?"

"Lunora? No. Or, at least, she said she didn't. It might have been a pose. We were big posers, as you might have been able to guess from that photograph you find so amusing."

"What about my mother, did my mother love you?"

"I have no idea. Sometimes she said she did, but she would always frame it in such a way, 'oh, to think of Reverend Warren's little girl in love with the devil himself.' Then she'd laugh."

"She thought you were the devil? Seriously? The literal actual devil?"

"A lot of the things she said, I thought she was being self-consciously edgy, or making jokes. But now I think she was serious more of the time than I suspected."

"Jokes? My mother? Hoo boy, you really didn't know her well, did you?"

"She didn't make jokes with you." He nods thoughtfully.

"No, my mother and father—Father Wisdom, obviously—they seemed to think having a sense of humor was basically the devil. I got in trouble for my temper and lack of submission, that's probably no surprise for a young werewolf, huh? But I got in almost as much trouble for my sense of humor. And, let me tell you, as hard as it is to keep from showing it when you get angry? It's so much harder to keep from showing it when something strikes you as funny. I would fake possession just to cover it up when I couldn't keep from laughing anymore. Just throw myself to the ground and start twitching wildly and screaming nonsense."

I'm smiling, so he smiles in return, but his eyes are troubled. "Fake possession? How does that work?"

"You really don't know any holy rollers? Pentecostal types?" He shakes his head. "Well, okay, the idea is that you get possessed by the Holy Ghost, wait, you'd say 'ridden' because it was invited. We'd say the spirit was *upon* us. So we'd speak in tongues or roll around on the floor or laugh uncontrollably. And that's a funny thing, now that I think about it. You couldn't *regular* laugh, but you could *holy* laugh. Which was different, becaue it wasn't because you thought something was funny? I don't know, even at the time it didn't make any sense to me. But I can probably still speak in tongues if I work myself up for it." I think about demonstrating this talent, decide against it. "So, okay, after she was pregnant with me, you did or did not look for my mother? I'm a little unsure of the timeline."

"I looked for her in the Los Angeles area," he says. "And online. But even as recently as that, it wasn't always so easy to find people online. Other than knowing in a general way that she was from Cajun Louisiana, and knowing her father was 'Reverend Warren' I didn't have much to go on. And not much hope. She left behind something that read like a suicide note. Now that she was carrying the Antichrist, she didn't want to bring about the destruction of the world after all. I assumed that she intended to kill herself and the baby at the same time." He stops, glances at me. "I'm sorry if this is upsetting to you."

"I'm not upset." I say this, but my voice is shrill and even I can smell the stressed out edge in my sweat. "Okay, I am upset. She never told me that my biological father was anyone other than John Wise, but she did used to say that when she was pregnant with me she had a vision that she was carrying the Antichrist, and with Wisdom's help she prayed, and by the miraculous power of Christ I was born a girl."

He frowns. "And that was a miracle because...?"

"Well, a girl can't be the Antichrist, you see."

"But why? If the Antichrist is the opposite of Christ, and Christ was male?"

"Don't try to figure it out, it doesn't actually make any sense. It's religion, right? Religion never makes any sense. I think that's why it attracts crazy people."

He frowns thoughtfully at me. "You think your mother was crazy?"

"I don't know. She died when I was nine, it's hard to make a judgment like that. But I know she saw things I didn't see. She'd point to them sometimes. 'Oh, look, 'Gashun, a bright spirit has joined us.' And it would just be, like, a sunbeam or whatever. When I was little I accepted that she had visionary powers I didn't understand, but in retrospect..." I shake my head. "I don't know. I wonder why she was so sure I was going to be the Antichrist, did she really think you were that evil?"

He chuckles. "Oh, I can answer that one. Early in our relationship, shortly after I showed her the wolf for the first time, she told me a story about something that happened when she was twelve. Her parents had gone to visit another family in the church and her little brothers each had a playmate their own age, but she was left alone, with the little boys playing and the adults talking, and she didn't feel welcome in either space. So she investigated the books on their bookshelf.

"Most of them were religious books. Bibles, Bible commentaries, a couple of books about politics. Then she found something that stood out because it looked more exciting than all those other books: *The Omen*, a movie tie-in novel about the Antichrist.

"She was a fast reader, and had finished most of the book

before the visit was over. But she never quite finished it. And she knew better than to ask to borrow it, or call any attention to the fact that she had read it. Because even though it was about the Antichrist, and had a lot of content borrowed from the religion her family practiced, she had a sense that it wasn't really a religious book, that it was more secular, more wicked than they would be comfortable with.

"She felt naughty for having read it. But it played with her mind afterward. She never knew quite how it ended. Did it end with the destruction of the world? The second coming? Something else entirely?

"But one thing that she did remember, was that the Antichrist in that book—a beautiful human-looking baby boy —was born of a jackal."

That wording sounds familiar, and images, movie scenes, flash through my mind. "Wait, I think I've seen this movie. They used a big hound dog and kept calling it a jackal. But jackals are really small, smaller than coyotes, there's no way one of them could birth a human-sized baby. There was a scene where a priest gets his head cut off by a sheet of glass and then Gregory Peck is supposed to kill his own son?"

"You've seen the movie? She never did. She told me she feared it would ruin the book for her. She didn't know what a jackal looked like, so she pictured a wolf.

"She used to make jokes—she acted like they were jokes— about how if we had a child together it would be the Antichrist. But after we had been dating just a few months, she took off, left that note, and I never knew any more about it." He smiles at me. "Until you gave that *Teen Mode* interview."

"Yeah, Jaime said it was the interview that put you all onto the fact of my existence. Do I really look that much like you?"

He shakes his head. "Other people see it more than I do. Mostly I look at you and see my mother."

We keep walking, and my eye is caught by a pink color, in

the grass. I go to pick it up. "Look, it's a King Cake baby. What's it doing out here?"

"It might have been dropped by a bird."

"It does look a little gnawed on." I hold it up. "We used to have little plastic babies just like this, but not for King Cakes. It was for anti-abortion marches. That was one of the things I used to get dragged to, was abortion protests. Like, we'd go into Baton Rouge and stand outside a Planned Parenthood with a big sign or something."

"Baton Rouge. Not New Orleans?"

"No, we never went into New Orleans. My father— Father Wisdom I mean—he used to claim it was dangerous for a Christian to go there, that the city was too much in the grip of Satanic Territorial Demons. So we'd go stand outside the Baton Rouge Planned Parenthood with these signs and all, and the idea was that we had to do it because we were saving babies. But then we wouldn't save actual babies. You know the story about Father Wisdom beating my little sister Ash to death, because that made it into the *Teen Mode* article, but we lost other kids too. Miscarriages, of course, but also I had a few younger siblings who died as infants or toddlers. But that was all okay because it was God's will."

Rage tightens my voice, and it becomes shrill, unpleasant even to my ears.

"The people who fight against abortion, like my parents used to do, they say they do it because children are precious, but they obviously think kids are cheap. Disposable. Mass-produced. Little plastic toys. And women too. Mothers. Disposable. Tools of production. Use 'em up and spit 'em out. Father Wisdom ripped his way through three women before I stopped him." I pause, startled by my own words. "I stopped him. Do you think I killed him?"

Leon looks confused. "He killed himself, didn't he? Or was the public account inaccurate?"

"No, he killed himself. But there's an argument to be made that it was my fault."

He continues to look confused. "Fault. You feel guilty?"

"Hell no. Well, not for that. I wish I'd stopped him sooner. Before he killed my little sister. I do feel a bit guilty for that. If it was all going to end with him dead anyway, I could have just killed him to start with and saved Sackcloth with Ashes."

Understanding dawns in his eyes. "I think I get it. You're asking me if you should feel guilty when you kill people to save other lives?"

"Am I? I guess I am. You've killed people, was it to save other lives?"

"Sometimes." He turns uncomfortable, evasive. He plucks a strand of dry grass, starts winding it around a finger. "I'm not the person to ask about this. I tend to think feelings of guilt aren't terribly useful. You feel guilty for killing your step-father, but also for not killing him. How is any of that helping you?"

Silence, while we both stare out at the ocean, watch dark clouds rolling in.

"Storm coming," I say.

"The weather is always changing out here."

A long pause, and my voice is tight when I say, "I loved my mother more than anything. She was my world. But she's also the person who made the decision to raise me in a torture cult led by my stepfather John Wise. I don't know if I'll ever be able to forgive her for that."

Leon says, "If you're not a Christian anyway, does it matter if you can't forgive her?"

"I guess you're right. It's just hard to think about how the person I loved most in the world was also the person who hurt me the most."

"The people you love most are always the ones who hurt you the most. Nobody else has that kind of power over your life."

We stop. One more step and it's nothing but water.

"Well here we are. The ass end of the ass end of nowhere," I say.

Long pause. We stare. I take a picture. Then we turn around and head back

10

A MASTERED WOLF

The next day, I go into the old gym for training and only Roman is there, fooling around with the fancy axe, spinning it, tossing it. Still not with my own dexterity, I notice with a feeling of satisfaction. He nods briefly in my direction but keeps his eyes on the axe.

"Rufus isn't joining us?"

"He has other business. And, I wanted us to get to know each other alone."

"Alone? Why alone?"

"You're nervous." His nostrils flare. "Why?"

"Because I assume you're plotting something? Possibly something weird and horrible?"

"Weird and horrible? That's what you think of our training?"

"Isn't that the point? To be weird and horrible? I assumed that was the point."

He laughs. Continues spinning the axe. It's starting to get on my nerves, so I take the axe away from him, begin spinning it myself, much faster and more expertly. He glares at me for a moment, then smiles. "You know the axe well."

"I do."

"Now it's my turn to be nervous. If you really wanted to kill one of us, in some ways, a wolf your size who really knows how to handle an axe is more dangerous than a wolf my size without an axe."

I throw the axe so that it whizzes past his ear, embeds itself in the rough, dark wooden wall that bears the signs of many bladed weapons over the last hundred years. "I trained with it when I was without my wolf, on the track and chase teams."

"Right, right." He pulls the axe out of the wall and starts playing around with it again. "The track and chase teams are mostly staffed by the wolfless, isn't it true?"

"Traditionally. Although there are an increasing number of trauma morphs like me who stay human on the full moon."

Without warning, he steps forward and uses the axe to cut off the two last toes on my right foot.

"Ow, you bastard, it's sandal season." I say this lightly, and the wolf makes no effort to emerge. But then he snatches up my toes to hold them in the palm of his hand.

"It upsets you when I do this," he says, nostrils flaring. "Why?"

"You stole my toes, of course it upsets me. It would upset you if I stole your toes."

"Do it." He holds out the axe with his free hand.

"Give me back my toes first."

"I want to know why it upsets you so much, for me to be holding onto them. They're not part of your body anymore."

Impatient, I grab the toes out of his hand, sit down on the floor, pointedly hold up my injured foot. The bleeding has stopped and the flesh is starting to knit up with an itchy tingle, but when I put the raw edges of the toes where they belong, there's a weird, almost magnetic feeling, as if the flesh of my body starts reaching out for the flesh of the toes, pulling them in. The itchy tingle intensifies, with a burst of discomfort that immediately dissipates into a sense of... satisfaction, maybe?

I wriggle my restored toes. "See? If you held onto them too long, I might not have been able to do that."

"I have never seen that before. It just knit right up!"

"I got the idea when I saw a TV show where a guy got his finger chopped off in some kind of industrial accident. He put it on ice and doctors were able to sew it back on, and eventually it healed and he had a usable finger again. I figured we could do the same thing, only faster."

"You lost a foot," he says. "I remember hearing that."

"But I didn't get a chance to do this, there was too much going on at the time. I think you have to do it pretty quick, before the limb has started to regrow, otherwise it doesn't take."

He shakes his head, smiles. "You really are cold-blooded, aren't you?"

"It's weird you would say that, when everyone else around here seems to think I'm an uncontrollable hothead."

"I admire cold-bloodedness." He uses the axe to chop off two of his own toes, waits a few breaths, then holds them against the flesh where they belong. He frowns. "It... what a strange feeling." He watches intently, starts to smell of spicy red panic. "It's not happening. Why isn't it happening?"

"It might take a bit longer for you. You're older than me."

He glares at me, wrinkling up his nose into a vaguely wolfy sneer. "I'm only in my early thirties, that's hardly decrepit."

"No, but Leon tells me our healing speed declines with age."

"There it goes." He exhales in relief, glances up at me. "You know this well, healing can be very uncomfortable."

"You were worried it wasn't going to work, I get it. I had that same thought when I got shot and didn't have my wolf. I thought I was going to die for real. Probably would have, if Leon hadn't shown up to help me."

"He saved your life."

"He did. And then he straight-up murdered the guy who shot me."

"That bothers you?"

"I don't know. You said I was cold-blooded, and I don't actually think I am. I think I pretend to be. But I think Leon really is."

"He can be." Roman smiles.

"Oh shoot. I attached my toes wrong, look." I hold up the foot. Instead of the toes descending in a line, the one second from the end is the shortest, the one on the outside is longer.

He laughs. "What can you do to fix it, cut them off again?"

"No, just a second." I kneel, become the wolf almost without thinking. We stretch our legs, briefly, don't even bother shaking out of our clothes, return to human still dressed.

"And just like that, everything's back where it belongs." I hold up the foot again.

He shakes his head. "Why did you fail the trial? You've clearly mastered your wolf."

"Maybe I have now. I hadn't then."

"Hmm." He starts taking down other weapons, playing around with them. Gives me a knowing look. "Do you ever think about how, if our father gets his wish, if wolf-shifters become entirely public, entirely known, your combat advantage disappears?"

"My combat advantage?" I frown. "Knowing how to handle an axe, you mean?"

"I mean, not looking dangerous. The way it is right now, most men would see a girl like you and assume you were helpless. Prey, in a sense. But if they knew you might be a wolf inside, they might not be so sure."

"Wouldn't that be a good thing? I think it would be a good thing if guys who thought about being jerks thought, 'Oh, maybe I shouldn't, she could be a werewolf, I might get eaten.'"

He laughs. "All right. But what about your friend, the very handsome boy who plays football?"

"You mean Edison. What about him?"

"I hear your bite has given him partial gifts of the wolf, which have enhanced his ability to play football. Now imagine that every player in the NFL is a wolf. That advantage disappears."

"Probably cuts down on the head injuries, though."

He shakes his head. "All right. But there's something else that troubles me. The more people know about us, the more people know how to kill us. Like these Veneray."

I nod. "You're not wrong about that."

"And what if their numbers are growing now, because our numbers are growing? What if we become just well enough known to inspire a punishing backlash?"

"Have you been talking to Pere Claude?"

"About this? No. Why? Does he say the same?"

"Similar. One of the big arguments between him and Leon is the matter of secrecy, and whether an uncontrolled trauma morph should be obliged to quarantine in order to maintain it."

"Well, the trauma morph restriction might be overly harsh. But I do think our grandfather has the right idea in general. He strikes me as very wise. And Leon, if I can be perfectly frank with you—although I admire him in many ways—but I'm afraid he's not always wise."

"No? I suppose not."

"A legacy of his red moon, I think, although that doesn't seem to trouble him as much now. He can be impulsive. And more driven by emotion than he thinks."

I nod. "Everyone is."

"Everyone?" He raises an eyebrow, skeptical. Snaps the

weapon in his hand, a kind of rusty hooked chain that belongs in a Hellraiser movie.

"Everyone." I nod firmly, pick up a different weapon, a kind of sharpened pole. "Did you ever meet Opal?"

"No. I didn't. She was the serial killer, correct?"

"Right. Our most infamous sibling. The Frat Boy Killer. Well, in order to be a serial killer at all, you pretty much have to be able to kill in cold blood. But why did she do it? To get back at Leon. She was really mad at him for, she thought, thinking of her as lesser when she turned out to be wolfless. Pure emotion."

"And she is still at large, is she not?"

"Right. She failed, in a way, because she didn't get Pere Claude and Leon to kill each other. But she created enough of a distraction that she escaped herself, so you could see that as success. And she might have helped the Strigoi create their own bitten wolves."

"Strigoi." He frowns. "And what are they?"

"Part of the Russian mafia."

He frowns. "The Russian mafia has bitten wolves now? And nobody thinks this is a problem?"

"Well, we don't know for sure that they do. And if they do, we definitely think it's a problem. But what are we supposed to do about it? I mean, it's like the Flint Savage outbreak. You can't un-bite a person."

He stiffens. Turns angry, defensive. "I suppose you think me and my brother are to blame for the Savage outbreak?"

"I didn't say that."

"We never imagined him doing anything as reckless as what he did. Never. Exposing multiple people without steering them through their first full moon? If we'd known what he planned, we would have stopped him."

"You would? And how would you have done that? Would you have killed him?"

He stares at me for a moment, then nods slowly. "Yes. To stop him, I would have killed him. And you did kill him."

"Pere Claude killed him. I just helped."

"Of course. You are very loyal to him, aren't you?"

"Pere Claude? I guess I am."

"Would you be as loyal to the next pere?"

"Would I?" Cold gut-punch of apprehension, dread. "You think Leon is angling to be the next pere, don't you?"

"Do you think that?"

"He tells me he isn't. But I don't entirely believe him."

He nods. "That's wise. Even if he is entirely sincere about his intentions now, there's no reason to think he won't change his mind." A smile. "Abby, if you're ready, I'll swear to Pere Claude that your wolf is fully mastered."

"If I'm ready? Of course I'm ready, I've been ready for three weeks."

"Let's get my brother and Leon to testify as well. They've been observing your progress."

We locate Rufus and Leon, then find Pere Claude in his office in the Grand Maison, the one next to my cabinay. A fan is going full blast, stirring the edges of the papers on his desk, but it's still oppressively warm. He's wearing little reading glasses, which some of the older wolves use for close-up work.

"Children and grandchildren," he says, nostrils flaring. He has a big smile on his face. "What can I help you with?"

Leon speaks up. "Abby has mastered her trauma morph, Father."

"Has she? Congratulations!" He hugs me. "Wonderful news! We must celebrate."

Just like that, I'm free.

11

THE MAISON

Steph is thrilled when I call to tell her I'm finally allowed to come back into town.

"That's wonderful, honey. So we can have a nice dinner on just about your real seventeenth birthday after all. You want to go to CharliQ's? What's your favorite thing they have?"

"My favorite thing?" I'm confused. "You mean, like, my favorite thing in the courtyard?"

She laughs. "No, silly, what's your favorite food?"

All the food I've ever eaten tumbles through my mind at once, swirling and jostling, bringing a rush of related memories. Pizza comes first. Vegetarian pizza was the first outsider food I ever loved, but then I remember the night Steph's ex-husband George came to kidnap his son Terry, posing as the pizza delivery guy, and now the smell of pizza always makes me feel a little bit nervous.

Next, all the things I've eaten as a wolf, things we killed and ate raw: ducks, pigeons, a whole deer, the guts of human enemies. The wolf gets excited to think about all this, glorying in her skills as a hunter, but my human self gets nauseated thinking about the stink and slime of entrails.

Falafel skewers come next, the ones Edison got for me at the shish-ke-bob place on our first real date, but even on that night I couldn't avoid getting in trouble, ended up in an argument with a super-religious guy on the Huskies football team, eye-flashed him and he got so upset that he knocked over a table.

And, of course, the long, leisurely afternoon dinner when Steph and I met Pere Claude for the first time. The cooks made me special vegetarian versions of every dish, and now I feel bad for making them go to so much trouble when just a couple of days later it didn't matter anyway, after I got shot in the head and lost a foot and gave up on being a vegetarian and just let the people of Bayou Galene feed me whatever kind of meat they wanted to.

"Abby? Is everything okay?"

I must have been silent for a long time. "I'm sorry, I was just trying to figure out my favorite food. How about if I don't choose? Just let Ms. Quemper make whatever she wants, I trust her."

"Okay, that's fine.What about birthday cake?"

"What about it?"

"What kind do you want?"

"Um, chocolate I guess." But then I think about the smell of hot chocolate with cyanide in it, Father Wisdom's final attempt at evil, when he tried to trick Justice and the others into poisoning themselves, I had to break into the New Harmony chapel to stop them, and I broke in by destroying the only thing in the chapel I ever loved, the stained glass Jesus with the black lamb on his shoulders.

"Chocolate, got it." She pauses. "How about tomorrow afternoon? I know it's a Tuesday but I'm still working at the bar on weekends."

"You're still working? Oh. What about the money from the Seattle house?"

"Well. I don't want to spend it all right away, kiddo. You know that."

"Okay, sure. Tomorrow."

"Looking forward to seeing you, honey."

"You too Steph."

I start packing up the things in my cabinay: clothes, computer, a small pile of books I'm in the middle of. For some reason I keep starting new books, reading the first three chapters or so, and then not finishing them.

But it quickly gets hard to decide what to bring. How long am I going to be in New Orleans this time? Am I going to go live with Steph? Go back to working at the Quarter maison? Move to the Seattle maison as soon as possible? Am I going to do what Viv suggested and try to get a college education?

Every different vision of my future seems to require different equipment.

I put things in my "take" pile and then remove them. I'll be in the city, I can get more shampoo. I have an impulse to bring my grandmother's shorthand diaries, but why? I've already done the transcription, and the whole set takes up a lot of space. Maybe it's better to keep everything to a single backpack?

"Abby?" Leon calls out from downstairs. "My father and I are ready to drive into town, are you packed?"

"Almost!" I call back, then quickly stuff a bunch of random crap into my backpack until it's full. Finally, I put on Grandma's red boots, hustle downstairs wearing the backpack, not caring to avoid the creaky places, every step ringing out like a bullet.

Pere Claude hugs me when I get down the stairs. "We're going into town now," he says.

"Great, come on," Leon shakes the car keys, turns around as if to lead us out.

"What's the big hurry?" I say. "Steph's doing a birthday

thing for me tomorrow, but there's nothing happening today, is there?"

"I have some errands to run," Leon turns around, smiles slightly. "Also, I'll be honest, once I know something is going to happen, I hate just waiting around for it."

"Oh, well. Me too."

"I noticed." He leads the way out to the big truck, the same one he took to the storage locker. "We're taking my dad to the Garden District maison, which has a lot more space than the one in the Quarter. And it's air conditioned. But Abby, I've been assuming you want to go back to the Quarter maison to resume your training with Etienne."

"You're taking me to one of the maisons? I thought I was going to stay with Steph. At least for a couple of days."

"Oh." He thinks about it, then shrugs. "Of course, whatever you want."

"I don't know, do you know something I don't? Maybe I shouldn't stay with Steph. Maybe she's too busy."

"No, it's fine," he says. "I'll drop you off at your loufrer's."

"Okay." But now I'm chewed up by self doubt. Did Steph want me to stay with her or not? Did we discuss it? Now I can't remember. I send her a text:

> They're dropping me off at your place I hope
> that's okay

I don't get a response right away, so I look out the window, fretting, as we cover the miles into New Orleans. Leon drives, with Pere Claude up front. I make note of the familiar landmarks that tell me I'm going into town. I've been to town only a couple of times in the past few months, always with a senior wolf as chaperone. But it's only now that we're heading into town for good that I start to wonder something: Leon does not have an officially mastered wolf, does he? And he has been staying in Bayou Galene, mostly. But I don't think he has the same restriction I have.

He's been living on his own for almost forty years, it would be a bit ridiculous for him to be under house arrest now, wouldn't it? On the other hand, doesn't Leon spending forty years in the outside world as a trauma morph kind of prove the restriction isn't needed?

As we get closer, I recognize more and more familiar markers, the ones that tell me, I'm going into town, I'm going to New Orleans, I'm going to see Steph, I'm going to see Terry, I'm going to see Morgan, I'm going to see Grandma Charli, I'm going to be somewhere that isn't Bayou Galene. A sense of anticipation, but gray, blunted, more like a memory of a sense of anticipation.

I'm always shocked at how short the drive really is. Bayou Galene feels like worlds away, but it's less than two hours away from the city.

Leon drives the car through the Quarter, and I'd sort of forgotten how narrow and crowded the streets are, this big truck seems to barely fit. When we get to Steph's house in Bywater, there's no parking right in front of the house; instead, there's a huge pothole and some orange cones.

"We'll just drop you off," Leon says. "If you need us, we'll be at the Garden District maison."

"Goodbye, granddaughter." Pere Claude leans over to give me a one-armed hug.

"Goodbye," I tell him, have a weird moment where I'm sure that this is the final goodbye, we're never going to see each other again.

"Are you sad?" he asks me, frowning. "You seem sad."

"No, it's just—I thought of something sad, it's nothing." I force a smile. "See you later."

They take off and I watch them go, still feeling odd. Forlorn. But why? I want to be here. I should feel at home here. But everything seems strange and off kilter. It's the pothole, I think.

Up on the porch, I knock, and the door opens. Somebody I don't know. Wait, this is Steph's boyfriend, I know him from his smell in her hair. He's a dark-haired guy, really average looking. Normal to the point of boring. Is that good? Maybe that's what Steph wanted. I don't instantly have a feeling about him one way or the other, which might be a good sign. George gave me the creeps even before he attacked me and I figured out who he was.

"I'm sorry miss, can I help you?"

"I'm Abby," I say. "Steph's friend?"

"Oh!" He nods, like he knows who that is, and I flood with relief. Then he calls out, "Steph, your friend Abby is here!" He smiles, sticks out a hand for shaking. "I'm Irwin Caine, Steph's boyfriend."

Steph comes to the door holding Terry on one hip, but frowning, frazzled. "Abby, I wasn't expecting you until tomorrow."

"Oh." I gulp back panic. "I'm sorry, I thought, I mean, I know we're having dinner tomorrow, but I thought—never mind, I can just go straight to the maison. I just wanted to—you know, touch base? I guess?"

"Oh." She sighs, runs a hand through her hair, I notice that her gray roots are showing, like she hasn't dyed it in a while. Also, Terry usually notices me right away and wants to be held, but today he hasn't seemed to notice me at all. He's gnawing on a big orange plastic thing and looks cranky and teary-eyed, not focusing on anything.

"He's teething?" I guess. This is one thing I have been through with babies before. My little sister Ash—

Never mind. I don't want to think about that right now.

"He is." Steph exhales: deep, long, frustrated. As if in answer, Terry throws himself back in her arms, wriggling like he's trying to escape, letting out an unpleasant high-pitched shriek, a noise I've never heard him make before. He tangles his fingers in her hair and she grimaces while he shrieks again.

"Here, let me." I take him, carefully extricating him from her hair. He scowls at me, says his name for me "Bah-bee!" In an aggrieved tone, like he blames me for his pain. Then he hits hits me with the orange plastic thing.

"Terry, no! No hitting!" Steph takes the baby back from me. "He's got to learn not to hit people. Apparently when he's in pain his first instinct is to lash out." She looks at me when she says this. Almost angry. Almost like she thinks it's my fault. Like she thinks I'm the one who taught him to do that.

I feel hurt. Like I want to cry. But I don't want to do it here. "Steph, please, I'm sorry, I just wanted to say hi, I didn't know it would be so inconvenient, I'll just go, we'll see each other at dinner. Okay?"

"Okay." She nods. "I'll see you tomorrow."

"Nice to meet you," Irwin calls out as I walk away.

It's a bit of a hike to the Quarter maison, but familiarity makes it go quickly.

The whole time I keep going over all the mistakes I made, all the stupid things I did, all the stupid things I've ever done. All the embarrassing things. Every time I ever screwed up or was awkward or said something I didn't mean.

Everything in New Orleans is familiar, but also, strange. Like when I was telling Leon about the new foot. The same in every way, except, my brain keeps trying to tell me it isn't the same.

The familiar streets to the maison, picking up on the scent trails of the people I know, plus other wolves, bitten and born, people I don't know, and a couple of wolves I know barely. Etienne's son, I think, is one of them. Etienne and his wife split up a few years ago and she remarried but he didn't. He says it didn't have anything to do with him getting shot in the head and losing his wolf, but sometimes I wonder. Raymond is here as well.

As I get close to the maison, people start pouring out to greet me: Babette, Barney, Etienne, and Nicolas, plus a wolf-less Varger woman I don't know, and a young male bitten wolf.

"Abby, welcome!" Etienne says. "This is Angeline and Christopher." He gives me a significant look when he pats Christopher, the bitten wolf, on the shoulder. He must know I was wondering about him. I didn't know the Varger ever had bitten wolves on staff at the maisons.

"Nice to meet you."

"We have more staff who are not here right now," Etienne says. "And you probably recognized my son Lucien and Roman's son Raymond." A brief apologetic smile. "We're a little busy here, sorry."

"Just more people for your welcome home party." Babette hands me a frozen margarita with a big straw. "Check it out, I bought a daiquiri machine."

And with that I get sucked back into the everyday life of the maison in the Quarter. Just like the bunker, it feels very different than it did last summer, more crowded, messy, tense, busy. As we pass through the house, the Snarlaway line rings and Etienne stops to answer. I hear him say huh, uh huh, and similar things. Then he writes out a little ticket and hands it to Christopher. "Standard attic visit, they think it's very large rats. Probably possums, is my thinking."

He nods. "Great. Should I go over there now?"

"Of course not, make an appointment for tomorrow," Babette says. "Right now it's party time!"

"Babs, you always think it's party time." I laugh.

"That's because it is. Life is just a party and parties weren't meant to last," she sings Prince at me, waltzing off toward the courtyard.

The courtyard has been fixed up for socializing more than it was last fall, with chairs and little tables and canopies. But also there are the signs that it's being used for collecting and securing new bitten wolves. Stray bits of cloth or leather obviously shredded by wolf claws. A completely shattered animal carrier on its side.

As everybody chats randomly, it becomes obvious that these people have been working together for several months, and I haven't been part of it. They have in-jokes that don't make sense to me, reminisce about dramatic events I wasn't around for. Babette called it a welcome home party, and I wanted it to be, but it doesn't feel like home. It feels more like when I visited Steph and Morgan's old house on Capitol Hill in Seattle. Like visiting a place that used to be my home. But now I'm just a visitor. An onlooker.

A ghost.

"Abby?" Etienne touches me on the shoulder. "Let's figure out where you're sleeping before the partying gets too out of hand." I grab my backpack and follow him upstairs, grateful for what feels like a social rescue. I have a purpose now.

He leads me to the second floor, where all the bedrooms are, to the end of the hallway, a little windowed alcove.

"It's not private exactly, but I was thinking you might be small enough to sleep comfortably on this chaise longue. Are you?"

He points. It's upholstered in worn purple velvet. "Yep, I've slept on smaller."

"Great, we'll get you some fresh linens."

He disappears, reappears with sheets. "I don't know if you'll want a blanket this time of year." He looks apologetic. "The Quarter maison still has no air conditioning, although we have thought about installing it, especially now that we're so much more busy. The Garden District maison got it last year."

"Just the sheets is fine. Thank you." Together we use the sheets to make the chaise longue into a bed.

He says, "You're probably wondering about Christopher."

"I am, yeah. We haven't had any bitten wolves on the team before, have we?"

"Not at the New Orleans maisons, no," he says. "Although Brooklyn has had a few. Anyway, Christopher has been a great member of the team. He's a New Orleans kid, ran away from a bad situation, homeless when he got bitten. So when he woke up here, he decided to stick around." He smiles but it turns tight around his eyes. "It's hard, Abby. The Flint Savage outbreak is not dying down the way we thought it would. The Varger have for years believed that the bite loses potency with each transmission so that eventually even the worst outbreak would end on its own. But we've seen no sign of that at all."

"Do you think you were always wrong? Or do you think there's something special about the Flint Savage... uh... wolf line? Is there a word for that?"

"I know what you mean, and we don't have a word for it. We never needed one before."

I sit down on the chaise longue that is my bed. He sits down on a window seat across from me. We stare at each other.

"Is it bad? It's bad, isn't it?" I say.

"I've never seen anything like it." He shakes his head. "And Leon, he's been digitizing the historic pere diaries, he's starting to think there never has been anything like it. Never. In the whole history of our people."

"Well it makes sense. An outbreak of this scale requires modern technology and modern travel, doesn't it?"

He nods. "I suppose that's true. There's so much we don't know. And that's why, the past couple of weeks, we've been doing something new. We're attempting to map, and ideally connect with, every bitten wolf in town."

"Wow. How many are there?"

"More than we could have guessed before starting this project. Babette has really been amazing."

"Babette? You mean, she actually stops partying long enough to do some work?"

Laughs. "I wouldn't say she stops partying, exactly. This job was basically built for her. She's a terrific scent tracker, plus friendly and attractive, so she finds it very easy to meet people. Offers them a drink from her flask, makes them laugh, invites them to lunch at Mid City Meats or a workout at the Rampart Hammerfit."

"Mid City Meats. Not CharliQs?"

"No, Charlaine Quemper has specifically requested that we not direct all these newfangled loup-garous to her place, and we respect that. The other maisons have started mapping their own cities in much the same manner. After the events of the past few months, we've realized that we need to bring the bitten wolves into our larger community. Many of them have been in the habit of avoiding us. They've heard of 'the rougarou' of New Orleans and they're suspicious of us. They think we're the cops of the wolf world?"

"Wolf cops." Laugh. "Sounds like a cheesy movie. But I get it. We were already thinking about that, in Meriwether, when we found out silver hurts bitten wolves even though it does nothing to the born. We need to be comparing notes about things like that, not avoiding each other."

He nods. "You're very right." Hand on shoulder. "It's really good to have you back. And I know now that your wolf is officially mastered, you could go anywhere, any maison would be thrilled to have you, but I'd appreciate it if you stayed here, at least for a while. Babette and I have been refining the techniques for training our people in scent tracking, developing a curriculum almost, and I think your input would be really valuable."

"Sure. Yeah." I shake my head, getting a little choked up. "Bon Dieu, Etienne, you always make me feel so good. Like a valued member of a great team. Why is it that you werewolves are either terrifying or the nicest people I've ever met?"

He laughs, but looks uncomfortable. "Terrifying? Who's terrifying?"

"Oh, you know. Vivienne."

He laughs. "Well, that's one kind of terrifying."

"And my father. He's another kind of terrifying. But I guess my grandfather is sort of terrifying and also one of the nicest people I ever met, so it's complicated I guess."

"It's the nature of the wolf, don't you think?" he says, with a smile. "A wolf is a fearsome predator, no? But also a loyal companion and protector. A wolf who doesn't show her fangs might be taken for a dog, a furry and playful friend to humans."

I laugh. I don't know if he meant to make me laugh, but he did. "Playful. Really. Can you play fetch with a wolf?"

He shrugs, eyes twinkling. "Try it, you might be surprised."

I laugh. He laughs. Then I think of something. "Etienne, has anyone told you that you could get your wolf back?"

"Hmm?"

"Arda's wound. It can be cured by a bite from a transforming wolf. I cured my father that way. I could do the same for you."

He nods thoughtfully. "Well. That's an interesting thought. But right now, I think, no. I do not have the gift of the trauma morph. I would lose my ability to be human during the full moons."

"And that's important to you?"

"I feel I have served my people well in this capacity. Maybe, after I get some of you younger wolves trained properly." He smiles. "Maybe then I would retire, and want my wolf back."

"Well. Any time. Just ask."

"I will. Thank you. Are you ready to go back to the party?"

I nod, feeling better than I have in days.

12

CHARLAINE QUEMPER

I wake up, heart pounding from the tattered remains of a nightmare I can't remember.

Check my phone, and it's already almost time for dinner with Steph, so I dress quickly and hurry off to CharliQs. But Steph's family isn't there yet. I check my phone again and see a text message from Steph:

> Running a bit late, see you at 6

I try sitting by myself for a while but start feeling bored and lonely, go find Charlaine Quemper in the kitchen where she's sitting up on a stool, supervising rather than cooking herself, directing a small army of younger Quemper family members and others: "Turn down the flame, Chas, you got it up way too high. Georgie, hon, use the big knife, that little one you got there is making you work too hard, let the knife do the work. Oh, hey, Abby, I wanted to talk to you about something, one moment. Adella, I'm putting you in charge of the kitchen until I come back, don't let it burn down, ya hear?"

"Yes, Grammy."

"Come on." She taps me on the arm and steers me into

the room that gets used as the office, where there's a phone and a computer and all the paper records. The picture of her and my grandma getting arrested is sitting out in the middle of the desk.

"They brought that? Good."

She nods. Picks up the photo. "Your father and grandfather came by yesterday with that and a couple of giant bottles of champagne. Got me thinking about the old days." She shakes her head.

"Are you willing to talk about the old days?"

She gives me a look. "You want to hear about the old days of the Civil Rights Movement? For real?"

"I do. Yeah."

"Are you sure? Because it was a lot worse than what they tell you in school."

"I went to school in a cult, everything they told me was lies. I want to hear the truth."

She nods. "All right, then. But you've got to understand, they killed more of us back then than they ever admitted to. We got beaten to death, or just disappeared. Your grandma had to save me from death or serious injury probably a dozen times."

"Who was trying to hurt you?"

"Cops mostly. When they were trying to break up protests. Keep the peace they said. But we were usually marching peaceful until the cops showed up."

"They still do that, Ms. Quemper. My friend Deena went to a demonstration in Seattle that turned into a 'riot' after the cops started hitting people with tear gas and rubber bullets."

She nods. "Back in the day, around here, they used dogs a lot." Unexpectedly, she smiles. "I swear to God I never saw anything funnier than a pack of six police dogs all coming straight after your grandma, these giant snarling German shepherds, regular hounds of hell, and Leah Evangeline so dainty and helpless looking, she just leans down and flashes 'em with those green eyes, growls a little. All of a sudden every single one of those police dogs is yelping and pissing themselves in fear." She chuckles, shakes her head, looks from me, to the picture, back to me. "You sure do look like her."

"When I saw the photo, I thought at first it was me and Izzy in vintage dresses."

"Vintage. Hmmph." She snorts. "That makes it all sound so quaint and far away. Like something for white tourists. It was a war, child. Another battle in the Civil War."

"I'm sorry. I just meant, Izzy looks like you. The same way I look like my grandmother."

"You flatter me, Abby. Isobelle is so much prettier than I ever was." She laughs, then makes eye contact with me, extremely serious. She'd flash if she had a wolf. "Izzy's been working for y'all loup-garous, I hear. Computers and so on. That right?"

"That's right, Ms. Quemper. And if your next question is what I think it is, then yes, the loup-garous are committed to protecting her."

She nods. "Good. They paying her cash money?"

"Um. I'm sorry, I guess I don't know."

"Hmmph." She makes a skeptical grunting sound. "Probably not then. You tell them to pay her. Tell your grandfather. He'll listen to you, they'll listen to him." She looks troubled for a moment. "Or, tell your father Leon. Your grandfather's got enough on his mind."

That look of trouble sends me into a panic. "What's wrong, Ms. Quemper? Is something wrong with Pere Claude?"

She stares at the photo for a moment, then shakes her head, forcing a little smile. "Oh, no, child, he's just old. Like me. I'm out there trying to train a bunch of kids how to cook right. How to live right. And I worry. Did I teach them enough? Can they carry on without me? Are they just going to keep on making the same damn mistakes?"

I nod. I pause, think about some of the questions I still have after reading my grandma's diaries. "Ms. Quemper, how did you meet my grandmother? She talks about you in her diaries, but she doesn't say how you met exactly."

"Oh, we met at a demonstration. She got between me and a couple of those police dogs." She laughs. "After that, we were best of friends."

"When did she tell you she was a loup-garou?"

"Kind of figured it out for myself. Watching her, the power she had. Little, like you, but she could break all the bones in a man's hand in a second, without working too hard. There was one time she did that, to get away from a cop that had her restrained, and the instant she did it, she went all to pieces, stepping away from him and sobbing. Even the man who got his hand busted, he looked right at her, and he assumed somebody else in the crowd must've done it." She chuckles. "All y'all loup-garous have that power to do violence, but your grandma, I swear, the greatest power she had was being able to turn on a dime and seem like like the sweetest, most timid and proper little white lady you ever saw. She could've strangled a man with her bare hands right in front of everybody and later on they'd still think somebody else must've done it."

She studies me for a long moment. "You could borrow a little something from her, I think. If you want my advice. You don't really know how to turn it off. And even as little as you are, if a man gets his hand broke and sees you glaring at him like you do, he's gonna know y'done it."

"I'm sorry, Ms. Quemper, I don't think I know how to do that. Turn it off, I mean. In the cult I learned to shut down entirely, but it's different. That was more like putting myself behind a blank wall. I couldn't just go back and forth. When I'm shut down I stay shut down."

She gives me an encouraging little hug. "I know. I know. You've already got so much trauma from that cult, it messes you around. Sometimes I think that's why they do it. Make sure we spend all our lives just coping, so we never have enough left over to fight for what's right."

I think about that for a moment. "You think they do it on purpose? I mean, hurt us on purpose?"

She shrugs. "You got a better explanation?"

"No, it's just blowing my mind a little." Slight laugh. "As much as I hated Father Wisdom, I still thought he believed that he was doing the right thing. What God would want."

"They do think it's right." Her expression turns hard. "They believe it's the right thing to do, keeping us down." She shakes her head. "You know, your grandma asked me, once, if I wanted the powers of the loup-garou. She would bite me, she said. 'Claude will be furious, but for you I'll do it.' And I thought about it, I really did. But then I told her, 'If I had the deadly power of you loup-garous, there's a long list of men who would have to die, and I don't think that would end well for anybody.'"

"No? Why not?"

She sighs. "Oh, child. Those powerful white men try to crush anything they get too scared of. I don't need them any more scared of me and mine than they already are."

"Oh." I think about it for a moment. "That's something my dad Leon warned me about. Sometimes when people are scared of you, they leave you alone. But other times they try to destroy you."

She nods. "That's about it. And if I thought for one moment that you could get rid of the evil in the world by killing a few bad men, you know I'd do it. But I don't think it works that way. I think you just have to fight evil wherever you find it."

I study the picture again. My grandmother's face. Like mine, but not like mine. Her expression is different. It's not rage. It's a kind of good-humored determination. A slight smile. She's looking right at the camera, seems to be asking, you see what this man is doing to me? It's ridiculous, isn't it? You see it, right? How ridiculous it is?

"Did you ever see my grandmother kill anyone?"

Deep long inhale. "I'm not sure. There was a man once— he was breathing when we left him, but—it still haunts me a little. The way his shin bone looked while it was poking out of his skin like that. The way he screamed. High-pitched. Not human, almost. It goes right through you." She shudders. "I said it was a war. We were fighting on the right side, but we still had to do things…"

She's silent for a long moment, and I speak up. "I'm sorry for everything you had to go through. But I still don't really understand why they do it. Why do they work so hard just to keep people down? Is it the money?"

She looks thoughtful for a moment, then shakes her head. "I don't know, child. Money's part of it, for sure, but it's more than that. A lot more. You should start out reading what Doctor King had to say about it, I think, if you never have."

Her eyes get glossy with tears and so do mine. "I haven't, Ms. Quemper. And I'm sorry."

She hugs me and I lean my head against her shoulder for a long time, trying to stop crying, grimly amused that I've been here maybe fifteen minutes and already ruined my eye makeup.

I know it's not possible, but I almost imagine that I can smell my grandmother, somehow, in the air around Charlotte Quemper, like a ghost, the same smell that permeated the storage locker. I inhale deeply.

"It's her perfume." She pulls away, giving me an amused look.

"What?"

"Come on now, I've known you loup-garous long enough, I can tell when you're picking up on some smell that interests you. Your grandmother used to wear a perfume, she had it made here in town at a little shop where you could have them make you a custom scent. Do you know this story?"

"I don't think so."

"Well. You might already know that Leah Evangeline's grandmother put her mother on a train from Paris to send her to relatives in New Orleans, because the Nazis were closing in. And the grandmother had this scarf she used to wear. Right before she put her daughter on the train that would take her to the boat that would take her to New Orleans, she took the scarf off her own neck, and unfolded it. It was a very fine silk, so it looked small around the neck, but when you opened it up it was much bigger than you'd ever think it could be. And when it was all unfolded, you could see that the abstract pattern of gold and white on a blue background, all the lines, they intersected in the middle to form a Star of David, the symbol of the Jewish people. So it was like a secret. And the mother and daughter never saw each other again.

"When Leah Evangeline was Bat Mitzvah'd, they were in Brooklyn by then, her mother gave her the scarf and told her the story. And Leah Evangeline asked, 'What's that smell? Is it Grandma's perfume?' and her mother just laughed, because she'd never noticed the perfume.

"Your grandma's wolf was just starting to think about waking up, so her sense of smell was on high alert, and she got a little bit obsessed trying to identify what perfume was on the scarf. She knew it had to be something that was available in Paris before the Nazis invaded. But that was all she knew.

"So, one day, in a Soho antique shop, she gets a whiff of it. A good strong whiff from an empty bottle, called Fleurs de Memoire. Flowers of memory.

"Not too long after this, her wolf comes for the first time, and she's got a lot of other things on her mind. The wolf, her move, her marriage. And then she loses her own mother to cancer. It gets her thinking about the scarf again, and that haunting scent, Fleurs de Memoire. So she starts looking in the New Orleans thrift shops for another bottle, maybe not so empty. She finds a little perfume shop where they make the scents custom for you, if you pay them enough. And she uncorks the bottle for them. Asks, do you think you could make something that smells like this for me?

"And damn, the little old man who runs the place, he knows the scent. He used to work for the Jewish parfumer who made it. They never came back after the war, but this guy, he remembers.

"So she and the little man strike up a friendship, and he makes her a new version of the scent, and she starts wearing it. You loup-garous don't go for heavy scents most of the time and she was no different. She wore it lightly. Barely there. But I got to know it. A cook needs a good sense of smell same as you loup-garous. And my nose never got so sensitive that I knew Leah Evangeline by just the smell of her sweat. But the smell of her perfume? I got to know it well. One time, for my birthday, she gave me my very own bottle.

"When she got killed, Claude told me I should take anything of hers that I wanted, anything that meant something to me, and I took that scarf."

She goes over to a drawer, takes out a wad of blue silk, shakes it out to its full square. Smells of the perfume, and my grandmother herself, burst forth as she shakes it. Right there at the center of the pattern, interlocking white lines and gilded threads that look like a purely random abstract, all come together to form a clear six-pointed star, white with a gold edge.

"That's beautiful," I say.

"Do you want it, child?" she says. "If you wanted it, I would give it to you."

"Oh, no, that's yours I've got my own thing from my grandmother." I stick out my foot with the red boot. "See? They've got pockets."

"The boots, I remember her wearing those." She nods.

"Maybe the scarf should be on display in a museum. The picture too. I've been thinking about starting one here in the restaurant."

She picks up a small bottle with a tiny amount of golden liquid in the bottom. It's labeled "Fantôme de Fleurs de Memoire" in a fine, neat handwriting that isn't my grandmother's—probably the perfumer.

"Phantom of Flowers of Memory?" I guess.

"Ghost, phantom." She nods. "Maybe it's not the most proper French, but this is New Orleans, we don't worry much about that. See, there's just a little bit left now. When it started to run low I tried to find the little shop myself, but it was long gone. So I started to use it very, very sparingly." She sighs. "The smell's probably not quite what it was, but it never went off entirely. It still smells like your grandmother to me. And to you too, it seems."

I nod. "It does." Then I stop. I just caught a faint whiff of Steph and her family, as if they're walking nearby. "Ms. Quemper, there's one thing I need to talk to you about before I forget. Did you know that my grandmother was probably murdered?"

"Murdered?" She looks troubled. "I heard she got shot by poachers who wanted that pretty red coat she had as a wolf?"

"That's what they wanted everybody to think. But she was probably murdered by Edwin A. Duke." I pause, as the name causes her face to twist into a look of disgust and fury. "You know him?"

"Know him? That fucking sumbich was number one on my list of men who needed to get eaten." She pauses. "I'd apologize for language but you're seventeen, child, I know you've heard worse."

I nod. "What happened, we think, is that she was going to run for office against him. And I guess he must have thought she had a chance to beat him, because he had her killed."

She shakes her head. "No, not that Duke, he didn't have to

think she had a chance. He would've had her killed just for having the nerve to try. He didn't think much of Black people, you could probably guess that, but that was nothing on how much he hated women." She pauses, shaking, sweat infused with stressed out rage. "God damn. Murdered by Edwin A. Duke! The sumbich is dead, but his son is still in politics around here. Junior acts himself a little more civilized in public, even come out against some of the worst things his father did. But who knows what he is in private. God damn."

"One more thing. Have you heard of the Veneray?"

"Veneray." She frowns. "Maybe. Aren't they a Klan offshoot?"

"They might be. But they're more loup-garou specific. Like, a secret society of werewolf hunters. And they were probably involved in my grandmother's death."

She shakes her head. "Figures. But no, sorry, I don't know anything special about the Veneray."

"Thank you, Ms. Quemper."

She pauses. "You can call me Grandma Charli if you want. We're family now I think."

"Thank you, Ms.—Grandma Charli." My phone buzzes with a text from Steph. "The Marchandes are here."

She puts a hand on my shoulder. "I guess it's time to start up the party, huh?"

"I guess it is."

13

SEVENTEEN

I head out into the courtyard of CharliQ's, where Steph's family, plus her boyfriend, are all gathered around one of the larger tables. Steph seems in much better spirits today. She's dyed her hair back to black with red tips, premature gray invisible once more. It still smells of the hair dye.

Terry is also in a much better mood. When Steph gets up to hug me, he also holds out his hands and says "bah-bee, bah-bee."

I give him a piggyback ride, around the courtyard, then into the kitchen, where Grandma Charli has resumed directing kitchen affairs. "Say hi to Grandma Charli, Terry."

"Hey there, children." She briefly touches him under his chin, then washes her hands. "But you get that baby out of my kitchen, now, babies are not sanitary, and they like to grab things."

I go back to the table, intending to return the baby to Steph, but Steph's dad smiles and holds out his hands. "Give him here, Abby, I want to enjoy him for a while when he's not screaming."

I lean in close, handing the baby over, but when Mr.

Marchande exhales I smell—a bitterness, a wrongness. In his sweat, in his breath.

"Mr. Marchande are you feeling okay?"

He wipes his forehead with a cloth, bounces Terry on his knee. "Just fine. Little tired maybe. I've been busy."

Steph's mom leans in with a laugh. "He's retired, supposedly, you'd think he would work less!"

"Musicians never get to retire."

"Not unless they get lucky." Morgan holds up his beer in a kind of cheers gesture. "We got lucky. Didn't we? With the money from the Seattle house?"

"We did." Steph looks down, oddly sad.

I take the glass from Morgan, inhale. "Wait, that's the Bayou Galene imperial stout, isn't it?"

He nods. "They had it on the menu. Guess they got a keg or something. It's really good."

"I know it's good, but you know it's two or three times as strong as regular beer, right? It's practically wine."

He laughs. "Maybe so, but I'm not a big wine fan. This stuff is really good, though."

Steph gives me a look. "Abby, I know you and Irwin met briefly under less than ideal circumstances. But here, I'm formally introducing you. Irwin Caine, meet Abby Verreaux."

"Nice to meet you. Steph talks about you a lot." He pumps my hand enthusiastically, but I'm confused.

"Steph, why did you give my name as Verreaux?"

"That's your family name isn't it?"

"My biological family. But you know my name is Abigail Marchande. You got me the ID that has that name on it. That's my name."

"Oh, I'm sorry honey, I didn't know. I thought you were using your family name now that you'd moved out there with your grandfather."

I reach down to the pocket in my right boot, take out my

Louisiana State ID, slap it on the table. "My legal name is still Abigail Marchande. Look."

Irwin frowns at it. "Wait, this says you're turning nineteen, doesn't it? I thought somebody said you were seventeen?"

Steph laughs. "Oh, that. Abby was born in a rural situation and didn't have a proper birth certificate, so when we went to get her some ID, we used my last name, and made her eighteen, for legal purposes. But she's really turning seventeen."

"A rural situation? I grew up in a cult, Steph."

She winces. "I didn't know you'd want to talk about that with someone you just met, honey."

Irwin says, "A cult, no kidding? Wow. What kind of a cult?"

"Christian."

Steph's mother jumps in to say "Protestant evangelical."

"You mean, not Catholic," I say.

She seems defensive. "Well, it wasn't."

"All religions are cults," Morgan says, firmly and a little drunkenly.

"Now, Morgan," his mother says. "Don't be rude. Mr. Caine might be a churchgoer himself."

"So?" He turns to Irwin. "Are you a church guy? Did I offend you?"

"I used to go to church with my mother, sometimes. Eastern Orthodox."

"Eastern? Isn't that interesting," Steph's mother says. "You all have a different Pope, isn't that right? Celebrate Easter on a different day?

"That's right," he says, smiling. "Mardi Gras Easter is on the first Sunday after the first full moon after the vernal equinox, while Orthodox Easter is the first Sunday after the first full moon after Jewish Passover."

"All that full moon business sounds kind of pagan to me," I say. Steph gives me a very sharp look, which I assume means "don't start talking werewolf stuff in front of my new boyfriend."

I say, "In the cult we didn't celebrate Easter at all."

"But you were Christian?" He looks confused.

"Well, we commemorated Easter. It was on Mardi Gras Easter, I think. I just don't think you could really call it a celebration."

"Really? What did you do?" Irwin seems genuinely intrigued.

"It was a two-day fast on Good Friday and—we didn't have a name for it so I'm going to call it 'Dead Saturday'— then on Easter Sunday, after a good long sermon, we'd finally get to eat pancakes. Wait, there was butter and molasses on the pancakes, I guess it was a feast after all, never mind."

"Dead Saturday!" Morgan snorts with laughter. "Good one, Abby."

"Holy Satuday," Steph's mom says, looking tired. "It's called Holy Saturday."

"Huh. I guess that makes sense, but we didn't call it that. Too Catholic, maybe."

"Interesting," Irwin says. "On Easter Sunday we had communion, followed by a feast of roasted lamb. We ate eggs that were dyed red to symbolize the blood of Christ. The lamb was usually cooked outdoors on a spit. A whole lamb, maybe more than one depending on the size of the congregation."

"So you ate Jesus three ways, interesting. Wait, that sounds like it belongs on a menu. Our special today: Jesus three ways."

Morgan cracks up, but Steph gets mad, barking out: "Abby! I know you think it's funny to disrespect people's religious traditions, but it's actually very rude."

"Sorry." I feel chastised but not repentant. Which is how I felt a lot of the time in the cult, now that I think about it. I butter and eat some of the bread that was put out in the middle of the table. The Varger don't avoid bread or other carbs the way fitness people sometimes do, but they don't always have it on hand either. Sometimes I really miss fresh bread.

Steph's mom says, "Irwin, is your mother still with us?"

"She's not, Mrs. Marchande. I lost her three years ago. She lived to be ninety-two, so I got a lot of time with her. I still miss her, though. I go to the deli near the Russian center just to get a piroshky like she used to make."

"The Russian center? What part of town is that?" I ask.

"East Jefferson. Near the hospital," he says.

"Metarie," Morgan says. "It's in Metarie."

"Russian. You ever hear of the Strigoi, part of the Russian mafia?" I ask.

"Abby!" Steph barks out. "That's rude!"

"It's rude to ask a Russian if he's heard of the Russian mafia?"

"Yes! If he were Italian would you be asking about the Italian mafia?"

"Sorry. But have you heard of them?"

He shrugs. "No, I'm sorry. I only know 'strigoi' as a word for a monster. Like, a witch who becomes a wolf or maybe a vampire?"

"Have you heard of the rougarou?"

Steph frowns ferociously at me. "No, Abby, I'm sure he hasn't."

"I have, actually." He smiles. "Local werewolf of the swamps, right? Also known as the loup-garou?"

"That's right."

Steph shakes her head at me. Izzy's little brother Chas— not so little anymore, he's gotten really tall in the last couple of months—comes out with the salad course, providing a welcome distraction. There's some mild drama around moving Terry from his grandfather's lap to a high chair, then, for a while, everybody gets comfortable again talking about food. I try to stay quiet, thinking that I have nothing good to talk about, nothing that won't turn into making Steph mad at me.

But now that I think about it, I'm kind of mad at her too. I never told her that I was using Verreaux as a last name, she just assumed it. Is she trying to disown me, now that I've connected with my biological family? I thought we had a stronger bond than that. Isn't that why we're here, celebrating my birthday? Or maybe we're not. Maybe this is about Terry's first birthday more than my seventeenth. Maybe this is Steph's way of saying goodbye.

"Abby, did you hear me?" Steph says.

"What?"

"I asked if you had school plans."

"Oh, sorry. I didn't realize you were talking to me. School plans. You mean, like, college?"

"Yes, I mean college."

"I don't know. My aunt Vivienne tells me I can get a bachelor's from a Bayou Galene school."

"You can? That's wonderful. You really ought to do that, then. If you can get a degree without even having to leave town, wow."

"What would you want to major in?" Irwin asks.

"I don't know. History, maybe." I finger the top of my grandma's boot, flash back to the glimpse of her unfolded scarf. "Did you know that my grandmother marched for Civil Rights with Charlaine Quemper back in the 1960's?"

"Did she? That's fantastic," Steph says.

"The same Charlaine Quemper who started this restauarant?" Irwin says. "Wow."

"Yeah. The more I find out about my grandmother, the more I wish I'd gotten the chance to meet her."

"Your grandmother isn't around?" Steph's mom says.

"She isn't, Mrs. Marchande. She got killed a long time ago."

"Killed!" She seems alarmed. "Oh, no!"

I realize I can't possibly explain the whole reality without going into a lot of werewolf stuff, and settle on, "Hunting accident. Very tragic."

"Oh, I can imagine. That's just terrible. Well, your grandfather is a lovely man. It's sad to think of him being alone for so long."

"He still misses her very much," I say.

We're interrupted again by the arrival of more food, the soup course. More innocuous food talk. Morgan gets another imperial stout in spite of Steph glaring daggers at him. The soup course talk hasn't died down until after the main course arrives, Morgan gets another beer and thinks Steph doesn't notice, but she does. Irwin continues to ask me innocuous questions you'd probably ask any seventeen-year-old, like, do I date, do I have a driver's license yet, what are my career ambitions. What books have I read, what books do I want to read, where have I traveled, where would I like to travel, what music do I like.

"Abby's a good kid when it comes to music," Steph's dad says, gesturing toward me. "She doesn't reject the good stuff just because it's old."

"Well, Mr. Marchande here gave me most of my education in modern music. I didn't really know music growing up, not even church music. I'd hear music sometimes, when we went to outsider churches, but John Wise didn't like it, so we didn't have any."

"No kidding." Irwin gapes at me. "Did you say John Wise? The religious writer?" I nod and he says, "He's the one who formed the cult that raised you?"

"Yes. John Wise was my stepfather."

"Well doesn't that beat all. I know you said you grew up in a cult, but I never imagined your stepfather was John Wise."

"Is that good or bad?"

"Just, strange is all. I've heard of John Wise."

"Did you hear about New Harmony, the cult he formed and nearly drove into mass suicide?"

"You know, I think I do vaguely remember something about a cult with that name, but I don't remember it being associated with John Wise. I thought I heard he has a new book coming out."

"Yeah, he's dead, that's my stepmother and brother writing the book in his name because his name sells." I shake my head. "How is it that you've heard a dead man has a new book coming out, but you totally missed it when that same man was busted for running a deadly torture cult?"

"Abby," Steph warns me, puts a hand on my shoulder. I realize I was starting to become angry, take a deep breath.

"Sorry. I'm not mad at you, I'm mad at the, I guess, the news media."

And that sparks everyone complaining about the news. Morgan, Steph's mom, and Irwin Caine seem to think the news is bad because it's too liberal, while Steph and I think it's overly conservative, and I don't know what Steph's dad thinks because he decides to start playing with the baby again.

I excuse myself to go use the restroom, then pause on the way back as I get a whiff of person-smell: Izzy, Deena, Edison, Edison's frat-bro friend Reed, and Edison's bandmates, Nora and Kennedy, they've all been here. Recently. Like, sometime in the last few days.

They're all here in New Orleans and nobody bothered to tell me.

Enraged, I barge right into the kitchen. "Grandma Charli, why didn't you tell me everybody was here in town!"

She gives me a look. I can't help it, I simmer down. She's good at giving looks. She would make a terrifying werewolf.

"Now, child, what are you so upset about?"

I tap the side of my nose. "I noticed that Izzy and my friends were here not too long ago. And nobody said anything to me!"

She nods. "Well. They arrived a couple of days ago. And their plan was to go out to the bayou to visit you. But then you let Steph know that you'd be coming into town. So, they're planning to hook up with you here in town."

"But they didn't—" I check my phone history. There is a text from Deena. It says:

> We're in New Orleans, I hear you are too.
> Text back to make plans.

It was sent last night, probably when I was busy with the French Quarter maison.

"Okay, I guess they did." I feel chastised again, maybe a little repentant. I'm still kind of new to the outside world, and I often forget to check for text messages. I know that about myself. I should be more tolerant when I think people haven't gotten back to me.

Grandma Charli gives me a moderately sympathetic look. "I know. You're going through that thing, I watched your father suffer. But it won't make you feel any better to get mad at all your friends."

"What? You watched my father? When?"

"Your grandparents ate here a lot, child, and of course they always brought your father along. I watched him grow up from a baby not older than little Terry out there, to a young adult just about your age. And he was always kind of a strange, moody kid. Smart. Thoughtful, even. But when he became a teenager, he started to have these real serious bouts of depression, I think, is what it was. He started to get angry with his father. And not everything he got angry about was even a bad thing to get angry about, if you understand me. You think we weren't angry, during the Civil Rights marches? But your father seemed to lose his sense for what was worth getting mad about. And he was a child in a lot of ways still. But he was also a physically powerful young man who could make people piss their pants in fear just by staring at 'em too hard."

"So I'm like him, huh? And I shouldn't be too much like him?"

"I didn't say that. Just learn from his mistakes, if you can. Don't get so messed up that you push away the people who care about you." She smiles. "Now, child, people are winding down with their dinner, I see, is it time for cake?"

"I guess it's time for cake."

"Good, good. We'll open the first giant bottle of champagne your father brought by. And I'll let people know."

"Let people know? Let who know?"

"Your friends of course. They wanted to let you have a nice dinner with Steph's family, but it's your birthday, they want a big party with cake and champagne."

Before too long, an enormous sheet cake is emerging from the kitchen, carried by three Quemper family kids, to a folding table all on its own. I'm given a crème brûlée torch to light seventeen candles, which I do. Singing, then I blow out the candles. Wonder briefly: am I getting trace amounts of were-wolf spit all over the cake?

Applause, then the Quemper kids start cutting the cake, dishing up pieces freely to everyone in the courtyard. A couple more members of the Quemper family, Izzy's aunt and uncle I think, wheel out the balthazar of champagne, inside a giant ice bucket balanced on a hand truck.

Together we open it warily, but it's not much more trouble to open than any other champagne bottle. As if summoned by the pop, which they probably were, people start pouring in. Basically, everyone I know. The French Quarter maison, the Garden District maison, and the crew from the bunker start pouring in. Pere Claude, Vivienne, and Leon arrive together and give me a present: a small notebook and a mini fountain pen. "From my mother's favorite stationery shop here in town," Leon says. "They should fit in the boot pockets. If she were still alive, she would have given you something like this, I think."

The Seattle group arrives all at once, wearing matching T-shirts for their band, which is apparently now called after the shared house Deena and Izzy and Edison have been renting together: Chez Lunatic.

"Abby! Come on, we have band stuff we have to talk about." Deena hustles us all outside the fence.

"Okay, just so you know? They know." She gestures at Reed, Kennedy, and Nora.

"They know? They know what?" I'm confused.

"You know." She taps the side of her nose. "Right?"

"Wolf stuff," I say, and everybody nods. "But how? Why?"

Edison says, "The band had a gig on the full moon and there was a wolf incident at the show." He looks a little worried. "I know your people are secretive about the whole wolf thing, and I don't want to get anybody in trouble. We haven't told the Seattle maison yet. But we thought you should know. Do you think we should tell anyone else?"

Do I think that? I look around, see all these eyes looking to me for guidance, and have a sense of foreboding that I can't explain. "You know? Right now, no. Things are, there's a lot going on. Do you all have questions for me?"

Deena says, "Not in the middle of the party, but we should get together later tonight or tomorrow." She hands me a Chez Lunatic T-shirt. "Welcome to the band."

We head back to the main party. I'm nervous to be keeping a secret from Pere Claude, but I feel strongly that it's not my secret to tell. Do we have to make everyone who knows about the werewolves into honorary werewolves? That seems like a convention that belongs to a different era. A pre-Flint-Savage era.

"Abby!" Morgan comes up from behind, drunkenly drapes his arm around my shoulders. He's quite a bit taller than I am, so this is awkward and I have to work to keep my balance. His breath has that sour Bourbon-Street smell of partially processed alcohol, and my brain automatically supplies a chemical name: butyric acid, also present in aged cheeses, which is why cheap powdered parmesan smells like vomit sometimes when you shake it on your pizza.

"Morgan," I say. "Maybe you should go home."

"No, I'm good. I'm good. I have to talk to you."

"About what?"

"Your father," he says. He leans into me, then points at Leon with his beer hand, splashing motor-oil black liquid on his fingers. Leon is standing up, talking to Vivienne with an intense, concerned look on his face. "That guy's your real father, right?"

"He is."

"Your father."

"You said that."

"No, I'm just…" He leans in, like he's going to whisper a secret. "He's a badass, isn't he?"

"He's a killer, if that's what you mean." I'm starting to get extremely irritated with drunk Morgan.

"Yeah?" he laughs. "For real?"

"For real."

"No, really?"

"I just said that. Yes, really."

"Is he like you?"

"Like me in what way?"

"You know, a werewolf?" he stage-whispers.

"You already know he is, Morgan, why are we having this conversation?"

"I want to be," he says. "You know what I want."

"You want to be a killer?" I pull away in confusion and discomfort. I know Morgan likes to hunt and likes guns, but this seems weird and disturbing.

He laughs. "Not a killer. I know you call me that. Because

I hunt and you're a vegetarian. But you're not a vegetarian anymore are you?"

"Not really, no."

"You know what I want."

"Except I don't know because you haven't actually told me. You're drunk and not making any sense."

"I'm not drunk."

"Morgan, you're extremely drunk. You need to go home and take a nap or something."

"No, you know what I want," he says. Pleading, almost. Urgent.

"I really don't. Why don't I walk you home and you can take a nap and we'll talk about it later?"

"You can't leave, it's your party."

"Fine, I'll get someone else to walk you home. Or call you a car or something."

"You won't do it," he says.

"I won't do what? Send you home? Because I think I will."

"You won't... bite me..."

"Oh, no, Morgan, what?"

He leans all his weight on me, like he's passed out, even though his eyes are open. His legs are noodles as I march him to a bench and prop him up against a tree, where he tilts over, not entirely passed out but most of the way there. He mumbles things that might be intended to be words, but they make no sense. After a bit he sinks further, his eyes close, and he starts to snore.

The snoring reassures me that he's breathing okay.

Steph comes up behind me, sighs in disgust. "So, he's done it again."

"Again? He's done this a lot?"

"Started to." She shakes her head. "Just in the last few months. You haven't seen it because you've been out there in the bayou." She waves her hand. "I don't know what's going on with him. I think he's depressed or something. But I've gone down this road, with the alcohol. He knows I have. And he still won't listen to me."

"Nobody ever listens to anybody, I think." I pause. I need to tell her about the bite thing. If Morgan has gotten it into his head where he wants to be a bitten wolf? I don't know what she could do about it, but she ought to know. "Steph? He said something to me—he was drunk and it was a little scrambled, but I think—"

But I'm interrupted when Irwin comes up behind us. "He's passed out, looks like. Do you girls need some help with him?"

"Sure," Steph says. "And the baby's going to start screaming again pretty soon, we should probably all just go home."

As if on cue, Terry begins to wail.

Happy birthday to us.

14

PASSION MORPH

I help Steph's family get to their car, carrying the baby while Steph and Irwin steer Morgan. Steph's dad is leaning on Steph's mom as if he's having trouble walking.

Everybody's falling apart. Terry isn't screaming, but he is chewing very hard on the orange plastic thing and glaring at me like he thinks his teething pain is all my fault.

After I get back to CharliQ's, the party starts to break up. Viv and Leon take Pere Claude away. We finish the second balthazar of champagne, almost all the cake is gone, the people I know are trickling out while the courtyard starts to fill up with people I don't know.

Babette taps me on the shoulder. "Are you ready to go? Your Seattle loufrer are meeting at a club."

"Sure, just let me say goodbye to Grandma Charli."

I find her in the office, sorting through some papers.

"Abby." She looks up briefly. "Adella doing all right running things in the kitchen?"

"Yeah, she's great. I just, the party's kind of breaking up and I was going to go somewhere else with my friends, I wanted to let you know I was going and say thank you."

She nods. "You're welcome. Happy birthday. And remember what I said about getting Izzy paid?"

"I should talk to my father or grandfather about it?"

"That's right. Oh, I got a present for you." She presses into my hands a tiny perfume sample bottle. "That's a few drops of your grandmother's scent right there. It's precious."

"It is, thank you."

I leave, find Babette just outside the gate. She pounces on the scent, sniffing eagerly all around me. "Bon Dieu, what is that perfume? Such a haunting scent. Beautiful and so sad, like flowers wilting after a funeral."

I hold up the bottle. "My grandmother had it made a long time ago as a re-creation of the scent her grandmother wore. I got this vial from Charlaine Quemper as a birthday present."

She takes the bottle from me eagerly and wafts it toward her nose. "Mmm, a rose note like the Chanel but darker, and is that agarwood? Orris root?"

"I don't know, perfumes are your thing."

We start walking. I put the tiny bottle in one of the shoe pockets and every step brings a fresh waft of scent. "What club are we going to?"

"Oh, they gave me the address, not the name. It's in the Quarter." We walk for a while, then Babette stops. "Wait, it's too hot for this." She takes off her white linen bolero jacket, which makes her bright blue slip dress seem very revealing all of a sudden.

A group of young men passing by on the other side of the street stop to call out. "Woo-hoo! Show us your tits!"

Babette notices me get angry, puts a hand on my shoulder. "They're not worth your rage." She stuffs her jacket into her shoulder bag and links my arm, pulls me forward. "You can't turn the wolf on every stupid man who calls out a rude thing, you'll never stop fighting."

"Are you sure? What if I just ate a few of them, to make

an example for the others?" I try to make it a joke and she responds by smiling, making her own joke.

"They'll give you indigestion, all that cheap body spray, ugh."

We follow the scent trail of the band to a little dive bar with a courtyard.

"We were just talking about New Orleans," Nora says, in her cockney accent. "How many werewolves actually live here?"

"All of them." A pause while everybody looks confused, then I say, "Sorry, that was kind of a joke. Bayou Galene is about a thousand people, maybe two thirds are transforming werewolves? And there are probably, I don't know, maybe as many as thirty here in town at any given time. Plus another thirty scattered among the maisons. But that's just the Varger, the rougarou. I don't know about bitten wolves or Cachorros or other wolf groups."

"So far we have mapped twenty-two bitten wolves here in town," Babette says.

I nod, then panic. "Oh, no, wait, Babette, I wasn't thinking. The band, they're not official loufrer."

"Hmmm?" She looks confused. "These are your loufrer, yes? I've met them before. Very pretty."

"No, my loufrer are my loufrer, but the others, Kennedy, Reed, Nora, they are, um, they just got sucked into it, they haven't been, you know, presented to senior leadership or anything."

She still looks confused. "If they know, they know. Yes?"

"But the, uh, the senior leadership doesn't know that they know." I briefly look at the others. "Becoming an official loufrer, it's a whole thing. It means you're one of the pack, like, an honorary wolf. Which gives you privileges, but also obligations." I turn back to Babette. "Wouldn't you say?"

"Oh. Yes, that is true." She shrugs expansively. "Well, I'm not one to put any obligations on anybody. Who wants wine?"

All hands raise, except Kennedy, who doesn't drink.

"Well, we have to get you something, cher," Babette says. "Tea? Coke? Sparkling water?"

"Plain water, thanks," they say.

Babette nods, excuses herself from the table and goes up to the bar. Reed goes up to help.

Kennedy shakes their head with a small smile. "I have never been in a town that wanted so badly to get me drunk."

We all laugh.

Nora says, "More than five hundred werewolves, that's a lot, isn't it?"

"It might seem like a lot of werewolves," Izzy says. "But the population of New Orleans alone is almost 400,000 people. The population of the United States is 330 million."

"So, it's not that many werewolves?" I say.

"Depends how you look at it. How many werewolves do there have to be before y'all become common knowledge? Nobody knows."

"Is that the end point then? Everybody knows werewolves are real?"

"Well, that's what we've been assuming. But that's another thing nobody knows."

Babette and Reed come back with three bottles of wine, one bottle of water, eight glasses.

I ask, "So, how did the band end up getting called Chez Lunatic? You had a different name before, didn't you?"

"We've had a dozen names," Edison says. "Usually when the lineup changed. Chez Lunatic became the name after Deena and Izzy joined the band."

"I'm not really in the band," Deena says. "I do manager-type stuff, arrange gigs, staff the merch table, send out the newsletter."

"You designed the T-shirts, babe," Izzy says with a smile.

Edison says, "And you helped me a lot with the lyrics."

"Oh, can I be the Bernie Taupin to your Elton John?"

"If only." He laughs. "Izzy got sucked in when she was helping us with the computer that we were using to program the effects pedals. She made the mistake of singing into a microphone, so we heard how great she sounds doing that."

She rolls her eyes. "Apparently it's like a curse. I'm from New Orleans so I can cook and I can sing, in spite of myself."

"That leaves Reed," I say. "I didn't know you were even into music?"

He grimaces. "Well. I'm not a musical member of the band so much."

"Wait. You got bit didn't you?"

He looks astonished. "You can tell? Is it in my sweat? Does that mean for sure I'm going to change?"

"It's hard to be sure. I'm sorry. But you should make plans assuming you will." I glance at Edison. "Thinking has changed recently about the best way to steer a bitten wolf through their first night. Restraints and sedation should be used only if absolutely necessary. If you can manage it, a senior wolf mentor and plenty of hunting space works much better."

Edison nods, puts a hand on his shoulder. "It's nothing to worry about, buddy. If you do change, we'll make sure you make it through."

"Thanks." But Reed looks, and smells, scared.

"How did it happen?"

"I was just there to watch the band." He shakes his head with a small smile. "Just there to see my buddy's band."

"Our set hit right at moonrise," Edison says. "During the third song, a girl in the front row starts screaming and ripping off her clothes. And that electric thunderstorm feeling filled the air."

"Edison was on it," Kennedy says. "Took off his guitar and did a stage dive right onto the screaming girl, carries her out of the emergency door."

"I was up at the front too," Reed says. "I thought she was having a drug freakout and tried to help Edison."

"That's when you got bit?"

"That's when I got bit."

"But he did help," Edison says. "I had some sedative on me and got her a little subdued, then I had more wolf equipment in the van."

"We followed him," Nora says. "We wanted to help too."

"So." Edison pours himself a glass of the wine. "The band did help. But they also saw a full transformation, first hand, and we had to tell them what was going on."

Babette jumps in to pour wine for all the drinkers, hands the glasses around. "Well, here's to all y'all," she says, clinking glasses. "Welcome to the pack."

"But I already told you we're not making them official loufrer," I say.

She shrugs. "They're part of my pack. Do y'all have questions?"

Kennedy says, "You said something about bitten wolves and born wolves and I'm still not sure how that works."

"Oh, simple." I smile. "There are people born to be werewolves, it's hereditary, we start transforming sometime in young adulthood. But if a born wolf bites somebody at the full moon, we might create a bitten wolf. And bitten wolves might create more bitten wolves."

"Are bitten wolves a lot different from born wolves?"

"A lot different? I don't know. Somewhat different. For example, bitten wolves take longer to change and they're bothered by silver."

Nora looks delighted. "Silver! You mean not all werewolves can be slayed by a silver bullet? The movies lied to me?"

"Well, none of us can actually be slayed by silver. Silver bothers the bitten, like an allergy. Slows them down, doesn't kill them. A single bullet is unlikely to kill any wolf-shifter, not unless you get a lucky head shot."

Barney and Raymond walk into the courtyard, carrying drinks. "Babette, I can't believe you were trying to party without us." Barney pulls up two additional chairs. "That is not like you at all."

Raymond smiles at me and it looks genuine. "Hey again, Aunt Abby. I'm sorry I was kind of rude to you before. I thought you were one of my father's friends and I don't like my father's friends."

Barney leans in toward him. "Aunt? Did you say Abby is your aunt?"

"Yeah, Abby is my aunt." He laughs. "Even though I think we're literally the same age. I just turned seventeen, didn't you just turn seventeen?"

I nod. "Yep. I guess we are about the same age then."

Barney bursts out laughing. "Seriously, Abby is your aunt? That is the funniest goddamn thing I've heard today."

"Why is that so funny, didn't you ever know anybody from a big family before?"

"I guess not big enough." He turns to Raymond. "So, Ray, is Abby more of a wine aunt or more of a flowered upholstery aunt?"

Raymond laughs. "Wine aunt, definitely."

"You guys, it's my birthday, you have to be nice to me."

Edison frowns at me. "Seventeen? You just now turned seventeen? But I thought you were eighteen back in August?"

My gut goes cold. Something about his expression. I force a laugh. "Seventeen, eighteen, what's the difference?"

"That means you've been sixteen the whole time we've known each other."

"Yeah?"

"Under eighteen."

"Not legally." I flash my ID. "See?"

"Right, you had just gotten that ID last summer. So I

thought you had just turned eighteen for real. And, wait, you're out of school too."

"That's because I'm a dropout." I laugh. Raymond laughs. Nobody else laughs. "Edison, come on, why is this a big deal?"

"I guess it's not a big deal, since we haven't done anything yet, but—"

"Edison! I can't believe you just announced that in front of everybody!"

"Announced what?" He looks puzzled.

"That we haven't had sex!"

He continues to look puzzled. "You want me to tell them we did have sex?"

"No! It's none of their business one way or the other!"

Deena stands up, glances at the sky. "Wow, look at those clouds, bet it's going to rain, huh?"

"It's New Orleans, so, probaby." I fold my arms, sink back into my chair. I'm still feeling upset but I don't want to let it turn into a big fight. "Anyway, everybody, please forget the last three minutes of conversation. So, Raymond. Do you like your father?"

He grimaces. "I don't know, sometimes. He's kinda conservative though. And he acts like he's the only one with a dominant wolf, you know what I mean?"

Nora jumps in. "Oh, now, you must tell us about all the werewolf politics. Alphas and betas and… whatnot. I've watched the shows, you know."

"I've watched the shows too," I say. "Do not go by anything you've seen in any of the shows. All lies."

"I heard that the whole alpha wolf thing was wrong anyway," Kennedy says. "That the guy who came up with it was watching wolves in captivity so what he saw in action was more like prison gangs. In the wild, a pack is a family, and the alphas are just mom and dad."

Babette says, "But aren't we more human than wolf? It's the human who obsesses over group hierarchy."

"I don't think that's quite true," I say. "I've had a lot of clashes with senior wolves where they want me to do a thing, we argue, and then because my wolf is more dominant, they back down in the moment. But they still want me to do what they say, it's not like they really gave up."

She laughs. "Senior wolves? You mean Vivienne, right?"

"Well, mostly her."

"Yes. See, Vivienne is more dominant than most wolves—more so than me or Etienne, anyway—so we think of her as a dominant wolf, and she is in the habit of thinking of herself that way too. But then she is so much less dominant than you or Nicolas. Nicolas is not a problem, because he's an adult, they rarely clash. But you! You're so young! So rash! So rebellious! And so rude! Using high personal dominance to counter your elders when your elders are clearly right." She laughs. "Yes, we've heard her complain about you a lot. She adores you, cher."

"What? You just made it sound like she hates me."

"You make her crazy, true. But she adores you, trust me."

Raymond turns to me, interested. "High personal dominance? Does that mean you have the stare?"

"If that means what I think it does, yes?"

"You have a special stare?" Nora laughs. "Oh, now you have to show it, darlings."

"It's not like that," Raymond says. "You have to trigger a dominance contest first. Like an argument or something."

"Or this." I make eye contact with Nora. Focus. It takes a while to find the wolf, and I keep her eyes in mine the whole time. I have to find the part of me that wants something from her. What do we want? Me and the wolf? Why would we flash Nora?

To prove that she's part of our pack. That we'll take care of her.

That's it.

"Nora." I say her name and let the wolf out in my eyes, feel the flash. "Nora, give me your wine."

She relaxes, smiles slightly, hands me the glass. "There you go, love."

The table laughs as I take the wine. She shakes her head, frowning. "What—what just happened?"

Babette takes her own wine and makes a cheers gesture toward me. "That was the dominance stare, friends. Abby has a good one. Very pretty, the green. Brown eyes like mine usually flash gold and blue or gray eyes like his—" she gestures toward Raymond. "Flash red."

"That was incredible," Reed says. "Like when car headlights catch an animal off the side of the road. But humans don't have that! The membrane that flashes back the light, I forget the name."

"Tapetum lucidum," Deena says. "Werewolves do. It's the only sure way to spot them when they're in human form. Check it out." She turns the flashlight on her phone and shines it around the table, elicits gasps from those who haven't seen it before.

"You were right about the colors," Kennedy says. "But I could swear Edison flashed gold, he's not a werewolf. Is he?"

"Um, it's complicated," I say.

"Abby bit me, I took a cure, there were lingering effects." He shrugs.

"Okay, maybe not that complicated."

"Does that happen a lot? Partial werewolves?"

"As far as we know I'm the only one."

Nora asks, "What would happen if you got bit again? Would you change all the way or stay the same?"

I nod. "Good question. It seems risky to try to find out though."

"Risky? In what way?" Reed turns nervous again.

"Um. I don't know, that's why it seems risky." I try to be

reassuring, but he's not buying it, he just pours himself more of the wine.

"Come on, Abby," he says. "Just tell me, okay? I can take it."

"All right, fine. Bitten wolves usually make it through their first night okay as long as they have people to look after them, which you do. So that's good. But sometimes they don't. Sometimes there's something, we don't know for sure but Nicolas thinks it might be an immune system response, sometimes they don't make it through their first night."

His eyes get wide and his sweat gets sharp and yellow with terror. "Explosive rabies. That's what that is, right? Werewolves who don't make it? Is that going to happen to me?"

"Oh." Shit, this is not going well. "No, no, I'm sure that won't happen to you."

"You're sure? How can you be sure?" He demands this, voice shrill and panicky.

"Because of the smell in your sweat," I say, with a big smile that probably looks fake as hell. "Your sweat definitely smells like somebody who is going to make it through his first night as a werewolf."

Barney says, "Clearly we missed something?"

"Reed got bitten last full moon," I say.

"That's rough," Barney says. "Good luck."

"Yeah, thanks."

"You're going to be okay," Edison says.

"Most wolves are okay if they have someone to look after them," I say. "Really. Especially if you have a mastered trauma morph who can stay human during the full moon."

"Mastered trauma morph?" Reed looks slightly alarmed. "Am I supposed to know what that is?"

"Most werewolves transform only at the full moon, but some of us also transform when badly injured. The 'mastered' part means that we're able to control it consciously. If you were to stab me right now, I could choose whether to shape shift or not. Make sense?"

Reed shakes his head, drinks some more of the wine. "I guess. It's still hard to believe any of this is real."

"So, trauma morphs, all right, what other kinds of morphs do we have?" Nora asks.

"Just the two. Regular and trauma." I pause. "I think?"

"Incorrect," Babette says, with an odd, bitter smile. "They never told you about the passion morph, obviously."

Barney snickers. "That's real? I thought it was just a bunch of dirty jokes."

Babette drains her wine glass and slams it down on the table hard enough to break, glass fragments driving into her hand, while her eyes flash gold. It's the first time I've ever seen her angry. "You laugh. She gets your respect and I get the snickers of a naughty little boy." She gestures at me with her bloody hand, wounds already healing. "Because she suffers to call her wolf. Pain gets your respect, pleasure gets your laughter. But the wolf is the same."

Barney shrinks back. "Babette, I'm sorry, I didn't, I mean, I didn't know. I thought it was just a bunch of stupid jokes."

"Wow," Deena says. "Passion morph. Does that mean what it sounds like it means?"

"Transformation at the moment of orgasm, yes."

"But why keep it secret?" I say. "I thought the Varger didn't have those kinds of anti-sex taboos."

"It's not a taboo." Babette is still smoldering as she begins to gather up the broken glass fragments. "It's a joke. You heard him sniggering about it. It's considered embarrassing. As if you always farted a lot during sex."

Barney makes a snorting noise as he tries to suppress laughter.

Babette continues to scowl, as she dumps glass fragments into a trash can. "But nobody ever talks about it. And we're encouraged to not engage it."

"To not have sex?" I ask.

"To not have orgasms. I assure you, I was alone the first time I discovered this particular gift." She sighs. "My parents treated it as something shameful, and I believed them. For a time. Until I stopped believing them. But it's why I go out to Bayou Galene as little as possible."

"But Babette, this is incredible. If it works like the trauma morph does, it means that if you trigger it once or twice in the last week before the full moon, you would be able to stay human during the moon. Just like me. And, Bon Dieu, maybe you could learn to fully master your wolf just by purchasing a vibrator!"

She laughs, impulsively kisses me on the cheek. "I love you, cher."

Barney looks sad. "I didn't mean to laugh, Babette, I just didn't know."

"Well now you do," she says, primly.

A lightning bolt sizzles across the sky, ending with an enormous crash.

A raindrop hits me on the cheek. "Uh-oh, it's starting."

It begins to rain with so much ferocity that we're all soaked by the time we gather our things and head back inside.

"Those of you who haven't been to New Orleans before? You have to be ready for a major rainstorm pretty much at any time."

15

LUNORA

It's getting late and we're all soaked, so everybody calls a car and goes back to wherever home is right now. Izzy and Deena are staying with Izzy's family. Edison, Reed, Kennedy, and Nora are all sharing a room in the Hotel Monteleone. Edison is friendly but distant when he says good night to me, with a hug but not a kiss.

I try not to feel hurt.

I fail.

The rest of us go back to the maison, where everyone is already asleep. We talk for a while, watching the lightning from the back porch, but it's obvious Babette is still in a bad mood, and one by one everyone else goes to bed except for Babette and me. It stops raining.

"It's late," she says, frowning up at the sky. "Are you tired?"

"Not exactly," I say. "I don't know, my sleep has been really weird since doing the heavy duty trauma morph training."

"Get a coat, let's go scent mapping," she says.

A few minutes later we're leaving the maison on foot. Babette is the most de-glammed I've ever seen her, in black leggings, a T-shirt dress, and a big, flapping black raincoat. Hood up, she jams her hands into the pockets of the coat and puts her head down and strides, or maybe stalks, forward with a grim determination. She's walking so rapidly that I find it hard to keep up with her.

"Are you still mad about Barney laughing?" I ask.

"I'm not mad," she says, but it's such an obvious lie that she cracks a smile. "No, I'm not mad about him laughing. I'm mad about why he laughed. Because he's right. It's a joke. I'm a joke. Usually I don't care. I make a point of not caring. I make a point of not caring about anything at all." She makes a growling noise deep in her throat.

"Babette, I'm sorry. I thought the Varger were different, because they're so much less screwed up than the cult, but they're patriachal too, I guess."

"Patriarchal?" She gives me a quizzical look. "You think this is political?"

"Well, sure. Isn't it patriarchal? To respect violence but not sex?"

"But we don't believe only men have the power of violence," she says. "That would be ridiculous."

"Well, yeah. I mean…" I struggle to explain it. "You can be sort of patriarchal, even if you're not all the way patriarchal. Like—oh! You know, how you call your hunt leader the pere, which means father, but women can still be pere? It's like that. That's what I mean. Because it's sort of equality but things are still tilted in a masculine direction. You see?"

She frowns. "Maybe. But you young people want to make everything so political, I'm not sure that's right."

"Young people. Listen to you. You're only nine years older than me."

"Nine years is a lot." She smiles. "Did I read that right, is your boy acting a little distant now that he knows you're under eighteen?"

"That's right," I growl.

"You're mad about that?"

"I'm not mad," I say, and it's obviously a lie. Is it always a lie when people say "I'm not mad"? "Okay, I am mad but I know I shouldn't be. It's like when I found out he wasn't monogamous. I can't get mad about who he is. If he's not willing to get physical until I'm eighteen for real, that's his choice. But I'm mad anyway."

"The heart is a beast, cher," she says, sounding more like the Babette I usually know. She slows down a little, pulls out her phone. "Where are we going?"

"Have we mapped the area around the Ashtown Theater?"

She taps a few times, says, "No, we haven't. Why there?"

"I don't know. It's a place my father went to see music in the 1980s, I was just curious about it."

"It's probably been torn down," she says, with a sniff.

"In Seattle it would be torn down, but in New Orleans it's probably been remodeled into high-end condominiums."

She laughs. "Point. Do you think I would like Seattle? Sometimes I think I need a change from this place."

"Seattle? I don't know, they have a much less laid back attitude about public drinking than New Orleans, I think you'd find it a rude shock. It's very beautiful there, though. Trees and water and hills. That's the thing I like about it."

"Your wolf awakened there, so she will always think of it as home," she says.

"What about your wolf? Did she awaken here or in Bayou Galene?"

"Bayou Galene. But some wolves are more restless than others, no? Less at home in just one place, more at home everywhere? The maisons need wolves like us."

"They do," I agree.

"I've been thinking about what you said, about mastering my wolf," she says. "I think I'm going to try it."

"You should. You totally should."

I stop. Inhale.

Babette also stops. Inhales.

"Bitten wolf, female," she says. "No?"

"Bitten wolf. Female. And I think I know her. I think she's my father's old girlfriend, Lunora."

Babette and I follow the trail, faint at first, growing stronger. We pass a corner store where she goes sometimes. And then, the old theater, which looks abandoned, but her trail goes right inside, to an unobtrusive side door. Babette raises her hand to knock, but the door creeps open before she makes a sound.

And there is Lunora, standing behind the half-open door, hostile edge to her body language as she studies us, frowning deeply.

A moment of shock on my part as I adjust to the fact that, just like my father, she's forty years older than in the photograph. Her face is pale, thin, mostly unlined, but her complexion has a grayish undertone that doesn't look entirely healthy. Long, wavy gray hair, heavy wolf sign in ears, nose, teeth. Enveloping robe of red-black velvet wrapped around her, nothing underneath. In the darkness her eyes gleam amber.

"Lunora?" I make it a question.

"Leon's daughter," she says. Not a question. She steps back, opens the door wider. "Well, you'd better come in. I've been waiting for you."

Inside, it's dim and the air has a heaviness to it, that speaks of a house that's been closed off, inhabited by one person who rarely leaves and rarely has visitors. An oppression, a solidness to her scent. It's not dirty in here, but it's very thick, very dark, lit mostly by candles, smelling of fire and honey, beeswax. Dried flowers scattered around the floor smell vaguely sweet, dusty. Like a tomb. Like a church. The walls have posters from shows in the eighties and nineties. If I spent long enough looking, I could probably find the show the ticket is for.

I say, "Waiting for us in the general 'other werewolves' sense? Or waiting for me, Leon's daughter, specifically?"

She laughs, goes to a refrigerator, pulls out a jar of liquid in an unsettling brilliant magenta. The refrigerator is so far the only sign that this place has electricity. "You want a drink?"

Babette takes it from her, sniffs. "Bon Dieu, what is in this? It smells sweet, dirty, and toxic as hell, like some uncanny distillation of every deadly substance ever known, the very essence of death."

"Excellent nose, my dear. Everclear and a few herbal poisons, wormwood, amanita, datura. It takes the poison for me to really feel anything."

"But the color?"

"An industrial colorant I use for fun. Not approved for human consumption, but it's probably the least toxic thing in there."

Babette takes a sip and I cry out, involuntary, "No!"

But Babette smiles. "That is absolutely the worst thing I have ever put in my mouth, cher. Which is a certain kind of accomplishment all on its own, I must say."

"Of course it is." She smiles. Holds it out to me.

"No, thank you. I don't want any poison."

"You know it won't kill you."

"I don't want any poison."

"Suit yourself." She sips from the jar. She points at me. "Her, I knew instantly as Leon's spawn, and I think I know why she's here. But you—" she points at Babette with a briefly dazzling smile. "What about you, gorgeous? What are you doing getting involved in all this Verreaux family drama? Get out while you can."

"Please, cher, you know I'm not a human, don't patronize me." But she's smiling when she says it.

"Oh, you think you're fucked up because you're a were-wolf? You don't know. There's a curse on that family, Leon would tell you. It goes way back. Nobody's fucked up like the Verreaux family is fucked up. She knows." She points at me. "I saw you on the television when that cult was getting raided and I spotted you right away. It's uncanny how much you look like he did back then, if he had been short and a girl. But I could see it in your eyes. You know the curse."

"I don't believe in curses," I say.

"You don't? Okay." She sets the jar down. "Would you like some tea?"

"Is the tea poison?"

She laughs. "No, it's just tea. I'll make some." She goes to the sink, demonstrates the theater has running water as she pours some into an electric kettle, plugs the kettle in. "Make yourselves… comfortable? I mean, sit anywhere you like, I don't care. I haven't had visitors in so long. I don't really like visitors, don't get me wrong, but I do sometimes welcome a distraction. Do you want some dried salted meat? I think that's polite in wolf circles, but I don't know a lot of other werewolves, I never learned the etiquette. I'm not sure I have anything sweet. Do you want tea cakes? Cookies? Scones? Any kind of carbohydrate? I'd have to go to the corner store but I could. I do sometimes, you probably noticed my trail out there. I'm agoraphobic, in case you couldn't figure that out. The hunt is the only time I go out and I don't usually go very far. I eat a few pigeons, I'm not proud. Don't worry, the dried salted meat isn't street pigeon, I also get a whole cow delivered here every so often, which means there's raw meat in a freezer too, if you wanted some of that. There are advantages to being born rich. I killed my father, which should have made it impossible for me to get his money, but nobody ever knew I did it, and I was a wolf at the time anyway, so that worked out all right. I don't live like this because I'm poor. God, listen to me talk, maybe I missed visitors more than I thought. Beautiful, what's your name?"

Babette startles, as if she had been almost hypnotized.

"Uh. Babette?" While Lunora was talking, both of us settled, cross-legged, onto cushions strewn across the floor.

"Babette. So French! You seem very French to me. Cajun, I assume, like most of Leon's people. You are one of his people? I think I can spot the difference between bitten mongrels like me, and the born wolf aristocracy, but sometimes I'm wrong."

"I'm born, yes. And I did spend a year in Paris. Studying. I adored Paris."

"Of course you did, a superb creature like you." She turns to me, her expression hardening. "And you. Tiny girl Leon. God, you remind me of him so much, how is that possible? What's your name?"

"Abnegation." I have no idea why I just gave my cult name. There's something extremely strange about being here, listening to Lunora talk, it's like falling under a magic spell. "Are you a witch?"

She laughs. "Do you want a tarot reading? I could give you a tarot reading, just a moment." The kettle reaches boiling, shuts off with a loud click. "Oh, tea first." She pours the water into a large glass beaker, where the leaves swirl around. It smells like good tea, no obvious poison. She takes an elaborate hourglass, turns it over. "Four-minute timer. Do you like the hourglass? It's a Terry Pratchett reference. Have you read Pratchett? I got it from a place in North Carolina. I get everything from everywhere. Mail order. Well. Internet now. I love the Internet. It's the best thing to happen to me in the last forty years. That's where I got all my tarot decks."

She takes up a large black velvet bag, shakes it a little, dumps some of the contents across the floor. Tarot cards, from several different decks all mixed together, falling in no particular pattern. "Hmm," she says, peering down at the chaos. "I see you already killed your father once." She picks up a card labeled THE HIEROPHANT that shows a Pope-like figure

and another one labeled DEATH that shows a familiar skele-
ton-on-a-horse motif, hands them both to me.

"No, I haven't killed him, Leon is alive." I'm confused. I've
seen people giving tarot readings in Jackson Square and it
does not look like this.

"Your other father," she laughs. "Does that look like Leon
to you? This one is Leon." She picks up a different card, one
that shows THE DEVIL, hands it to me. This particular devil
does look a bit like Leon, showing a thin man with red hair
wearing a black suit and tinted glasses. His eyes are yellow,
slitted snake pupils.

"You might have to kill him too, of course," she says. "But
that path hasn't been walked yet." She hands me a card that
shows a swirling white design I recognize as the satellite image
of Hurricane Katrina. It's called WHEEL OF FORTUNE.
"Everything's turning soon, and I'm not sure where it goes
after that. Tea's ready." She pours from the glass beaker
through a strainer, two mugs, hands them to us. "I'd offer milk
and sugar, but I don't have any, sorry. How's the tea?"

"It's good," Babette says, sipping. "I don't need milk or
sugar."

I inhale. It does smell all right, but I still don't trust it. I
take a cautious sip. It is good. Another cautious sip. "Thank
you."

"You're welcome." She sips directly from the glass beaker.
"I could read your tea leaves too, but it'll just show me all the
same things the cards do. Does Vivienne still have a crush on
her brother?"

Babette and I choke on our tea in unison. I speak first.
"Does she what?"

"Vivienne was completely hung up on Leon when she was
young, didn't she tell you? Oh, of course not, why would she
tell you? Well. At the time, it was obvious to me, and also to
Leon. They're not genetically related so it's less creepy than
you might think. But of course, you're wolves, you'd know that

too. By smell. You know, it's so funny, before I had the wolf, I didn't have a sense of smell at all, not even a normal human sense of smell. When I met Leon, I didn't know he was a werewolf at first, of course, that's not the kind of thing you find out right away, but I knew he had a very strong sense of smell, because he was always talking about it. Do you smell that, what's that smell. It was so funny sometimes to watch him react to smells. Like watching a dog stand in the corner and bark at nothing. You tell yourself it must be ghosts. Anyway, his little sister hated me. I don't blame her, though, I am fairly dislikable. Which reminds me, is Leon still addicted to the berserker drugs?"

"I don't... I don't think so?" I glance at Babette, hoping to get some kind of anchor in the real world. Talking to Lunora is making me feel like I'm having an attack of vertigo.

"Well. Back in the day, he worked hard to recreate some of the fabled potions from the pere diaries. The formulas were frustratingly vague, he said. Still, he developed something, and started using it, and damn, if it didn't seem to make his depression better. Oh, that's it! That's why you look so much like him. You have that same nihilistic despair in your eyes."

She moves with shocking supernatural swiftness, caresses my face. "Do you use the drugs? I wouldn't, if I were you."

"I don't."

"Good. Hold to that. They change you."

My breath catches in my throat. My head pounds. Maybe the tea was tainted after all. "Change you how?"

"They devour your conscience. That's what he wanted at the time. He didn't want to be so burdened with self-doubt. He didn't like feeling so guilty after he killed people."

I let out a tiny, cautious breath. "And how did the berserker drugs help with that?"

"If you take them regularly, they destroy your ability to feel certain emotions. Remorse. Empathy. Love. Wait, I have some honey, do you want honey? I like the way it smells, it was one of the first things that actually smelled good to me. When my sense of smell started to emerge, after Leon bit me, it came even before the wolf, but it was terrible. Everything smelled like garbage, like rot, decay, death. That stopped happening eventually." She shakes her head, stirs honey into her tea. "But the memory of it lingers. Like a ghost in the back of my mind, every smell seems to carry the possibility of its own corruption. You know how everything alive carries within it the inevitability of its own death? Like that."

She sips the tea. "Anyway. Did they tell you the berserkers were all about the killing frenzy? Because that's only useful in the middle of a battle. What they wanted, the berserkers of old, was the ability to kill in cold blood. It's harder than you might think, unless you're born to it. That's why your family is cursed. Back in the old country, the Norselands, you specialized in supplying berserkers to the warring kings. It made you rich, for a while, until one of your young bersekers took liberties with the daughter of the king and you were exiled. Do you know why you took the family name of Verreaux? It's the French spelling of an old Norman word, varou, means werewolf. Do you ever wonder why your family has the biggest, fanciest house in town, or the biggest, fanciest tomb? That's why. Used to be there was only one wolf family, and it was you. That changed over time, of course.

"What you don't know, because they won't talk about it now, is how that core Verreaux family made their money in the new world. Your people never kept slaves, they'll tell you that, and it's true. But that's because they weren't farmers. They were hunters and they were traders. You think they were too good for the slave trade? Think again. Of course, that curse, the curse of blood money, that hangs over a lot of the wealthy families around here. But your family would do things only a werewolf can do. You supplied bloodhounds. For enough money, you would track the people trying to escape slavery and bring them back to the men who claimed to own them. That's where the Veneray came from. Before they started hunting our kind, they used our kind *as* hunters."

I gasp. "So you know about the Veneray?"

"That's right. Before the war, the Veneray engaged werewolves to hunt and kill for the benefit of rich men. But after the war, those rich men started to get worried. They didn't need you to hunt people anymore, you see, and they got worried that you'd turn your hunting skills on them. They made a few efforts to exterminate you entirely, which didn't go well, so they settled on a policy of containment."

"But how could you know all this?" I ask. "Until recently Leon didn't even know the Veneray were real."

"It's not in the pere diaries." She nods. "They were ashamed of it, I guess, so they took it out. That's why Leon didn't know. But I heard it from my father and his Veneray contact. I used to record the conversations he had in his study. That's how I knew about the plot."

"The plot?" A sense of dread starts coiling in my gut. She's talking about the plot against my grandmother. "What did you know?"

"I knew my father intended to send a couple of men onto the hunting grounds on the full moon, that they would be in a truck, and would have high-powered rifles. Leon didn't think they'd manage to seriously hurt anyone, so he thought it would be a good distraction to keep his father away during my first night as a wolf. I wasn't so sure.

"Then, after they killed his mother, he had the nerve to get mad at me! As if I hadn't told him exactly what was going to happen. You ever notice how men always do that? You tell them what's going to happen, they don't listen to you at all, it happens just like you said, and then they get mad at you? Like you caused it. Like it's your fault they didn't listen."

"Not only men," Babette says.

"Hmm." Lunora sniffs, skeptical, then smiles. "Oh, but I

can't possibly argue with someone as winsome as you. Of course you're right. Not only men."

"You told Leon it was going to happen." I feel like the world is tilting away from me. "You told him and he did nothing?"

"That's correct. Oh, I have something for you." She goes over to a shelf, finds a small velvet bag, hands the bag to me. Inside are several tiny little cassette tapes, unlabled. "These are from after Leon left town, but before I killed my father and his Veneray contact. About a week's worth. I haven't listened to them for forty years. The little tape recorder stopped working decades ago and I never replaced it."

She cocks her head, as if listening to something, then says, "You know, as lovely as this has been, I think it's time for you to go. Even you, precious."

Babette and I stand up.

"Thank you," I say. "For the tapes. And the tea." I hand her my mug and the tarot cards.

"Of course. Oh, one more thing." She caresses my face again, makes hard eye contact, not a dominance flash, more of a sincerity flash. "The family curse runs strong in you, I can see it. Don't go the way your father did. When the dead wolves talk to you, listen to them."

"The dead wolves? You mean the ancestors?"

"The ancestors, yes. It's funny, they talk to me, even though I married into the family, so to speak. But I know they talk to you. That's another thing I can see in your eyes. The same way they talked to him. But he never listened. That's why he shouldn't be the hunt leader."

"What? What do you know about it? Has he talked to you?"

"Not for forty years, obviously. But some things you just know. Anyway, it's been lovely, maybe see you around."

She hustles us out the door, where the sky is getting light. Babette and I turn to each other with dazed expressions.

"That is probably the weirdest thing that has ever happened to me," she says. "Wow. But she said some things, I wasn't sure what she was talking about. The Veneray? The plot? You seemed to know."

"Yeah. I know."

"You want to fill me in?"

"I'm not sure. Maybe it's just cursed Verreaux family business."

"Abby, please. I thought you didn't believe in curses?"

"Not magical curses. But maybe other kinds."

"Well." She looks up at the sky. "I say we take a car back to the maison and get some sleep before we talk any more about it. That poison drink messed me up more than I wanted to let on."

16

A VERY EXCLUSIVE CLUB

Back at the maison, Babette drops off right away to sleep. I watch her breathe for a while, slightly worried about the effect of Lunora's poison, eventually fall asleep in a chair.

DRINK IT, DRINK IT, DRINK IT

> *Justice is holding out a communion cup of bright magenta nuclear waste*
>
> *Future's so bright I have to wear shades*
>
> *If you really believed in the ancestors you would drink it and trust them to protect you*
>
> *Get away from me Justice*
>
> *Don't you trust them?*
>
> *I don't I don't I don't I don't*
>
> *In the distance, a mushroom cloud of bright acid green, the same color as my eye flash, signals that it's time for the world to end*

I WAKE UP SUDDENLY, HEART THUNDERING, ALREADY IN A combat-ready crouch. It's daylight and the house smells of fresh coffee. I grab the bag of tapes and head downstairs. But only Barney appears to be home. He's on a laptop computer, drinking coffee, and I corner him.

"Exactly the person I was looking for!"

"Uh?" He gives me a confused look.

"Do you have any idea how to play one of these?"

I hold up one of the mini tapes. He peers at it curiously for a moment, then laughs. "I think there might be a mini cassette player in our museum of lost technologies."

"Can the output be digitized?

He shrugs. "In theory. They're probably set up to do that kind of thing at the bunker, you want to take this out there? How urgent is it?"

"Too urgent for me to want to go all the way out to the bunker before listening to it. Thanks, I'll see if I can find the tape player."

"Well, hold on, I'll help."

He follows me to the storage room, which has a collection of defunct computers and other electronic equipment, some items already gutted for parts, plus cables, accessories, attachments, all of it neatly binned, stacked, and labeled, but still bewildering. The heavy electronic and metallic smells remind me of the way Mardi Gras beads smell when you first open the bag.

With Barney's help I find the cassette player, which is designed to play full size tapes but has an adapter for the mini tapes. Right next to it is a player for 8-track tapes like the one I found at Beckford Manor.

I pop the mini cassette into the player, press what looks like the play button, and nothing happens. "It's broken." I hold it out.

He turns it around in his hands. "Nah, it needs power. Should take a plug adapter." He ruffles around a bit then turns back to me holding out the plug. "Here you go, that should fit."

I plug it into the wall, press play, hear a man clear his throat, a telephone rings, a man says "Hello?" I stop it.

"Perfect, thanks Barney." I look around the storage area. "Wow. Why do we have all this stuff?

"Superstition?" He laughs. "I don't know. I mean, there was probably a reason at one time, and then we kept on doing it even when there wasn't a reason. Except now there is a reason again. So I guess it was all good. Where did these little tapes come from, anyway? I guess a wolf would probably know by smell."

"Leon's ex-girlfriend Lunora. Babette and I visited her last night and she gave us these tapes. They might contain details on the Veneray plot to kill my grandmother."

"But wasn't your grandmother killed a long time ago?"

"Forty years. Yeah."

He frowns. "But you said it was urgent."

"It's urgent to know the truth about the Veneray. They might still be an active threat."

"Oh? Okay." He frowns. "Wait, who are the Veneray?"

"Legendary secret society of werewolf hunters. As in, hunting after werewolves."

He makes a skeptical face and shakes his head. "No, y'all are just messing with me, you cannot tell me the passion morph is real and then the very next day you try to tell me there are secret werewolf hunters. I refuse to believe it. Do you want headphones?"

"Oh, yeah, thanks."

"Here's a good pair, they're wireless, which won't work in the old tape player, but they have a plugin adapter thing some-where around here." He starts rifling again. "You went out with Babette last night? Was she upset?"

"She started out that way, but I think meeting with Lunora

was such a weird experience that it pushed everything else right out of her mind."

"Good or bad?" He hands me the adapter. "Oh, you're going to need a second adapter for the headphones, the tape player has the wrong kind of plugin."

"Good or bad might be too simple of a way to look at it."

"Is she mad at me?" He holds out the second adapter. Looks so lost. So small. And I realize, all of a sudden, that he's hung up on her. He's subtle about it, usually. But the instant I think it, it seems obvious.

"Not exactly? She's mad about what you said, but she'll forgive you if you take the right attitude in the future. Maybe she'll even date you, I can't promise anything."

He winces. "I can't, Abby. Wolfless can't date shifters."

"Why not?"

"We just can't, okay?" he snaps out.

"But what about your parents? Isn't your father wolfless?"

"It was a different time. Just drop it, please?"

"Of course, I'm sorry, I wasn't trying to bother you. Is it okay if I use the big desk?"

"Yeah, sure. If you don't answer the phone it'll ring through to Etienne's cell phone, so you can just ignore it."

In the desk drawer I find a permanent marker, label the tapes 1, 2, 3, etc., count twelve of them, briefly despair of how long it's going to take to listen to them all. Luckily, this tape player seems to have been designed with transcription in mind. There's an index counter that can be reset, a pause button as well as a stop button, and a button that will play it back at 1.5, 2, and 3 times the original speed. I make extensive use of this, after a few minutes of listening to Beckford in real time, calling people on the phone to sell them minks, possibly sell them cocaine, and bet on losing sports games. I can tell the "losing" part because he gets angry and tries to explain how he doesn't really owe the money he owes.

Listening to one-sided Beckford monologues turns out to

be emotionally draining. I find myself disliking him intensely. He's angry and pompous, the kind of man who will actually say on the phone "Do you know who I am?" Above all, he's boring.

As I sift through his phone conversations, making notes in shorthand with my brand new fountain pen, it occurs to me that, without really thinking about it, I have been assuming Lunora was fully justified for murdering her own father.

But did he really deserve to die, just for being a pompous, boring jerk?

Did he abuse Lunora in some way nobody's ever talked about, not even Lunora herself?

On the third tape, I finally hit something interesting: a voice that isn't Beckford's. I stop, listen in real time and write down all the words:

"Beauregard. Welcome. Are you here to pay me?"

"You dealt with the rougarou problem, yes?"

"I slaughtered that bitch. Yes."

"But I heard there was fallout. Thibodaux Taxidermy? People were killed, the body was taken?"

"It was the Verreaux boy. Her son Leon. I set things up so that he'd know who did the deed, and think she was killed for her pretty red coat. He went to the taxidermy shop, took revenge, and left."

"Well, Beckford, where did he go? Don't you think we need to kill him too?"

"He's basically a teenage runaway at this point, so I'd say no."

"Has he been bitten yet?"

"Based on the carnage at the taxidermy shop, I'd say yes."

"Then obviously we have to get rid of him. He could spread the contagion, bite others."

"But he'll be lying low, hiding from his father. And his father will be in mourning. They won't make any more trouble for you. I have to get out of here, Gil. I really do."

Long pause, sounds of walking, breathing, moving objects. "Beckford, if you took care of the problem the way you said, why are you so afraid?"

"The goddamn wolves are right outside my goddamn door, Gil. I have to get Lunora away from here. She's been acting weird for the last couple of months, I think maybe she's pregnant. And if so, it's his. Leon's. I don't want her getting it into her head to run off and join him wherever he is. Claude Verreaux has made me an offer on this property, I'm going to take it."

"Run off and join him? You think she's in contact with the boy? Knows where he is?"

"I don't know. She might be."

"Then use her to find him and kill him. You'll get your money when Leon is dead."

"God damn it, Beauregard, you can't do this to me. I already killed the bitch, the bitch was our deal, give me the money."

A long pause. "Beckford, do you know where the Veneray come from?"

"I don't care." He sounds irritated.

"For years, the rougarou were our paid servants. We hired them to be our most powerful bloodhounds. They were fast. They were strong. They could heal deadly injuries. And they could track by scent better than the best dog, maybe even better than a wolf. There never were any better hunters anywhere. But they betrayed us. We decided the time had come to put an end to the werewolves, once and for all. We sent a dozen strong men out here, heavily armed. But they never returned. After three failed attempts, we changed our tactics. Just trying to kill them, animal violence, that was playing on their territory. We had to contain them using the powers where humans have the advantage. Law. Money. Politics.

"For a hundred years, we never stopped watching them,

but we acted only rarely, and always with caution, so they wouldn't clearly see our hand. Do you understand? We became a rumor to them. We see them clearly, but they don't see us. If they saw us clearly, we wouldn't live long. They still excel at pure animalistic violence."

Beckford makes an annoyed grunt. "But Gil, everything you've said makes it sound like even more of a mistake to try to kill the boy. I don't have the faintest idea how to track him down, and the attempt could tip the rest of them off. You're the one who told me that you only get one chance with these wolves. If the first stroke fails, you're dead. Well, we took a lot of trouble to set up the stroke that killed the bitch. And now you want to send me running half-cocked after the son? No way."

"Hm." Sound of liquid pouring into a glass. "Do you know how the Veneray have persevered over the years, keeping our secrets, keeping the rougarou in line? Father to son. Always. We don't bring in outsiders. We keep the faith."

"Faith?" Beckford makes a scoffing noise. "What faith?"

"We protect humanity against the monsters. Do you realize what the rougarou could do to this world if they were ever to step out of their little Cajun village?"

"They're werewolves, Gil. It's weird to realize werewolves are real, sure, but how do they threaten the whole world? Surely you're being melodramatic."

"The bitch was running for office, Beckford. Political office. Don't you understand what that means?"

"She was going to fight you on the refinery, I know all that. Millions of dollars at stake. I get it."

Pounds table. "You do not. The rougarou can make more of their own kind, Beckford, whenever they want. If they wanted to, they could create vast secret armies. Infiltrate every power structure we have in this country."

Almost I can hear Beckford rolling his eyes. "Gilbert, I'm not one of your Veneray klansmen, don't give me all that crap about secret armies and sacred duties. You hired me to do a job, I did the job, and now you're not paying me. That's the issue here."

"Kill the bitch's son. Then you get paid."

"God damn it, Gil! Why would I do anything more for you now, when you've already failed your side of the bargain? Deal with the boy yourself, I'm out."

"If we pay you twice as much, will you kill the boy too?"

"No. Three times as much. He's on the run, he's going to be a lot more trouble to kill."

"Fine. Three times as much. But you don't get any of the money until you bring us his head. Kill him in human form, so we know for sure it's him. You bring us a wolf's head, we don't know, we can't tell them apart."

"Fine. I'll do it."

Sounds of the other man walking out of the room.

I rip off the headphones, excited, run to find Barney. "Barney! What does the name Gilbert Beauregard get us?"

He takes off his headphones. He was playing a video game. "What?"

"The name. Gilbert Beauregard. Possible Veneray. Look up what happened to him in 1982."

"Okay, sure, but it can take a while to find information from that long ago. Not everything was online then, we have to go into different archives. Is it okay if I get the rest of the computer team involved?"

"Of course. This is official business. Get everybody you can get."

I go back to transcribing, but I'm restless, impatient, find myself pacing around while I fast-forward through conversations that aren't nearly as revealing as the one with Beauregard.

Finally, Barney comes back to find me. "Abby? We might have something. Doctor named Gilbert J. Beauregard, Junior. Gilbert J. Beauregard Senior disappeared in 1982, boating accident but no body. Junior lives here in New Orleans, the Lakewood neighborhood."

"Do we have an address?"

"We do." He holds up his phone, map highlighted.

"Well." I stand up, locate Grandma's boots. "Let's go."

"Right now? Just us?" He frowns. "Shouldn't we have backup? If you really think this guy is Veneray."

"I don't want to go in all guns blazing. He won't give me any information if he feels threatened."

Barney shakes his head. "You're seeking justice for a forty-year-old murder, you can't wait twenty minutes?"

"Fine. Twenty minutes."

Barney sends out the information to the rest of the team about where we're going, while I pace around restlessly. Finally he shakes his head, gets up, grabs the car keys. "If you're just going to pace around in circles, we can go out there. But don't confront this guy until we have backup!"

"Barney, I'm not confronting anybody. We're just collecting information."

The Lakewood neighborhood isn't a part of New Orleans I've seen before, but it's got a lot of what Vivienne calls "McMansions," large, in-your-face houses designed to look imposing, but not especially beautiful.

"This is the right block," Barney says, driving slowly past a large, white house, reminiscent of Beckford Manor without the ironwork. A man, older than Leon but younger than Pere Claude is out in the yard, poking at some flowers.

I don't know how I know, but he's the one. "Gilbert J. Beauregard Junior," I say, out loud.

"Maybe," Barney says. "We should—oh, shit!" Behind us, a police car burps, flashes its lights. We pull over and Barney begins fumbling for license and registration, smelling of panic. The cop raps on the windshield. Barney rolls it down.

"What's the problem?" he says, voice shrill. "What did we do?"

"Do you live in this neighborhood?" the cop studies the paperwork, hands it back.

"I'm sorry I thought this was a public street," Barney says.

"You were driving extremely slowly. Like you were casing the joint," the cop says.

"We were looking for an address," Barney stammers out. He's so nervous he might explode.

"Who?"

"Gilbert Beauregard," I say.

"Oh." He thinks for a moment. "What did you want to talk to him about?"

"I'm, um, I think his father might have been my biological grandfather?" This was the opening gambit I had prepared for Beauregard, and I have no idea if it's going to work on the cop. But he looks thoughtful.

"Your name, miss?"

"Alice Weber."

He nods. "Okay, then, why don't you get out, I'll conduct you over to Mr. Beauregard."

I give Barney what I hope is a reassuring look. "Great, thanks. Frank, I'll text you when I'm ready to get picked up, okay?"

Dazed, Barney nods. I get out of the car, smile at the cop in what I hope is a sunny, harmless way. The cop gestures, and I follow him to the man we spotted working in his garden.

"Hey, there, Mr. Beauregard sir, this young lady wants to talk to you about your father." The cop glances my way. "Alice Weber, was that it?"

I nod. "That's it."

Beauregard smiles. "Well, sure, Dave I'm always happy to talk to young people. What is it, miss?"

"I, um. Well. I think your father might have been my biological grandfather?"

He smiles "Why sure." He glances at the cop. "Thanks, Dave, I'll take it from here." The cop makes a little salute gesture and walks off. Beauregard peers at me for a long time, shading his eyes. "It's hot out here, you want to talk in the rec room?" He gestures toward a small standalone building near the pool.

"Sure." I feel a quiver of apprehension. He isn't buying this. He knows who I am, or what I am. But how? And if so, what would he be planning?

He pauses, right outside the door, smiling. "Let me go first, hon, there's a security code. You can't be too careful in this town."

I nod. Watch as he opens the door, shiver in the rush of chilled air from inside. Beep, beep, boop, beep, boop, beep. A British woman's voice, accent more posh than Nora's, says "Your alarm has been disabled."

"Come inside." He gestures, I follow. He shuts the door. Inside it's dim and cold and smells like Scotch, cigars, pool chalk. Instinctively I make note of potential weapons. Pool cue. Metal-tipped darts. Fireplace poker. Cocktail knife. Ice pick.

"Would you like a beer?"

"I'm not old enough, thank you."

He just laughs, opens the refrigerator, takes out two cans of Abita Springs. He hands me one, pops his own, sits down on one edge of a giant plush leather couch.

I sit on the other side of the couch, nervous, perching, hands clasped at my knees, conscious of how short the skirt is, bare legs against the cool surface of the leather. I'm still dressed for my birthday yesterday and I haven't showered. Do I smell sweaty to him? Would an ordinary person be able to learn to recognize the peppery snap of werewolf sweat?

The beer cracks properly and smells correct, so he's not trying to poison me with the beer. I sip. Smile awkwardly. "I don't drink a lot of beer," I say. "I'm only seventeen."

He laughs. "Seventeen is when I drank all the beer. Are

you sure you're not one of Cissy's cheerleader friends? You look so familiar."

"No, sorry. I don't know anyone named Cissy. Your father died a long time ago, based on what I've been able to find, is that right?"

"He died in 1982."

"How old were you then?"

"Nineteen. I was in college."

"Were you close to your father?"

Chuckle. "Close enough. He was paying for my college, anyway. And you think he was your grandfather?"

"That's where the trail leads. My grandmother was a, uh, she was a…"

"Hooker?"

"Exotic dancer." I sound defensive. "Back in the 1960s. She used to do entertainment at private men's clubs, was your father involved in one of those?"

He nods. "He was. He spent a lot of time at the club, even while I was growing up in the seventies. My mother thought it was fine, as long as he provided plenty of money. And your mother?"

"My mother?"

"Your grandmother was a stripper, what about your mother?"

"My mother was very religious. But we don't get along. She didn't want me to look into this. She never wanted me to know anything about my grandmother or my grandfather."

"You're not religious?"

"No, sir."

He laughs. "You kids aren't, I hear. You think it's intolerant. Old-fashioned. Isn't that what you think?"

I shrug. "I don't know, sir. I don't know what other people think. For me, it's just not an important part of my life. Was your father religious? Those old men's clubs, they were kind of like a religion, weren't they?"

"Were they?" He sips his beer. "Well, they had their rituals, and their secrets. And back in the day, you know, they didn't used to let in Jews or Catholics. But that was already changing by the time my father was involved."

My gut coils in rage, apprehension. Something about the way he said the word "Jews" makes me sure he must know who I am. But I swallow. Try to maintain a neutral facade. "No Catholics? In Louisiana? How was that even possible?"

He laughs. "Well, it was a very exclusive club. They didn't let women in, of course. None of the clubs did, not until the 1970s and all that women's lib stuff came along. A lot of them had a kind of ladies auxiliary for the wives, and there were certain events where the whole family would be invited. But the real club was always men only. Then they started saying, 'Oh, you can't keep women out.' The clubs changed. They started dying. When they weren't a place you could go to get away from the wife, there was no reason for them to exist anymore. That's what I think."

"Did your father ever bring you to the club?"

"Once I turned eighteen, he brought me in a few times."

"What was the club? The name, I mean. Masons, Shriners?"

"Shriners are Masons," he says. "He was a member of the Azphokites."

Not that I expected him to just come out and say "Veneray" but I'm still thrown.

"Azphokites? I've never heard of them."

"Well. They were a secret society."

"Were? They're not still around?"

"Come to think of it, they might be." His demeanor changes, his smile turns smug, he thinks he's being clever. "They still meet up in Baton Rouge, I think. Yes. Near the capitol building. High rise."

"You think? Are you teasing me? You're a member aren't you?"

"If I told you, it wouldn't be much of a secret, would it?" He looks down at his phone, smiles. Outside, a car drives up. Inside me the wolf tenses. He called somebody when he typed the code in, more Veneray, maybe cops. The wolf gets ready to fight.

His voice has a pleasant tone when he says, "I know who you are, Abnegation. And I know you're his daughter, her granddaughter. We know everything. We knew he was back, Leon. We know y'all are building an army of new wolves out there. And we've been waiting for him to send someone. If he thought sending a harmless-looking little girl like you was going to put us off, well, we're here to show him that he's wrong."

The door opens. Four bitten wolves enter, large men with an air of violence about them, Strigoi? Why did I think Strigoi? Right away they shoot me, a single bullet, but there's something in the bullet, a poison or a sedative. Not enough to knock me out, but I decide to make a show of passing out anyway, crashing face-down into the fireplace tools with a loud clatter. The poker is under me.

I lie still, willing myself to heal from the drug as fast as possible.

Gilbert says, "Down already? I thought this would be tougher. Unless she's not really one of them after all?"

"She is one," says one of the men, nudging my side with his foot. "Just little. We take head, yes? Send to Leon?" His Russian accent is thick. I was right, they're Strigoi.

"Yes, but don't do it here, I don't want blood getting everywhere."

One of the men bends down, reaches out to pick me up. But the few seconds of rest have given me a chance to fight off the sedative, and I have the fireplace poker. I roll over to my back, bringing up the poker, letting gravity, his momentum, my wolf strength all conspire to send it deep into his gut, at an upward angle all the way to his heart.

He gasps, falls forward on top of me. Dead? His heart isn't beating, anyway. I get ready to use his body as a shield in case they shoot me again—

Leon is here.

Kicks open the door. Crack! Crack! Crack! Three Strigoi necks snap hard and the men fall, unconscious, maybe dead.

That was fast.

Bootheel hard to the crotch of Gilbert Beauregard, who grunts, falls backward, flailing, lands heavily on the floor, rattling the glassware. Leon places the same bootheel on the other man's neck, carefully, not hard enough to cut off his oxygen. Green eyes flash.

"Lie still." Voice in a low growl.

Gilbert obeys, relaxing, eyes going blank.

"Abby." Leon continues to stare at Gilbert. "If any of the Strigoi move, poker through the eye into the brain."

"Got it."

He says, "Gilbert J. Beauregard Junior, are you a member of the Veneray?"

Blank, he answers: "Like my father before me and his father before him, I am loyal to the brotherhood of the Veneray."

"What is the purpose of the Veneray?"

"To control the power of the rougarou. The werewolves. We keep them in line."

"You tried to kill my daughter Abby, why?"

"To send a message to the rougarou, do not send your people after us."

"You called Strigoi, why Strigoi?"

"They're tough. They know how to kill werewolves."

"The ones you called are werewolves themselves. Why kill rougarou wolves and not Strigoi wolves?"

"The Strigoi serve us. We pay them. We don't fear them."

"Who else is in the Veneray?"

"I can't tell you."

Leon keeps his foot on the other man's neck, crouches down to bring his face close, increase the force of his stare. "Gilbert. Who is the leader of the Veneray?"

"Edwin A. Duke, Junior. But you can't go after him."

"Why not?"

"He has protection. We all have protection."

"What kind of protection?"

"We know more than you think." Beauregard smiles. "We always did. The bitch…" He trails off, passing out. Leon makes a disgusted growling noise, stands up, considers the scene for a moment, then takes one of the Strigoi bodies, uses him as a kind of puppet, makes him shoot Beauregard in the head.

Leon steps back, considers the scene again, frowns. He takes a cloth out of an internal pocket of his jacket. "Hand me the poker." I do. He wipes it off with the cloth, tosses it to the floor near the fireplace. He picks up the beer I was drinking, sniffs, pours it out in the bar sink, crushes the can, puts the can in the pocket of his jacket. Then he takes off his jacket, hands it to me. He takes off the rest of his clothes, hands them to me. "Abby, wait for me outside."

I take his clothes, wait outside. I assume he's going to go to wolf form, but I never smell the lightning. Instead, I hear and smell guns firing. Blam! Blam! Blam! Blam! Blam! The reek of Strigoi blood oozes, then overwhelms me as Leon opens the door, walks out naked and covered in blood. Slams the door behind him with the heel of his foot. Jumps into the pool, emerges wet and smelling of chlorine, holds out a hand for his clothes. I hand him the clothes. He dresses swiftly, takes his phone, sends a text. I watch the blood dissipate into the pool water until it becomes invisible.

"I just texted Vivienne. She and Régnault will take care of the scene. We should get out of here." He walks to the car, and I follow. Why do I follow? I keep doing whatever he says instantly, no questions asked, that's not at all like me. As if I have some instinct to follow him as hunt leader right now. I sit in the passenger seat, crumpled in on myself, thinking, while we drive away. After a few minutes, he explodes.

"Abby, what the hell were you thinking coming here alone?"

"I had it handled. Didn't you see my poker?"

He growls, shifts lanes, revs the engine. "That was not *handled*, Abby! You were on the ground and surrounded by powerful enemies!, moments away from being killed! You obviously went in there without any kind of plan at all."

"No, I had a plan, my plan just didn't work out. My plan was that I'd ask him questions and he would answer them. I just wanted to talk, I didn't know he'd call in the Strigoi."

"You didn't know." He makes another growling noise, this one much deeper in his throat, and his sweat turns a sharp molten red, like lava. "How did you not know? These men killed *my mother* and you didn't know they were going to kill you?"

"Well I didn't know killing me was going to be their first move! I've had Strigoi try to kill me before, you know. And I handled it!"

"Strigoi. Not Veneray." He fumes. "You've never tangled with the Veneray before and you had no idea what you were getting into. You can't keep doing that, Abby. Just running off on your own." We're stopped at a light and he stares hard at me, flashes green. "Come to me first next time."

But the flash just makes me irritated. "Oh, just like you obeyed your father when you were seventeen?"

Tight-lipped, he pulls into traffic again, gives me a side-long glare. "This isn't about me and my father."

"No? What did you do with the Strigoi?"

"Staged a shootout. Made sure there was a lot of head damage, hopefully that will keep them from healing and coming after us."

"You killed five people."

"Yeah?"

"If I killed five people like that, I'd be in so much trouble with Viv."

"Don't try to distract me." He glares. "You need to leave things to the adults sometimes. Or at least consult with us before you act."

"Maybe." I look down, hate admitting that he might be right. "What do we do next? He said they know more than we think. He knew you were back, and he knew I was your daughter, and he called me Abnegation."

"Your identity isn't very secret, not after the *Teen Mode* article."

"But the *Teen Mode* article doesn't talk about you at all. I just say that my biological father wasn't Father Wisdom. When I gave that interview I still thought you were dead. So how do the Veneray know this stuff? What's their information channel?"

He makes a small growling noise deep in his throat. "Maybe it's always been worse than we thought. We put all this effort into keeping our existence secret, while the people most dangerous to us have always known everything and it was never a secret at all."

He glances at me and his face is pure cold rage. "I think it's time I paid a visit to Edwin A. Duke, Junior. Are you in?"

"Of course I'm in. Let's go."

EDWIN A. DUKE, JR

Leon and I drive north up Highway 61, a stretch of road that always inspires complex feelings. It's the road to New Harmony, but it's also the road where Steph picked me up and changed my life for good. I stare out the window, wondering what I've gotten myself into.

"So. I'm in. What exactly am I in?"

His answer is clipped, businesslike. "Our first step is to interrogate Junior. His answers will determine our next step. Our ultimate objective is to determine the power and goals of our enemy, assess the current threat, neutralize it. If possible, we will also obtain justice for the murder of Leah Evangeline Verreaux forty years ago."

"Okay." I think for a moment, digest all of that. "I'm still in." There's silence for a moment, but it's a tense silence. Leon seems to have gone into a certain mode, one I've seen him in before, right after I got shot in Los Angeles. He's ruthless, cold, efficient. Deadly.

"What you did in there, that seemed very well-practiced," I say.

He gives a tiny shrug.

"So, have you done that kind of thing a lot? Burst into a place, bust heads, cover it up?"

He hands me the crushed beer can, changes lanes. "What do you think?"

Silence for a while. He's not interested in chitchat I guess.

I ask, "Are we going to kill people?"

He frowns for a moment, negotiating traffic, then gives me a quick sidelong glance. "Maybe. If we're right about these men, who they are, what they've done, they might try to kill us, and we will need to defend ourselves. Is that going to bother you?"

"I don't know." I answer honestly. "These are all pretty bad men. Enemies. But it still kinda bothers me to think about killing them. I talked to Lunora."

His face goes gray and blank with shock for a second, then a slight smile. He says, "Lunora? My ex-girlfriend Lunora?"

"Yeah, we found her as part of that whole mapping all the bitten wolves project. Babette and I talked to her. She's living in the old theater, the one where you took that picture from the Cure concert."

"Bon Dieu. I'm glad she survived. How did she seem?"

"Kinda nuts? But informative."

"Informative?" His expression turns grim again. "What did she tell you?"

I take a deep breath before asking: "Did you really know the attack on the hunting grounds was coming and just let it happen?"

Long, long pause. His voice is quiet when he speaks. "I didn't think they'd succeed in hurting any of the wolves."

"So you betrayed your people."

He turns defensive. "I wouldn't do it today. I wouldn't have done it then, if I'd known what was going to happen."

"But you knew it was wrong. And you didn't care."

"I cared. I just did it anyway."

"Were you trying to get revenge on your father? For the trauma morph restriction, maybe?"

"No. Not that."

"What was it then? You knew it would hurt him."

"I told you, I had no idea they would kill my mother! I didn't know they would succeed in killing any of us. We're not that easy to kill, Abby. I didn't know about the Veneray connection."

"But you knew there was a chance they would hurt somebody. You had to know."

"It seemed like a small chance. And I was young. Stupid."

"You were seventeen. I'm seventeen, I wouldn't do it."

His anger smolders, tickles my nose like the smoke from a match. "Are you sure? Absolutely sure? You wouldn't do something that might endanger the Varger, if you thought the chance of harm was small, and the thing you wanted to do was important?"

"Making your girlfriend a werewolf was that important?"

"I was trying to save her life! And I knew that my father would try to stop me, if he knew. Maybe you've never seen that side of him, but he's actually fairly prejudiced against the bitten."

"No! He's not a bigot."

"Not in the ways you're used to. And he doesn't hate the bitten, not exactly. He's always been very courteous and respectful toward individual bitten wolves. He just thinks of them as less important, the same way you might think of people who aren't members of your own family as less important."

"No, it can't be. Pere Claude congratulated me, when I brought Andrew the bitten wolf in safely. He said it was well done."

"Of course he did. But he would also have congratulated you if Andrew was dead and there had been no other injuries."

"I just don't believe you. Pere Claude isn't prejudiced against the bitten. That's ridiculous. It would be in your mother's diaries—"

Grandma Charli's voice comes back to me.

She would bite me, she said. 'Claude will be furious, but for you I'll do it.'

Claude will be furious.

A memory flashes: Pere Claude's rage, like thundering boulders, directed against Flint Savage. He was disgusted by the idea of making the gifts of the wolf something you could purchase with money. But also, there was a deeply visceral quality to that rage. It wasn't just the most angry I've ever seen Pere Claude, it was the most angry I've ever seen anyone.

"The taboo," I say, resolve crumbling. "The taboo that says you never make a bitten wolf on purpose. He really believes in it, doesn't he?"

Leon nods. He smiles slightly, sympathetic. "Abby, I'm not telling you this to make you think poorly of my father. He inherited that prejudice from his father, who got it from his father. It goes back a long way. You've heard of the berserkers of old, yes? The fearsome warriors who could not be stopped? Well, if all you want is a fearsome warrior, a bitten wolf on berserker drugs will do just as well as a born wolf. They're not quite as indestructible as we are, but that doesn't matter when you can create them by the dozens every full moon.

"According to our traditions, we were exiled from the Norselands because the bitten-wolf berserkers got so out of control that the kings turned against all wolf shifters. That's where the taboo comes from.

"I know what I did turned out badly and we all paid a steep price for it. But I really was trying to save Lunora, and I really did have reason to believe that, if my father had been anywhere near her on that first moon, he might have taken her for an enemy and killed her himself. Do you understand?"

I shake my head. Fold my arms. Stare out the window. "I don't know. I don't think I understand anything anymore."

We drive for a while in silence. He glances over sometimes, opens his mouth as if he wants to say something, but each time just exhales, clamps his lips, shakes his head.

Eventually he pulls off the highway. "There used to be a shopping mall this way, on the edge of town. We'll need suits to blend in at the capitol. Think of how your aunt Viv dresses."

The shopping mall still exists, although it has a somewhat shabby look, and is now called NEW ORLEANS OUTLET COLLECTION. Leon regards it with a strange expression I can't quite read, like, a sad smirk. "I remember when this place opened. In the early 1980s, malls were the future."

"The future of what?"

He laughs. "You know. The future."

We drive around a ruined parking lot, find a store called PROFESSIONAL FOR LESS, park next to it. Outside, the weather is hot, heavy, oppressive. He looks around at the decrepit state of things, inhales deeply, shakes his head. "My mother hated the malls, back then. Called them sterile. Thought they were killing off the retail in the downtown core of towns all across the country. Creating dead inner cities in the middle of active but soulless suburbs."

"Was she right?"

"I don't know. I don't spend a lot of time shopping. I do know that my downtown Los Angeles property was cheap for its size when I bought it in the 1980s, but it's very expensive now. I think maybe things run in cycles."

We head into the store and before long, we're both looking extremely respectable in gray linen, carrying leather briefcases and wearing lightly tinted sunglasses that could pass for eyeglasses.

"The UV coating helps keep people from seeing the eye

flash," he says. "And glasses can do a lot to make you look...
harmless." Small smile.

"Thanks, I'll keep that in mind the next time I show up
somewhere to kill somebody." I think I'm making a joke, but
am I?

We look at ourselves side by side in the mirror. We do look
very professional, and I've never seen our resemblance jump
out so strongly before. Something about the not-quite-
matching gray suits, the way he's slicked his hair back and I've
put mine up in a bun, you can see that we have the same
cheekbones, similar eyes.

He nods. "We won't look out of place in the capitol." He
glances at my boots, thinks for a moment. "They're not professional, but a lot of women wear different shoes in and out of
the building, change into pumps at their desk, you can probably get away with it. Let's go."

We walk out wearing the new outfits, put our other clothes
in the trunk, start driving again in silence. Him mentioning his
LA properties has reminded me of a question that nags at me
sometimes: when he was in Los Angeles, what did he do for
money? Viv was acting in movies under the name Roxy Void,
but what was Leon doing?

Because, sometimes, especially today, I get the impression
that maybe whatever Leon was doing in Los Angeles for
money, it involved killing people. And I'm not sure I want to
ask him about it because I'm not sure I know what to do with
the answer. If he told me "no" would I believe him? And if he
told me "yes" would it change anything?

"You're quiet," he says. "Do we need to rehearse what
we're going to do when we get to the capitol building?"

"Sure. What do we do when we get there?"

"First of all, I need you to agree to follow my lead."

"You want to be my hunt leader?"

He sighs. "Do you object? If you won't follow my lead, we
can't do this." He pauses, and when I don't answer right away,

he gets agitated. "Abby, are you with me or not? If not, I'll do it without you, that's fine. I just need to know."

I get agitated in return. "Forget it, Leon, you are not ditching me! We are doing this together! Whatever it is we're doing!" I pause. "What is it we're doing, anyway? Visiting Junior in his office, and then?"

He shakes his head. "I'm not entirely sure. That's why I need you to follow my lead. I don't know what we're going to find once we start looking, so we'll have to recalibrate our strategy as we go. We can't be working at cross purposes."

"Okay." I say this, and we can both hear the lack of total commitment in my voice.

"Abby, if you're having doubts…"

"It's not that." I stare out the window for a moment, gather my resolve. "Leon. Tell me the truth. Were you ever a professional killer?"

Sharp intake of breath. He holds for a moment, then blows it out. "Well. I knew this conversation was probably coming someday, but I didn't know it would come up right now."

"No? We're heading off to confront our enemies, maybe violently. It seems like the perfect time to me. Anyway, I know the answer is 'yes' because if it were 'no' you'd just tell me."

A long pause, while he changes lanes and his heart races, sweat all spiky and red with tension. "Why do you need to know, Abby?"

"Why don't you want to tell me?"

"Because I'm not proud of it?"

"No?"

"No." He says this firmly. "I was blackmailed into doing it."

"Blackmailed? Okay, I didn't see that coming. How did you get blackmailed into being a hit man?"

"When I first got to Los Angeles I worked as a bodyguard. I was good at it. I met a lot of people that way. And I rarely had to do anything violent. I specialized in shutting down threats before anything got to that point. You know our gifts. Smell the powder of the smuggled gun, or the sweat of the person unusually stressed out. Notice the person changing direction suddenly, or hiding behind the curtains.

"But there was one incident where I had to show the wolf a bit more than usual, and there was a man, a kingpin of the LA underground, who knew about wolf shifters, saw me do it, and knew me for what I was. He came to me for a contracted hit. Offered a lot of money and a threat: if I didn't do it, he would expose me."

"Expose you how?" I try to picture it. "I mean, who would he tell? Are there Veneray in Los Angeles?"

"I don't know. I've never encountered them. It may have been an empty threat. But at that time I was still worried about what would happen if my father found me. So I told myself it was a service. My reasoning was, these men—and it was always men—were going to get killed one way or the other. And I could do it without guns. Without collateral damage."

"Plus you'd get the money."

Long pause. Then he says, "Yes, I did get the money."

"Was it a lot of money?"

Another long pause. He nods, slowly. "Yes. It was a lot of money."

"When did you stop? Or did you stop?"

"After a couple of years, the man who was blackmailing me got killed himself."

"Did you do it?"

"Let's say, I didn't prevent it. After that, I went to stay with the Lobos for a while, detoxed, all that good stuff." He sighs. "The whole clean desert living thing didn't work out, obviously, but when I went back into Los Angeles, I never went back to the business. I tried to avoid the people who used to ask."

Silence while I digest this information. I'm not sure if it makes me feel better or worse about Leon. Maybe it's better to just know, rather than continue having vague suspicions. Clear the air. Get the truth.

But is this the real truth?

I realize I'll never know.

"All right. I'll believe you."

He frowns. "You say that like you don't actually believe me."

"I'm willing to follow you for now. I said I was in, I'm in." I fold my arms tightly, stare out the window at the encroaching urbanization as we draw near to Baton Rouge. "You know, I never realized it before, but Viv is probably cranky all the time because this style of clothing is really uncomfortable. Like, I thought those weird itchy prairie dresses we had to wear in the cult were bad, but a suit? Bon Dieu, it's pure torture."

A pause, then he chuckles. "Most suits nowadays have stretchy fabric built in, you should try some of the things we wore back in the 1980s."

At the Capitol in Baton Rouge, we park in a visitor lot, walk through the park to a side entrance specifically for visitors. Bored workers peek into our empty bags, have us put keys and phones into a bucket, send us through a metal detector. We pass.

We take an elevator up to the main floor, and I have a flash of memory when I hear the female elevator voice say, with a sexy lilt, "First floor."

"Wait, I've been here before. Father Wisdom took us on some kind of field trip. He was talking to a, to a legislator who was a friend of his, I think. They were both part of some government Bible group. The rest of us took a tour. I remember that elevator voice. I couldn't believe how seductive she sounded, and I couldn't tell if I was the only one who noticed."

Leon laughs. "I don't know who picked out that voice, but Viv complains about it a lot." He studies a directory, then says, "We're taking the stairs up. Keep close with me, we might have to stare somebody down."

Slip into the stairway, up to the fourth floor. Close the stairway door quietly. Walk down the hallway with a firm purpose, swinging our briefcases.

Leon knocks on the door.

A young man opens it. Frowning. His badge identifies him as Clancy Claremont, page. "Do you all have an appointment?"

Leon lowers his glasses to look deep into the page's eyes, and I catch the green flash. "Take us to Edwin A Duke, Junior."

Blank, the young man turns around, walks toward an inner office, opens the door. "Sir, you have a couple of visitors."

"What on earth? Blast, Clancy, I told you no visitors—"

The man at a desk stands up, preparing to be outraged, to tell us to go away, but then he catches Leon's eyes. Even before getting flashed his face falls into a shocked, blank, surrendered look, like he knows who we are and why we're here.

"Abby, close the door." Leon points. "Tell the page to leave for the day."

I make eye contact, flash. "Hey, Clancy, it's time to go home. Have a good night."

"Thank you." He leaves. I shut the door, turn back around, watch Leon step forward, menacing. He's about the same height as the other man, and more narrowly built, but I can still see it in their body language, one of them is capable of killing the other with his bare hands, and it's not the politician.

Leon says, "Edwin A. Duke, Junior, are you a member of a group called the Veneray?"

"Yes."

"Was your father also a member of this group?"

"Yes. He brought me into the group."

"What is the purpose of this group?"

"To control the rougarou."

"What are the rougarou?"

"Cajun werewolves."

"Do you know the name, Leah Evangeline Verreaux?"

Small nasty smile. "My father talked about her. Always called her that bitch. Sometimes that red bitch. It was funny, because she had red hair and she was a communist."

"Do you know he had her murdered?"

Laugh. "My father had a lot of people murdered."

"Have you ever had anyone murdered?"

Another laugh. "Nobody does that anymore. You don't have to kill people to get them out of your way. Killing backfires, a lot of the time. Brings attention where you don't want it."

"The Veneray knew I was back in Bayou Galene, how?"

Junior laughs. "Oh, my. Do you not know? You rougarou, you have cops you call, who are friendly to you? We own the cops. You use the Internet to coordinate your activities? We own the Internet. If we wanted to drive you all from that little town, we could do it in a heartbeat. Turn it into an oil refinery parking lot. You exist because we allow you to exist."

Leon advances slowly, step by step, gaze steady, murderous. "Bravado. You've tried to destroy us before and failed. When and where do the Veneray meet?"

"I don't…"

Leon presses harder. "Edwin A. Duke Junior, where and when do the Veneray meet?"

He gives up. "Three days before the full moon, in the club at the top of Masterpiece Towers. It's a regular Azphokite meeting until midnight, then the others leave and the Veneray remain and do our business."

"That's tonight. You're getting us into that meeting."

He glances at me. "No women in the Azphokites."

"No? No women at all?" I frown. "Not even bartenders?"

"Oh, well. Cocktail waitresses. Of course."

Leon says, "Abby, do you think you can be a server?"

"Sure. I've bartended before, remember that party we did in Los Angeles?"

Leon nods thoughtfully, staring at Junior. "Very well. I need to make some arrangements before the meeting, probably an hour or two, can you guard Junior here? Don't kill him unless you absolutely have to."

"Not unless I have to."

Leon leaves, shutting the door behind him. For a long time Junior stares blankly. Then shakes his head. Seems to wake up a bit.

"So. You're his daughter?" I nod. "Are you in school?"

"No."

"My daughter is about your age I think. She's going to start college in the fall."

"Good for her."

"Please." His voice takes on a begging, piteous tone. "Please don't let your father kill me. Don't do that to her. She's a good girl."

"Is she? Hmm."

He frowns. "Please. I just mean—you're a good girl too, aren't you?"

"Am I? What makes you say that?"

"Come on. I know you're a good girl. Deep down. Don't let him make you do things you don't want to do. Your father is a murderer you know. Leon Verreaux, Evangeline's son? I've heard about him. You know he killed three people at Thibodaux Taxidermy?"

"Only three? Huh. The way people talk about the massacre, I thought it was a lot more."

"It was very bloody, the way he did it. Extremely violent.

Ripped them apart. Until recently I thought we killed him a long time ago."

"'We' meaning the Veneray?"

"Yes. My father said we had, when he told me the story. He said it was the last time we'd taken any direct action against the rougarou. 'We killed the bitch and the son of the bitch, and the rest of them have stayed in their proper place ever since.'" He pauses, seems to notice my expression. "I'm sorry, I don't mean any disrespect to your grandmother."

"Hmm." I look away from him, to quell my own temper, study his shelves. I smell Scotch and cigars, where are they? There. I uncork the bottle, take a sip. It's good. "Why is it always Scotch and cigars anyway?" I take one of the cigars, sniff it closely, still don't get the appeal.

"You smoke cigars?"

"No, I don't smoke, I just like to ruin it for other people." I drop the cigar on the carpet, crush it under the heel of my boot. "I do like Scotch, though." I take another sip from the bottle. "So, what's it like being a rich white man with political power?"

"Excuse me?"

I gesture with the bottle. "Tell me about your life. What's it like getting everything a person could want without having to work for it? Do you get bored, is that why you try to hurt people?"

His demeanor changes, as he slips into a more comfortable place for him. He draws his shoulders back, voice taking on a deeper, more condescending tone. "Now, listen, I know you 'woke' kids want to tell me how privileged I am, but I worked damn hard to get here and I work damn hard every day of my life."

"Pft." I sip from the bottle again. "You inherited a job from your father, *Junior*. You say you work hard and maybe you do, but do you honestly think you work harder than the person who cleans the toilets around here?"

"Now, listen, girl, not every person is suited to every kind of job. You wouldn't want a janitor doing brain surgery, now, would you?"

"Nice try, but you're a politician, Junior. That's more like being a reality TV star. No real qualifications other than having a certain kind of personality. Ambitious, narcissistic, likes to hear himself talk?"

"There's a lot more to it than what you know. I happen to have a law degree."

"Congratulations. My aunt also has a law degree. But I know you don't have to have a law degree to be a politician."

He's fiddling with something in his desk. "You know that bottle you're drinking from is my most expensive Scotch? It cost me five hundred dollars and a trip to Canada."

"Yeah? I noticed it was good."

He puts a snifter on his desk. "Would you mind coming over here to pour me some of it?"

"Sure." I take a step forward, lean over, splash Scotch into the snifter.

He points the gun at my chest. Finally. As if I didn't know what he was fiddling with under the desk.

"Just back away, darling, it'll be okay. You tell him I had a gun, you had no choice."

I take a step backward, morbidly fascinated by this little scenario. He's changed demeanor again, a bit of mobster about him now. "Tell Leon I had no choice?"

"It's okay, I won't hurt you." He takes a step forward.

"Your buddy Gilbert Beauregard tried to have me killed."

"It was nothing personal. Gil would have tried to kill any rougarou who showed up. I see now that was a mistake."

I set the Scotch on a little end table. No sense spilling it. "A mistake?"

"A mistake, I'm sorry." He takes another step forward.

"You're sorry."

He steps closer. Close enough that we could touch each

other. He smiles, the smile of a man who feels that he's back on firm ground, back on top.

"Sorry, *bitch*" and then he pulls the trigger.

Well. Tries to. Strangely, his fingers are all broken, and I have the gun.

He shrieks, thin, high-pitched, and I think about what Grandma Charli said, about the man with the broken shin, how that high-pitched scream of pure animal pain doesn't sound human.

We were on the right side, but…

Prey. That's the sound of prey caught in a trap, and the wolf stirs in excitement. She likes that sound. She likes the bright yellow curry smell of his pain and fear. This man is an enemy. It's good when your enemies become prey.

"What did you do," he manages to say, panting, voice weak. "What did you do?"

"I broke your hand?"

"Oh, God. God, it hurts. It hurts."

"I bet it does. You got a lot of little bones in there, I made sure to break all of them."

He collapses into a chair. "How did you—are you like him? Like Leon?"

"Yeah, I'm a werewolf. Did you not know that?"

He shakes his head. "I didn't. I didn't."

"The Strigoi goons who showed up at Beauregard's place knew. They were going to chop off my head."

"We called Strigoi because they know how to deal with the rougs, that's what everyone says."

"You didn't know I was a werewolf but you hired Strigoi werewolf killers anyway?"

"We knew your father, or one of the others, might show up too. We had to anticipate a fight."

"Oh, I get it now. You didn't hire them for me. You hired them for him. Wait. You thought Leon might show up and you only sent four goons? What the hell were you thinking?"

"They're Strigoi, we thought four was a lot." Panting. "God, my hand hurts."

"Yeah, it's swelling up, you might want to put some ice on that. We'll wait until Leon gets back, though. I'm curious about something. You know the werewolves are real—as in, we turn into literal wolves on the full moon—and you know Leon is my father—and you know he's a werewolf—but you still didn't know I was? I'm just trying to understand your thought process."

"We don't know when you do it. What age, I mean. And we weren't sure if they always do it to the girls. We knew your grandmother was one of them, but… God this hurts."

"I bet it does. So, when you say 'do it' you mean… the bite? Like, as a rite of passage into adulthood, if you're found worthy, an adult werewolf bites you?"

A look of interest. "Is that how it happens? We didn't know the details."

"Well, if you don't already know, I'm not telling you."

Pause. "Does it interfere with your fertility?"

"Dude, I'm seventeen, don't be gross."

"We assumed that's why they don't always do it to the girls. Because it's hard for a female werewolf to bring a child to term."

Is it? I wonder. It was hard for my grandmother, but when she talks about her miscarriages in her diary, she makes it sound like it wasn't a common problem for the other women in town. Just her own bad luck.

He continues, "So we thought that maybe they do it to women only after they've had a couple of children. Your grandmother—"

"What about my grandmother?" I grab his hand and he shrieks.

Leon enters, nostrils flaring. "You broke his hand."

"He tried to shoot me."

"Hmm. In that case, you showed impressive restraint." Looks at hand. "I bet that hurts."

"It does. God. It does." His gaze to Leon is pleading, as if now he's looking for mercy from the other man. Male bonding or something.

Leon pokes the hand and Junior screams again. "Don't try to shoot my daughter, she's been shot a lot and really doesn't like it." He gives me a slight smile. "Ready to go?"

18

MASTERPIECE TOWERS

The three of us head to the nearby office tower, on foot, Leon gripping Junior's arm the whole time. Junior seems nervous and annoyed, squinting at the setting sun, scowling at Leon, at me, but not daring to do anything.

We enter the lobby, head to a special elevator that requires Junior's key card. Up to the "penthouse" floor which is actually the thirteenth based on count. I wonder about that particular superstition. The wolves care about the number thirteen, but don't fear it. They consider thirteen moons to be a moon year. Thirteen moons without a new bitten wolf and a temporary maison closes down. Thirteen moons without a transformation and you're considered to have Arda's Wound. Thirteen years old is when they start preparing you to be a wolf.

Up on the thirteenth floor, we get out into a lobby area. Leon sniffs, nostrils flaring. "Abby, the kitchen is that way." He points.

I nod, head in the direction of the kitchen smells, find a corridor partially concealed by textured mirrors. A young woman carrying an empty tray notices me and frowns thoughtfully.

I say, "New cocktail waitress?"

She nods, gestures for me to follow, into a bustling kitchen and bar. Young women hurry smoothly back and forth carrying trays of drinks and snacks. They're all rendered oddly interchangeable, in short black knit dresses and stunning jeweled chokers, hair slicked into buns, makeup flat and pale. All the prep work is being done by an older woman and a man, both dressed in the black pants and white apron more common for kitchen staff.

The woman making cocktails, Gretchen by her nametag, looks up at me. "New cocktail waitress," I say.

"Oh, good, we're short staffed tonight. Did anybody get you a uniform yet?"

"No."

She sighs. "Well, they're back there, near the bathroom." She waves her hand in the direction. "The makeup counter is there too. You don't have any tattoos, do you?"

"I don't."

"Good. Sometimes we can cover them up, but it's a pain." She looks down at my shoes. "Red. They should have told you to wear black. But I guess they'll do, these men rarely look any farther down than your tits anyway. We'll get you a choker after you're in the dress, go."

The dress hasn't been laundered since the last person wore it, and it smells distractingly like her, her perfume. I come back out, Gretchen looks me over, frowning. "What are you thinking? Take off your underwear! And use the nipple tape, it's at the makeup counter."

"Take off my underwear?"

She rolls her eyes, takes my shoulders, spins me around to where I can see myself reflected in the silver side of a steel refrigerator. "It makes lines under the dress, see? Pantylines? Bralines?"

"Oh." I see what she means, go back to remove my underwear. I spend a good deal of time entirely naked, or wearing just sweats or just a bathrobe, why should it feel weird to wear a short dress with no underwear? But it does. I come back out, she nods approval. "Go do your makeup while I pick out a choker."

I find the makeup counter. Freshen my hair bun. Find the nipple tape. Do my makeup so that I have the same flat, pale look as the other girls. With the help of Babette and Vivienne I've sort of learned to put on makeup, but I don't think it will ever be something I do naturally, as an everyday part of my grooming, the way they do. It always feels like a costume, like I'm making up for a performance.

Gretchen nods approval. "It'll do. Hold still." She fastens a choker around my neck, rubies, three strands, the whole thing about two inches wide, cool and heavy. Tiny sharp gems that sparkle, balanced with smoother, larger stones in a teardrop shape. She spins me around so I can see the effect in a small mirror, and the quick-flashed glimpse sets my heart pounding. It looks like a slit throat, as if I'm dead already and don't know it.

I finger the rubies. "Are these real?"

Behind me, I almost imagine that I can hear a little girl laughing. A pretty laugh.

"Yes they're real." She looks amused. "But it's registered, do not think for one moment you can walk out of here wearing it. And if you try, these guys will hunt you down and kill you."

"Will they." I finger it. They'd try, maybe, but they'd hit rubies first.

"Ready? These men, you serve them in a particular way, come here." She gestures, leads me to a large one-way mirror, where we can see the whole room but it's obvious they can't see us. "So, the first thing is, you do not interrupt them when they're talking. Not ever. You watch, and when you see one of them has an empty glass, you go up and you stand there. You don't say anything until he talks to you, and he might not say anything, it might be all body language. Like, you make a little gesture at the empty glass, he hands you the empty glass, you point to the empty glass like 'do you want another one?' and he nods and you come back here and get him another one. No words at all. Got it?"

"Sure. So if he doesn't want another one, or if he wants something different, he'll speak up?"

"He will. So, another thing is, they don't pay. It's all part of their club dues. But also, you can't let them see you writing anything down. If you get a bunch of orders all at once and have to write them down to keep them straight, there's a pad of paper back here for it." She points. "And they like to move around, so you have to remember who's who, you can't just tie it to a table or seat. It helps to give them little nicknames in your head." She points at the men. "Red Tie, Big Gut, Weird Sideburns, Extremely Freckled—huh, that one is kind of hot actually, looks a little like Eddie Redmayne don't you think?"

With a weird jolt I realize she's pointing at my father. "Uh. Well. He seems younger and more athletic than the other guys, I guess."

"Yeah, he does. I bet he's a new recruit. But, even if they happen to be older-guy hot, if they flirt, blow them off as smoothly as you can. Don't flirt back, but don't get mad either. If it gets too awkward, make an excuse, and come back to the kitchen."

"Got it."

"And, finally, you do not prep any drinks or food yourself. You give the orders to me or Joel and we put the items on your tray for you."

"Sure. Is that a union thing?"

She laughs. "Darling, please. It's so you don't mess up your makeup or your dress. But also it lets us more accurately charge their club for the overall amount of alcohol consumed. We don't charge each individual man for his drinks, but we do make them pay. You'd best believe it."

"Okay, got it.

"I think you're ready to go. Good luck."

I drop my face into a neutral look. Shut myself off. Don't think about anything, just let them tell me what they want to drink, go back to the bar, get the drink. Everybody seems to want a martini, a Manhattan, an old fashioned, something simple and mostly alcoholic. It's so easy it becomes almost hypnotic. My face is blank, eyes distant. But I listen. I hear them talking about business deals, stock sales, things that mean nothing to me, but they might mean something to some-body. Those words are in my head, and I have a pretty good memory. I can't walk out of here wearing this ruby choker, maybe, but I could walk out of here knowing that Fred Manson is short-selling his Initech stock because he's heard the economy is going to take a severe downturn soon. If I knew what to do with that kind of information, it might be worth far more than the ruby choker. But I don't.

Some of the men look at me with a leering appreciation, or make vague flirty comments that I ignore, as instructed. But really I'm invisible to them. They see a body, a face, but they don't see me. Even without the uniform and the makeup making us look interchangeable, we're still invisible to them. Commodities. Products. They look at me and take pleasure in what they see, but it's not much different than when they sip their perfect Manhattan and take pleasure in its artfully finessed balance of flavors.

It's obvious from the way they talk that they see every-body in their lives that same way. Their wives, their children, their mistresses, their employees: everyone is a product to them, a service, a possession, prized or despised, but either way, not a person, just a collection of things they value or don't value. My daughter isn't beautiful but she's good in school, maybe I'll send her down the frigid lawyer route. My son got another DUI, it looks bad, I need to get him a driver. My secretary is quitting, that bitch, do you know anywhere I can get a girl who still knows how to take dictation?

After a couple hours of serving them I hate all these men with an intense deep-down loathing.

I think about what Grandma Charli said: A long list of evil men who need to get eaten. Once you've decided that it's okay to kill people, then you always have to wonder, would the world be better off if I just killed this guy? Would it make more trouble or less trouble? And that's a lot to think about. I don't know that I've decided it's morally okay to kill people except in self-defense, but I'm not sure I've ruled it out either.

"Your hair is so red," says one of the men, the one called Big Gut, when I bring him his old fashioned. Leering. "Is that natural hon?"

"It's not a wig," I say.

He reaches out to touch it.

He's drunk.

And I really, really want to do him some kind of violence.

Maybe I'm as bad as my father. These men, they make me so angry. The way they act like they own me. Like I'm nothing to them. A cocktail waitress. An object.

Leon, I think, is bored. He makes eye contact with me a few times, gives a small smile, but a little shake of his head. Not time yet. We're still waiting for midnight.

At one point, I'm refilling my tray, one of the other girls, Emerald based on her choker, says something and I mention that it's my first night.

"Oh yeah? Have they talked to you about the rougarou yet?"

"No, what?"

"Yeah, some of these guys…" she gestures. "They're into the occult or something. They think werewolves are real. The Cajun ones anyway, the rougarou."

"You don't say." I nod, making a show of thoughtful

consideration. "As in, literal shapeshifters? Or some kind of metaphorical werewolf?"

She laughs. "You know, it's hard to tell sometimes." She checks the clock on the wall. "Oh, if it's your first night, remember last call is at eleven twenty and the staff all has to leave at ten minutes to midnight. That ten-minute thing throws people sometimes. And we leave through that door." She points to what looks like an emergency exit. "There's a staff elevator back there."

Apprehension curdles in my gut. "Ten minutes to midnight? Why the ten minutes?"

"It's a ritual thing with them. They have a saying, 'If it's midnight it's already too late.' But it probably started because of some weird liquor law, don't you think?"

"Probably. Thanks for the warning." Emerald leaves and I think about what to do. Leon is waiting for midnight proper, because Junior lied to him. Well. Not exactly a lie. Not a direct lie. People often say "midnight" when they mean "around midnight." With the pressure of Leon's gaze on him, it might have been difficult to lie outright. But it was easy to be evasive, to casually use a common idiom, knowing it would be interpreted in the wrong way.

It's already almost last call.

I find a coaster and a pen, write:

THEY DO IT AT 11:50 PM

Hope that's clear enough. Carry out a tray of drinks, take one to Leon, who frowns at me. We've spent the evening avoiding each other. I put the coaster down on a side table, note facing up, champagne flute on top of it.

He takes a sip, reads the coaster, nods, turns it around to hide the note, sets it back down. In spite of my apprehension, this part is almost fun, like we're planning a heist. I touch the rubies at my throat.

Last call. I bring out a final tray of gin martinis, serve them, collect empties, go back to the kitchen. The staff is clearing out rapidly, dropping their jeweled chokers through a slot into a safe, changing back into street clothes.

I head to the main room again, make eye contact with Leon, who indicates with a little nod where I should stand. It puts us at opposite parts of the room, maximum coverage. Junior is sitting next to him.

The non-Veneray men start to trickle out.

Junior stands up, casually, like he's going to the bathroom or something, starts walking. Leon and I both watch closely. He must feel our eyes on him. What does he think he can get away with?

But the other Veneray also know what time it is. A few seconds ago, Leon and I were at opposite points of a very rough circle, but now the circle has moved out to surround him. It seems very casual. Men meandering about with drinks in their hands. None of them even looking at Leon. But their purpose is clear.

Junior blows on a whistle, shrill and shockingly loud. All eyes turn to see him pointing at Leon with his broken, puffy hand.

"Veneray men, kill the w—" But he never finishes the sentence, because his neck has been snapped and he's falling to the floor with a glazed look, Leon standing behind him.

Some of the Veneray reacted quickly enough to the word "kill" to reach for their guns, but find their hands broken, just like Junior did.

Only one of them manages to get off a shot, and it goes right through Leon's jacket. That man also gets his neck snapped.

Before anyone else has time to react, Leon howls once, a true wolf howl from a human throat, and it sounds uncanny even to me. It's a howl that means, the hunt is on. Rising and falling and reverberating in the air, a silvery knifelike sound.

Roman and Vivienne enter the room, Vivienne all strut and attitude, playing Roxy Void, and Roman in black, holding a sword. Why a sword? Looks cool, I guess, and they probably had to be ready in case the Veneray had more Strigoi goons. But their most impressive weapon is Rufus, who enters in wolf form, full attack mode, snarling, growling, showing teeth, eyes glowing red.

As one, the Veneray react with extreme fear, seeing their worst nightmare come to life: their ancient enemy in his most fearsome aspect, right here in their sanctuary.

Some of them scream, some piss themselves a little.

They seem to have given up fighting, and stare blankly at wolf-Rufus, hands limp at their sides. Leon booms out in a commanding voice, "Veneray men, pay attention. You killed my mother forty years ago, and it was intended to send a message to my father—stay in your place. He, it seems, heeded that message. The rougarou and the Veneray have existed in a stalemate for those forty years. But today, that peace was broken. Abby?"

I step forward. Leon gestures toward me. "As you can see, my daughter is very young and not particularly fearsome. She went to one of your members, Gilbert Beauregard, just to talk to him, to get information. But he summoned four Strigoi to murder her. Now your Strigoi are dead, and Beauregard too."

Gasping. "No, not Gil!"

"You saw what happened when Edwin A. Duke, Junior ordered me killed, what happened when your men tried to draw their weapons, when one of them fired. You do not want to start open war with us. You will not win such a war. Rufus?"

Rufus transforms back into human form, and there is even more gasping. One man, Obvious Toupee, faints entirely.

Red Tie stands up. "Mr. Verreaux, I do believe there has been some kind of a misunderstanding here. I swear to God until this moment most of us thought y'all rougarou were just eccentric Cajun environmentalists."

Evil Facial Hair raises a hand. "I knew you were real were-wolves but I thought you only transformed on the full moon."

Leon makes a disgusted growling noise in his throat. "Well. You were wrong, weren't you? Know this. The rougarou are stronger than you. Faster than you. Able to heal injuries that would kill you. We can become the wolf at any time, not just the full moon. We can stay human at any time, including the full moon. And, perhaps most importantly, we can track you by scent. You do not want to start a war with us."

Facial Hair says, "No. No, you're right, Mr. Verreaux, I don't believe that we do."

"This is your only warning. If you or anyone connected to you comes after any of us again, all of you die. Every man in this room. We will ensure that all of our people know you by scent. Abby, Vivienne, please collect the underwear from each of these gentlemen. Socks. Underpants. Undershirts."

Frozen for a moment, they gape at him. I say, "You heard him, gents. Strip."

Gritty with fear, they begin to take off their clothes. He's not making them take off all their clothes just for the scent. We could collect socks alone for that. He wants them humiliated. He wants them to feel defeated, small. He wants revenge. In a way, he's quenching a forty-year-old thirst.

Part of me is right there with him. I hate everything about these men. I want them to suffer. But I also have misgivings. This doesn't seem right. It's too theatrical, involves too many people. It could provoke a backlash.

I shake my head. Well. Leon wanted me to defer to senior wolfy authority, and that's what I'm doing. Now I've got a big stinking armful of Veneray underwear to prove it.

Leon says, "Abby, would you know these men again if you encountered their scent trail?"

I nod.

"Roman, Rufus?"

"Of course."

Vivienne says, "Come on, Abby, we're going to distribute

the clothing as widely as possible before these men have a chance to think they're going to have other options."

She struts out again. I follow. All the way into the elevators, the parking garage, her car. She doesn't break character until we're in her car and heading out onto the street, then her face twists into a spasm of disgust. "God, I hate men like that. Some of them are probably Azphokites, I'll bet you anything."

"They're all Azphokites, Viv. The Veneray are a subset of the Azphokites. Like the Shriners and the Masons, I guess."

"They are? God *damn* it." She slaps the steering wheel. "That's the last thing we need."

"Is that worse? Why is that worse?"

"The Azphokites... they're super well connected. Wealth, power, media, the whole package. If they notice you, it's not good."

"They're enemies?"

"They're enemies. They're *the* enemy. If you're female, they're your enemy. If you're gay, bi, trans, they're you're enemy. If you're Black, indigenous, any person of color, they're your enemy. If you're Jewish, they're your enemy. If you're Muslim, Buddhist, atheist, Wiccan, any minority religion, they're your enemy. If you're moral, they're your enemy. And now, apparently, if you're a wolf, they're your enemy. Figures. God damn it. It's been Azphokites the whole time."

"How do you know about them?"

"They're very active in Los Angeles, deep into the movie industry. I tangled with them as Roxy Void."

"That sounds interesting. You going to tell me the whole story someday?"

"Maybe." She grins. Then her face falls. "I don't know what Leon is thinking, getting into it with the Azphokites. He did not discuss this with me first, he just told me what to do and I did it. Same old story."

"You think his whole thing of making them strip was

wrong? I thought so too. He was doing it for revenge, but revenge doesn't always work out the way you want."

"No it doesn't." She sighs. "I know he's hoping they'll back off after this, realize the smart thing to do is leave us alone. He seems to have been right that they had no comprehension of our real power."

"But it could also be a mistake to show them what they're dealing with too clearly, right? What if they get afraid of us in the wrong way and try to destroy us instead of leaving us alone?"

She shakes her head, with a grim look. "Well, they have tried to destroy us before, and failed. I guess I don't know how scared to be."

"But that was the old days, when they tried that. Right? I mean, nowadays they could drop a nuclear bomb on us."

She laughs. "I suppose they could. But that would endanger their precious oil refineries, so I don't think they would. Also, a nuclear bomb, even a little one, would attract a lot of attention, don't you think?"

"But that land mine that killed Pere Claude's father, do you think that was them?"

"It might have been. But it only killed one of us, even so." She briefly puts a hand on my shoulder, trying to be comforting. "I'm not saying you shouldn't worry, little one, I'm worried too. But we shouldn't get carried away imagining all kinds of terrible things that aren't very likely to happen."

"Maybe." The sun catches my eye and I check where we are on my phone's map. "Are we heading west? To Bayou Galene?"

"Yes?"

"Shouldn't we take this stuff to the maisons first? They have the trained scent trackers."

She thinks for a moment, nods. "You're right. And men like that tend to live and work in bigger cities. In fact, we should distribute pieces of clothing to all the maisons, like we did with Flint Savage. Just in case some of them think they're going to flee the deadly rougarou by running off to Los Angeles or New York." She takes the next exit, gets on a different highway heading into New Orleans.

"Viv, is Leon really going to expect us to kill all of these men if any one of them comes after us?"

She shakes her head. "I don't know. It seems like a lot, doesn't it? There were a dozen men in that room."

"I don't know if I can do it. Be an assassin. Just kill people in cold blood."

"It's fine. You don't have to be the one to do it." She nods, looking grim. "Most people have trouble killing in cold blood."

"Even werewolves?"

"Especially werewolves." A sad little smile. "The wolf part doesn't really think in what you'd call an abstract way. A wolf kills an enemy, but who's an enemy? Somebody who threatens you right this instant. It's the human part of us that seeks to kill in more strategic ways. Revenge. Money."

"Viv. There's something something Lunora told me about Leon."

"Lunora?" She goggles at me for a second, so stunned that she almost drifts the car out of her lane, says, "Shit" and corrects it. "Lunora. Leon's old girlfriend Lunora?"

"Right. Babette and I found her as part of the scent mapping project."

"She's still alive? Actual Lunora? And living in New Orleans?"

"Yeah, but she's a recluse, that might be how you missed her for so long. She said that Leon abused the berserker drugs because they have a side effect, an artificially created socio-pathic personality, and he wanted this, because he wanted to be able to kill people in cold blood. To get revenge for his mother."

"Yes?"

"You don't seem surprised."

"I'm surprised you heard it from Lunora, but she's not wrong." Big sigh. "I remember him talking about it."

"When you knew him in Los Angeles, was he working as a hit man?"

She startled. "Bon Dieu. He told you that? Or did Lunora know somehow?"

"I asked. After I saw what he did to Beauregard. So it's true?"

"It's true." She nods. "But I don't know any more details than that. I made it a point not to know any more details."

"Viv, you're going to think I'm terrible. My father Leon has saved my life at least once, probably twice. But I don't really trust him."

Small, huffed-out laugh. "I don't know what to tell you about that. Pere Claude is your hunt leader. You trust him, you don't have to trust Leon. Are you asking me if I think you're misjudging him?"

I nod. "That's it. Do you think I should trust him?"

"Oh, little one, that's such a complicated question. There's no obvious answer. I've trusted Leon many times. Trusted my life to him, in fact. And he has come through for me. Many times. But he's one of those people, there's something hidden inside him, like a dark place you can't touch, or a room that's always locked. And I don't know what's in there. I'm not sure he does either. But I do think some of the things he does, they come from that place."

"Some of the things he's done." I take a deep breath. "Viv, did you know that Leon knew about the attack on your mother before it happened? He knew Lunora's father was sending people out to harass the wolves on the full moon. But he didn't do anything to stop it, because he thought it would keep your father busy while he was helping Lunora on her first night as a wolf."

Her eyes stare straight ahead at the highway and fill with

tears. "I knew," she says. "He involved me in his plans. I didn't have a wolf yet. So I'm the one who guarded Lunora during the first part of the night, when he was still out with the wolves in the field."

"What? He didn't tell me that. I confronted him about all this and he admitted everything—I thought it was everything —but he didn't mention you."

"He probably thought it wasn't his story to tell."

"Lunora said you didn't like her, because you had a crush on Leon yourself."

Now she laughs. "Oh. Well. Ha. That's not why I didn't like her. We just didn't get along. Sometimes people don't. You know how I say Leon has that dark place you can't touch? Lunora had it too, only it was bigger and also completely deranged. For Leon, I think that was a lot of the attraction. He was fascinated by her." She shakes her head. "That fascination is why I didn't like her. Leon was my best friend when I was growing up, that's what she took away from me. Did I have a romantic crush? Not really. Maybe. A little. In a way. But what I hated was that all of a sudden my best friend didn't seem to care about me anymore. I was just his annoying wolf-less kid sister tagging along. I wanted him to care about me again, so I'd do pretty much anything he asked me to. And then I'd hate myself for it. Because everything I did was just helping him move further away from me."

"So what happened that night? Did you and Lunora try to kill each other?"

"No, we didn't, which was lucky for me, it turns out. None of us actually knew how dangerous a bitten wolf could be on their first moon. But I did feel guilty. For going behind my parents' backs in the first place, and then after what happened to my mother, I felt so bad about it. I hated Lunora, hated my brother, even hated my father. I blamed him for making us go behind his back. For being so stubborn. Unreasonable, I thought at the time."

"At the time. You don't think that anymore?"

"Well, the Flint Savage outbreak has got me thinking that maybe my father was right. The taboo is there for a reason. You don't make a bitten wolf on purpose, no matter how good you think your reasons are. Because you might make a Flint Savage."

She inhales, as if she's about to say something more, but I hold up a hand.

"My phone is ringing, just a second." It's Steph.

"Abby." Her voice shakes. "Abby, where are you?"

"In a car with my aunt Viv, why?"

"Abby, my dad collapsed. He's in East Jefferson Hospital. He's in a coma. They're not sure he's going to wake up."

19

WEREWOLVES, THEY'RE EVERYWHERE IN THIS GODDAMNED TOWN

Viv drives me straight to the hospital. "If you need anything, call."

"I will."

"Oh, and, you might want to put on some pants and take off that fancy choker?"

I reach my hand up to my neck. I had sort of forgotten I was wearing anything other than a standard collar feed. "Wow, thanks. Except I don't have any pants."

"Here." She tosses me some sweats from the back seat. "These should fit okay if you roll up the cuffs. I just find that places like hospitals aren't very comfortable if you're a young woman dressed up for a hot night on the town." Slight smile. "Everybody assumes you're on drugs or something, it's weird, I've been there."

"Well, if I'm going to be sitting in hospital chairs I definitely don't want bare legs. Thanks, Auntie Viv." We hug.

"Best wishes, little one. I hope your loufrer's father is well."

Just inside the doors I find a restroom, stop to change clothes and wipe off most of the makeup. Viv was right, her sweats do fit me okay if I roll them up. I put the ruby choker into one of the boot pockets.

Sometimes you have to run off with nothing but the clothes on your back.

When I find the hospital room, Steph's dad is in a bed, unconscious and full of mysterious tubes. Steph's mom and Morgan are both sitting in weird awkward looking chairs, Steph's mom holding the baby. Steph and Irwin have been in here, but I don't see them.

"Abby, thank you for coming." Steph's mom rises and hugs me.

Terry holds out his hands and says "Bah-bee" with a weary sadness that seems very inappropriate for a kid barely a year old. I take him and hold him tight.

I make eye contact with Morgan. "Where are Steph and her boyfriend?"

"Steph and Irwin went to the Russian deli to get dinner, they're not back yet. Abby, could we go out and talk?"

"Sure." I hand the baby back to his grandma and we head into the hallway, find a private little alcove. "Abby, my father has pancreatic cancer. Pretty advanced, so he must have been sick for a while, even though he never said anything about it. According to the doctors, his prognosis is not good. They don't even expect him to wake up."

"That's rough."

"Abby. I'm going to ask you something, okay? Something big."

My gut lurches. I think I know where this is going. "What is it?"

"Would it cure his cancer if you were to, you know, if you were to bite him?"

I shake my head. "Morgan, I'm just not sure. There are so many things that could go wrong, and even if it works, well, after that he'd be a werewolf."

"And what's wrong with that?" He's angry. "I've spent a lot of time around your people in the last year. There's nothing wrong with being like you are. You call your abilities the 'gifts of the wolf,' don't you? Not the 'burdens of the wolf' or the 'curses of the wolf.'"

I sigh, frustrated. "Maybe you don't remember what you said to me at the party, because you were too drunk, but I remember. You want to be a bitten wolf yourself."

"And what's wrong with that? Abby? What exactly is wrong with that? The power of your people, it's amazing. Anybody would want it, once they'd seen it."

"Maybe that's true." I think about Flint Savage and his idea of charging money for it. And then I think about the traditional taboo against making a bitten wolf on purpose. It would be easier if I didn't have to make these decisions. If I already knew I wasn't going to do it. Because I don't want to do it. Maybe Steph's dad, to save his life, but Morgan? It doesn't feel right and I don't know how to explain why.

"Maybe," I say, reluctantly. "If we do this thing and your dad makes it through okay, maybe after that. I'd consider biting you."

"So you will bite my dad?"

"If Steph wants me to." I nod. "We should go to the Russian deli and talk to her."

"Yeah. We should." He turns grim. "If she's there."

"If she's there. Why do you think she's not there?"

"I don't know, she's been gone longer than I expected and isn't answering her phone."

"That doesn't mean anything." My heart pounds. "You know it doesn't mean anything."

"I guess there's only one way to find out."

We go back into the hospital room.

Morgan says, "Hey, Mom? Abby and I are going to go to the deli ourselves, do you want anything?"

"No, no thank you." She smiles. Wipes her eyes. "No, I'm fine."

In Morgan's truck we head to the Russian deli, which isn't far. There's a large eating area outside, people eating little dumplings in sour cream and a bright red soup made from beet. They look happy and the food smells good.

But I get a whiff of Strigoi, too, one of Beauregard's bitten wolf goons. Not too recent, but it worries me. What if the Strigoi have gone after Steph as a way of attacking the rougarou? And just how many Strigoi bitten wolves are there?

I call up the scent tracking app and drop an anchor for the bitten wolf. Morgan notices me.

"What are you doing?"

"Um, you know the Russian mobster guys, the Strigoi? Some of them are bitten wolves now."

"Where?" He looks around suspiciously.

"None of them are in here right now. Just their scent traces. We have this app, look. If you pick up on a scent, you drop an anchor like this, and if you follow it, it gets your route and sends it back to the server. The information from all our phones gets coordinated, so we get a complete scent picture."

"Wow, so high tech." He laughs a little. "Somehow I didn't expect that from y'all."

"Yeah, we use technology like other people, go figure." I make a quick circuit of the room just in case I missed something. "Morgan, Steph hasn't been here at all and Irwin hasn't been recently."

"They didn't even come here?" Morgan starts to get a bit panicked. "Really? That's not good. Where the hell are they? Are they drinking? I bet they're drinking. How do we find them?"

I think about it. "I have an idea. I'll get the wolves on it. You go back and help your mom with the baby."

He frowns. "You just want me to leave you here?"

"Morgan, you know that app I showed you? If we get three or four scent trackers working together with that app, we can cover a lot of ground quickly. I'll call Etienne, see who's available. Most of them know Steph, but if they don't, we can drop into the Bywater house and pick up a clothing item."

"You still have a key?"

"I do." I slap my red boots, just to make sure. Not only do I still have a key to the Bywater house, I still have a pricy ruby choker. "We'll find them, Morgan. We're good at this stuff."

"I suppose you are. Okay. But if you find her and you need any help, call me. All right?"

After he leaves, I sit down at a little table outside and call Etienne.

"Abby, hello. Vivienne has already stopped by with the Veneray clothing items."

"Did she? Good. But this isn't about that. My, uh, you know my loufrer Steph? Her father is sick in the hospital."

"Oh no! I'm so sorry to hear that."

"Yeah, well, she and her boyfriend left to get food at the Russian deli, supposedly, but they never actually made it here. And we don't know where they are so we think she might, uh, she might be drinking again. You know she has a problem with that."

"I do, yes. You want our help to find her?"

"If you could. If you could get the scent trackers on it."

"Of course. Where do we start?"

"Well, I don't know. I'm at the Russian deli, I'll probably start here, I saw a few bars in the neighborhood. If she's not here, she's probably in the Quarter, Marigny, or Bywater. But if she's not in any of those places, I really don't know. At that point she could be anywhere in town, I guess. They took Irwin's car, so maybe they went somewhere he likes. But I don't really know anything about him."

"Got it. We'll find her."

"Thanks, Etienne."

I hang up, feeling a little better knowing that Etienne is helping me.

If Etienne wanted to be pere, I would follow him.

Why am I thinking about that? Anyway, he can't be pere

without a wolf, I already know that. How can you be hunt leader if you can't lead the hunt?

I close my eyes for a minute, inhale deeply, trying to get a sense for whether Steph has been anywhere near here recently. No? Maybe? I have a sense, so subtle that it might be my imagination, she's—that way.

I drop an anchor, start walking. At first I'm convinced I must be going the wrong way, since this seems like it's all residential. But then, one of the houses has the words RUBY'S ROADHOUSE METAIRIE painted on the side. I see a red beer light in the window above the door. And I hear the sounds of a band tuning up, a couple of taps on a snare drum, a few strokes of an electric guitar. This is the kind of place Steph would go. It looks fun. Both of us are drawn to the sounds of a band tuning up.

But as I get closer, I realize she was here and left. There's a car in the lot that smells of them, must be Irwin's car, and they both left on foot—that way.

I close my eyes, get a firmer handle on her person scent, which always makes me think of dark blue velvet. But right now it's spiked through with the reek of alcohol. She was very drunk when she left here. It makes me sad, then angry, then sad again.

Their trail leads into a residential neighborhood, then to a small house that seems to be Irwin's. I knock on the door. No answer. I try calling Steph's phone again. Still no answer.

"Steph?" I call out louder. "Steph, are you in there?"

I hear voices, then a solid thump and breaking glass, like the sound of somebody falling over. "Steph! Steph!" I try the lock. It holds. I kick in the door, splintering the wood.

Steph is okay. She's standing up, not obviously injured. Looks like she knocked over a small end table and is now trying, with drunken clumsiness, to clean it up. She notices me, sparks in anger. "Abby, what the hell are you doing here? You just busted down his door."

"You didn't answer when I knocked and I heard a thump, I thought you might be hurt."

"The hell," she says, voice thick and slurred. "God damn it, you werewolves."

"Huh?" Irwin says. He's sitting on the couch holding a bottle of Russian vodka.

"Werewolves," Steph repeats, drunkenly, pointing at me and dropping to the couch, her own vodka bottle in hand. "Her."

"Steph, no," I say. "Steph, please. Please come home? I'll call us a car." I move to put my arm around her, but she shakes me off.

"No," she says, irritated. "I'm not going anywhere with you. We're fine. Just leave us the hell alone. Get out of here."

Irwin sips from his bottle, looking confused. "What was that about werewolves?"

"They're everywhere in this goddamned town," Steph says. She waves her free hand. "Everywhere. The goddamned-fucking loup-garou. They follow you around. Track you like prey. How did she know we were here, Irwin? She tracked us. And they're so violent, did you see what she did to your door?"

I know Steph is drunk, but she's giving me a hard, dull, angry look I've never seen from her before. I want to cry.

"Steph, please. The baby," I say. "Think about Terry."

"My mom has the baby," she says. She starts crying. "My mom has the baby. My mom can take care of the baby. My dad is dying, Abby did they tell you that? My dad is dying. Goddamned werewolves."

"Werewolves killed your father?" Irwin says, confused.

"They won't help," Steph says. She takes a step forward, leans into me with her foul Bourbon-Street breath, says "You won't help him will you? You won't do it."

"Won't do what, Steph?" But I think I already know. Steph had the same thought as Morgan. It's been scrambled by a bottle of vodka, but it's still there. Steph wants me to bite their father.

"After you sober up we'll talk about it."

"I'm sober," she says. Then laughs. "A little. I'm not as drunk as you think."

She takes a step forward. Then collapses forward, hitting her head on the coffee table but still somehow not spilling the vodka bottle. Blood pours down her face, a shallow forehead cut that bleeds and bleeds.

I call Etienne, and he and Nicolas show up with the car to take Steph to the hospital, leaving Irwin behind passed out on his couch. She's bleeding profusely from her forehead, only semi-conscious, and doesn't resist us. But then when we try to check her in, she wakes up a little more, gets really angry and starts yelling, and the hospital makes us take her away.

"Concussions can make people belligerent," Etienne says, apologetically, as we lead her out.

Still bleeding, we take her to the French Quarter maison, where we lay her out on the couch. She mumbles something unintelligible, then starts snoring. Etienne goes to fetch the first aid kit while Nicolas and I watch her.

"I'm sory," Nicolas says. "I'm really sorry this happened."

"Me too."

"I don't know much about recovery from alcohol addiction, is this going to set her back a lot?"

"I don't know. I don't know much about it either." I pause. "I thought you were supposed to keep concussed people awake for twenty-four hours?"

"That's mostly a myth," Nicolas says. "We shouldn't leave her entirely alone, but she can sleep. I'm not sure we could keep a drunk person awake anyway."

"Yeah, I don't know how to do that. In movies and stuff they use coffee but I don't think it actually works."

Etienne brings me the first aid kit and a warm, wet cloth I can press against her forehead until the bleeding stops.

"Do you need anything else?" Etienne asks.

"Maybe some sports drink or something? If she wakes up thirsty. Oh, and, um, maybe a bucket in case she wakes up sick."

He brings me those things. The sports drink is a very bright purple that reminds me of Lunora's magenta poison cocktail. For a while Etienne and Nic sit with me. When Steph's wound stops bleeding, they help me put a bandage on it. They ask me if I'll be okay on my own. I say yes. I move from the chair to the floor, prop myself against the couch so that I can feel the warmth of her body, and know instantly if she wakes up. Then I go to sleep.

"The baby, where's the baby!" Steph is sitting up straight, panicked, and I'm instantly awake too.

"Your mom and Morgan have Terry," I say.

"Oh, God." She looks ill, starts coughing, and I push the bucket into her hands. She uses it. A couple of times. It's one of the worst things I've ever smelled.

"Abby." She looks miserable, fingers the bandage, winces. "My God, what have I done?"

"It's okay, Steph. Irwin left the car at the bar, you walked to his house, that's where you hit your head."

"I don't remember." She starts crying. "I don't remember any of it. I don't even remember deciding to take the first drink. We were going to the Russian deli to get food. We were going to get food and bring it back because hospital food is so terrible and Irwin said we could get pierogies and..." She breaks down sobbing, while I stroke her hair. Then I lead her to the bathroom. She uses the toilet and the shower, with the door slightly propped open so I can rush in if she needs help.

I lead her back to the couch. She sips some of the sports

drink. Cautiously. Wincing, like the liquid hurts her. "I need to go back to sleep I think. I'm sorry. I'm really, really sorry."

"I know. Do you want a blanket?"

She gives me an incredulous look, a slight smile. "Sweetie, it's eighty degrees in here."

"I know, but... never mind. You just go back to sleep now."

I resume my place on the floor, check my text messages. Maybe if Steph recovers quickly enough I can catch the Seattle people today, before their plane leaves.

But my latest text from Deena drives every other thought from my head:

Scratch that, they moved up our flight to 1pm bcs of the hurricane

20

A POORLY ORGANIZED DEPRESSION

I go backwards through my texts from Deena, see that she was trying to arrange lunch for everybody at CharliQ's. But their flight to Seattle, originally scheduled for 7 p.m., is now leaving at 1 p.m. So they have to head off to the airport right now.

I sigh. That's the way everything seems to be going today. I grab one of the maison laptops and find hurricane information. Pax isn't a named hurricane yet, just a "poorly organized depression." But if it organizes, and keeps to its current course, it looks like a direct hit on New Orleans.

Traffic is already getting ridiculous as people leave town. There's no officially ordered evacuation, but after Katrina a lot of people don't wait around anymore, they just start driving north and west right away if they can. Outside, the air is heavy, hot, still. But it won't be still for long.

The members of the maison start gathering in the main room. It's awkward, with an unconscious Steph taking up the entire couch, but nobody says anything. They just glance her way, then sit on the floor.

Etienne says, "It looks like most of you have heard about the storm?" Nods all around. "And there's a really good chance it's going to hit right around the full moon tomorrow."

More nods. "We've had this happen before, the full moon and a hurricane at the same time, but not for quite a few years. Because of the Flint Savage outbreak, we really need to have the city maisons staffed, but it's voluntary. If any of you need to evacuate—"

"Where would we go?" Barney says. "It's not going to be better out at Bayou Galene, is it?"

"That's hard to say at this point. We won't really know which part of the state gets hit harder until the hurricane is closer to making landfall."

Nicolas and Vivienne enter. Nic says, "Are we making plans for tomorrow?"

Etienne nods. "We are. We're determining who's going to be in town, who's going to be in Bayou Galene, and who might want to relocate outside of the likely hurricane zone."

"I need to be in Bayou Galene," Vivienne says. "With my father."

"I'll be in town here," Nicolas says.

Etienne looks thoughtful. "Abby?"

"Town," I say.

There's some more discussion, but I'm distracted. Because Edison is standing outside.

I go out to confront him, have to stop and catch my breath. He looks so good in that scruffy jean jacket. Like he's going to invite me onto the back of his Harley and we'll ride off into the sunset to do crimes like Robin Hood. But I'm also annoyed. I fold my arms. "What are you doing here? Don't you have a plane to catch?"

"We wouldn't all fit in one car, so I got my own." He gestures at a car sitting across the street with its engine running.

"Wow. It's just waiting there while you talk to me. Don't they charge you for that?"

"They do." Shy smile as he looks down at his feet, blushing a little. "I have something I wanted to give you." Out of the pocket of his jacket, he pulls a white root vegetable tinged with magenta, hands it to me.

"Okay, way to make my day more surreal. You just handed me a turnip. Why did you just hand me a turnip?"

"Rutabaga." He laughs. Nervously. Why is he so nervous? "When I thought you were turning nineteen I had this thing planned. I was going to take you to a BDSM 101 class. Because last summer you seemed kind of interested when we went to that one club?"

Now I get embarrassed. "Uh, yeah, I guess I was kind of interested maybe."

"Me too. I thought it was something we could explore together. You know. Two total newbies? Making all the embarrassing mistakes together? Tying our knots wrong and applying incorrect terminology?"

"Using the equipment upside down?"

"Yeah. But the one thing I know about BDSM is that you need a safe word. Because BDSM involves role play, like, where you're saying 'no, no, no' as part of the, I think they call it a scene? You need something to say if you really do want it to stop. So it needs to be something that would never come up as part of the scenario. Something weird and non-sexy. And there's like, a sacred rule of BDSM that if you say the safe word everything stops immediately, no questions asked. If you're tied up they release you, if you're getting whipped they stop whipping you, if they're freaking you out by reading select Biblical passages they stop talking."

"Biblical passages? Just what kind of BDSM did you have planned, Edison?"

Another shy grin. "I don't know, I kind of had this idea that maybe it would help you process religious trauma if we did, like, inquisitor and witch scenarios? Maybe swapping who's who?"

I start laughing. Surreal, sweet, bizarre, ridiculous, I can't do anything other than laugh. "Okay. Bon Dieu. Yeah, sure, I would try that with you."

"So, I already had my safe word all picked out. And it's rutabaga."

"Yeah? I don't have a better one. So I guess it's my safe word too."

A much deeper, sexier smile, the wicked tempter grin I'm used to from him. "So that's our safe word. Until you're eighteen. Rutabaga."

I stare at the unglamorous vegetable in my hand. I'm so mad at him, but also so charmed. I try, for a moment, to stay mad, and trying to stay mad causes it to fail entirely. He's trying to protect me and himself, I guess. How can I be mad about that? We hug. "Okay, Edison. See you in a year."

He laughs. "We can see each other before then. I hope we will. Just, you know. Rutabaga."

"Okay. Yeah. Get on back to Seattle and make sure your buddy Reed survives his first night as a werewolf."

He waves, gets in the car. I watch it pull away, tossing the rutabaga from one hand to the other. Do I know what rutabagas taste like? Their smell is very mild. Similar to turnips and parsnips, which I'm pretty sure I have eaten. Now I wonder if I want to eat this particular rutabaga or if I want to find some way of hanging onto it forever.

A car pulls up, releases Roman. He seems frantic, highly stressed out. "Abby!" he says. "Is my son in there?"

"Yeah, you heard about the hurricane?"

He pauses, looks confused for a moment, then nods. "The hurricane, right."

"Why, what did you think I meant?"

He shakes his head. "The hurricane. I just—never mind. Is it okay if I go right in?"

"If you know the door combo." I grin slyly at him. "Do you know the door combo?"

"Door combo?" He looks confused again.

I point at the digital lock. "Digital lock. So if you show up naked you can still get inside."

"Oh." He laughs. "The things you people think of."

But we never have to enter the code because Raymond opens the door. "Dad. What are you doing here?"

"I need to take you back to Bayou Galene for the full moon," he says. "Before the hurricane."

Raymond frowns. "I was going to stay here. I've never seen a hurricane before."

"You'll see the hurricane in Bayou Galene," he says. "Come on, son. I want you by my side for this. To make sure you're safe. Don't make me stare you down."

Raymond rolls his eyes. "Fine. Let me go pack."

He leaves. Roman and I stand on the porch. "Are you going in?" I ask Roman.

He sighs. "I don't want Raymond to think I'm crowding him."

"Hmm, okay." I think for a moment. "You know, you said you got your hands on Flint Savage's notes about the injection technique, I'm curious about a few things."

He smirks knowingly. "Planning to make a bitten wolf yourself?"

"What? No. Of course not."

"You can tell me. Is it your loufrer? The one sleeping it off in there?"

"No." I pause. Take the plunge. "It's her father. He's dying of cancer. In a coma right now. And she and her brother have both asked me if I would do it. Bite their father, in the hope it will cure his cancer."

He smiles. "You're going to break the taboo."

"I guess, yeah. It wouldn't be my first time breaking a taboo."

"No. I suppose not. You must know that I had no idea of such a restriction when Rufus and I made Savage one of our pack. I don't know if I would have followed it, had I known. But I didn't know."

"Did you do it for money?"

"No." He's stern. "We were partners. At that time we trusted him. We thought he shared our vision."

"Yeah? What was that vision?"

"It was about fitness. And bringing wolf men together in a shared space that catered specially to our needs."

"Wolf men. No women?"

"Our original idea was that the male Hammerfit and the female Hammerfit would be separate facilities, in order to allow our customers to be casual about nudity. We had an idea that we would provide a more Scandinavian fitness experience."

"Scandinavians are casual about nudity?"

"They are. Quite."

"So you've been to Scandinavia?"

"Finland and Sweden. Lovely countries. I'd like to return someday. In Stockholm I caught a whiff of what I thought might be another wolf shifter, but I didn't have a chance to explore further. I think we might look for some of our kin in the far north, among the Saami people."

"Yeah? That sounds cool. I'd like to see Scandinavia. Of course I'd like to see anywhere, really. I want to see Brooklyn, where my grandmother came from. And Disneyland. I've been to Los Angeles but not Disneyland. Oh, and a volcano. I really want to see an active volcano. Don't they have those in Hawaii? I want to see lava."

"Well, you're young, there's plenty of—" He pauses. Looks sad. "Time, plenty of time. If you want to do the injection method, your saliva needs to be kept fresh. Warm. Mix it with a saline solution to make the injection process easier, but keep things close to body temperature. Exposure today, tomorrow, or the next day is best. Because of the hurricane you'll prob- ably want to make it the day after the full moon." He frowns thoughtfully for a moment, nods. "Definitely. You do not want to be shepherding a brand new bitten wolf tomorrow night."

"Good idea. And that'll work? The day after the full moon?"

"It works as well as the day before. Before the injection do a scratch test. Shallow scratch, rub a very small amount of saliva into it, watch for a strong immediate reaction, which might indicate an allergy. It won't be enough to cause a change. Everything else, I think you know, you've helped people through their first full moon before."

I nod. "Is my own saliva best? If he's allergic, will he be allergic to all wolves or just me?"

He shakes his head. "That I don't know. Savage always used only his own saliva."

Raymond comes out carrying a backpack. "Ready."

"Great, come on." He steers the boy away, stops, turns back toward me with a slight smile. "Good luck, Abby."

I watch them go, then head inside. Steph is awake and drinking some of Etienne's café au lait. He's the only one who always makes it with chicory. "Abby," she says. She looks miserable, but more like herself. "I was just talking to my brother. We need to get to the hospital as soon as possible."

"We do?"

"My father. He's declining rapidly. He might not have much time."

21

THE HOSPITAL

My brother Nicolas drives us to the hospital.

"Do you want company?"

"No, that's fine, thanks." I would welcome him most of the time, but I don't want any Varger nearby when I talk to Steph and Morgan about breaking the taboo. "You can just drop us in the loading zone here."

Once we're out of the car, I pull Steph aside, into a shaded area. "Steph, I don't know if you remember——"

"If it happened last night? Probably not."

"Morgan asked me if I would bite your father."

"If you would bite him?" She looks horrified and confused. "Why would you do that?"

"In the hope of making him a werewolf and the hope that would cure his illness."

Comprehension dawns. "Oh. Oh." She looks upset. "Was I on board with this?"

"It was hard to tell. Are you?"

She paces around looking physically uncomfortable. "I. Wow. I don't know. I really don't. How——how likely is it to—do you think it would actually work?"

"It's hard to say. It might. That's the best I can do."

"Oh God." She runs her hands through her hair. Presses up against the wall of the hospital. Sinks against it. "This is really it, huh? He's basically going to die right now if you don't do anything."

"It's hard to say. My brother Roman said it would be better to bite him on the day after the full moon, hoping the hurricane will have passed by then, but we might not have that much time."

"No. No, we might not. God." She buries her face in her hands for a moment, then raises her head, looks me right in the eyes. "Abby, you have to. I think. If it could save him? You have to try. It's like an experimental cure, right? At least it won't bankrupt us." Small sad smile.

"So you want me to do it? I will."

"Oh, God." She gives me a shaky smile. "This is really not where I saw things going a couple of days ago when we were having dinner."

"No. Me neither."

"So how do we do this? You can't just transform right there in the hospital can you?"

"I don't have to. After the Flint Savage outbreak, we know that the injection technique works. I just need to, uh, drool in a cup and have a hypodermic handy."

She laughs, weakly. "Well. Let's see what we can do about that."

We enter the hospital. There's a medical supply shop that has hypodermics and saline solution.

Her father's room is full when we try to enter. Steph and Morgan kick out a few of his musician buddies. They're solemn. Holding their hats. They salute us when they leave. "When he passes, let us know, we'll give him the biggest second line this town has ever seen," one of them says.

"We will, thank you." Steph hugs them, they leave. Steph holds her mother for a long time, then says, "Mom, you've been up all night, you're exhausted, you should go home and get a little sleep, Morgan and I have got it for now."

"I can't," she says, swaying on her feet. "I have to be here if he passes. I can't—I can't just let him go."

"Just a couple of hours, Mom," Morgan says. "The baby needs a break too, he's been at the hospital all night."

"The baby, right." She frowns, chews her lower lip. "I'll call Lula Mae Hebert from church, she's always asking about the baby, she'll help."

"She'll help," Morgan says. "I'll call you a car, okay? You shouldn't drive this tired."

"No. No, I shouldn't. I guess you're right."

After Steph's mom and Terry have been successfully sent back to the Bywater house, it's just me, Steph, Morgan, and their dad, unconscious.

Morgan says, "Steph, how are you feeling?"

"Hungover. Abby told me you asked about our father."

"She did?"

"About. You know. Biting him?"

"Oh, that, right, right. Well?"

"I think she should do it."

"Okay." He nods. "Okay, so, it's happening now? Right now?"

"I'd wait until after the hurricane, but we're not sure he'll survive that long are we?"

"They kill people during hurricanes," Morgan says. "If they think they're terminal anyway? They just unplug 'em. No matter what the family says. It's now or never."

"All right." I glance up at the globe of camera in the corner. "We should obscure what I'm doing from the camera. I need to do a scratch test."

We arrange ourselves, tight together, holding hands, like we're praying. I hope we're obscured from the camera. Even more so, I hope nobody is paying attention, because everything I'm about to do would look extremely suspicious.

"You need a knife?" Morgan holds out his enormous red Swiss Army knife. I accept, use a sawblade that I think is designed for scaling fish, scrape it across the skin of his father's arm, avoiding all the many tubes going in and out. Then, feeling a bit ridiculous, I lick the wound.

Nothing.

"Okay, no allergic reaction, that's good. I'm going to drool into a cup now, this is going to look weird."

Drool, saline, hypodermic. I hold it up. "Steph? Morgan? This is your last chance to change your mind. There's no going backwards. I can't un-inject him. And the cure Edison used, I don't have any of that available right now. So this is really it."

"Do it," Steph says.

I inject. I've injected people before, bitten wolves deep into the first moon frenzy, but those injections felt like doing battle. This seems different and I'm worried I'm doing it wrong. But it seems to go okay. I pocket the hypodermic, and wait.

"When do we know if it's working?" Steph says.

"I don't know."

"Is he going to wake up before tomorrow night? Because getting him to a safe spot might be trouble if he's still in the coma, they won't want to let us take him out of here," Morgan says.

"I don't know, I said. I don't know how long it will take."

"He looks the same," Steph says. She sounds frustrated. "He looks just the same."

"I keep telling you I don't know how long it will take. I've never done this before."

"Never?" Steph looks alarmed. "I thought you had. Haven't you? What about George?"

"That was an actual bite and it wasn't on purpose. I bit my dad on purpose, but that was also an actual bite. I've never injected anyone before."

"You bit your dad?" Morgan frowns at me. "Why did you bite your dad? Isn't he a born wolf?"

"Yeah, but he had a head injury that prevents transformation. If that happens, you can restart the transformation by getting bit by another born wolf? But it doesn't always work. So he'd been going around getting his kids to bite him, then my bite finally did the trick." I laugh. "Okay, that sounds really weird, doesn't it?"

"So that means your bite is a good bite?" Morgan says, anxiously. "Like, a strong bite?"

"I don't know if it works like that, exactly."

"How does it work exactly?" Steph asks. She's starting to get freaked out, I can tell. "What's actually going to happen to him?"

Now I'm getting frustrated. "Steph, Morgan, I already gave you the last chance to say no, I can't un-bite him now, why weren't you asking me these questions five minutes ago?"

"I don't know!" Steph says. She runs her hands through her hair. "God, my head hurts. I shouldn't have to make these kinds of decisions with a hangover."

"And whose fault is that?" Morgan says.

"Irwin," she says. "I shouldn't date ex-drinkers anymore. If they fall off the wagon, they take me with them."

"Irwin's fault," Morgan says. "Right. He held a gun to your head?"

"Morgan, that is not the point! Anyway, don't act like you're—you were so drunk after Abby's birthday party that we had to carry you home!"

"This isn't about me, Steph! Anyway, I was at a party and I was walking distance from my house and everybody knew where I was. You told us you were going to the Russian deli for dinner and Abby says you never even went there at all! She had to track you!"

"Oh." She frowns. "I wondered why I was at the loup-garou house. Did you all track me by scent?"

"We did." I stare at the floor, flashing back on her face, her voice, that strange dull anger, all directed at me.

The god-damned-fucking loup-garou.

"I'm sorry you had to do that."

"Stephanie, girl, is that you I hear?"

Her father's voice. Clear. Strong.

We all turn. His eyes are open

"It's me, Dad," Steph says, taking his hands, tears beginning to stream down her face. "It's me."

22

SECOND LINE

Since Steph's dad is sitting up and talking, the hospital lets us take him home without too much fuss, but they're very concerned that he needs to come back after the hurricane and talk about a cancer treatment plan. He nods agreeably but when we get him in Morgan's truck he sighs.

"Kids? I know what the doctors say, but I just don't know about all that cancer treatment business. Eat up all that money we got from the Seattle house, and for what? Another couple of years on this earth? Is that worth it? Your lives are just beginning."

"Dad," Steph says. "We have something important to tell you." She glances at me. "Abby, do you want to show him?"

"Here in the car? Can't we park somewhere first?"

"We'll need privacy," Morgan says.

"What about the maison courtyard?"

"You want me to park in the Quarter?" Morgan is incredulous. "The traffic is already getting pretty bad."

"Okay, what about your house?"

"Mom's friend Lula Mae is probably going to be there," Morgan says.

"Can't we just, you know, tell her to leave for a few

minutes? It doesn't actually take that long. And your mom probably should be there too."

"She should," Steph says. "Mom needs to know."

"Well, I don't know what y'all got planned, but it sounds pretty exciting," Steph's dad says, with a small, nervous laugh.

We get to the house and find that Lula Mae, who's been up all night with a teething baby and is starting to get worried about the hurricane, is only too happy to get sent home.

"Thank you so much," Steph tells her. "This means a lot to us."

"So glad to help," she says. She takes Mr. Marchande's hands fervently. "And it's so good to see you up and walking around, Roderick, I was praying for you, God answers. Bless you!"

"God, right," I mutter, under my breath. Steph gives me a warning look.

"Take care of yourself Lula Mae," Steph's father says. He takes the baby from her and starts trying to make him laugh.

Steph's mom, asleep on the couch, stirs. "Roderick! Is that you? Oh, Rod!" She embraces him passionately. "I was so scared I'd never hear your voice again. Is this a dream?"

"Maybe I died after all and went to heaven," Steph's dad says, half-jokingly. "What do you all think?"

"I'm pretty sure I'm not dead," Morgan says.

"Good, if you're not dead, the rest of us probably aren't either," I say. "Steph, is it time?"

"I guess it is." She takes Terry from her father. "Dad? Mom? Abby has something pretty extraordinary to show you. And once you've seen it, we've got a lot to talk about." She turns to me. "Abby? You ready?"

"Ready." I sigh. Close my eyes. Reach deep inside. The wolf is right there, easy to find. I invite her to show herself and she yawns, stretches —

We shake ourselves out of our clothes, yawn, let out a howl: well, here we are.

Pad over to each one of our family in turn, stick our nose into their hands, a greeting. Then back to our pile of clothing, curl up and—

I stand, awkwardly, holding my clothes in front of me. "Excuse me a second." I scoot into the bathroom, get dressed properly. Still wearing Viv's sweats. I come out. "I suppose you have questions?"

Everyone is standing there, looking stunned, blank. The first person to actually react to me is Terry, who squeals excitedly and holds out his hands toward me. "Bah-bee woof-woof!" he says. "Woof-woof!"

I take him from Steph, who doesn't resist. "The baby gets it," I say, whirling him through the air briefly, while he laughs. But I'm a little disturbed that Steph and Morgan seem so stunned. They know what I am. They've seen the wolf before. What's the problem?

Morgan speaks up next. "Well, you all saw that, right? Abby turned into a big red wolf, and then back into a little red-haired girl?"

"Loup-garou," Steph's dad says. He's smiling a little. "I'll be damned."

"I need to sit down." Steph's mom collapses onto the couch, fanning herself with a church program.

"Yeah, Dad, they're real," Steph says. "And there's more."

"More? You don't say."

Steph's mom continues to fan herself. "My goodness. My goodness. Miss Abby, have you been a loup-garou this whole time or did it just come on you all sudden-like?"

"This whole time, Mrs. Marchande."

"Well. My goodness. What a world. No wonder you—well. What about your people out there in the bayou, do they know about this loup-garou business?"

"They're all loup-garous too, Mrs. Marchande."

"They are? My goodness. You don't say. Even your grandfather?"

"Especially my grandfather, Mrs. Marchande. He's the head loup-garou."

"Well, now. He's a lovely man, your grandfather," she says. "A lovely man. Are all loup-garous like that? Why do we fear them so much?"

"A loup-garou has a lot of power to do violence, and power can be misused. But overall we're just like other people. Some good, some bad."

"Of course, of course," she says.

"We have gifts, too," I say. "Gifts of healing. It might be our most important power."

"Healing? Laying on of hands? You call out to God?"

"No, not like that. We heal ourselves. A loup-garou can heal all kinds of things that would kill a normal person. Injury. And also illness."

"Illness." Her face goes blank with wonder. "Oh my. Are you saying what I think you're saying?"

I nod. "We can make more loup-garous with a bite. It doesn't always work, but if it does, it means, the bitten wolf gets all the gifts."

"Child, you have to do it!" she says. "Right now! You have to bite him!"

"Well, hold on now," Steph's dad says. "What's involved in all this? What does it mean to become a loup-garou? There's got to be more to it than just healing, otherwise everybody in the whole world would become a loup-garou. We wouldn't have hospitals anymore, we'd just have places you could go to get bitten."

"There's not that many of us to start with," I say. "My brother Nicolas, he's a loup-garou, but he's also an epidemiologist, and he's talked about that. There's almost eight billion people on the planet and probably less than a thousand loup-garous, even including all the bitten."

He nods thoughtfully. "All right. And why aren't there more of y'all?"

I think about it. I don't know if I can explain the taboo, and take a different tactic. "Well, you know, the bite doesn't always work. And, um, the circumstances—because I can turn into the wolf at will, I can bite you on purpose. But most loup-garous can't do that. So usually a loup-garou only bites when they're in a fight."

"Ah." He nods thoughtfully. "So what's going to happen to me?"

"She hasn't bit you yet, Roderick," Steph's mom says.

He shakes his head. "No, Emalee, I don't think that's true. I think it was her bite that woke me up out of that coma." He makes sustained eye contact with me. Not flashing, not yet, but getting there.

I nod. "That's right, Mr. Marchande."

"We asked her to," Steph says. "Morgan and I. We didn't think you'd make it through the next few days otherwise. I'm sorry. But if you're upset, blame us, it was our call. Abby just did what we asked her to."

Steph's dad sighs. "I don't know how to feel about that, children. I really don't."

"We thought of it as being like an experimental treatment," Steph says. "We're next of kin, we gave permission."

"You didn't ask my wife, though."

"I would have said yes," she says. A defiant lift to her head. "You better believe it. I would have said yes, child, you go on and bite him with your big old loup-garou teeth. I would. If it might save him. You do it." She turns to me. "Is it going to save him? Do you think?"

"It's hard to say. The full moon is tomorrow and with the hurricane, I don't know what's going to happen. Morgan, if you can help me steer him through? I can stay human, that'll increase his chances, Mrs. Marchande. But I'm sorry, there's no guarantee."

"No there isn't," she says. "No guarantee about tomorrow. Ever. So we do it today. I'm gonna call up all our friends, anybody who's not leaving town before the hurricane. I'm gonna call them up and we're gonna have ourselves a party."

And that's what we do, for the rest of the day. We have a party. Invite all their friends who are still in town.

After a while, the rain lets up for a time and some of his musician friends decide we're going to have the second line right now, "Why wait until he's gone? We can just have another one then." They start parading through the neighborhood, playing all the old New Orleans classics, Mardi Gras songs, party songs. Steph's dad is a keyboard player, which isn't a typical part of a marching band, but he pulls out a thing called a melodica, a small keyboard you blow into that sounds like a mobile pipe organ, and he makes it work.

We pick up people from around the neighborhood who hear the music and come out to join, sometimes playing their own instruments, more often just dancing, waving their fancy parasols up and down, handing beers to the people in the parade. It's so much fun that I almost forget to be sad. But we know he's saying goodbye. Because even if he lives, even if it all works out exactly the way we want it to, everything from now on is going to be different.

23

HURRICANE PAX

On the morning of the full moon, the weather in New Orleans has been getting steadily worse. Around eleven a.m. they call it: we are now being hammered by Hurricane Pax, no longer a poorly organized depression. Steph's boyfriend Irwin stops by the house. He's apologetic and Steph is cold toward him. So maybe he's her ex-boyfriend now.

With Morgan and Steph's dad we talk logistics, pick City Park as our site. There's a large forested area that should have plenty of space to run around and animals to hunt. During a hurricane, we assume nobody is going to be using the park for entertainment purposes.

I go to check in at the Quarter maison. I have the uncomfortable feeling that I'm recreating my father's mistakes from forty years ago, isolating from the other wolves in order to steer my own bitten progeny through his first night. But I can't tell them what I'm doing, can I? Or can I?

I don't really know how the senior wolves, like Etienne or my brother Nicolas, feel about the taboo. Would they understand? Or would they try to stop me? And would that compromise my ability to help Steph's dad?

"Abby!" Etienne greets me at the door. "We thought

maybe you'd changed your mind and left town with your loufrer. You haven't been answering your phone."

"Sorry. I was at the hospital."

"I'm sorry." He hugs me. "It's rough to have everything happening all at once like that."

"Yeah." I nod. "Everything is going wrong at the same time, it's like we've unleased a curse."

He looks thoughtful. "If you wish, you can spend the night protecting your loufrer family, rather than working here at the maison."

"What, really? You really think that would be okay?"

"Of course. I've been talking with the Garden District maison and we believe that the lack of tourists here in town means that not only are we unlikely to get any new bitten wolves, even if we do, they won't be in a position to cause much trouble. The malls are closed. There isn't a Saints game. Nobody is partying on Bourbon Street."

"I guess you're right. There isn't going to be the kind of public gathering that would make an unexpected wolf really dangerous." I smile, suddenly relieved, and a little suspicious. I just got leave to do exactly what I want: protect Steph's family tonight instead of working for the maison.

"Anyway, I'll be here and I'll be staying human," Babette says, raising a hand. "So you don't have to worry about it migarou, we have everything covered."

"You hope you'll be staying human," Etienne says, gently. "It's your first time, Babette, you still don't know for sure it will work."

She shrugs and goes back to reading on her phone.

"What about Nicolas?" I ask. "Barney? Did they go to Bayou Galene?"

"No, Barney is taking a nap," Babette says. "I'm not sure what Nic is doing right now but he didn't mention leaving town, so I'll assume he's going to be here."

"Hey, Babette? If you're staying human, you want to have

something rigged up for in case you go to wolf form after all. Like a little backpack where you can put your phone and some hypodermics full of sedative."

"A little backpack?" She laughs. "Seriously, migarou?"

"I need one myself, come on."

We spend the next couple of hours sewing ourselves little backpacks with elastic straps, wear them under loose sweatshirts.

"It feels a bit odd but I can live with it," she says, wriggling her shoulders. Smiles.

"We're ready for the moon, I guess."

"Not quite," she says. "If we're both staying human, we need to do something about our hair. French braids?"

"French braids, of course."

We braid each other's hair, which is just about the only thing that could have calmed me down even a little.

"You're really good at this," I say, testing the braid. It's tight and sure.

"So are you." She grins, testing the braids by moving her head around. "I feel like one of those wrestling women, you know. Not the theatrical ones, the one who wrestle in cages. The theatrical ones never braid their hair, that's how you can tell it's a performance. A real warrior braids their hair."

"Sorry, I don't watch wrestling."

"No? You might like it. A bit like our sparring. But not so…" She gestures. "Kinetic, I suppose you would say. They don't throw each other around. You know, if there were a type of wrestling that was all wolves, it would be something to see."

"Would it? I guess. But who would watch it?"

"Oh, you see, we would pretend it was the theatrical kind of wrestling. We would have to pretend we were faking it."

I laugh. "Then why bother?"

"Wolves would know the difference."

We're sitting up in the alcove where my chaise longue bed is set up, staring out at the wild weather. Babette says, "It seems like deepest night already doesn't it? The sky is so dark and ominous. The rain pounds, the wind howls."

"It's true. I should get back to my loufrer."

She smiles a little sadly. "Of course. You need to protect him through his first night."

"What? What are you talking about?"

"Migarou." She shakes her head. "You aren't as stealthy as you think. With your loufrer's father dying, it was obvious what you would do. And I understand."

"Oh no. Does Etienne know?"

"He won't say, if he does. You're safe." She hugs me. "Cher, the taboo may have protected us once, but in the days of the Flint Savage outbreak, what's the point? You might as well try to save a life. So go. Take him to City Park. That is your job, after all. To look after any new bitten wolves tonight. It doesn't matter so much if you're the one who bit him, does it?"

I hug her enthusiastically. "Thank you, Babette. Thank you. I appreciate it."

I get ready to walk through the gathering storm back to Steph's family. The streets are already flooding, so I take off Grandma's boots, put my ID and phone into a plastic bag, roll up my pantlegs. I hand the boots to Babette. "If you could put these in a safe place?"

She nods, sniffs at them. "Your grandmother's perfume is still there, but what is that?" She unzips the other pouch and pulls out the ruby choker. "Bon Dieu, where did you get this?"

"Oh. I kind of forgot about that. It came from the Veneray. You should ask Viv what to do with it."

"It's gorgeous," she says, holding it up to her neck.

"Yeah, but it might be cursed."

"Cursed? Because it looks like a slit throat?"

"Because there might be a Veneray who thinks it was stolen and is looking for it."

"Ah, yes." She puts it back in the pouch, zips it again.

"Well, into the storm."

"Good luck." We hug, and I leave to wade through my first hurricane in the city.

It's never taken me so long to walk to Steph's place from the maison, and every moment it seems like the wind blows harder and the flooding gets deeper. I knew I was going to get soaked and didn't bother trying to protect myself against the rain, but I think that was a mistake. The rain is pelting me hard and I think I'd feel better with a raincoat even if I got just as soaked.

It's not cold, but even so, the strong wind and soaking rain make me feel chilled. Like being in a swimming pool that isn't quite warm enough.

When I knock on the door of their house, Steph's dad opens it.

"Well, look what the storm blew in," he says, good-humoredly. "Guess it's pretty bad out there?"

"It is."

Morgan frowns. "Should we—do you think—we can wait for the full moon inside my truck?"

"We can. But we should probably not be in the truck when the moon rises. Mr. Marchande, I have some sedative that will help calm you down, but a lot of the time the new wolf goes into a kind of frenzy."

"A frenzy? That doesn't sound good."

"It's mostly driven by the new hunting instinct. As long as you can run and chase after something, you'll be fine, but if you're confined, that's when the frenzy happens."

"Will we know when the moon is coming?"

"We will. I'll feel it. Probably you too. Why don't we plan on waiting in the car until it's just about time, then we'll both get out. If you start to change, I'll give you that sedative. Not until you start to change, though. The formula is too strong, if you're not actually a bitten wolf, it might kill you. Then I'll change shape myself and we can hunt together. Your first night will go better if you hunt with a senior wolf."

"Senior wolf." He snorts. "You're seventeen."

"But I've been a wolf longer than you." I smile. "That's what counts."

"All right, let's go," Morgan says. "I'm getting nervous, if we don't leave soon, the flooding will be too deep even for my truck."

He was right, there are places where the water is several feet deep and if the truck wasn't raised up so high, we wouldn't be able to make it through. Visibility is terrible. We're staring at the world through a solid sheet of water. If there were any traffic, or if he didn't know the streets so well, we'd probably get into an accident or drive right off the road.

City Park has a gate at the entrance, but Morgan just sighs and drives around it. "Priorities," he says. We probably ruin some landscaping, but after a major hurricane, who's going to notice?

Deep into the park we find some unflooded high ground and wait for moonrise. Silent, for a while. I think about my Seattle friends, probably sitting with Reed just like this, waiting.

Steph's dad says, "Abby, tell me what it's like to be a loup-garou."

"In what sense?"

"Do you like it?"

"I don't know. I guess." I try to answer honestly. "I don't really have anything to compare it to. Because I was born to it, I was always a loup-garou, even before I knew I was. Before I changed shape for the first time, the wolf was already a part of me."

"Is that so, huh? Born to it. But me, I got bit. By you. Right?"

"That's right, Dad," Morgan says. "Two kinds of wolves. Two kinds of loup-garou. Born and bitten."

"You don't say." More silence. Then he says, "I suppose that means your family who are loup-garou, your grandfather and that brother you mentioned, they were born to it as well?"

"That's right."

"Do you know other wolves who came to it by getting bitten?"

"Sure, quite a few."

"And how do they feel about it?"

"Pretty good." Smiling, I can answer honestly. "I never met a bitten wolf who really regretted it."

Morgan gives me a look. "Hmm, imagine that. Everybody you know who becomes a bitten wolf is happy about it."

"If they make it through the first night," I say. "Not everybody makes it. We talked about this. Sorry Mr. Marchande, not to scare you or anything. But the first night can be rough."

He nods. "I do consider myself adequately warned." Another pause. A particularly strong gust of wind rocks the truck back and forth. He asks, "Why the first night, in particular? What makes that one night so special?"

"Well, we don't know for sure, but the theory, from the more science-minded wolves I know, is that it's mostly because your brain has to make so many adjustments, and the process of doing that is very, uh, chaotic? But by the second moon, those changes are mostly already made. We like to help you through the first three moons if we can, that's considered ideal, but the really crucial one is the first one."

"Is that a fact," he says. Nodding. Thoughtful. He's obviously still having a bit of trouble believing all this is real.

That's how it goes, when you're not raised in a wolf culture. There's always a part of me that thinks it can't possibly be real. But is it good or bad? That's the thing I don't know. Are we being selfish, trying to hoard the gifts of the wolf only for those born to it? Or are we being sensible? What would it really look like, if a significant percentage of the population became bitten wolves? What kind of a world would that be? More cruel or less cruel? More brutal or less brutal? Steph was put off by the violence of the trauma morph trial, but regular humans are the ones who fight wars and slaughter people by the millions. Wolf violence has an intimacy to it. Humans mass-produce death.

I have a brief, horrific vision of a war zone, weapons exploding, children on fire running, screaming—

I startle awake. I hadn't realized I was falling asleep.

"Moon's getting close isn't it," Steph's dad says.

"It is," I say.

"Time to get out?"

"Time to get out."

"What should I be doing?" Morgan asks.

"Just, be alert, I guess. I don't really know what's going to happen."

He nods. Hugs his father. "Good luck, Dad."

"Thanks, son. Hope to see you in the morning. But if I don't—" He gets teary. "If I don't, you should know you've been a good son to me, and I appreciate this wolf thing, that it's you doing the best you know how. But if it fails, you should know, I had a good life. With all of you. And I'm glad I got to spend that time with my grandson."

More hugs, then we get out of the car, bracing ourselves against the wind and the rain. I'm grateful for Babette's firm, assured French braiding, because otherwise my hair would be getting in my eyes and mouth.

But something is wrong. A smell. It's not a right smell. Some kind of chemical? Blood. Dead meat.

"Huh. It smells like somebody's been dragging a big deer carcass around," I say.

Steph's dad frowns at me. "Is that what that is?"

And it starts.

24

THE CULL

Born wolves usually change in an instant, so fast, it can't be observed with the naked eye. Bitten wolves change slower, more like shape shifters in the movies. Steph's dad collapses, panting heavily, begins to twitch, and moan. It doesn't sound good. Bitten wolves usually seem pretty happy with their situation, but from the outside, listening to them, it sounds like they're being tortured.

I watch as he gradually shakes and shivers his way into becoming a gray-furred wolf with golden eyes. Earlier, I thought I might transform and hunt with him, but I'm too worried by those odd smells: the chemicals and the deer carcass. I want to keep my human brain active, figure it out.

Once Steph's father is fully transformed and shaken out of his clothing, he runs off in the direction of the deer carcass. I run after him. Other bitten wolves are approaching too, drawn by the smell.

Lured by it.

This is a trap.

"Veneray." I say it out loud, like a curse, and put on a fresh burst of speed. This is the next battle in that war. My father didn't scare them in the right way at all. He scared them the wrong way. They're escalating.

Up ahead, a ruined structure, concrete, two deer carcasses sprawled across it, a dozen wolves eating, mostly bitten. Is the meat poisoned? Is that what's causing that weird chemical smell? I take out my phone, text Etienne, Babette, Barney:

> Something weird going down in City Park
> Bitten wolves lured here with deer carcasses
> Chemical smell

I sigh. Maybe I'll get in trouble for breaking the taboo and biting Steph's dad, but that doesn't matter now. Whatever is going on here, I need backup.

A noise catches my attention and I put the phone away. Try to identify the noise. Hard, because the hurricane is pretty noisy, it could have just been some debris flying—

Spot something that looks like a giant duck blind, as it flaps in the wind. A big tarp covering up a white truck.

That sound again. Metallic.

A sharp explosive sound, hot stink of gunpowder, a familiar pain: I've been shot. Abdomen. Probably not fatal even if I were a normal human. I shake off the pain and run at full speed in the direction the bullet came from, that truck behind the duck blind, leap onto the top of it. Below me, a male voice says, "My God, what is that thing up there, is that one of them?"

The men shoot up through the roof, smell of their panic yellow and pungent, wild shots failing to hit me and making my job, punching through the roof, that much easier.

"What are you doing here?" I demand. But I didn't make eye contact first, it has no force.

"Shit, shit, shit," one of them is gibbering, reaching for a different weapon, one that looks like a rocket launcher. Probably is a rocket launcher. Instinctively, I reach out to snap his neck before he can aim.

The other man is moaning, swooning and bloody, victim of a wild shot from his companion.

Eye contact. Strong flash. "What are you doing here?"

"It's a cull," he says, blankly. "They sent us to do a cull."

"Who's they? Who's us?"

"Order from the mayor's office to Nola PD. The rabid dog problem has gotten out of control the last few months, so we're taking out a bunch of them tonight."

"Rabid dog problem? You think you're killing rabid dogs?"

"No, not ordinary dogs." The fear in his sweat oozes stronger. "Monsters."

"Monsters. You mean the loup-garou? Shape-shifters? People?" My voice comes out in a fierce growl.

"Monsters," he says, softly.

I hear another vehicle approaching. I can't leave this guy free, should I kill him? I need to kill him, don't I? Snap his neck? I killed his buddy.

But wait. I might need to ask him some more questions. I shouldn't kill him yet. But I can't let him go free either.

Fretting, fretting. What to do? No wonder Leon just kills people.

The car stops. Etienne and Babette get out. "Abby? Abby, where are you?"

I don't have time. Break all the bones in the man's trigger hand, like I did to Junior. Break one of his ankles for good measure. He moans in pain but he's alive.

I stand up so that they can see me over the top of the car. "Etienne, Babette, look out! This is some kind of ambush."

A volley of explosions, white light, acrid smoke, and a smell like rotten garlic. I don't see either Etienne or Babette anymore, they're lost in the smoke. The wolves that were hit directly with this new ammunition are burning, howling in pain, a thin shrill keening that spindles all my nerves like a silver dagger. Smell of burning wolf hair and scorched flesh.

A scream emerges from my throat, seemingly without choice. I scramble to where I saw Etienne and Babette fall.

Etienne is lying on the ground, his body a bloody, burned mess, still burning. I smother the flames with mud, which stops the burning, but he's badly hurt and doesn't seem to be healing at all. "Abby," he says. Weak smile. "It's…" He trails off. Eyes staring blankly. No breath. No heartbeat.

But he can't be dead, not one of our people.

(Not even one with a wolf five years gone?)

(Shut up shut up shut up)

What do I do? I have competing instincts, to stay with him, and to hunt our enemies.

Enemies. He can't possibly heal if they don't stop shooting at him.

I run toward the direction the other shots came from, dodge another volley of those burning, explosive shells. I catch up with Babette, on the ground, both legs shattered and burning. I slather mud over the flames and they go out. She nods gratefully. "White phosphorus, I think that's what this is. You have to…" She passes out, but she's breathing. Again I have competing instincts, to find Steph's dad now and help him, or to hunt our enemies.

Enemies. Before I can help the wounded, I have to stop them from getting more wounded. A gust of wind clears away some of the foul smoke, and I spot the other concealed truck. If I just keep running toward them in this trajectory, they'll get me the way they got Babette.

I get an idea. I run the opposite way, back to the truck I already attacked, thinking I'm going to grab the rocket launcher. Can I figure out how to use it? I've seen them used in movies and TV, never in real life. But they're not designed to be complicated. I wish I had Morgan. But it would take time to get Morgan here, and I need to stop them now. Maybe forget the rocket launcher? They also have a regular gun. I've fired a regular gun before.

Damn it, I'm not sure what to do now.

I open the door of the truck, shove out the injured man, who shrieks again as his broken hand and foot make contact with the ground. The keys are in the lock. I don't have my license yet, but I do know, in a general way, how to drive.

Ignoring the dead man (the man I killed) I start up the engine, drive it through the grass until I can see a clear path between me and the other truck. I think about it for a moment, leave the engine running in neutral, take the rocket launcher and wedge it in to where it will press down hard on the accelerator, as the engine revs in neutral.

Put it back in drive. As it starts moving forward, I leap out, land with a roll. Back on my feet, running toward Babette. If I did this right, the trucks are going to crash into each other, which will hopefully injure the humans enough to keep them from firing more of the white phosphorus at the wolves.

Brilliant white shrapnel and a vast cloud of choking smoke explode as the trucks collide. I crouch down to protect myself, rush forward in a crouch, find Babette lying where I left her, hit by a couple of small pieces of the burning substance, but otherwise okay, starting to get that gaunt look we have sometimes after healing severe injuries.

"You made it go boom," she says, with a slight smile.

I smother the places where her skin is burning. "Will you be okay here for a bit while I find Steph's dad?"

"Well you did blow up the bad guys."

"Right, but I don't know that there aren't more bad guys. Babette, it's bad, I got info from one of them, he said the mayor's office sent the Nola PD to do a cull."

"A cull?" Her voice is thick with rage. "The mayor?"

"Right. It could be the whole city's turned against us. I don't know."

She sits up, wincing in pained determination. "Where's Etienne? They got him bad."

I point. "I smothered the burning. I don't know if he's going to survive. He's been too long without a wolf."

"Help me up. Take me to him." She uses me to help her to her feet, and leans on me heavily, steps awkward and halting. The pain in her sweat is intense, a bitter reek that inspires pity and horror and a little bit of fear. Anything that can do that kind of damage to one of our kind is something to be very worried about.

She looks down on him. (His body) "Help me get down again?"

I do. She sits, clasping his hand. "I don't think he's breathing. None of his wounds are healing."

"I know. I'm sorry. I have to go try to help Steph's dad."

I scoop up a handful of mud, ready to smother any part of him that's burning.

But when I find him, he's already still. Not badly burned. His neck seems to have been broken. I don't know how it happened, and maybe I don't want to know.

This way, I can imagine he died quickly, without pain.

Just an accident.

One of the many things that can go wrong on a wolf's first night.

I use the mud on any wolves who are still burning, although a lot of them seemed to have figured out the trick and rolled in the mud themselves. But half of them are already gone. No longer burning, but lying still in a way that tells me they won't be waking up in the morning.

Morgan is here. Behind me.

"Abby? What's going on? I heard explosions and saw smoke. And that smell, what is it?"

"White phosphorus," I say.

His look turns to one of horror. "White phosphorus? But that's a military weapon."

"This was ordered by the mayor's office."

"The mayor? No, it can't be. Why would somebody do that?"

"To kill werewolves. Look around you."

His face goes gray with horror. "My father?"

"I'm sorry. I think he's dead. But we won't really know for sure until the morning."

"Those mother fuckers," he says. "Are you sure it's the mayor? I voted for that guy."

Sirens in the distance. "Do you hear that?"

"Hear what?"

"Fire engine. Somebody might have reported the explosions. We need to hurry."

"Hurry doing what?"

"Get the wounded into your truck."

Morgan drives his truck up to the battle ground, and together we get Etienne and his father into the truck. But Babette is already healed enough to walk, and she doesn't want to come with us.

"Sorry, migarou. I have to go kill the mayor."

"Babette, no! You can't just kill the mayor. Can you?"

"Well. I guess I'm going to find out," she says. Gives me a strange, feral grin, runs off into the stormy night.

I go to check on the wounded man I left behind. Apparently, he had a gun on him and tried to use it with a broken hand, only to get killed and partly eaten by pissed-off werewolves. I just leave him there.

Morgan and I drive back to the maison. The weather is still terrible, but a little better than it was when we drove out here. It's only been a couple of hours since moonrise.

Barney is the only person inside, when I work the code and push open the door. He hops up from the computer, worried. "What's going on, Abby? Etienne and Babette said something was happening in City Park."

I hold the door open for Morgan, who carries in his father's wolf body, lays him out on the floor.

"Bon Dieu, who is that?"

But Morgan says nothing. Only goes out to the car again, and carries in Etienne's body.

Barney stares, while his eyes fill up with tears. "He's going to be okay, isn't he? Isn't he? He's a wolf."

"He hasn't transformed in five years. His healing gifts are weak," I say.

"What, you're just giving up on him? How could you? Abby, how could you!"

"I'm not giving up, Barney. But you know there's nothing we can do for him other than keep him safe, make sure there's no more damage."

"But…" he struggles, unable to formulate words. "But it's not possible. Who did this?"

"The mayor."

"Abby you don't know that for sure," Morgan says.

"The men doing it said they were from the Nola PD and it was the mayor's order. A cull. Dangerous rabid dogs."

"The mayor. God damn it, the mayor?"

"Babette went to kill him."

"What? No. I should help her."

"Barney, no. Don't. You can't help her." I think about it. "Do you think I should help her?"

"No, you can't, you have to protect Etienne," Barney says. "You're the only wolf now."

I think about arguing. He's already dead, I can't protect him from that. But instead, I nod. "All right. She's an adult with an active wolf, she can make her own choices. I guess she'll either succeed or realize she's in over her head and give up."

"We've got other problems too," Barney says. "Before you

walked in I thought my news was going to be the worst news of the night."

He pulls up a hurricane progress map on the big screen. Points. "See where Pax made landfall?"

"Bon Dieu, that's a direct hit on Bayou Galene."

25

AFTERMATH

"I still don't understand," Morgan says. We've both been pacing around the maison while the wind howls outside and the rain hammers the walls, fretting, unable to sit still, possessed with an urge to do something, but no idea what to do. "Why did they go to so much trouble just to kill a few wolves?"

"They probably would have killed more if we hadn't been there to interfere," I point out.

"But even in a worst case scenario, they were never going to get more than a dozen or so." He frowns, picks up a Snarl-away-branded ballpoint pen, starts clicking it. "It just seems like so much trouble to go to."

I nod. "Yeah, it does. And they sacrificed four officers to do it."

"What?" Morgan stops clicking, frowns at me. "Four?"

"They had two cars, two officers in each. All of them ended up dead."

He frowns intensely at me. "Any of them killed by you?"

I pause. Remember the visceral sensation of the man's neck cracking under my hands. "Uh. Yeah?"

"Good," he snarls, clicks the pen with renewed ferocity.

Barney rips off his headphones and says, "Good God, if you two can't sit still, can't you go out to the garage and spar or something?"

"We can't spar, he's not a wolf," I say.

"Fine, don't spar, punch the walls, I don't care. Just—wait, I just got some footage from Bayou Galene. Holy shit, look at this."

It's a brief clip, only thirty seconds or so. It shows the Grand Maison getting buffeted by wind and rain, and then, part of the roof rips right off and goes flying.

We watch it again and again, hardly able to believe what we're seeing.

"The wolves are probably okay," Barney says. "Don't you think?"

"Unless somebody drove onto the hunting grounds with a bunch of white phosphorus weapons."

He doesn't have an answer to that. Instead, numb, we watch the roof of the Grand Maison go flying out into the night. Again. And again.

After a while Barney says, "I think I can finally get a stable connection with the other maisons, hold on." He starts dialing people in on the big screens: Los Angeles, San Francisco, Seattle, Las Vegas, Chicago, Montreal, Brooklyn, Miami. We get the Garden District maison, and then last of all, the bunker.

"Hey everybody," Barney starts the meeting. "Some of you have heard, we had a situation here in New Orleans."

"Hurricane Pax."

"Worse than that," I step into the camera. "There was a coordinated attack on New Orleans wolf shifters, supposedly ordered by the mayor's office."

A lot of shouting and chaos for a moment as everybody reacts, then Brooklyn says, "What kind of attack?"

"Two vehicles dragged deer carcasses through town to create a strong scent trail leading to City Park. When the wolves showed up and started eating, there were Nola PD officers in hidden cars who started firing at them with white phosphorus."

More chaos as the people who know what that is react with shock. Seattle speaks up. "White phosphorus? What is that?"

"It burns," says Los Angeles. "Clings to the body, a bit like napalm, keeps re-igniting until you smother it, creates a lot of smoke and confusion, and, most importantly, does a tremendous amount of tissue damage."

"Enough to kill a wolf-shifter?"

"It did," I say. "It killed several bitten wolves." I inhale, about to share the bad news about Etienne, but somehow I can't bring myself to say it. It's like my tongue doesn't want to work.

"What is it, Abby?" Seattle and I worked together, he sees the distress on my face.

"Etienne," I say. Instead of chaos, this is met with stunned silence. "Etienne was hit badly. And he doesn't seem to be healing."

"Is he dead?" Garden District asks. "For real?"

"I don't think we can know for sure until the morning," I say. The others nod. "But I think—I think if he were going to be able to heal this injury, he would have started healing it by now. I'm afraid his wolf is too long gone and the injury was too severe."

Almost everyone on camera is obviously holding back tears, sniffling, eyes glossy. Etienne has been main director of the track and chase teams for more than five years. Everybody knew him. He trained most of us, especially the scent trackers.

This is a serious blow.

"What about Bayou Galene?" we ask the bunker. "We saw the footage of the Grand Maison. What's the damage out there?"

"The good news is, the bunker and the public house were

both designed with hurricanes in mind, no real damage to the structures, and they both have generator power. Every non-wolf in town is hunkered down in one of those places and I think we're going to be all right. But half the buildings in town are just gone. Rubble."

"What about the wolves in the hunting grounds?"

"They're probably better off than anybody here in town."

"No strange cars driving up? No smoke, no explosions?"

"No. Nothing like that."

We stay hooked into the other maisons, but with no new disasters it turns into reminiscing about Etienne.

We don't really know for sure he's gone! I want to shout. But I know it's not much of a hope. I flash back, suddenly, to the moment when my older sister Chastity tried to revive our sister Ash, using a kind of "outsider medicine" I now recognize as CPR. Where did she learn to do it, I wonder? Was it in a book? It was probably in a book.

There are no books about helping werewolves heal. There's folklore, aphorisms like "the only thing a wolf really has to fear is starvation" but nobody knows. Nobody's studied it in any kind of scientific way, not until very recently.

Since I've known Etienne less than a year, I don't have much to contribute. Mostly I listen. Eventually I curl up in a corner of the couch and sink into a dark brooding nightmare that feels like still being awake.

He did it, says my grandmother. *They made a deal, you see.*

I startle awake. It's morning. Light streaming in. The storm over.

Etienne and Steph's dad are still dead. I can smell them now. The decay starting in their tissues. You don't come back from that. The tears start to prickle in my eyes, tears of mourning, but also, rage.

The words echo in my mind. They made a deal, who? Who made what deal?

I remember Roman. In town. Right before the hurricane. Insisting that his own son come back to Bayou Galene with him.

Roman knew about the attack.

What if he and my father made a deal with the Veneray? After Viv and I left? What if they agreed to look the other way while the Veneray made this attack?

But why?

I stand up. "Where's Nic?"

"Nic?" Barney wakes up in a panic. "He should be coming back by now. Do you think something happened?"

But we don't have long to panic before Nic appears at the back door, naked. He walks in, dons a robe, hugs me. "Abby, I know something went wrong last night. I heard the wolves howling."

"Oh, Nic, it's awful. The mayor's office ordered the Nola PD to do a cull. They lured all the wolves to part of the park by dragging a deer carcass through the streets, and then shot at them with white phosphorus. And they got Etienne."

He kneels down near Etienne's body, strokes his hair. "You said the mayor ordered it? Are you sure about that? That's a pretty serious accusation."

Barney says, "Guess what the computer team found?"

He pulls up security camera footage from outside the mayor's office. Clearly shows Babette. Stark naked except for the ruby choker. She smiles up at the camera, blood on her teeth, then makes a gesture at the camera, as if she's throwing something, and the image winks out.

"Bon Dieu," I say. "Is the mayor dead?"

"If so, it's not official. They might be trying to work up a story that doesn't involve werewolves."

"We should take Etienne out to Bayou Galene," Nic says. "His family."

"Right," I say. But Morgan speaks up. "Abby, please, help

me with my father first?" He's been crying, his eyes and nose are red, raw-looking. "It's morning and he didn't change back. I think he's really gone."

"Of course." I go to embrace Morgan. "Of course I'll help your family. Then we'll go out to the bayou after that."

Morgan and I take their father home. I wait in the car while he breaks the news, before we take his body inside. The whole family is weeping. Hard. This is the worst day I can imagine. Steph's dad and Etienne both, and whoever did that—

I think about Roman. The Veneray.

But I can't jump to conclusions. Not based on a half-remembered fragment of a dream. I can't.

Leon did almost exactly the same thing forty years ago. Let an attack happen to distract while he did something else.

Okay, but, no, it doesn't make any sense. Pere Claude was with him in Bayou Galene—

What if the attack in town was to distract me?

Okay, that's just the purest paranoid speculation, why would Leon care what I was doing—

She threatens your plans

Damn it, more dream logic. What plans?

Instead I focus on helping Steph's family. We spend all morning in a kind of vigil, with candles, Steph's mom running a rosary through her hands. She asks, "What happens to his, I mean, what do we do with his body? The church won't let us bury a, a wolf, they won't let us…"

She breaks down again. More hugs. And I say, "We'll take him out to the cemetery in Bayou Galene. We'll let him sleep with the other wolves. He should have a place in the Verreaux crypt. I bit him, right? That makes him part of my family."

We drive out, slowly, on heavily damaged roads. Not much traffic, but there are a few places where we have to get out and physically remove debris from the roadway.

As we approach Bayou Galene, the damage gets more and more extreme. Roofs torn off, entire buildings reduced to piles of rubble. Cars and trailers picked up and tossed around like children's toys, turned upside-down, caught in the branches of the live oaks.

Everything seems strange, as the landmarks that usually tell me we're getting close to Bayou Galene have been flattened, or damaged to the point of being unrecognizable. The new brewery pounded into sheets of metal, the convenience store pierced by tree branches, the poor Grand Maison missing a large part of its roof.

"My God," Steph's mom says, voice shaking. "The hurricane just destroyed everything."

"Not everything." I point to the public house, squatting, concrete, intact. I never thought before about why it was built in a hexagon like that, assumed it was just a stylistic choice. But now I realize it was a hurricane-proof design. It's never been tested so much, but it passed the test.

Almost the entire town is gathered in the public house, wolves and non-wolves alike, which makes it very crowded. But it's quiet, somber, everyone still in mourning. The werewolves flare nostrils as we carry Steph's father inside, lay him out on one of the tables.

"Who is that?" somebody asks me.

"Loufrer," I say. "Where's my brother Nicolas?"

"Cemetery. We all took Etienne to his family crypt a couple of hours ago and did the howl, but some people stayed to do the vigil."

I nod. That fits with what I know of Varger funeral customs. They don't do a second line. "Where's Pere Claude?"

The words "Pere Claude" seem to go right through everyone, stunned and lost looks and my heart seems to stop for a moment.

"What. Happened. To Pere Claude?"

A few minutes later, I'm storming my way into the Bayou Galene mayor's office, where Leon is brooding over a computer, Roman and Rufus standing behind him.

"Leon!" I try to boom it out, but my voice doesn't do that, it doesn't boom. Instead I growl low in my throat. "What did you do last night? Where are Pere Claude and Vivienne? Did you kill them in order to claim the pereship?"

He frowns. "What? Abby what are you saying? Don't be ridiculous."

"If you didn't kill him, where is he?"

"When the old pere leaves, we don't know where he goes. I told you that. That's by design."

"What about Vivienne? She wasn't the pere. Where did she go?"

Leon stands up. "Abby, I don't know what you're accusing me of, but my father —" he pauses. "Roman, Rufus, could you leave us alone?"

They nod, and leave.

"Abby, my father wasn't able to lead the hunt last night. So I stepped in to do it. Viv attended my father, kept him away from the other wolves. I led the people because I had to. Please understand."

"Nice story. So where are they now? Pere Claude and Vivienne?"

"I don't know, because I'm not supposed to know. How many times do I have to tell you that?"

"Liar. Does Viv have her phone? Give her a call."

"Abby, please. You still don't know our ways very well. It would be bad for everyone here to know where my father is, to still be looking to him for leadership."

"Did you know about the attacks last night? The ones in town?"

"I heard about them, yes. Devastating. Etienne was a great man, wolf or no wolf."

"Did you hear about them before they happened? Did you make a deal with the Veneray?"

He scowls. "Abby, what are you saying? You were right there when I spoke to the Veneray. You know I didn't make a deal with them."

"I was right there at first. But then Viv and I left. For a while it was all men in the room. I don't know what you men said to each other. And don't pretend you wouldn't just look the other way while something like this happened. You did it once before."

He turns angry. "Abby, I told you about that, I wouldn't do it now. Not after what they did to my mother. Not the Veneray."

"What about the mayor's office?"

"What?"

"Didn't they tell you? It was the mayor who ordered the attack on the wolves last night. A cull, they said. The mayor killed Etienne."

He shakes his head, gives me a frustrated look. "Abby, what? Why would you say that? You're just being paranoid. The mayor wouldn't do a thing like that."

"The men from the Nola PD who were trying to kill the wolves, they seemed to think their orders came from the mayor's office."

"The Nola PD?" He turns pale. "Abby, what did you do?"

"What did *I* do? What did *you* do?"

"Did you kill cops?"

"Of course I killed cops!" I slam my fist on the desk. "And you would have done the same. Unless you're a traitor. Are you a traitor, Leon?"

"Abby, you're—I warned you about this, remember? You still haven't recovered from the permanent black moon. You're paranoid. Delusional."

"Delusional! Leon, I watched Etienne get slaughtered, and Steph's dad was killed, and Babette was almost killed, and half a dozen bitten wolves were killed—this happened right in front of me, I am not delusional."

"Abby, please calm down." He puts a hand on my arm. I shake it off.

I fling open the door. "Hey everybody! Listen up. Leon! I accuse you of betraying your people. Once forty years ago. And again last night. You are not worthy to be the pere. I challenge you for the position of hunt leader."

"You're challenging me for the pereship?"

"I just said that."

"Abby, no."

"Not willing to fight me? Does that mean I win by default?"

"This is ridiculous. If you lose you'll be exiled."

"What about if you lose?"

He doesn't answer right away. I say, "So the contest is rigged, you're telling me. A wolf like me can't be the pere because I won't win against you in combat. Your system is fucked up." I punch him in the face.

He rubs his jaw, shaking his head. "Don't. Please don't."

"Fight me. I'm officially challenging you for the pereship. Fight me. Defeat me in combat, you asshole, do it. You think you already know you're going to win, well, prove it." I punch him again. And a part of me is right there, screaming the rightness of this. Screaming that he should not be the pere, it's wrong wrong wrong, he's a traitor, his leadership will mean the ultimate destruction of all our people.

And another part of me is wailing, *No, Abby, no, stop it, you're being insane, this isn't the way…*

But it seems like I can't stop myself. I punch him again. He still won't fight back.

I kneel down, reach for the wolf. But she's not right there, like she has been before. Damn it. And I smell—is that berserker drugs?

Pepper and lightning, the world turns upside down, as a large white wolf takes my neck in his jaws and bites.

Just hard enough to prove he wins.

Not to kill me.

Just to draw blood.

Our fight is over almost before it began

And I lost.

26

THESE BOOTS ARE MADE FOR WALKING

"This isn't exile."

Leon smiles slightly. We're in the office of the Mayor of Bayou Galene, him at the desk, me on the other side. Sitting. Calm. Feels like a job exit interview. *Your performance has been somewhat disappointing...*

"It's not exile? What is it then?"

I look down at the desk, where my new identity is laid out in a series of objects: a passport, a drivers' license, a cash card, actual cash. And a plane ticket to London. One way.

Leon says, "Temporary. Because of your youth and the informal, impulsive manner of your challenge to my authority, this is not considered a permanent exile and you are not considered a true ghost wolf."

"Considered." I pick up the passport. "Considered by whom? Who's doing the considering? Exactly?"

He takes a deep breath, continues. "The term of your ghosting is temporary. If you wish, after your eighteenth true birthday, if you are ready to accept my authority as pere, or the authority of whoever is serving at that time, you can return. But until then, you must not have any contact with the

Varger, or our allies. That includes your own loufrer. I'm sorry. It hurts, I know, but this isn't a punishment."

"Easy for you to say."

He sighs. "It's not a punishment," he repeats. "It's a practicality. Now, you have enough money in that account that you should be comfortable for the whole year, as long as you're frugal with it. Do you remember when we talked about the Scottish village where my parents went on their honeymoon? A little town called Drochlemore just north of Inverness? You should go there. Lots of sheep."

"Sheep." I shake my head. "They won't like wolves."

"Or, go wherever you want, as long as it's far away from here." He rubs his eyes, gives a weary sigh. I guess it's tough when your power grab happens on the same night as a hurricane that flattens half the town. "I still don't know what possessed you."

"The spirit of my grandmother."

He glares at me. "Don't joke about that."

"It's not a joke." And it isn't, but I'm not as sure of myself as I pretend. If my grandmother truly was with me, was she the voice telling me to do it, or the voice telling me not to? I want to say I'm sure. But I'm not sure. So I'm cooperating. Going along with this exile that isn't an exile. I have so many doubts. I doubt Leon. I doubt myself. I doubt my choices. I doubt his choices. Maybe he's right after all and a year backpacking around Europe is exactly what I need. Clear my head. Get away from everything.

I pick up the passport, check the name and age. I decided to make myself twenty-one this time, no fooling around. After everything that's happened, I should be able to go to a bar. My new name is Abnegation Asher. Maybe Abnegation is my cult name, but it still feels like mine. Abnegation, but not Self-Abnegation. Steph named me Abby, and that's still a part of my name. But I was never really Abigail Marchande. I know that now. Even if the terms of my exile didn't involve no contact with my loufrer, it would still seem like a good idea to leave them alone. I'm bad news, Lunora was right about the family curse. Steph's family should stay well away from all us loup-garous from now on.

Except for one thing. "Leon. Izzy's grandmother asked me to make sure of something. You loup-garous should pay her cash money for her computer work. You hear?"

He looks startled for a moment, then nods thoughtfully. "Yes. I hear."

"What happened with the mayor and Babette, anyway? Is he dead? Is she dead?"

"Babette's current whereabouts are unknown, but the mayor is dead. His office claims he was killed by hurricane debris."

"Was he working with the Veneray? Was the cull their idea?"

"We still don't know." He says this firmly, but I don't believe him. It's all connected. What Viv said about the Azphokites. They're your enemies. Unless you make them your allies. And maybe that's what he did. Cut a deal. Maybe he even thought it was the right thing to do, to protect the people. That would make sense. It's how Leon does things. Not with an evil intent, exactly, but with a ruthless and amoral lack of concern.

I gather up the things on the desk, the artifacts of Abnegation Asher. "Vivienne told me once that you had a place inside you that was like a locked room. And she thought, maybe even you don't know what's in there."

We stare at each other for a moment. Not a dominance flash. Just a stare. He says, "What do you think she meant by that?"

"It was a warning. Lunora told me that you never listen to the ancestors, and that's why you shouldn't be the hunt leader."

"Lunora told you that?" He frowns. "Why would she know anything about it?"

"She swears the ancestors talk to her and she listens. I'm just telling you these things because I don't want your pereship to be a disaster. Even though I already know it will be."

"You're still paranoid," he tells me. But is there just the hint of doubt on his face? "You haven't recovered from the permanent black moon yet."

"No? How long do I have to wait, do you think?"

He shakes his head, a hint of sympathy in his eyes. "I'm sorry. I really don't know." We stare at each other for a long time, not a dominance contest but still something uncanny about it, as if we're trying to read each other's minds, and almost succeeding.

I say, "Etienne told me once that our sense of smell can seem almost like psychic abilities. Can I read your mind? Not exactly, but I can read your sweat. You're not as sure of yourself as you pretend to be."

"Who is?" A long pause, then he says, "Oh, here." He leans down, then sits up straight, puts Grandma's red boots on the desk. "You left these at the maison, I thought you might want them for your trip. You said they fit you well."

"They do." I nod. I take the boots, comforted and then enraged by the smells of the women who worse those boots before me, my grandmother and Vivienne. "It's funny, you got both of the women who wore these boots before me killed, am I next?"

"Abby," he barks out sharply, upset. "I did not kill Vivienne. I don't know why you're so stuck on that."

"Paranoia," I say. I slip on the boots, put the artifacts of Abnegation Asher into the secret pockets, stand up, see how it feels. "So that's what I get, huh? A plane ticket and some boots, take a hike, see you later?"

Very slight smile. "You're a wolf, Abby. What do you really need?"

ACKNOWLEDGMENTS

For helping me get Hunting After Ghosts into print, a big thank you to:

- My first readers Carol and Ulysses, who talked me down from turning this into two books, as well as offering loads of other helpful advice.
- My editor Shannon Page,.
- Michael Kinsella, who suggested the white phosphorus as anti-werewolf ordnance.
- My spouse Paul M Carpentier, for meticulous proofreading as always (any remaining typos are my fault), and also for driving me around Cajun country during a tropical storm and not getting us stuck in a flood.

ABOUT THE AUTHOR

Julie McGalliard is a writer, data scientist, and occasional cartoonist. She lives in Seattle and has traveled to New Orleans a lot.

Follow her adventures at https://www.gothhouse.org/author/juliemcgalliard/

Photo by Andrew S. Williams

 facebook.com/jmcgalliard

 twitter.com/mcjulie

 instagram.com/jmcgal

CPSIA information can be obtained
at www.ICGtesting.com
Printed in the USA
BVHW041826180522
637434BV00010B/52